ABOMINATION

ABOMINATION

GARY WHITTA

Whitta

Published by Inkshares Inc., San Francisco, California
www.inkshares.com

Edited and designed by Girl Friday Productions
www.girlfridayproductions.com

Cover design by Jason Gurley
Map by Jonathan Roberts

ISBN: 978-1-941758-33-5
Library of Congress Control Number: 2015930180

First edition

Printed in the United States of America

For my wife and daughter.

Judge not, and you will not be judged.
Condemn not, and you will not be condemned.
Forgive, and you will be forgiven.

—Luke 6:37

After the fall of the Roman Empire, chaos
and bloodshed swept across the remains of
Western civilization like a plague.

Consumed by feudal warfare, Europe plunged into a
centuries-long era of illiteracy and cultural desolation
from which few historical records survived.

Some believe that the true history of this dark age was
deliberately concealed by its surviving scholars.
Too incredible to be believed, too terrible to be retold.

Until now.

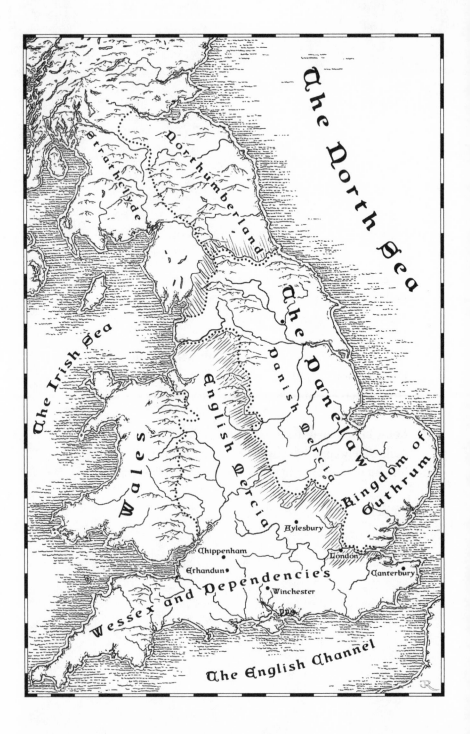

ENGLAND
888 AD

ONE

Alfred was tired. It had been a long, hard war, and though he had won it, he had barely rested since. He knew that the peace would not last long. For an English king, he had learned, it never did. There was always another war.

He had spent his entire reign defending his homeland and his faith against the hordes of Norse barbarians from across the sea. For nearly a century, they had been arriving in fleets of longships, raiding England's coastline and laying siege to its villages and towns, their incursions growing more daring—and more bloody— with each passing year. When Alfred was still but a boy, Danish invaders had established permanent footholds across England, seizing all of East Anglia and Mercia, two of the largest kingdoms in the land. Danish power spread so far and wide after that, and so quickly, that within three short years only Wessex remained unbroken. The last free, sovereign kingdom in all England. Alfred's kingdom.

He was not King then, nor did he have any wish to be, but he would soon have the crown thrust upon him. The Norse wasted no time in attacking Wessex. Alfred's King and elder brother was for a short time successful in repelling the invaders. But after that, defeat followed defeat, and when the King met his death shortly after his army was routed at Reading, his crown passed to Alfred, his sole heir. And so it was that by his twenty-first year, Alfred had become England's only remaining Anglo-Saxon king, and in all likelihood its last.

For a short while, Alfred had considered surrender, and with good reason: the Norsemen were notorious for their brutality and lack of mercy. Other English kings, those who had not fled, or who had refused to yield, had been tortured to death when their walls inevitably fell. The Danish king at the head of the invading force, a godless thug named Guthrum, was driving deeper into the heart of Alfred's beloved Wessex, sacking every town and village before him. Alfred's army was forced to retreat as far west as Somerset, where the seclusion of its tidal marshes afforded him time to regroup. Summoning men from the neighboring counties, he set them to building a fortress from which they could rally and stage attacks. Tired of running and hiding, Alfred finally began to take the fight to the enemy.

He defeated the Norse in battle at Ethandun, driving them all the way back to their stronghold and laying siege to it until he starved the heathens into surrender. It was a decisive victory, but the Norse were still too many and too widespread to be driven utterly from the land. Tired of bloody battles and dead men in numbers more than he could count, Alfred offered armistice to his hated enemy, Guthrum: if the Norse agreed to lay down their arms, they would be granted their own lands in the east. The English territory they already occupied would be formally recognized as the Danelaw, a kingdom in which Guthrum and his people could— and would be expected to—live in peace.

And so it was agreed. And so Wessex was saved.

Throughout his kingdom, Alfred's subjects, grateful to have been spared the horrors of a Norse occupation, began to call him Alfred the Great. It was a title that did not sit well with him, for he did not see greatness within himself. He had studied the life and campaigns of that other "Great," Alexander III—the Macedonian king who had been driven by a firm conviction in his own greatness, one so deeply held he believed it was his destiny to conquer the entire world. And so he had; by Alfred's age, Alexander had vanquished the vast Persian army, once thought invincible, and had gone on to preside over one of the greatest empires the world had ever seen, ruling all of Asia Minor from the Ionian Sea to the Himalayas. Alfred, by contrast, had barely managed to hang on to his own little kingdom.

Alexander had famously never lost a battle, while Alfred had lost many. Far too many.

He would not lose another, he told himself. In the years following the Danish accord, Alfred refused to grow complacent. He went to London, a city sacked and ruined during the Norse invasions, and restored it to life, buttressing it against future attack. Alfred's own royal palace at Winchester was fortified similarly, as were villages and towns throughout Wessex, until every man and woman within his kingdom's borders could feel secure that the horrors of recent years would never visit them again.

Everyone except Alfred. Wessex was as safe as he could make it, and yet he did not sleep easily. Every messenger and scout brought fresh reports of Danish naval activity, fresh rumors of a coming invasion. And now, Guthrum, long rumored ill, was said to be on his deathbed.

Though the Danish king was a barbarian, Alfred had come to respect him—and more importantly, to trust him. In the years since the armistice, Guthrum had always held his word to keep the peace. But it was known that many ambitious and hot-tempered men of war among the Danelaw Norse were waiting to take power after Guthrum's death. Men who would have no respect for the treaty their predecessor had honored. And the only thing Alfred feared more than another Danish invasion from across the sea was a Danish uprising from within England's own borders.

And so here he sat, on his throne at Winchester, as uneasily as he ever had. He had sent word to his military commanders throughout the kingdom to be on close watch. After all, it took days for word to travel here from the Danelaw; for all Alfred knew, Guthrum might already be dead. Even now, as he sat here, Danish forces could be massing under some new king in preparation for an attack. But he had done all he could. Now all that was left to do was wait, and worry.

"Your Majesty?"

Alfred looked to the page standing before him; he had been so lost in thought he had not heard the boy approach. "What is it?"

"The archbishop requests your presence in the courtyard," said the page. "He says he has something you must see."

Alfred groaned. Aethelred, the Archbishop of Canterbury, was the last man he wanted to see today, or any other day. Though Alfred cherished his Christian beliefs, he did not likewise cherish the man who was leader of his church. The archbishop had been inherited along with the rest of Alfred's kingdom, and there was something about the man that had troubled him from the beginning. Had Alfred's reign been one of peace, he likely would have moved to replace the prelate, but he had been too busy fighting a war against the Norse to also embroil himself in a battle with the church. In recent months, however, he had come to sorely regret having not done so, and never more so than at this moment. What Aethelred had to show him was certain to sour his appetite and send him to bed with nightmares. As if sleep was not hard enough to come by these days.

Alfred gave the page a reluctant nod. "Tell him I will be there presently."

The page bowed low, then hurried away. Alfred sat a while longer before making his way to the courtyard. Whatever fresh horror Aethelred had in store for him, he was in no hurry to see it.

———•◦❧◦•———

Five months ago, Aethelred had come to Alfred in feverish excitement. During the rebuilding of London, a common laborer had by chance discovered a cache of ancient Latin scrolls buried beneath the earth. The laborer brought them to his parish priest, who, so startled by what he saw within them, rode them to Canterbury himself that same day.

Aethelred, too, recognized in the scrolls something remarkable the moment he saw them. They were old, so old that the Latin text they contained, some earlier, arcane form of the language, was barely understandable even by his most learned priests. But what they were able to translate both chilled Aethelred's blood and excited him so he could scarcely keep his hands from shaking. The scrolls spoke of powers even more ancient than they. Of incantations and rites that could change the shape of flesh, create new life from old. Of the power to make any man who wielded it into a god.

It took Aethelred and his most senior scholars months to decipher the text of all nine scrolls. When at last their work was finished, Aethelred brought it to Winchester and presented it to his King as a way to finally secure peace for all the English kingdoms—to annihilate the Danish threat, once and for all. When Alfred heard the archbishop's promise that he could accomplish all this without a single drop of English blood spilled, he was intrigued; when he heard how Aethelred intended to do it, he did not know whether to be appalled or simply think the man mad.

It took a demonstration for Aethelred to prove to his King that his mind had not taken leave.

Aethelred had one of his curates bring forth a hog appropriated from the castle's livestock. Alfred, and everyone at court that day, was at first amused to see the leashed pig pulling the hapless curate along by its leash as it sniffed the stone floor. Was this some kind of jest? At best, Alfred thought, Aethelred might embarrass himself before the entire royal court. Which would give Alfred just the excuse he needed to ease the man quietly from his seat at Canterbury and replace him with someone less irksome. The poor man had obviously been working too hard. It was time.

The curate threw a half-eaten apple before the pig and backed away as the animal scarfed it down. Few noticed the look of pale dread on the young priest's face as he retreated; all eyes were on the pig, a common beast running loose in this highest of halls.

As the pig chewed greedily, Aethelred cautioned the royal guardsmen standing nearby to be at the ready, then threw back his arms with a flourish. Courtiers exchanged awkward glances; some of them giggled. *This is already enough to finish him*, Alfred thought to himself from his throne. *The Primate of All England, waving his arms about like a court jester performing a conjuring trick.*

And then Aethelred began the incantation. The giggling stopped. So did the amused glances. All eyes were fixed on Aethelred as he mouthed the ancient words decrypted in Canterbury.

The language was familiar, and yet not. *What is that, some kind of Latin?* Alfred wondered. Only one thing was certain: as Aethelred continued with the incantation, his voice slowly rising, a chill descended upon the room. Though none understood the words, every man and woman somehow knew that there was something *wrong* about them. As though they had come from a place not human. Several of those watching felt a strong urge to leave the room, and yet their feet would not carry them. They were rooted to the spot, paralyzed, unable to look away.

The pig, who had been happily devouring the apple, suddenly dropped it. Its jaw went slack. Its head twisted and turned in an unnatural circular motion, as if tortured by some infernal sound only it could hear. It let out the most horrendous, piercing squeal, then fell sideways onto the floor, where it lay still.

For a moment the room was eerily silent, all present rendered speechless by the bizarrely morbid display. Aethelred had, seemingly, killed this animal without laying so much as a hand on it. With the power of words alone.

It took Alfred to break the silence. "I demand to know the meaning of this—" The pig squealed—louder than before—cutting

Alfred's words short. Then its body jolted back to life, writhing on the floor through a series of violent spasms.

Some postmortem reflex? Alfred glanced up from the stricken beast to Aethelred and saw the broad grin spread across the archbishop's face. As though full of delight in what he knew was to come next.

Something burst from the belly of the pig, blood spraying across the floor. Several onlookers shrieked in dismay, and those standing closest backed away in revulsion as another protrusion erupted from within the pig's body, then another, each glistening with dark, viscous blood as they unfolded and took form. Bony, jointed, stalk-like appendages, resembling the limbs of some monstrous insect, they slipped and slid across the smooth stone floor like the legs of a newborn calf trying to stand.

And then the *thing*—it could no longer reasonably be called a pig—rose up on its six newly formed legs, each bristling with thick, fibrous hairs. The creature's jaw unhinged and dropped wide, revealing a mouthful of sharply pointed fangs. The royal guardsmen drew their weapons and Alfred watched with grim fascination as the creature ambled forward. Its eyes were wild and bloodshot, searching the room, seemingly half-blind and in the grip of some rabid fever.

The beast lifted its head, opened its jaw wide, and howled—an appalling sound that defied nature and raised gooseflesh on the arms of every person present. The callow young guardsman who stood closest to the beast moved to strike it down with his sword. Before Aethelred could warn him off, the guardsman's blade came down on one of the beast's spider-like legs, releasing a spray of black blood that splattered his tunic. As the beast screamed, the guard tried to draw back his blade for another blow, but it was stuck fast in the bone and gristle of the beast's leg. Wounded and enraged, the pig-thing wheeled, wresting the sword from the guard's hand. Before he could withdraw, the beast lurched forward and its two front legs closed around his waist like pincers.

As the young man flailed helplessly, his comrades came to his aid, some trying to pull him free of the creature's grip, others hacking at it with their swords, the screams of the beast and of the guardsman in its grip mingling in a hellish cacophony. Then the creature's pincers closed tight and the young guardsman vomited blood as his body was sliced in two. The beast threw both lifeless halves of the man aside, trying now to defend itself against the other guards, who were stabbing and slashing at it furiously. But it was too late; the thing had sustained several grievous wounds and was bleeding out quickly. Weakened and dying, it finally toppled, gasping, blood bubbling up in its throat. The guard captain moved in, sword drawn high, and with all his strength brought the blade down, taking the monster's head clean off. For a few moments more it continued to move, its chest heaving, its arachnid legs twitching reflexively. And then, finally, it was still.

His face spattered with the blood of the beast, the guard captain glared at Aethelred. Alfred stepped down from his throne and marched across the room to the priest, who had not stopped smiling during the whole bloody episode, and who smiled still.

"Did you enjoy the demonstration, Sire?" asked the archbishop.

"I did *not*," hissed the King through gritted teeth, his fists clenched.

Aethelred's smile arched wider. "The Danes will enjoy it even less, I suspect."

TWO

Alfred ordered the throne room cleared of all but his guards before interrogating the archbishop about the horror they had just witnessed. Aethelred calmly explained that while he had taken care to ensure accurate translation of the scrolls' incantations, their precise recitation was still something of a work in progress. Had the guardsmen not slain the beast, it likely would have died within minutes anyway, as had the other test subjects on which the archbishop had performed the rite in Canterbury. But he was confident that with more time, and a meager portion of the kingdom's resources, he could perfect the process—and thereby transform the common creatures of the realm into an army of savage war beasts that would strike fear into the hearts of the Norse. In time, he went on, these beasts could be brought under control and trained to kill not just the Danes but any enemies of England who might yet present themselves.

Alfred, still fuming, had the archbishop escorted to his chambers and convened with his ealdormen to seek their counsel. And though none denied the abhorrent nature of the event they had all witnessed, the great majority nonetheless argued that what Aethelred had brought before them should not be rejected out of hand.

All shared Alfred's concerns about the possibility of fresh hostilities with the Norse, particularly in light of Guthrum's ill health.

And though Alfred had done much to bolster the kingdom against attack, Wessex still bore the wounds of its long conflict with the Danes and could scarcely afford another open war so soon after, in blood or in treasure. The council's advice to Alfred was near unanimous: as sworn defenders of the realm, it was their duty to be strong as much in stomach as in purpose. They could not allow their distaste, intense as it might be, for Aethelred's proposed methods—*unconventional*, one ealdorman euphemistically called them—to curtail what could be a potent opportunity to secure a peaceful future for Wessex, and for all England. So powerful was the promise Aethelred had brought them that, in all their conversation, no man present dared utter the one word that privately haunted each of them. *Witchcraft.*

And so Alfred had reluctantly agreed. Aethelred and his entourage from Canterbury were to be quartered at Winchester and provided with whatever they needed to perfect their arcanery.

God only knew how many poor beasts suffered and died in the archbishop's twisted experiments during the months that followed. Alfred had lost count, when he could no longer stand the sight of the wretched abominations Aethelred conjured daily.

At first none of them had lived long. The malformed things borne of each dog and mule and horse on which Aethelred practiced his art either collapsed and died after a few minutes or had to be speared by pikemen when they turned on the archbishop or his assistants. Over time, as Aethelred made refinements and corrections to the pronunciation and cadence of the incantations written in the ancient scrolls, and to the accompanying hand gestures described therein, the monsters he brought forth began to live longer. For hours, then days, then indefinitely. But one thing did not change. In every case, no matter how long-lived, the beasts were viciously aggressive from the moment they were birthed.

They would attack anything, without provocation—even each other. Aethelred once watched as two hunting dogs, brothers from the same litter who had never shown any aggression toward one another, were transformed by the rite into a pair of scaly, ridge-backed hellhounds that proceeded immediately to tear each other apart. Fascinated, he made a detailed note of it in his journal.

Aethelred also discovered that with subtle changes to the summoning, he could create many varied forms of beast from each base subject. He could turn a swine into the same quasi-arachnid he had created in Alfred's throne room, or with a minor rephrasing, bring about a kind of horrific, beak-nosed, oily skinned jackal. All of these experiments were carefully documented by Aethelred's apprentices in an ever-growing bestiary. Aethelred practiced tirelessly each day for months on end, creating dozens of variations, until he was satisfied he had exhausted all possible permutations for each base subject. A cat could become only so many things, he learned, and when there was no longer anything new to be created from a cat, he would start again on a goose or a badger or whatever poor, unsuspecting creature was next on his list. In time he learned to bring forth all manner of creatures with flawless specificity, down to the length of the tail and the manner in which it breathed fire. The ones that breathed fire were his favorites; the day he discovered that particular variation prompted one of his most enthusiastic journal entries, and fire-breathers now warranted their own section in the bestiary.

But for all Aethelred's accomplishments, the problem of control remained. He had enlisted all of Alfred's most skilled animal handlers—men who had broken the wildest horses and could train a feral wolf to eat from the palm of one's hand—but none could tame any of Aethelred's creations. Increasingly it seemed that these beasts were beyond any form of mastery, though Aethelred himself stubbornly refused to accept that. While he insisted that he could eventually control them, Alfred's impatience grew. Finally, the King, already haunted nightly by visions of the things he saw in the courtyard each day, decided that he had seen enough.

When a leathery reptilian monster that had once been a fox pounced on the handler who was attempting to feed it a haunch of meat and took the man's arm off at the shoulder instead, Alfred went into a fury. He told the archbishop that he wished to see no more of his "progress" until the priest could prove that the beasts could be controlled. Otherwise, what use were they in battle? They were as likely to attack their own handlers as any enemy they might be set upon. Before the King stormed out of the courtyard that day, he warned Aethelred that if this final problem were not solved, and soon, he would put an end to the archbishop's experimentation altogether.

Now, two months later, Alfred returned, albeit with reluctance. He had seen many horrors in war, but none compared to what he had witnessed here in his own courtyard since the archbishop began his experiments. The ground was now scarred and pockmarked like a battlefield and stained dark by great swaths of dried blood. The timbers of many of the surrounding structures were charred black and white by fire. And most noticeable of all was the nauseating stench of sulfur that hung ever present in the air. The entire courtyard was rank with it. Alfred pulled from his sleeve a cloth that he kept for these unhappy visits and held it over his nose and mouth as he strode across the bloodstained quadrangle. Even the strong perfume in which his apothecary had soaked the cloth was not enough to mask the smell entirely.

Aethelred was waiting for him, dressed as always in the ecclesiastical finery befitting his high station, and with an air of confidence. Alfred had not seen him in weeks; the archbishop had kept to his King's command, not once requesting Alfred's presence since that poor trainer had been maimed, and so Alfred assumed he must have good cause for doing so now. He found himself wondering what he hoped for. Did he want Aethelred to succeed in attaining mastery over these beasts, and by extension, over England's enemies? Or did he wish for failure, which would finally give him reason to shut down this whole loathsome undertaking and unseat Aethelred from Canterbury? *Something I should have done long ago*, Alfred told himself once again.

"Thank you for joining me, Your Majesty," Aethelred said as the King approached.

"After the failure of your last demonstration, I must assume you would not ask me here without good reason," Alfred replied.

Aethelred ignored the slight and simply nodded. "Indeed. I think you will be most pleased with our progress since you were here last."

Alfred sighed, in no mood for a preamble. "Can you control them or not?"

"I doubt we shall ever be domesticating them as pets, but for their intended purpose—as weapons of war—yes, I believe I can now control them. It has not been easy, but this is the breakthrough I have been working toward."

Alfred just looked at Aethelred expectantly. If the archbishop was fishing for a compliment, some kind of recognition for the hours he had dedicated to creating these heinous aberrations, it would not be forthcoming.

"Very well, then!" Aethelred declared, and he turned to the guards standing nearby. "Stand ready, if you please!" A dozen of Alfred's best and most battle-seasoned pikemen were already in position, their arms drawn. All were hard men, but from their expressions it was clear they would sooner be patrolling the Danelaw border, freezing in some remote watchtower, or mucking out the castle's pigsties. Anywhere but here. Nobody wanted this duty. Those who were assigned it rarely slept well.

Close to them was a small troop of servants carrying buckets filled with water, ready to douse anything that the archbishop's beast might set ablaze. That lesson had been learned hard, when one of the first "infernals," as Aethelred liked to call them, put a torch to the courtyard's old wooden stables with a single breath. The fire might have spread and consumed the castle's kitchens and library but for the fast response of a hastily improvised bucket brigade. The stable was beyond salvage; on Alfred's orders, its blackened timbers were left standing as a reminder, and now the dousers stood ready before every incantation.

Satisfied that all was ready, Aethelred signaled the apprentice across the yard who manned the gate to the pen that held the test animals. The apprentice raised the latch on the gate, and as it swung open with a rusty groan, Alfred shuddered; he had come to abhor that sound. He had heard it many times: it was the sound that presaged the squawking and screaming as some poor, damned creature found itself transformed via Aethelred's words. *What manner of beast has he selected for today's bloody show?* Alfred wondered.

For a moment, nothing happened. Alfred was puzzled; usually the penned animal emerged immediately into the yard, happy to be released from its confinement, unaware of the grim fate that awaited it. He glanced at Aethelred, who appeared briefly embarrassed before gesturing impatiently at his apprentice. The apprentice looked at first hesitant, but in the face of the archbishop's glare, reluctantly stepped inside the pen to coax out its occupant. He disappeared briefly from view, but Alfred could hear him cajoling the beast. *Get out there, go on. Go on! The archbishop is waiting! Don't you dare embarrass me or I'll see you gutted!*

Alfred blinked in puzzlement as another man emerged from within the pen. Stripped to the waist, barefooted, rib-thin, pale, he looked as though he had not eaten in days. The apprentice was behind him, shoving him toward the center of the yard.

Alfred turned to Aethelred. "What is this?"

"A breakthrough," replied the archbishop.

Alfred looked back at the half-naked man, and now recognized the signs: the emaciation, the faraway look, the whip scars across his back. The leggings were those worn by his own infantrymen. The man was a captured deserter, one of many who routinely languished in the castle's stockade. Desertions had risen lately, particularly here at Winchester, as men increasingly decided they would rather take their chances on the run than risk being assigned to yard duty under Aethelred and subjected to the nightmares that had traumatized so many of their comrades.

"Explain this now," Alfred demanded.

"I have observed that transformation greatly diminishes the base subject's cognitive faculty," said Aethelred. "A dumb animal, even a well-trained one, retains not enough intelligence to recognize even basic commands. But a *man* . . . a man survives the process with intelligence to spare. Enough, I believe, to be reliably controlled."

Alfred's face turned a paler shade. He stared at Aethelred, aghast. "You cannot be serious."

"Our mistake was using animals to begin with," said Aethelred. "We learned much that was useful, but this practice was never intended for use on the lower forms of life. I am sure of that now."

Alfred glowered at Aethelred. "I will not permit this."

"Sire, must I remind you what is at stake here? The godless barbarians in the Danelaw are growing in strength, and awaiting their moment to launch a fresh attack upon us. With Guthrum dead or dying, that moment will surely come soon. We must use every means at our disposal to defend this realm and our faith, or risk seeing them both destroyed by a race of heathen savages."

"I was uncomfortable enough with you experimenting on beasts," said Alfred. "I will not abide this . . . this *witchcraft* to be practiced upon men!"

Aethelred raised an eyebrow. "Witchcraft? Your Majesty, this is the very farthest thing from it. The discovery of the scrolls was no accident. It was a gift from God himself. He favors us with this knowledge—this *power*—and intends for us to use it. He has seen the crimes these Danish heretics have perpetrated against his church. Monasteries razed to the ground, holy relics destroyed, good men of cloth put to the stake and burned. Theirs is a war against God himself, and he has blessed us with the means to smite them in his name."

"The God I believe in would never mean for such blasphemies to walk upon his earth," said Alfred. "Whatever the origin of those scrolls, this cannot be their purpose." He had grown tired of his word being challenged. He turned to the pikemen standing nearby and gestured to the ragged prisoner standing in the center of the yard. "Send this man back to the stockade. And see that he gets a hot meal."

As the pikemen moved to take the prisoner away, Aethelred drew back his arms and began an incantation. He had become well practiced, and more than proficient enough to say all the words he needed in just a few moments. Alfred, though fast to realize what Aethelred was doing, was not fast enough.

"Stop him!" he shouted to the guards, who raced toward the archbishop. But Alfred could see that the prisoner's body was already contorting, racked by a sudden onset of painful convulsions. Aethelred completed the incantation just as the guards seized him by the arms. He did not resist; his eyes were locked on his subject, now doubled over in agony. The poor man's eyes bulged as though they might burst, and he opened his mouth wide, letting out a tortured scream.

Alfred grabbed Aethelred by the collar. The deserter was on his knees now, arms folded tight around his midsection, and he stared blindly at the ground, apparently trying to cough up something caught in his throat.

"Undo it now!" the King commanded.

"I cannot," answered Aethelred, as he watched with fascination. "It must take its course."

Helpless, Alfred looked back at the prisoner. All eyes in the yard were on that man now. He had fallen onto his side, and now he convulsed, kicking wildly in the dirt as he clawed at himself,

raking bloody fingernails across his chest and neck as though trying to crawl out from inside of his own fevered skin.

And then he did exactly that. His rib cage swelled against his
chest, then burst clean through it like the points of a dozen bone
swords. One of the fire dousers dropped his bucket of water and
fled; the others backed away in horror as the prisoner's entire torso
seemed to turn itself inside out. He wailed in agony, his organs
spilling out onto the dirt as some dark, wet thing emerged in their
place. And then the rest of him began to split open and come
apart, the skin of his arms, legs, and head peeling away as pulsat-
ing, bloody shapes sprouted from within.

Alfred stared at the thing that just moments ago had been a
man. It reared up on new hind legs while tentacled appendages
slithered and unfurled and felt around at the ground beneath
them. The man no longer had a head; instead, a tangled cluster of
long saliva-coated tongues protruded from the riven stump where
his head had once been. They licked and lashed around the beast's
shoulders, which were now covered by some kind of armored
bone plating. What little was still recognizable as a man hung limp
around the creature's misshapen waist, a macabre belt of flayed
human skin.

The beast made a sound not of this world, a dreadful, tor-
mented howl. Alfred felt as though an ice-cold stone was growing
in the pit of his stomach. "Kill it," he cried out. "For God's sake,
kill it!"

Several guardsmen moved to surround the abominable creature, pikes thrusting outward to hold it at bay. It roared and lashed
out with a tentacle that wrapped around the staff of the closest pike
and pulled, bringing the pikeman along with it. Before he could
retreat, the tentacle coiled around his waist and squeezed, crushing the man's ribs. He let out a strangled, gurgling cry, muffled
when another fat, wet tentacle wrapped around his face and tore
his head from his neck. Blood spewed from the pikeman's neck as
the beast tossed his lifeless body aside. His head was given to the

tongues, which grasped at it and pulled it down inside the monster's neck, swallowing it greedily.

The other pikemen were attacking now. But this was not like the pig-thing, nor any of the creatures Aethelred had conjured before. This one was heavily armored, and the pike-heads merely glanced off its thick hide. The beast whirled around and skewered an unsuspecting soldier with a boned claw that sank deep into his chest and out his back. He slid backward and fell, dead before he hit the ground. A third pikeman was grabbed around the ankle and flung across the yard with such force that Alfred heard the man's bones break when he hit the stone wall. Five desperate men still surrounded the beast, which was yet unhurt and becoming more enraged.

"Let me stop it!" Aethelred cried. "Before it kills us all!"

Alfred was loath to let the man free even for a moment, but he knew he must act quickly, and he had few other options. He nodded to the guards to release the archbishop. Shrugging free of their grip, Aethelred raised his hands in his contorted sorcerer's grip and shouted a command that neither Alfred nor any man present could understand, though they all recognized it as the same arcane language used in the incantations.

The beast stopped instantly. It had two men cornered and would surely have killed them both within moments, but instead it turned to face Aethelred, suddenly docile. Aethelred spoke in the strange tongue again, and the beast approached, seemingly compliant.

As it shambled toward the archbishop, Alfred and the other men standing nearby took cautious steps backward, but Aethelred raised a hand to reassure them. "It is all right," he said. "It will not harm anyone else—unless I command it to. It is perfectly under my control, of no danger to us or our troops in battle. But set against the Danish horde . . . a very different matter."

The beast stood at least seven feet tall and towered over Aethelred, who yet showed no fear of it. Alfred stiffened as the archbishop reached out to pet the horrendous creature with the affection one might show to a beloved dog. In response, the beast gave a miserable whimper. To any sane man, the sight of this vile, wretched thing would inspire a combination of fear, pity, and disgust. Alfred saw the way Aethelred looked at it—in admiration—and he knew: *he has gone mad.*

Aethelred was so besotted with his creation that he did not notice the pikemen, now regrouped and taking position behind the beast. With a nod, Alfred gave them the order they were waiting for. They lunged as one, driving their blades hard into the creature's back, finding the tender muscle and flesh between its thick plates of bone. The beast let out a hideous screech and sank to the ground, its limbs giving way. Before it could recover, the pikemen were climbing up onto its back to stab it again and again, driving their pikes deep. Aethelred protested, but none were listening. The beast finally slumped forward onto its belly, its tongues thrashing like rattlesnake tails for a moment longer. And then, at last, it was dead.

More pikemen rushed into the yard, attracted by all the screaming and commotion. Alfred pointed to Aethelred. "Take this man and place him in the tower under guard," he ordered. The pikemen surrounded the archbishop, taking him firmly by each arm.

"You did not need to kill it," said Aethelred, still thinking more of his precious experiment than of the four men who now lay dead. "There was much we could have learned from it."

Alfred was barely able to contain his fury. "I have learned all I needed today. I learned that I have allowed these experiments of yours to go too far. Well, now I am putting an end to it. To all of it!"

"And discard all the progress we have made?" Aethelred protested. "This was my most successful subject yet. If you will only hear me out—"

"Nothing you can offer could possibly justify this atrocity!" Alfred bellowed, red with rage. "How many others have there been? How many men did you mutilate before this poor bastard here?"

"None that you would not have put to death anyway," said Aethelred. "All came from the lists of condemned men."

"I would never condemn any man to such a fate as this! I tolerated this foul enterprise because of your assurance that it would allow us to wage war without spilling the blood of Englishmen!"

"Sire, one man transformed is worth twenty of any other! In strength, in resilience, in aggression! See here what this single one did, and imagine the havoc that a hundred such beasts could wreak upon our enemies! A mere hundred, compared to the thousands we might lose in a conventional battle."

Alfred's tone lowered, but he remained no less resolute. "I will not suffer this curse to be put upon even one more man, be he condemned or not."

"The transformation need not be permanent," offered Aethelred. "I assure you, given more time, I can find a way to reverse the effect—to restore them to their original form when they return from battle."

With a heavy sigh, Alfred rubbed his brow. "I've had about as many of your assurances as I can take. Guards, see the archbishop to the tower. There he will stay, until I decide what to do with him."

The pikemen marched Aethelred away, leaving Alfred to survey the carnage in the yard before him. He shook his head, cursing himself for being so foolish as to believe that this could ever have come to any good.

Barrick and Harding, the two largest and least obliging of Alfred's jailors, marched Aethelred roughly up the stone steps of the spiral staircase. Torchlight flickered on the walls as Barrick unlocked the heavy oak door to the solitary cell atop the tower and Harding tossed the archbishop inside. He landed in a pile of dank straw, with barely time to right himself before the door slammed closed again and the key turned in the lock.

He dusted himself off and straightened his robe. For a moment he sat there in the dark, listening to the idle chatter of the two guards now standing post outside. And a thin smile played across his lips. *Alfred is more blind than I thought,* he delighted in thinking to himself. *After all that he has seen, he actually thinks that he can cage me.*

Alfred had convened his senior counselors in the war room. All by now had heard of the slaughter in the yard; some had seen it for themselves. Though months ago all had voted to explore Aethelred's proposal, they had, like Alfred, grown increasingly uneasy with where it was leading. Today's events had been the final straw. None needed convincing that it was time for this ill-advised episode to be brought to a close. Alfred had already ordered all record of it destroyed, including the accursed scrolls that had begun it all. The only question now was what to do with the Archbishop of Canterbury himself.

"He is finished as archbishop, and in the church. That much is certain," the King declared to unanimous nods of approval. "The senior clergy will not dispute it. Many of them were also disquieted by what Aethelred was doing here. For that, I will apologize and ask them to put forward a successor of their choosing."

"What, though, is to be his fate beyond excommunication?" asked Cromwell, one of Alfred's high reeves and a trusted military advisor. "Is he to be charged with a crime? Is there to be a trial?"

"If Aethelred is guilty of a crime, then I am equally guilty for condoning it this long," Alfred said. "And a public trial of such a . . . bizarre nature would only spread superstition and fear throughout the kingdom."

There was a long pause before anyone spoke again. This time it was Chiswick, another of Alfred's war counselors. His special responsibility was to manage the army's apparatus of spies and subterfuge, and he could often be relied upon to suggest unconventional solutions to difficult problems.

"Perhaps, then . . . an accident?"

Alfred and the others looked at him.

"It is well-known from here to Canterbury that the archbishop was engaged in dangerous work, though not the exact nature of it," Chiswick went on. "Perhaps he died in faithful service to his church and his King. Aethelred is largely unloved. I doubt many would pry into the truth of things."

All now looked to Alfred, who found himself disquieted by the notion. "I love the man least of all, but to simply execute him . . ."

Chiswick leaned forward. "It seems to me your options are few, Your Majesty. He cannot continue as archbishop, and a trial, as you rightly say, would be a catastrophe. And he certainly cannot be set free; this dark knowledge he possesses makes him far too dangerous."

A cold shiver ran down Alfred's backbone. *Yes, it does, doesn't it? How could I have been so stupid?* He turned to the guard captain standing nearby with a sudden urgency. "Triple the guard on the tower! And I want the archbishop gagged and his hands bound! Do it now!"

Four guards raced up the tower steps. One of them carried a length of strong rope and a cloth for a gag. They did not understand their orders, but there was no question of their captain's urgency. They took the steps three at a time.

They arrived at the top of the stairs to find the cell door at the end of the short hallway wide open and hanging half off its hinges as if it had been beaten down with bare hands, its heavy oak beams splintered and smeared with blood. But no ten men could have broken down that door. Stranger still, it looked as though it had been broken into from the outside.

They approached gingerly, swords drawn, calling out the names of Barrick and Harding to no response. The torch that lit the hallway had been broken free of its iron housing and lay on the floor, flickering. The frontmost guard picked it up and held it out to shine inside the darkened cell.

Something warm and wet encircled his arm. He dropped the torch in shock—and was pulled suddenly forward, disappearing into the darkness of the cell. And then came the screaming, while the man's helpless thrashing was cast in shadow on the cell walls by the light of the fallen torch.

The screaming ended almost as quickly as it had begun; the shadows went still. For a moment, silence. The three guards outside the cell now had their swords drawn, yet dared not venture farther, their hearts pounding in their chests. And then they jumped back in alarm as their fellow guardsman fell forward out of the darkness and collapsed, blood spilling from a gash across his neck so deep that his head hung to one side, askew.

Barrick emerged from the darkness behind him. Or what had once been Barrick. Now he—it—was some kind of wolf-like monstrosity, its sinewy body covered in gray, matted fur. It walked on its hind legs with four more limbs to spare—long muscular arms with great razor-clawed hands.

What was once Harding slithered out from behind the wolf-thing and up the wall. Some kind of giant two-headed lizard, its leathery skin was covered with sharp, bristling spines, and a clubbed tail swished lazily back and forth as it crept toward the three guardsmen.

The closest of them panicked and foolishly lunged at it with his sword. The lizard easily dodged the blow, then responded by spitting a gob of sputum that burned like acid through the man's breastplate. The guard dropped his sword, screaming, trying desperately to unbuckle his armor, but before he could unfasten even one strap, the acid was through to his flesh and he collapsed to the ground, writhing helplessly, his final screams echoing along the stone hallway.

The two remaining guardsmen looked at their fallen friends in horror. And then Aethelred stepped out from the cell.

He smiled.

"Drop your swords, and you have my word that you will not die here today."

They did as he commanded. Aethelred raised his hands and, looking into the eyes of the two men before him, began to recite the words he had spent months perfecting.

And within moments, they were his as well.

THREE

Two horsemen arrived atop a gentle hill and looked down at the open country before them, a sprawling valley of fields and farmland, dotted by a few modest cottages that could barely be called a village.

"This can't be it," said the first rider.

"The bloke back at the inn said this was it," said the other. "Five miles along the only road east, you'll see it when you get to the hilltop."

"I know what a knight's estate looks like. If there were one here, we'd be seeing it, believe me."

They saw a lone man below, pushing a plow through one of the small farm plots the land was divided into.

"Let's ask him."

They rode down the craggy hillside, careful to avoid the rocks and divots. Many parts of England's rolling countryside were picturesque and pleasant to ride; this was not one of them. One wrong footing on this terrain could mean a broken ankle for a horse and perhaps a broken neck for its rider.

Arriving at the valley floor, they cantered over to the man working the field, a powerful sweat on him as he drove a deep furrow through the earth with the plow. Cast in heavy iron, it looked better suited to be drawn by a horse, but the man pushed it along unaided, as though he knew no better. The two men on horseback exchanged a look of amusement. Farmhands were not renowned for their intellect, but one that did not even know how to work such a basic tool? Wonders never ceased.

The peasant was turned away from the hillside and, consumed by his laborious task, seemed oblivious to the riders who had just arrived behind him, even as one of their horses gave a loud snort.

"Oi! You!"

The plow stopped. The peasant turned and raised his hand, both to shield his eyes from the sun and to wipe away the sweat that soaked his temple. He appeared a particularly uncivilized specimen, his face smeared with dirt, his long hair a stringy, tousled mess.

"What?" he said.

The two riders shared another look, this time not amused but annoyed. Did this peasant not recognize their uniforms? The royal insignia on their tunics?

"*What?*" the first rider said. "Is that any way for a commoner to address two of the King's men?"

The peasant took a step forward, out of the glare of the sun. He could see them better now.

"Oh. Right you are."

The riders waited for some gesture of respect or humility to accompany the peasant's realization of who they were, but none came. He simply stood there, squinting up at them, as though his original question still stood. *Well, what?*

Now the second rider spoke. "You do know that plow is meant to be pulled by a horse?"

"Of course. I'm not an idiot," said the peasant. "The horse is sick. He has a bellyache."

The first rider was growing impatient. "We are in search of—"

"I should have known those carrots were suspect."

"*Stop talking.* Where is Sir Wulfric's estate?"

The peasant chortled to himself. "I'd hardly call it an estate."

"So you do know of it?"

The man turned and pointed to the far side of the field he was working. Smoke drifted from the chimney of a modest farmhouse at the edge of the village beyond. Both horsemen looked puzzled, and the first one spurred his horse closer, glowering down from the saddle impatiently.

"We are in no mood for games, friend."

"What games? That's his house there."

Now the second rider spoke again. "That house is far too meager to be the seat of a knight."

"Well, to be fair, Wulfric also owns this field, and that one there, and that one over there," said the peasant, pointing. "All rich soil, good crops. Not bad if you ask me."

"Sir Wulfric, peasant!" the first rider scolded him. "Be mindful how you refer to a Knight of the Realm."

"And not just any knight," added the second. "The greatest of all knights."

"Yes, I've heard the stories," said the peasant, who seemed to be growing tired of this conversation himself. "Greatly exaggerated, for the most part."

The first rider had finally had enough. He dismounted and marched over to the man, giving him a black look.

"Now look, peasant. I've had about enough—"

The sun, still setting over the hill, now cast its light upon the silver pendant, wrought in the shape of a scarab beetle, that hung on a loop of leather around the peasant's neck. It was a simple design, but one familiar to every man and boy sworn to the King's service. That same medallion had been seen by all who had ever passed through the army barracks at Winchester, in a painting that hung in its main hall. It was depicted hanging around the neck of Sir Wulfric the Wild. Knight of all knights. The man who had saved King Alfred's life and turned the tide at the Battle of Ethandun, and with it the entire war against the Norse.

The rider's legs quaked, and for a moment he thought they might give way entirely. Instead he sank to one knee, bowing his head before the dirt-faced peasant. "Sir Wulfric, please accept my most humble apology."

"Oh, *shit*," the second rider exclaimed under his breath. He hurriedly dismounted and knelt at his comrade's side.

"This field is too muddy for kneeling," said Wulfric, who despite his station had never grown comfortable at the sight of any man subjugating himself before another. All men were equal in God's eyes, so why not also in the eyes of men themselves? "Rise."

And they rose, now regarding this grubby farmworker with the kind of reverent awe normally reserved for gods and kings.

"I apologize," said Wulfric as he pulled a rag from his pocket and wiped the dirt from his hands. "But the long days in the field can grow dull, and I must find my amusements where I can. Now, what does Alfred want?"

Wulfric left the plow in the field and made his way back to the house as the King's riders departed the way they had come. It was still early in the day and there was much land left to sow, which now would have to wait. As a rule, he had little time for the commands of kings—but Alfred was more than just a king. He was a friend, and one who had done more for Wulfric than he could ever repay. And so Wulfric, though he detested the thought of picking up a weapon ever again—and that was certainly the only purpose for which Alfred would call upon him—knew he could not refuse.

As a young man Wulfric had been a smith's apprentice, learning how to forge a sword and make it strong, but not how to wield one. That was for others. The very thought of violence made his stomach roil like a live fish writhing in his belly. Like all Englishmen, he had been raised Christian, but his father had also encouraged Wulfric to think for himself, and so to take from the holy teachings what he would. Of what he knew of the Bible, a single verse had always spoken to Wulfric more than any other: *Love thy neighbor as thyself.* He wished no man to raise a hand against him, and so he would not against another.

That was until the Norse came.

He was raised in the town of his birth, a small place called Caengiford. London lay just a few miles to the southwest, and it was there, when Wulfric was seventeen, that the Danish marauders had come, smashing the great walls the Romans had built centuries ago, claiming the city for their own, killing anyone who did not have the good sense to flee before them. Wulfric could still remember the displaced and the wounded coming through Caengiford, horribly burned, missing entire limbs, mothers still carrying the bodies of babies that had been trampled or flung against the walls by the barbarians from across the sea.

Wulfric had refused to be shielded from such sights. He wanted to see. Though he did not understand the suffering he witnessed, he knew that turning away from it, trying to pretend it was not real, was somehow irresponsible. And he knew that these horrors could as easily be visited upon him and his. He just did not realize how soon.

The Norse arrived in Caengiford the next week. A raiding party sent to hunt down those fleeing the city found Wulfric's village instead, and since their nature was to destroy all before them, they set about burning it to the ground. Wulfric barely made it out alive, slipping through an open window at his mother's insistence while the Danish brutes outside hammered at the door. He escaped a moment before they burst through, and he ran into the forest as fast as he could, never looking back. Thus he did not see his mother's and father's fate, nor that of his four younger brothers, too little to run. But his imagination served well enough, and even years later, he could not bring himself to think of it but for when old memories came unbidden, in nightmares.

After escaping the destruction of his village, Wulfric stole a ride on a merchant's cart until he was discovered and thrown off. After that he walked. He had no destination in mind, nowhere to go. Wherever the Norse were not, that was good enough for him. He lost count of the weeks he traveled alone, sleeping by the side of the road, eating whatever he could find in the woods or, on a good day, whatever might fall—or be encouraged to fall—from a passing cart. One day he asked a passerby where he was and discovered that he had wandered as far as Wiltshire. He made his way to a small town and, after demonstrating his ability with hammer and tong, was taken on by the local smith. There he earned his keep making farming tools and shoes for horses, and as time went on, ever-increasing numbers of swords. Alfred's war against the Norse was not faring well, it was said, and weapons were needed to arm the men being pressed into service from every county.

It was a smith's job to check the weight and balance of every sword as it cooled from the forge, but Wulfric always found an excuse to leave that task to the other apprentices. Even holding a sword felt wrong to him; the thought of running a man through with one made him queasy. He tried to tell that to the King's recruiters, when they rode into town to muster every able-bodied man they could find, but all he got was a firm clip round the ear and orders to report to the barracks at Chippenham by week's end or be marked a deserter.

Wulfric weighed his options and thought briefly of running. But he knew of the army's relentless pursuit of cowards who defied the King's commission, and he did not relish living another long while on the run, much less the punishment were he to be caught. And so he arrived at Chippenham on the very last day before he would have been declared an absconder. There he was given livery and a wooden sword to practice with and thrown immediately into mock combat. In a time of peace, his training might have followed a more unhurried pace, but the Norse were advancing on every front, and there was little time to do else but throw new recruits into the thick of it and hope that they could fight, or learn to in short order.

Even a mock sword felt ugly in Wulfric's hand, yet he found that although he had no wish to fight, he undoubtedly had a knack for it. More than a knack—an instinct. On his first day sparring in the training yard, he went right at the master-at-arms, a bearded, barrel-chested soldier with more years of combat experience than Wulfric had on this earth. Armed with only a blunted blade of wood, he fought with such speed and ferocity that the instructor wound up on his backside, stunned. The other trainees applauded and hollered, but Wulfric was more surprised than anyone; it was as though some other entity had taken possession of his sword arm, of his entire body, driving him forward. In those few seconds, he had become someone else entirely, someone ugly and brutal and merciless. In other words, exactly the kind of person his superiors were looking for. It was noted that while there was little artistry in the way Wulfric fought, there was a savage purity to it. He fought more like a Norse than an Englishman—a fact that would, in time, chill the blood of both alike. The Norse had a name for men like Wulfric, men who fought and killed without fear or mercy or grace. *Berserker.*

The nickname stuck fast. Throughout the Chippenham ranks he became known as Wulfric the Wild. Wulfric hated the name, but not the respect that accompanied it. Nobody cuffed him on the ear anymore. Instead, from then on, Wulfric was watched closely by his trainers, marked as one of a few who had something special, something that could be used to great advantage out on the field. When it came to battle, as it inevitably would, he and others like him would be placed close to the King to afford him the greatest protection.

Battle came sooner than expected, in the deep cold of midwinter and on Twelfth Night, no less. Wulfric and the other trainees had been enjoying the last of their Christmas rations on the night the Norse stormed the walls of Chippenham.

Alarm bells sounded, rousing sleepers from their beds as, outside, barbarians poured over the walls and battered down the gates of the English fortress. Officers rushed to the barrack rooms to mobilize as many men as they could. There, a sergeant who knew Wulfric grabbed him by the collar and sent him in the other direction from his young comrades. He went where he was bid and found himself outside the royal chamber itself, where Alfred's personal guard and a troop of other heavily armed men were moving the King to safety.

It was the first time Wulfric had seen Alfred, though he thought he might have spied the King once before, looking down on the training yard from the parapets. But there was no mistaking this time: Wulfric was just a few feet away from the King as the man was bundled from his room half-dressed, having just moments before been roused from his royal bed.

"Wulfric, come here, lad!"

Wulfric's master-at-arms, the man he had charged and put on his back that first day in the yard, was beckoning urgently. When Wulfric approached, he felt the leather bindings of a sword hilt pressed into his hand. It felt so much heavier than the wooden dummies he had been practicing with. He looked down and saw the metal blade glimmer in the torchlight. The first true sword he had ever held as a soldier.

"Stay with the King! Stay with the King!" the master-at-arms bellowed, and he pushed Wulfric along with the rest of Alfred's company as they rushed the King along the hallway. It was all happening so fast. Outside could be heard the sounds of battle— the clash of metal on metal, the roaring of fires, the screams of wounded and dying men. Sounds Wulfric had not heard since fleeing his village two years before.

It was outside that Wulfric killed his first man. He brought up the rear of Alfred's protective huddle as they exited the hallway into the chill air of the courtyard. Wulfric's first thought was how bitterly cold it was and how he wished he'd had time to grab his warmer tunic before he'd been herded out of his room. Then he heard a war cry that curdled his blood and turned to see a giant

Norseman charging at him, face hidden behind a long braided beard and a battered metal helm. The warrior was easily twice Wulfric's size, and looked to him more like an ox that had learned to walk on its hind legs. But that was all the observation he had time for before the Dane was upon him, swinging an oversized hammer that was unlike any weapon of war Wulfric had ever seen—and he had forged many.

Wulfric jumped backward to avoid the first blow, but the Norseman was quicker than his size suggested, and his second attack came too fast for Wulfric to anticipate. This time he managed only half a dodge before the maul struck him in the shoulder and knocked him to the ground. He looked up, dazed, to see the great bull of a man bearing down on him, hammer overhead in preparation for the killing blow.

But Wulfric had not lost hold of his sword. He swung low, slashing the Norseman deep across the ankle. The Dane cried out and went down on one knee, dropping the hammer. He drew a knife from his belt, but now it was Wulfric who surprised with his speed. He leapt back to his feet and swung his sword upward like a farmer chopping wheat with a scythe. It caught the Dane on the underside of the neck and buried itself deep in his throat.

As the giant's blood sprayed out onto the cobblestones, time seemed to slow, and Wulfric noted that it was curious how blood appeared black, not red, in the pale light of the moon. And then time resumed its normal rate again, and Wulfric drew back his sword. The motion pulled the blade free from the Dane's neck and brought him crashing to the ground. Wulfric stepped back to avoid the dead man's blood staining his boots as it pooled out toward him, then ran to catch up with King Alfred and his men.

The ox was the first man Wulfric killed in battle, but far from the last. Many more were to come in the months ahead. Alfred and his company, along with the rest of those who managed to escape the disaster at Chippenham, retreated south to the Isle of Athelney in neighboring Somerset. The small island provided a bottleneck that protected them from the type of frontal assault suffered at Chippenham and afforded Alfred time to regroup.

Not that he had much left to regroup; most of his men had been killed or captured, and the small force that remained could scarcely defend itself, let alone stage a counterattack. But Alfred refused to be cowed, even after a crushing defeat and with so few resources at hand. He sent word to every nearby village and town, commanding men to rally to his banner. And rally they did. After several long months of rebuilding his army, Alfred took it back onto the field and met the full might of the Danish host at Ethandun.

It was to be a bloody morning, not least for young Wulfric, who, since first drawing blood in the battle against the ox, had discovered that he now had not only a talent for killing, but a taste for it. After the fall of Chippenham, the Norse had hounded Alfred's retreating army halfway across Wiltshire before finally breaking off pursuit. Along the way, there had been several bloody skirmishes, in which Wulfric had claimed many more Danish heads. In each battle, it was as though some inner savage that usually lay dormant within him awoke and asserted control until the fight was over. After the killing was done, Wulfric could feel nothing but remorse for the lives he had taken. But when he was in the thick of it, bloody sword in hand, it was as though he had been born to do this and nothing else. None who fought alongside him, who witnessed this transformation, could disagree. And over time, Wulfric's nickname, given in jest after that first day in the training yard, began to strike his comrades-in-arms as wholly inadequate.

But on that day at Ethandun they saw something else entirely. Wulfric had already killed at least twenty Norsemen in the battle—the royal crest on his tabard had entirely disappeared behind a thick coating of Danish blood—when he wheeled around to realize King Alfred was nowhere to be seen. Lost in the reverie of slaughter, he had broken the one rule his master-at-arms had given him: *Stay with the King!* He searched the melee, cutting down any Dane unfortunate enough to stray within striking distance, until he caught sight of the King on his horse. And even from fifty feet away, Wulfric could see that Alfred was in trouble. The Norse were swarming his position, cutting down his personal guard, making their way closer to the man Wulfric had taken an oath to protect.

Wulfric surged forward and reached the King just as a powerful Dane dressed in furs and mail reached up and pulled Alfred down off his mount. With the King defenseless on the ground, the Norseman drew back his axe for the killing blow. That was when Wulfric charged into the fray, piercing the Dane's mail armor with his sword. The barbarian slid off Wulfric's blade, dead, even as three more moved in to finish the job he had started. Wulfric, breathing hard, took up a defensive position between the Norsemen and his King.

The first man to attack went down quickly: Wulfric dodged the Norseman's swinging sword and slashed him across the back with his own. The second and third came at Wulfric together, thinking to better their odds. It did, but not nearly enough. Wulfric ran his sword through the open mouth of one, but when the blade became stuck in the back of the man's skull and could not be pulled free, he let it go, and took on the other man unarmed.

This one carried a crudely formed cudgel, little more than a heavy hunk of wood with iron spikes hammered through it, but deadly enough, especially at arm's length. Wulfric, driven by the war spirit that possessed him in battle, knew that his best chance was to get in close. He waited for the Danish brute to take a big, lumbering swing, ducked under it, then charged at the man, tackling him to the ground. The Norseman was still by far the stronger and would doubtless prevail in a hand-to-hand grapple, but Wulfric would not let it come to that. He drew a stiletto from his boot and drove it into the barbarian's right eye, deep enough to skewer his head to the ground beneath.

Wulfric fell back onto the ground, exhausted. More English soldiers now rallied to the King's side, surrounding him. Two men helped Alfred to his feet. None did so for Wulfric. They had not witnessed the encounter; to them he was just another common infantryman, not worthy of their concern. But one man had noticed: Alfred. As he was escorted to safety, his eyes never left Wulfric, the young man who had just saved his life.

Alfred went on to a great victory at Ethandun, and the war turned after that. Alfred routed the Danish host and pursued the surviving rabble all the way back to Chippenham, where the rest of the Norse were by now garrisoned. With the Danish king, Guthrum, sequestered inside, Alfred saw his chance to break them once and for all. Thus, with his entire force arrayed around Chippenham's walls, Alfred began a slow siege. After two weeks, the Norse within were starving, their will to resist broken. In desperation, Guthrum sued for peace, and Alfred offered the terms that would at last bring the war to an end.

After his triumphant return home, Alfred's first order of business was to have the young infantryman who had saved his life at Ethandun brought before him. Wulfric had no idea why he had been summoned to the royal court, and so was surprised when he was told to kneel and felt the flat of Alfred's sword touch first one shoulder, then the other. "Arise, Sir Wulfric," the King said. And the young man who once swore he would never so much as hold a sword rose, a knight.

Wulfric was a common man with no noble heritage, and so it was explained to him that all knights must have a coat of arms to signify their house. With little heraldic precedent to draw on, Wulfric decided to take as the symbol of his house a cherished memory from his childhood. His father had taught him as a boy to identify all manner of curious beetles and bugs, and Wulfric's favorite among all was the scarab beetle. His father had explained that its armored shell made it hardy and resistant to all manner of hostile conditions. Wulfric, who knew the hard life of a peasant, had liked that. He also liked that the scarab's favorite pastime was to collect dung. And so it was that years later, wrestling with the fact that he was no longer a commoner but a Knight of the Realm, he thought it the perfect way to remind himself of his lowly beginnings. For what could be more lowly than an insect that spends its days half-buried in shit?

Once Wulfric had a coat of arms by which his house could be known, all he needed was a house. Alfred granted him his choice of castles and lands up and down the kingdom, but Wulfric would take none of them. Instead he settled on a house and a plot of land where he could raise turnips and carrots and perhaps find a wife for himself. If God were willing, perhaps he would even see fit to bless him with a son or daughter, but Wulfric would not ask for anything he had not yet earned. To his mind, all he had done of note was kill men in battle, and he did not see why that should ever be rewarded.

When Wulfric stepped through the door, Cwen, his wife, turned in surprise from the stove where soup was cooking. "You're back early," she said. "Did you forget something?"

By God, that soup smells good, Wulfric thought as the aroma hit him. Of all the reasons he had chosen Cwen for his wife, her cooking ranked only second. *Well, perhaps third*, he thought to himself.

"Yes," said Wulfric wearily. "I forgot, if only briefly, that I will never be out of Alfred's debt."

Cwen did not appear to like the sound of that at all. She placed her hands on her hips and frowned at him. "Please, not that look," Wulfric said as he sat. "How about some of that soup?"

"It's not ready yet," said Cwen, softening not even a little. "What do you mean? Those riders I saw on the hill, they were the King's men?"

"He's summoned me to Winchester."

"And of course you said no."

"I could hardly do that. Not after everything he has done for me. I must at least go and see what he wants."

Cwen stepped out from behind the kitchen table. She was getting bigger every day. The child was due in only a few months. That was why Wulfric was out on the plow, though the horse was sick. When his son was born—somehow, Wulfric knew it was to be a boy—he would not want for food to eat, nor any of the things that Wulfric had gone without as a child. He would be the son of a knight. Perhaps Wulfric would ask Alfred for that castle after all, so that his son might grow up in it.

"You've got it backward," Cwen said sternly. "You've always had it backward. It's Alfred who owes you, not the other way around. He'd be dead if not for you."

"I only did what I was sworn to do," said Wulfric. "What any soldier would have done in my position. But Alfred did not have to knight me, nor set me up for life the way he did. Look at all that I have—more than I ever dreamed. My own house, my own land." He rose from the table and took his wife by the hand. "My own wife, the most beautiful in the world."

"Save your flattery," said Cwen, though the faintest hint of a smile suggested that it had made its mark. "I am quite sure Alfred did not grant me to you."

"True, but I would not have won you had he not made me a knight."

"I didn't know you were a knight when I agreed to marry you."

"If I were not, I would never have had the courage to ask," he said, close enough now to kiss her. And kiss her he did.

They kissed, and made love, and later Wulfric got his soup, and they ate together by the hearth.

"Don't think," Cwen said, looking up from her bowl, "that with a few fine words and a quick roll on the bed you can buy me off. You're not disappearing off on some campaign. I want you here when the baby is born. I *need* you here."

"Who said anything about a campaign?" Wulfric replied.

"Do you take me for a fool? Why else would Alfred send for you? I've heard the rumors about the king in the Danelaw. They say he's nearly dead and that the Norse may rise up again under some new warlord."

"Rumors, that's all," said Wulfric. But Cwen knew him well enough to know that while he might wish that were true, he did not believe it. She reached over and took her husband's hand.

"Wulfric, look at me. I know Alfred is your friend, but I am your wife, and this is your child." She placed her other hand over her bulging belly. "I want you to promise me, here and now, that you will not let him send you on some new war against the Norse."

Wulfric squeezed her hand tightly, met her eyes. "I promise."

Satisfied, Cwen smiled and returned to her soup.

"I'm sure it's nothing, really," he said. "Maybe Alfred burned another batch of cakes and wants to borrow you for his new head cook."

Cwen laughed, and kissed him on the forehead, and rose to fetch them both another bowl.

Early the next morning, Wulfric left his house with a saddle and provisions for a long day's ride over his shoulder. He unbolted the door to the stable, and his horse, Dolly, peeked out from the gloom inside.

"How are you today, old girl?" he asked. Dolly did not reply until Wulfric brought the saddle down off his shoulder and slung it over her back. She stamped a hoof and snorted unhappily.

"Oh, stop complaining," said Wulfric as he fed her a handful of oats. "You had all of yesterday off. Today, bellyache or not, we ride. We're going to see the King. And I'll bet you his carrots are a lot better than ours."

FOUR

Wulfric arrived at Winchester early that evening. He had ridden tirelessly throughout the day, eating his lunch in the saddle, stopping only so that Dolly could briefly rest and drink and get her oats. Wulfric hated the thought of being away from Cwen and the little one for even one night, and he would do whatever was in his power to avoid a second. Perhaps, he thought, Alfred wanted only a small thing, and in making such good time he could be back home with his family tomorrow.

Perhaps. The King was not wont to send riders to summon his most trusted knight over a trifle, but still Wulfric had entertained himself on the journey by imagining all the reasons Alfred might want to see him that would allow him to be home before the next sunset. By the time Alfred's castle appeared on the horizon, Wulfric had been forced to accept the gloomy truth that those reasons he could think of could be reckoned on one hand. And none of them seemed likely.

The guardsmen on watch atop the castle battlements had spied Wulfric coming along the road from some distance away, and the great fortress's gates rumbled open as he approached. Dolly's hooves clopped across the drawbridge, and as Wulfric passed beneath the barbican into the outer yard, he was reminded why, as much as he loved Alfred, he rarely enjoyed visiting his friend's royal seat. The guards and other men-at-arms who met him as he

entered gazed at him in quiet fascination, as though some mytho-
logical hero made flesh stood before them.

To many of these young men, of course, that was exactly who
Wulfric was. Sir Wulfric the Wild. The man who had killed more
Norsemen than any other in the Danish campaigns, by more than
double. The man who had single-handedly slaughtered a dozen
barbarians in defense of the King's life and then refused the lavish
lands and riches offered him in reward. The man who, it was said,
the King trusted and listened to above all others, even the Queen
herself.

Wulfric tried to avoid the eyes of the man who took Dolly's
reins for him as he dismounted, but he could feel them boring
into him. This would be the story of his visit here, he knew. An
unremitting parade of genuflection and reverence that would soon
have Wulfric itching for home, where the merest suggestion of any
such display would earn him a hard rap on the knuckles with a
wooden ladle. He liked that far better than this.

He hoped at least to avoid visiting the barrack where that
god-awful painting of him hung. Wulfric had refused to sit for
it, and so the artist had been forced to make do with whatever
descriptions and drawings he could garner from others. The result,
Wulfric had thought when he first saw it, was ridiculous. He was
depicted holding a shining sword aloft in an absurdly heroic pose,
all puffed up with pride, a trait that Wulfric had taken pains to
avoid his entire life. The artist had even restored the part of his ear
famously lost to a Danish axe at Ethandun, as if it were better that
he appear invulnerable. But Wulfric liked his ear the way it was. It
served as an ever-present reminder to himself that death was never
more than an inch away, that even the most celebrated warriors
were as mortal as any other.

It might have been useful to the young soldiers who passed
through here to be reminded of that also; as it was, the painting
would inspire in those men only a naively romanticized notion
of heroism, one that would be roughly dispelled in their first real

battle. The only thing rendered with any accuracy at all, Wulfric thought, was the scarab pendant that hung around his neck—they had, at least, got that right. *Yes, definitely avoid the barracks*, he reminded himself. Then he thanked the man who stabled his horse and made his way across the yard toward the inner bailey and the castle's central keep, where Alfred resided.

Just being here in the royal household, with all its trappings, made Wulfric uneasy. The idea of royalty had always struck him as inequitable, an attitude no doubt inherited from his father. *No man is greater than another by birth*, he had taught his young son. *Only by deed.* But Wulfric was also a man of God, and kings and queens, many believed, were chosen by God himself, for he alone knew who among the people had it within themselves to lead their country to its rightful destiny.

Having witnessed firsthand what Alfred had accomplished, Wulfric found that belief difficult to argue against. The crown had been thrust upon Alfred at a young age, after the untimely death of his brother, and he had, through sheer courage and audacity, turned years of bitter and bloody defeat at the hands of the Norse into the unlikeliest of victories. He had brought England back from the brink of annihilation. Now, thanks to his guidance, it was safer and stronger than ever. Could any other man have done such a thing? Could Wulfric? He doubted it.

Though Wulfric knew as well as anyone not to use the name *Alfred the Great* in the King's presence, he believed it to be warranted. For he was a great King and, more than that, a great friend. He had not needed to reward Wulfric for doing a soldier's duty, but everything Wulfric now counted as a blessing in his life he owed to his friend's generosity. The two of them had spent countless hours together, eating and telling stories and slowly coming to the mutual realization that in another lifetime they would have been brothers. As it was, in this one, they practically were.

———•◦⦂◎⦂◦•———

"Wulfric!"

Alfred strode briskly across the Great Hall and clapped his arms around Wulfric in a fond embrace. And in that moment, with all royal formality dashed away by that informal gesture, Wulfric's unease lifted. They were surrounded by enough timber and stone in this one room to build Wulfric's house twenty times over, yet Alfred's greeting made him feel as though he had simply wandered over to visit his neighbor, Brom, to borrow a loaf of bread. He was in the company of a friend first, his King a distant second. He returned the embrace warmly.

As they separated, Wulfric could see that all was not right. Alfred looked tired and haggard, as though he had not seen a good night's sleep in some time. Whatever predicament had led him to summon Wulfric was no doubt the cause, and Wulfric wanted nothing more than to know the nature of it, but it was not his place to ask.

"My thanks to you for coming so quickly," said Alfred, as cheerily as he was able. "How was your journey?"

"Uneventful," Wulfric replied. "I made good speed, which I hope to also on my return." He wasted no time letting Alfred know how keen he was to be on his way.

Alfred laughed. "You've only just arrived and already you're planning your trip back?"

"Your invitation is never anything less than an honor," said Wulfric. "But I am reluctant to be far removed from Cwen at the moment."

"Ah, how is the beautiful Cwen? Wait, she's not sick, is she?"

Wulfric beamed in the way only an expectant father can. "Far from it."

Alfred knew that look. He had six children of his own. A grin spread across his own face, and he grabbed Wulfric by the shoulders and embraced him again, more firmly. "God bless you, you horny bastard!" he exclaimed with a laugh. "How far along?"

"Six months, thereabouts. Her back aches and she waddles like a duck, and last week I swear I saw her eat a piece of coal. But for all that, she is still the most beautiful woman I could ever hope to lay eyes on, much less have married."

"She is that," Alfred agreed. "Do you hope for a son or daughter?"

"Cwen gives no mind to that and prays only that it has its health. As do I, although whenever I dream about it, it is always a boy."

"I have no doubt of it," Alfred said, the smile fading from his lips. "I pray that we might have you home before he is born."

And something inside Wulfric sank like a stone.

They ate dinner together that night in Alfred's private chamber. Wulfric had no appetite. He had suspected, of course, that his hope of returning home the next day was a fantasy, but now it was confirmed. Whatever task lay before him was to be measured not in days or even weeks, but in months.

Alfred seemed determined to put off discussing anything of import for as long as possible, leaving Wulfric to nod and smile politely as he privately tortured himself with questions of what lay in store for him. He cringed as he remembered the promise he had made to Cwen just before he left. *What are your words worth*, he asked himself, *if they crumble into dust so easily?* But to whom did his allegiance belong? His beloved wife carrying his unborn child? Or to his best friend and his King, to whom he owed everything he had? He found himself praying for some hope of returning home without having broken his covenant with either.

"Do you believe in witchcraft, Wulfric?"

Wulfric's attention returned suddenly to the table. The King had been talking for some time, but the oddity of the question was such that it stood out from all the rest.

He waited for Alfred's face to crack. The King never had been able to keep a straight face when telling a joke, but Alfred's expression now was as somber as Wulfric had ever seen it, even during the darkest days of the war. This was not a jest. And there was something unsettling about the look in Alfred's eyes. It suggested that he knew more, much more, about the subject he had just broached than he had yet volunteered.

Wulfric thought carefully about his answer before speaking. "I've never seen any evidence of it."

"You've seen no evidence of God, either," Alfred replied, as though anticipating the answer. "And yet you believe."

"God was with us at Ethandun," said Wulfric. "We could not have turned the tide of battle otherwise. I remember you said so yourself."

"*Direct* evidence," the King retorted. "Something before your very eyes that defies all nature, and science, and reason. Something that cannot be explained."

"Then no. But faith is the evidence of things not seen, is it not?"

For a long moment, Alfred did not speak. He simply fingered the stem of his goblet and stared into the blood-red surface of the wine within, lost in some dark thought.

"I have seen things," he said at last, his voice not much above a whisper. "Things that have led me to question my own faith. And may cause you to question yours."

A gust of wind howled against the window. Wulfric could not tell if the room had suddenly grown colder or if it was his imagination. Either way, Alfred's demeanor troubled him. These were not the words of a rational man, and Wulfric had never known his King to be anything but.

"Why am I here?" he asked, finally.

"In the morning, I will show you," said Alfred as he rose from his chair, prompting Wulfric to do the same.

"I am not tired," said Wulfric, determined to get to the source of whatever was causing this uncharacteristic behavior. "I came a long way. If this is why I am here, if you have something to show me, show me now."

"In the morning," said Alfred. "The things I speak of should not be seen so late before sleep."

Wulfric did not sleep. Instead, he tossed and turned restlessly through the night, partly because the bed, though far more comfortable and spacious than his own, was not his own. He had rarely spent a night away from home since making his new life there, and when he did, sleep did not come easily. He missed the feel of his own pillow, lumpy as it was. He missed the smell of whatever Cwen had been baking, left out to cool overnight. And most of all, he missed Cwen, the warmth of her back as he nestled himself against her, his hand on her firm, round belly, feeling the gentle stirring of his unborn child within. All the luxuries and appointments of Alfred's castle only reminded him how far he was from them.

But mostly he did not sleep out of concern for his friend. He had seen Alfred drawn and wan before—many times while on campaign—but never like this. Wulfric knew better than most the strength of the man, knew that it would take the gravest of matters, more grave even than war, to weigh so heavily upon him. Alfred's words repeated incessantly in Wulfric's head as he shifted uncomfortably beneath the bedsheets. *I have seen things that have led me to question my own faith.* Wulfric knew that Alfred's faith in God went to the very core of his being. It made him the man he was, had given him the strength to drive back the Norse even when all seemed lost. If all the horrors of battle, of seeing comrades bloodied and cleaved all around him, could not shake this man's belief, then what in God's name could? It was a question Wulfric could not solve, though he racked his brain, and it haunted him still when the first cock crowed and one of Alfred's pages arrived to fetch him.

Alfred was waiting for Wulfric in the Great Hall. He made no offer of breakfast, nor did he enquire how Wulfric had slept; it was plain enough to see. While the King last night had seemed determined to delay the matter at hand, this morning he was equally determined not to tarry. He escorted Wulfric from the hall and through the castle's winding hallways until they arrived at a door with which Wulfric was not familiar; he thought he had seen all of the castle in his time here, but this was new to him.

The door was constructed of the heaviest oak and barred by an iron gate that appeared to have been added recently. Two guards stood watch by the entrance. Wulfric did not like it here. He had never much cared for small spaces. Looking back now, he realized that the walls and ceiling had been gradually contracting as they progressed along the hallway, so that now they stood at the end of what felt more like a tunnel. He was already beginning to feel distinctly uneasy.

"What is this?" he asked.

"The dungeon," Alfred replied. He nodded to one of the guards, who unlocked the iron gate and swung it open, then did the same with the door behind it.

"Here," said Alfred. He produced an embroidered cloth and offered it to Wulfric. It was damp, and there was an almost overpowering, but not unpleasant, odor from whatever the material had been soaked in. Wulfric was no herbalist, but his friend Aedan, who owned the field neighboring his, grew many types of fragrant plants, and so he recognized the smell—a concoction of lavender and mint. It was not unlike the perfume Cwen had made for herself from the bushel of herbs Aedan brought them as a welcoming gift when they first set up house, and for a moment Wulfric found it comforting; it smelled to him of home.

Then the dungeon door opened with a creak and something else rose up out of the dank, musty air within. Wulfric could not identify it—he had never before smelled anything quite like it—but it was foul. He immediately pressed the cloth against his nose and mouth, but even the strong aroma of the perfume only partially blocked out the stench. Wulfric looked at Alfred and noticed that he had no such cloth of his own. "Where is yours?" he enquired.

"It pains me to say that I have grown accustomed to the smell," Alfred replied. He lifted a flaming torch from its cradle on the nearby wall and they began their descent.

Wulfric followed the King down the winding stairs, the two of them led by one of Alfred's guards while the other remained above, locking and barring the door behind them. All trod warily as they descended, Wulfric most of all; the dank stone steps felt slippery underfoot, and his mind was racing with thoughts of what might await them at the bottom. Winchester's dungeon was reserved not for deserters or common criminals, who typically languished in the stockade, and not for high-ranking enemies of the crown, who were sent to the tower, but for the worst and most despicable of those who sought to harm Alfred's kingdom. Who was down here? A captured Danish spy with tidings of a fresh plot? A foiled assassin? Or something beyond even his busy imagination? Wulfric did not know whether to feel relief or dread in the knowledge that he would find out soon enough.

With each step, the fetor wafting from the darkness below grew more powerful. Wulfric twisted the cloth Alfred had given him to wring out more of its perfumed scent, but it was no use. Even with the cloth pressed firmly against his face, the stink was so strong by the time they reached the bottom of the steps that Wulfric could barely keep himself from retching. What the hell was it? Sulfur, perhaps? Similar, but worse.

Even in the bright light of their torches, the narrow corridor at which they arrived gave up little. The stone walls on either side extended for only a few feet before disappearing into the deepest, most impenetrable blackness Wulfric had ever seen. This was no ordinary darkness, not simply the absence of light; it was as though something down here was *radiating* darkness, filling every corner of this dungeon with it. Wulfric was not a man easily unnerved, but at this moment he was gripped by a powerful desire to retreat up the steps, to be away from this place. Still, he stood firm.

The guard, his torch lighting the way, led Alfred and Wulfric down the narrow corridor, passing cell after empty cell. Though the flame burned brightly, it stubbornly refused to reveal anything more than a few feet ahead. It should have cast at least a dim light down the tunnel's entire length. Here, it shrank to an isolated sliver of light in a sea of unyielding black.

Wulfric began to hear something. A scratching sound in the dark up ahead. Snorting and snarling. Some kind of animal. It sounded to him sickly, or wounded, but not in any way that he had ever heard, and he had tended many an animal on his farm. He shivered as his suspicion grew that whatever was being held down here fell into that last dreaded category—the thing beyond his imagining.

The guard came to a halt. "Go no farther," he warned. Before them a line had been daubed across the floor in woad, and a few feet beyond, the iron bars of the final cell at the hallway's end could be dimly seen in the flickering dark. This cell looked different from the others. The lower half of the bars were ridden with rust and a strange, greenish corrosion; they were pitted and scarred as though something had been chewing at them, and some were still dripping with a wet, viscous saliva.

Something behind those bars was moving, something primal and ugly, scratching and snorting around the floor of the cell. Whatever it was, it lived low to the ground. But Wulfric caught only brief, partial glimpses of it in the dim light. For a moment, he thought he could discern a clawed foot, like that of an oversized cat. But then the torchlight reflected a glimmer of reptilian scale. Was his mind playing tricks with him, down here in the darkness?

The guard used his torch to light another that hung from the wall. He waited for its flame to bloom fully and then tossed it low against the foot of the iron bars. Wulfric jolted back in alarm as the creature within let out a shriek, amplified by the close stone walls, that set the hairs along his arms and neck on end. The creature retreated from the flames, into a dark corner of its cell, but then it slowly came forward again, into the light, and Wulfric at last saw the full nature of it.

It moved across the rotten straw lining the cell floor on six squat, lizard-like legs, each webbed foot bearing several large, horned claws. Its body was scaled but shaped like a potbellied hog, and it had the snout and tusks of one, too, although its lidless eyes were distinctly reptilian, bright red with slitted yellow irises. The unnameable thing approached the fallen torch, sniffing at the burning embers through the bars. And then the thing reached through and snatched the torch with its mouth, wrestling with it for a moment as it tried to pull it through the bars. Finally it dropped the torch, then grabbed it again by its tapered end, pulling it through the bars longwise. Wulfric watched in morbid fascination as the beast opened its jaws wide, revealing rows of slavering, needle-like fangs, bit down on the torch with a loud crunch, then shredded it to splinters in a frenzy before swallowing it down, flames and all.

The guardsman took a step back, ushering Alfred and Wulfric with a raised arm as he did so. A moment later, after swallowing the last of the torch, the beast belched out a hot burst of bright orange flame. In the brief eruption of light, Wulfric saw that much of the cell's walls had been charred black by fire.

Against his better judgment, Wulfric found himself moving closer, unthinkingly stepping across the line on the floor. Alarmed, the guard reached out and grabbed him by the shoulder, but it was too late. The beast caught sight of Wulfric and went wild. Slavering like a rabid dog, it threw itself hard against the bars, screeching as it clawed at the air. As the guard tried to pull Wulfric back, an impossibly long tongue uncoiled from the creature's mouth and snapped around Wulfric's wrist. He cried out and tried to pull free, but the beast was stronger. It scuttled backward, toward the rear of the cell, dragging Wulfric with it.

Alfred grabbed Wulfric's free arm and dug in his heels. But even their combined strength was not enough. As the two of them were dragged closer to the beast, the guard drew his sword and began hacking frantically at its tongue, severing it only on the third strike. Finally free, Wulfric and Alfred fell backward onto the floor. The wounded beast rolled onto its back as well, howling and kicking its feet hysterically.

Moving quickly, the guard drew a dagger from his belt and slid the blade under the piece of severed tongue that was still constricted around Wulfric's wrist. With a hard jerk upward, he cut the tongue free, and it fell to the floor, still writhing like a fish flapping on a riverbank. Alfred stood ready with a skin of water, spilling it onto Wulfric's wrist the moment the thing was removed. His flesh sizzled, wisps of smoke rising, and Wulfric saw a bright red welt encircling his wrist where the tongue had taken hold of him. The top layer of skin had been burned away by the beast's saliva.

"It spits acid!" Alfred barked. "That is why we go no farther."

Wulfric was still vaguely in shock. He took the water skin from Alfred and drank deeply. He looked back at the cell. The creature seemed to have calmed. It now lay slumped on its belly at the front of the cell, its head skewed sideways, and chewed lazily on the bars like a dog with a juicy bone. Wulfric watched as its wounded, bleeding tongue licked against the iron, covering it in its corrosive slobber.

"I ordered all the others destroyed," Alfred explained. "This one, despite my reluctance, I kept. For who would believe the story on words alone?"

"What in God's name is it?" Wulfric asked, still breathless.

"There is one thing of which I am certain," said Alfred grimly. "Whatever it is, it was not created in God's name."

FIVE

Alfred told Wulfric the whole story as they left the dungeon and headed back toward the Great Hall. Along the way, they visited Alfred's personal physician, who ministered to Wulfric's wrist. It could have been much worse, the doctor observed as he applied a salve to the wound and wrapped it; there had been one man who had lost a hand to that beast the same way and another who had not returned from his visit at all. Visits to the dungeon were strictly regulated now, and none were made without the King's permission.

By the time they arrived at the Great Hall, Wulfric had heard all. Of how Aethelred had discovered the arcane scrolls and devised a plan to use them, as a way to bolster England against future Danish threats without endangering English lives. How the plan had sounded so promising at the time. How Aethelred had been given license to conduct his experiments, in hopes of perfecting a way to control the transformations and the abominable creations that resulted. How Alfred had finally shuttered the whole endeavor when he learned the full, sickening truth of where Aethelred's obsession had led him. And of how Aethelred, using the dark skills he had mastered, changed the very guards assigned to imprison him into monsters who then aided his escape from the tower.

Wulfric's head was swimming long after Alfred had finished recounting the tale. He sat in silence at the heavy oak table at the center of the hall and stared into the distance as his mind attempted to reconcile it all. He had been raised to believe in the existence of things beyond his understanding, forces invisible to him and far greater than himself. But to actually see such things with one's own eyes was another matter entirely. No known scientific or natural phenomenon could account for what he had witnessed down in that dungeon or for the tale the King had told him afterward. And he agreed with Alfred—no God that he held to would ever create something so diabolical, so wicked, so utterly without virtue. Something so . . . *hellish*.

"This is Chiswick," announced Alfred, snapping Wulfric from his thoughts. Wulfric stood to greet the man and, as always, found himself not knowing quite where to look as the King's counselor bowed to him. Chiswick was bull-necked, bald-headed, and stocky, an unremarkable-looking man save for the ugly scar that ran diagonally across his face from just beneath his left eye and across the bridge of his nose and both lips, ending just beneath the right side of his chin. Wulfric had seen enough war wounds to recognize this as one, probably inflicted by a Danish longsword years ago. Though the scar was unsettling to many, Wulfric found himself reassured by it. He gave more weight to the words of men who had learned the price of war firsthand. They tended to speak truth more plainly.

"It is my great honor, Sir Wulfric," said Chiswick, as he completed his bow. "The King has regaled me with the tales of your heroism many a time."

"It's a fine line between heroism and duty," Wulfric replied. "I prefer to think of it as the latter."

"Chiswick is my most senior military advisor and chief spymaster," said Alfred. "Very little happens in the kingdoms without his knowledge. He has been endeavoring to keep track of Aethelred since his escape. Chiswick?"

Chiswick unrolled a map of lower England across the table, positioning goblets and candlestick holders at its corners to hold it in place. The map was heavily adorned with annotations in Chiswick's own hand.

As he studied it, Wulfric was immediately taken back to the Danish war. Often had he stood in Alfred's tent with the King and his war council studying campaign maps and discussing strategy. The more senior of Alfred's advisors had bristled at a commoner being invited to such high-level meetings, but Alfred, having come to know Wulfric after Ethandun, had insisted on it. *All these nobles and knighted men tell me only what they think I want to hear*, he had told the young Wulfric. *Their desire to win my favor by constantly agreeing with me will get us all killed. I need men courageous enough to disagree with me when I am wrong.*

And so Wulfric had done as he was asked and spoken the truth as he saw it. Alfred's highborn advisors had had no choice but to suffer his presence, restricting their objections to furtive looks among themselves, particularly when the King took Wulfric's advice over their own.

"Aethelred left here with six of our own men that he perverted to his will," Chiswick said, pointing to Winchester on the map. "That was twenty days ago. Since then we have received numerous reports of disturbances throughout the northeast quarter of Wessex. Commonfolk fleeing their homes, claiming to have been attacked by rabid beasts like none they have ever seen. With each fresh report, the number of beasts grows. I believe Aethelred is working his way toward the Danelaw border, and that his army grows larger with each new town and village he enslaves along his route."

To Wulfric it all still seemed so unbelievable. He had sat in dozens of military briefings just like this one, and yet nothing like it at all. This was more like something from a nightmare, or a ghost story told around the campfire by journeymen to frighten one another. It could not be real, and yet he could not deny what he had seen with his own eyes. It took a while for his mind, still racing, to focus and find its first question.

"How large is his force, by the most recent report?"

"The villagers we have spoken to are not the most reliable," Chiswick answered. "Many are in shock, babbling. But the most coherent among them said they reckoned close to a hundred."

Wulfric took a moment to contemplate that. A hundred of those . . . *things* . . . such as he had seen in Alfred's dungeon? The thought chilled him.

"Where is he now?"

"The last known sighting was here," replied Chiswick, gesturing to a small town about sixty miles short of the boundary where Wessex ended and the Danelaw began. "At his present rate, he could be at the Danes' border by month's end."

"And his intention when he gets there?" Wulfric asked.

"He first proposed this force of beasts as a deterrent against another Danish invasion," said Chiswick. "But now . . . I hesitate to try to predict the actions of a man so clearly mad, but I believe he intends to launch some kind of preemptive attack into their territory."

"If he seriously intends to attack the Danish on their own ground with so small a force, I suspect this problem will take care of itself soon enough," offered Wulfric.

"A hundred may not seem like many," said Alfred, "but in our experience, just one of these beasts is the match of a dozen armed men. Who knows how many more Aethelred will have acquired by the time he reaches the Danelaw? With this power he employs, his enemies do not fall on the battlefield—*they become his allies.* Soon he could be using it to turn the Danes on themselves."

A silence settled on the Great Hall for a moment. Alfred waited while the full implication of that sank in. Wulfric had become an expert at war, in both theory and practice, but this was no longer war as he understood it. The rules had changed. In the old way, the way it had been for thousands of years, both sides lost men in battle. But under Aethelred's new rules, the victor converted the vanquished into his own ranks and grew more powerful with each conquest. It was a terrifying idea, both strategically and in other ways that troubled Wulfric far more deeply.

It was Chiswick who broke the silence. "Our concern is not a war between the Danes and Aethelred's army, if one can even call it that. It is that any kind of attack from within Wessex will be perceived to be in the King's name. If Aethelred breaks the accord and attacks the Danelaw, it will stir up an already precarious situation and perhaps lead to a counterinvasion."

"And another all-out war," Wulfric observed. It was a strange thing, he thought, to be considering ways in which to prevent an attack against the Norse, after all the times he had helped to plot them. He had no love for the Danes, after all they had done to him and those he loved, but the kingdom simply could not afford another war.

"My advice is simple," he said. "Dispatch the full force of your armies to intercept Aethelred before he reaches the Danelaw. Crush him quickly, with overwhelming force, and end this thing before it begins."

"Would that it were that easy," Alfred responded with a heavy sigh, looking to Chiswick.

"Our forces are scattered throughout the kingdom," said Chiswick, pointing to various annotations on his map indicating the disposition of infantry encampments and other military assets. "Even at best speed, they have little chance of assembling into a force sufficient to overwhelm Aethelred before he reaches the Danelaw. And even were it possible, committing such a force would leave the rest of Wessex ill defended should the Norse seize the opportunity to attack from elsewhere along the border. No, our best chance, we believe, would be to take him by surprise using a small, swift, mobile force, one specially formed for this task."

Wulfric scratched his head, confused. "If Aethelred's force is equal to more than a thousand men, what chance does a small contingent have against him? Most likely you would only be sending more men for him to enslave."

For the first time, Alfred allowed himself a smile. Wulfric knew it well, the wry look the King adopted when he had a bright scheme. "Aethelred is not the only one with magickal tricks up his sleeve," he said. "Come with me to the chapel. Thank you, Chiswick."

The priest paced up and down before the stone altar of Winchester's chapel. He had been told to await the King's presence, and so far he had been waiting for more than an hour. Yet it was not the waiting that bothered him but the worry of what would be expected of him when the King did at last arrive. He had been practicing all hours of the day and night and was confident he had mastered what had been asked of him. But he also knew, more than most, what was at stake—and the price of failure, both for himself and for the men who would be placing their lives in his hands. One small mistake, one mispronounced syllable or moment of hesitation, would spell disaster.

The irony had not escaped him. He was not by nature cut out for the martial professions; he had entered the priesthood largely because it was a path of peace. But that path had now twisted in an unforeseen way and was leading him into the very thing he had hoped to avoid—a war, and not just any war, but one fought with weapons more horrendous than anything ever before conceived by man. A shiver ran through him, only partly because it was cold in the small stone-walled chamber.

He heard the chapel door open behind him and spun around to see King Alfred enter with a man he did not recognize. He looked to the young priest like a commoner, but the steeled look in the man's eyes suggested he was more likely a soldier of some kind. The priest swallowed deep and corrected his posture as they approached.

"Your Majesty," he said, bowing low before the King.

"Cuthbert, this is Sir Wulfric," Alfred said. The priest's eyes widened a little; he might not have recognized the scruffy-looking man standing beside the King, but he most certainly knew the name. He was standing in the presence of not one living legend but two. He looked to Wulfric and tried to conjure something to say, but could not think of anything that would not make him sound like a complete idiot.

Alfred sensed the priest's awkwardness; he had grown used to it by now and knew it would be merciful to move swiftly to the business at hand.

"Cuthbert was a junior cleric under Aethelred at Canterbury," the King explained to Wulfric. "He has a keen aptitude for languages, so the archbishop put him to work studying the scrolls. He was the first to successfully decipher what had baffled many other more learned scholars."

"If I had known what lay within them, I would never have consented to it," Cuthbert was quick to offer. He had seen what the archbishop had wrought in Winchester's courtyard, from the words he had helped to decode, and the guilt lay heavy on him. He felt responsible for every twisted, malformed monstrosity the archbishop had brought forth and wanted now only the opportunity to help set it right again.

"I say it not to assign blame," Alfred said, placing a reassuring hand on the cleric's shoulder. "That is set squarely on Aethelred's shoulders alone. I mean to say that you are among the brightest of Canterbury. And perhaps now our brightest hope."

Cuthbert felt briefly uplifted by the compliment, only to grow even more nervous as the King's words reminded him of the responsibility that now weighed upon him. He placed a hand to the back of his neck and rubbed nervously.

Wulfric did not know what to make of the callow, fidgety little man who stood before him. Little more than a boy, really. There had been many like him during the war, pressed into service despite their protests and their tears. Most of them had not survived long. But behind all the awkwardness and jitters, Wulfric recognized a spark of something in the boy's eyes—a keen intellectual curiosity that he remembered once burning within himself as a young man, before war had made it a luxury to be swept aside. In a way he envied Cuthbert. Before the Norse came, he had often dreamed of joining the clergy himself and devoting himself to a life of quiet scholarship. *In the next life*, he told himself.

"You came with Aethelred to Winchester?" he asked Cuthbert.

Cuthbert nodded. "I was one of many he brought from Canterbury to assist him with his . . ." He hesitated, looking for the right word. "His . . . experiments. I dared not refuse, but I feigned a sickness contracted on the journey so that I might have as little hand in it as possible. Many of us were not comfortable with what the archbishop was doing. Few of us had the courage to refuse or question him."

"What became of the other clerics when he escaped?"

"One tried to stop him. He was turned, God help him. The others fled shortly after for fear of being punished for complicity in his crimes."

"But not you."

"I have no family, no means, nowhere else to go. I cannot return to Canterbury. And even if I could, I would not. I have vowed to help somehow undo what I helped to bring about, and I told His Majesty so."

Wulfric smiled; he was beginning to like this man. Oftentimes a fretful demeanor like Cuthbert's could be mistaken for spinelessness, but the more Wulfric took the measure of him, the more he was convinced that Cuthbert was no coward. From his own hard-won experience, he knew that true courage was not the absence of fear but doing what must be done in the often-paralyzing presence of it.

"In Cuthbert's study of the scrolls, he discovered that they contained more than just the words of transformation," Alfred explained. He looked at Cuthbert. Still ridden with nerves, it took the cleric a moment to realize that the King was expecting him to continue the tale.

"Oh! Yes. The scrolls also contained detailed descriptions of several other quite interesting invocations, some of which I believe were intended to be used to counter the transformative effect. Put simply, I believe it may be possible to bless an object—such as a suit of armor—with a ward of protection that would dispel any magick directed at it."

Wulfric looked at Alfred with puzzlement. "I thought you had ordered the scrolls destroyed."

"I have been working mostly from memory," explained Cuthbert. "I have a very good one."

"Does Aethelred know of this?" Wulfric asked him.

"No. By the time I deciphered these counterspells, I had seen for myself what the archbishop was doing, and I decided it was best not to pass on any further knowledge to him. When he asked me, I told him that the rest of the scrolls were beyond my ability to translate."

Wulfric was impressed. A nervous little milksop this young priest may have been, with a lifespan likely measured in seconds on any field of battle, but Wulfric's father had taught him to value intelligence and sharpness of mind more than any other quality, and it was fast becoming clear that Cuthbert had no shortage of either. Still, it was difficult not to feel extreme unease as he considered the strategy that Alfred had proposed with such confidence. Kings, Wulfric contemplated, were always more sanguine about their war strategies than were the men charged with carrying them out on the battlefield. He gave Alfred a skeptical glance, such as few of those at court would dare attempt.

"*This* is your plan? Magickal armor?"

"I'm sure by now you would agree that Aethelred's magick is no fantasy," said Alfred. "If the arcanery with which he conjured these monsters is not in doubt, why should we not have as much confidence in the other spells gleaned from the very same scrolls?"

"I look at this as I would any other weapon of war," said Wulfric. "I will believe in its usefulness once it has been proven in the field. How exactly do you propose to test this?"

"I thought we might put the armor on you and throw you at Aethelred," said Alfred with a sly smile.

Wulfric turned again to the cleric. "Does your knowledge extend to anything we might use offensively against Aethelred and his horde?"

Cuthbert looked puzzled. "I'm sorry, my lord . . . such as what?"

Wulfric glared at him, irritated. "I don't know! A rain of fire? Enchanted arrows? You tell me, you're the expert!"

Cuthbert looked down at the floor, embarrassed. "No, my lord. Nothing like that, I'm afraid."

"So you can protect me against this conjurer's magicks, but not against the beasts he creates."

"For that, my friend, you will have to rely upon your sword, and your wits, as you always have," said Alfred, with a smile that he hoped might foster some encouragement. It did not succeed.

Wulfric sighed. It was becoming increasingly clear to him that there was to be no escaping this dire duty—not only for the debt he felt he still owed Alfred, but because the more he saw and heard of Aethelred's sorcery, the more he genuinely feared for the chaos and destruction it might spread. He could refuse and go home, but then how long might it be before war or something even more terrible arrived in his village, threatening his wife and child? No, this mad priest had to be stopped. And if he would not do it, then who would?

"I will want to choose the men I take with me," he said to Alfred with the weary tone of reluctant acceptance.

"Of course," said the King, trying not to show his relief.

Cuthbert was still standing there, quietly wringing his hands. Wulfric looked to him now with a nod. "Starting with him."

Cuthbert's eyes widened in alarm. "Excuse me . . . what?"

"If this campaign is to be successful, my men and I will rely heavily on your knowledge. Your *unique* knowledge."

"Yes, yes, of course," stammered Cuthbert, with the beginnings of what felt a lot like panic. "But I can discharge my duties here, enchant whatever armor you require before you and your men depart. Anything you—"

"That will not be sufficient," Wulfric interrupted with a wave of his hand. "This magick of yours is unproven. We may require your expertise to maintain or adapt it as needed. And we will almost certainly encounter situations that will require improvisation. You will serve us best in the field."

Cuthbert could hear his own heartbeat pounding in his ears like a drum, and darkness seemed to be creeping in from the corners of his vision. His knees felt weak. His stomach tightened. His mouth was suddenly so dry he could barely speak, but his keen sense of self-preservation somehow compelled the words to come forth.

"My lord," he offered meekly, voice cracking. "With respect, I am a scholar, not a soldier."

Wulfric clapped his hand heartily upon Cuthbert's shoulder, and the cleric's legs almost gave way beneath him.

"My friend," Wulfric said, "as of today, you are both."

Cuthbert was dismissed, and as the priest scurried off in the direction of the nearest outhouse, Wulfric and Alfred walked back from the chapel to the courtyard where Wulfric's horse was stabled. For a while, neither man spoke. But the pall of unspoken words hung over them both until Alfred was forced to say something. Anything.

"Where will you start?" he asked.

"I will find Edgard," said Wulfric, with no hesitation. He had already thought that far ahead. "There is no battle, no campaign I can conceive of, that I would fight without him at my side. Once he is with me, the others I need will follow."

Alfred nodded his approval, and they walked several more steps without a word. Wulfric gazed at the stones between his feet, deep in sober contemplation. "Of course, first I must give the news to Cwen," he observed, his voice lower now, as though speaking to himself.

"How will she take it?"

"Truth be told, I do not know which I fear more—Aethelred's army of abominations or her reaction," replied Wulfric, only partly in jest. "I promised her I would never go to war again. That was her one and only condition when she agreed to marry me."

"You are not going to war," offered Alfred. "This is a singular mission on behalf of your King—and frankly, your God. Cwen is a woman of faith, is she not? Surely she will understand that."

Wulfric gave it thought. "A crusade," he said, finally.

"Just a small one," suggested Alfred wryly, with a smile that he noticed Wulfric did not return. Alfred knew his friend well enough to see that there was something more on his mind, something even he was reluctant to voice.

"Is there anything else you would ask of me?" he said. And that was enough to stop Wulfric in his tracks. The knight turned and looked at Alfred hard, with something as close to anger as the King had ever seen directed at him.

"I have only one question to ask," said Wulfric. "How could you have been so blind as to not see where this madness, this . . . *heresy*, would lead you?"

Alfred looked about him as though searching for an answer. And Wulfric saw now in his face things he had seen many times in other men, but never in his King. Remorse. Guilt. Shame.

"I have asked myself that question many times. I have also asked God. So far, neither of us have an answer. All I can offer is this: Everything I have done in my life, including this horrifically misguided venture, has been compelled by a single aspiration—to protect and defend this kingdom. So it pains me more than you can understand to know that my actions may have now put it in greater peril than any Norseman ever did. But that is why I ask you now, not as your King, but as your friend, to help me this one last time. To help unmake the wrong that I myself have made."

Wulfric looked at his King. Alfred found his expression impossible to read, and he waited, for some gesture of understanding or, dare he hope, absolution. But all Wulfric gave was a single nod before he turned and walked away toward the stable where his horse was waiting.

"It will be done," he said, without looking back.

When Wulfric arrived home, it was worse than he had feared. Cwen bawled and cursed and threw everything at him that her heavily pregnant state would allow. Alfred had been wrong, of course—not about Cwen being a woman of faith, but in suggesting that it would help her understand why Wulfric had to leave her when her belly was ripe and she needed him most.

Wulfric knew that Cwen would never have believed a story of monsters and magick, so he told her instead a tale of a dangerous band of heretics led by a deranged priest who was spreading blasphemies and had to be dealt with—it was, after all, still true, in a manner of speaking. But invoking duty even to both God and King carried little weight with Cwen, whose priorities now began and ended with the gift she carried inside her. *Tell Alfred he can stick his little crusade up his arse!* she had screamed at him between bouts of hurling copper pots from across the kitchen. *God does not want you chasing mad priests a hundred miles away—he wants you here with me and your unborn child! How can you do this to us now?*

This is why warriors should never marry, Wulfric later thought to himself as he packed his saddlebag and nursed a bruise on his forehead from a milk jug that Cwen had aimed particularly well.

Because war is a jealous mistress. She has a way of calling us back to her, long after we thought we had bid farewell for good.

Wulfric mounted Dolly and headed out that same evening. He had hoped to at least stay the night, but Cwen had told him in no uncertain terms that the only place he would be sleeping would be the stable. And so he rode into the night, heading east, to where he knew he would find Edgard. At the top of the hill, he stopped and looked back, hoping to catch sight of Cwen watching him from the doorway or the window. But there was no sign of her. Sadly, he turned away and spurred his horse on.

SIX

Wulfric sat cross-legged in the center of a grassy meadow, idly considering a curious flower he had picked, a type he had not seen before and could not identify. It was a quiet moment, among the few he had known in many a month, save for sleep—and even that was, more often than not, a breeding ground for the nightmares that now plagued him. And so he tried to find some peace in each rare moment of quiet solitude, such as this one. Although, truth be told, having little else to occupy his mind only made it more difficult to ignore the pain from which he could find no relief.

Even now, months after that misshapen beast had attacked him in Alfred's dungeon, Wulfric still bore the wound around his wrist—as fresh as though it had been inflicted yesterday. He had tried every salve and treatment he knew, but still he felt it burning under the bandage in which he kept it wrapped. At times it felt as though the beast's tongue were there still, a phantom appendage encircling his wrist like a white-hot manacle, eating away at the layers of his flesh. Just another wretched aspect of Aethelred's black magick—wounds that refused to be healed by medicine or even by time.

Wulfric was pulled from his reverie by the sound of footsteps in the soft grass behind him.

"The men are wondering if they are to sit here all morning, or if you plan on giving the order to attack," said Edgard.

Wulfric glanced up at his fellow knight. Just as Wulfric was one of the few men in Alfred's kingdom who had earned the right to speak to his King as an equal, Edgard was among the few who enjoyed a similar privilege with Wulfric. Every other soldier in England, even the most senior officers, addressed Wulfric with a degree of reverence that made any kind of useful or honest conversation impossible. But not Edgard, a knight who, like Wulfric, had once been a common man enlisted in Alfred's army. He had fought alongside Wulfric in almost every battle against the Norse, before Ethandun and after.

They had liked each other instantly, from the first time they had broken bread around one of the enlisted men's campfires. They were from the same county, they learned. Their families had bought fruit from the same local market and even knew a few of the same people. And both were men blessed—or cursed, perhaps—with an innate talent for battle. They had much in common and quickly became inseparable on the battlefield. Before long, the two of them had saved each other's lives more times than either could remember. At first they had kept score in a running contest over bragging rights, but after a while, both men had lost count. Save Alfred himself, Wulfric knew of no man in all England he would more readily trust with his life. And so Edgard had been the first Wulfric had sought to enlist in his campaign to hunt down Aethelred and his army of the damned.

Edgard, unlike Wulfric, had not been so humble as to refuse the lavish lands and titles Alfred had gratefully offered them both after the war. But as it turned out, he had grown restless in his retirement. He was tired of his castle, expensive to maintain and impossible to heat, and even more tired of his wife, who nagged him incessantly. In truth, he had never much cared for her to begin with, but he had always wanted children more than anything, and she was the youngest of five sisters, the other four all having borne sons to their husbands.

Fate had decided that she would bear Edgard none, though not for the want of trying. When the arguments inevitably came, she never failed to remind him that she was of fertile stock, and so the fault must lie with him. Edgard had come to resent her, and his damned drafty castle, with all its empty bedchambers that should by rights be filled with the laughter of children. And so when Wulfric had come knocking on his door with an offer to fight by his side once more, Edgard asked no questions about the nature of the enemy or even the size of the reward; he simply seized the opportunity to ride away from all that reminded him of a life unfulfilled. *Ending life comes to me much more easily than creating it*, he had reflected sadly to Wulfric as they rode from his castle together.

Edgard had not looked back to see if his wife was watching him ride away. He had not even told her he was leaving.

Together they had wasted no time in marshaling the most potent small force of fighting men ever assembled. Nearly a hundred strong, they were handpicked veterans of the Danish campaigns, men Wulfric and Edgard knew could tip the balance in any engagement, and who would even the odds against Aethelred's beasts. Alfred had tried to warn Wulfric that just one such beast was the equal of a dozen men. *Not the men I plan to set against them*, Wulfric had told himself.

Most of the men Wulfric and Edgard sought to recruit had at first laughed at the tale told them of Aethelred and his abominations. Some did not; they had heard stories in alehouses and around campfires of villages overrun by unspeakable shape-shifting horrors led by some dark warlock. But none hesitated to join; they would follow Wulfric and Edgard into battle against any enemy, no matter how improbable.

Their force assembled, Wulfric and Edgard had ridden northeast, tracking Aethelred's own path toward the Danelaw border. Those among Wulfric's men who had at first scoffed at his story became believers as they followed the trail of horrors the crazed archbishop had left in his wake. They had all seen settlements sacked by the Norse, but never anything like this. There were no bodies, no wounded. Instead, entire towns and villages had been emptied, leaving behind nothing but eerie desolation. As they surveyed the silent ruins of the first ghost town they encountered, Wulfric reminded his men of what the King had said of Aethelred. *His enemies do not fall on the battlefield—they become his allies.* Hardened men all, not one of them passed through that town without a shudder.

They had eventually caught up with Aethelred just outside Aylesbury, a small market town he had plundered for souls that very morning. It was not a moment too soon; Aylesbury was perilously close to the Danelaw border. And then there were no skeptics left among Wulfric's men, for now they saw what lay before them with their own eyes: a great herd of nightmarish, oil-black beasts, their forms beyond imagination, slithering and lurching their way across the land as they howled and wailed, a hellish cacophony that in sound alone inspired revulsion and despair. And at their head, the lone figure of Aethelred, leading them onward like some demonic shepherd.

The creatures' irregular shapes and movement made them difficult to number from a distance, but Wulfric had estimated the herd to be at least five hundred strong—the combined populations of the dozen or so villages and hamlets Aethelred had descended upon along his path now transformed into the grotesque horde lumbering along under his command.

Wulfric was a student of war, of battle tactics. He had thought long and hard during his pursuit of how best to confront Aethelred and his minions when he finally caught up with them, and had decided ultimately on the plan of attack that had always served him best—straight at the heart of the enemy, without fear or hesitation. Wulfric knew that Aethelred would be relying partly on the psychological fear his abominations struck into the hearts of all who laid eyes upon them. But Wulfric had neutralized that particular

asset by selecting men he knew would not freeze or waver in the
face of even the most terrifying enemy. *Aethelred's army is no different from any other we have faced and defeated countless times*, he
had reminded them the night before. *A mindless horde of barbarians and animals without honor, or wits, or God on their side.* He
reminded them also that Cuthbert had been working tirelessly to
bless the armor each of them wore with the protection that would
render Aethelred's other advantage useless in battle.

The speech had worked. In the morning, Wulfric and Edgard
rode their force of a hundred men right at Aethelred, across an
open field, their horses' hooves thundering in the earth, swords
drawn, unafraid, roaring bloody murder at the tops of their voices,
so loud they rivaled the howls of Aethelred's monstrous herd.

At first, Aethelred seemed to relish their approach. Standing
defiant and unafraid before his army, he focused his attention on
Wulfric and the tip of the oncoming spear. He raised his hands,
bony fingers dancing through the air like a virtuoso harpist playing an unseen instrument as he recited an incantation. But his look
of defiance slowly turned to one of consternation as Wulfric and
his men kept coming, seemingly immune to the spell that should
by now have contorted them into yet more broken and willing
servants.

Cuthbert had done his job well. Wulfric's armored breastplate
shimmered with an iridescent glow as the protective seal the young
cleric had placed upon it absorbed the brunt of Aethelred's magick
like a lightning rod and dissipated it harmlessly.

Aethelred cursed and began to prepare another incantation,
but Wulfric's army was by now just fifty yards away and closing
quickly. And so Aethelred panicked and retreated into his horde,
commanding them to attack as he did so. His monsters surged
forward to meet Wulfric's brigade. In the moments before they
clashed, Aethelred found himself wondering why this small force
of men, outnumbered by five to one and outmatched to a far
greater degree, was not fleeing at the mere sight of his army, as so

many had done before them. He could only assume that they were fools, or mad. But if he could not add them to his numbers, his beasts would surely make short work of them on the field.

Aethelred's arrogant assumption was soon proved wrong. His army was a fearsome sight to be sure, but it had never before been tested in battle; any enemy encountered before now had either been turned or had fled in terror. This was his vile children's first real taste of combat, and Aethelred discovered to his dismay that unlike Wulfric's band of war-hardened veterans, they had no belly for it at all. In the initial chaotic throes, his monsters struck down several men, lashing out wildly with claw and fang and tentacle, but Wulfric's cavalry hit back even harder, hacking and trampling a bloody swath through Aethelred's mob, leaving abominations maimed and bleeding and shrieking in agony in their wake.

The shape of the battle changed rapidly after that, and Aethelred's monstrous host collapsed into panic and disarray. To the surprise and delight of Wulfric and his men, it quickly became apparent that these hellish beasts were not so fearsome when confronted on equal terms—more akin to an unbroken horse, they spooked at the first sign of danger. Soon the entire horde was scattering and fleeing before Wulfric's surging forces, even as Aethelred made a desperate attempt to maintain some semblance of discipline among them. Though Wulfric's men were still engaged with several beasts that were doggedly fighting back—mostly those that had become enraged after being wounded—the archbishop could see that it was hopeless. With so many of his forces fled and his own magick rendered null, the battle was all but lost.

And so he sought instead to make his escape, marshaling a small group of his more obedient servants—those first few he had turned during his escape from Alfred's tower. With them, he scurried away amidst the chaos, down an escarpment to the edge of a nearby forest, where he disappeared into the trees while Wulfric's men finished off the rest of his beasts.

Wulfric lost twenty men that day—which was better than he had expected for having put well over a hundred beasts to the sword and scattering the rest to the winds. Now only Aethelred himself and whatever few abominations he still controlled remained a threat.

From then on, it became a hunting expedition. Wulfric and Edgard tracked the archbishop day and night, hoping to find him before he had the opportunity to replenish his numbers. The trail led them all the way to Canterbury, Aethelred's seat, and to the cathedral where this whole horrific misadventure had first begun.

And now here they were, precisely four months from the day that Wulfric had ridden away from his wife and unborn child. It had been a long campaign, arduous for both body and spirit, but it was almost done, and he was almost home. His army was encamped not far outside Canterbury Cathedral. Aethelred was known to be inside, licking his wounds. One final battle to close the book on all of it, and Wulfric could at last return home. He would meet his son, by now a month old, for the first time, and make things right with Cwen. At last, he would begin his new life as a husband and father both.

But as anxious as he was to do all of that, he would not allow haste to be his undoing in these final hours. Aethelred had been bested in battle and his magick neutralized, but Wulfric knew better than to underestimate his opponent even now. He knew Aethelred to be a cunning man, a defiant man, and whatever he had been doing for the past three days holed up inside his cathedral, Wulfric felt sure that it was something more than simply waiting for him and his men to break down the door and finish him off.

No, Aethelred would not go down so easily as that. He surely had one final card still to play. The only question was, what?

Wulfric was still pondering that as Edgard looked at him, one eyebrow arched, waiting for an answer to his question. "That is why we're here, isn't it? To attack?"

Wulfric gazed across the plain at the spires of Canterbury, shrouded in morning mist. "We will attack when I have a better idea of what awaits us within, and not before," said Wulfric. "We know what awaits us within. Aethelred and at most a few dozen of his hellhounds—far fewer than we have already done away with. Why do we wait?"

They had kept a close watch on the path Aethelred had taken back to Canterbury as they followed, taking note of any settlements or towns he might have harvested for reinforcements. So far as they could discern, he had passed through none, opting instead for the most direct route back to Canterbury—meaning he could only have conscripted any individuals or small groups encountered along his way. Perhaps by now he had also turned Canterbury's own staff and other retainers, but even then the numbers could add up to no more than Edgard was estimating. The sorcerer was trapped and under siege, his forces depleted, his magick useless. He was ripe for the finishing. *Unless* . . . The word ate away at Wulfric like the burning ring around his wrist.

"He's been in there for days," he observed with a nod toward the fog-shrouded cathedral in the distance. "Doing what, God only knows. Perhaps refining his magick to counter the wards on our armor. Perhaps training his remaining forces to better stand their ground, to fight more fiercely. Perhaps something we have failed to even consider. I don't like it."

"What evidence do you have to suggest any of this?" Edgard asked.

"None," admitted Wulfric. "Only a bad feeling. Like the one I had before Chippenham. Remember that?"

"Hmph," grunted Edgard, gazing out at the horizon. The two men had many differences on matters of war—from infantry strategies to the best way to silently cut a man's throat—and had often debated late into the night, but Edgard had to admit that when it came to ill portents before a battle, Wulfric's gut instinct was almost never wrong. He sighed.

"Wulfric, the only way for us to know what awaits us in there is to go and find it."

Wulfric let the flower that confounded him fall from his fingers and stood, turning to look at his men, assembled not far behind him.

"Perhaps not," he said. "Bring me Cuthbert."

Edgard passed the order to a runner, and a few minutes later they saw the little cleric dashing across the field to where his commander stood, huffing as he ran, breath clouding in the morning mist. "It really is a wonder that boy's still alive," said Edgard with amusement as he observed Cuthbert's awkward gait, his ill-fitting robes hanging off his willowy frame as though slung over a poorly made chair.

"That boy's the reason any of us are still alive," replied Wulfric. Cuthbert had come to earn his respect over the course of this campaign. High-strung and brittle he may have seemed at first blush, but when it mattered, he had proven himself no coward. At Aylesbury, Cuthbert had insisted on staying with the men until the last moment to ensure that every one of them had a freshly placed blessing on their armor, as well as on that of their mounts, before they entered the fray, in case the protective power of the spell—at that point, still an unknown quantity—should diminish over time. In doing so, he ventured far closer to Aethelred's horde than he had thought himself capable. It was not until later, after the battle had ended, that he realized he had forgotten to place a protective blessing upon his own vestments and had left himself vulnerable to one of Aethelred's curses. It was only by happenstance that he had not been targeted and turned into some dire beast that his own comrades would have been forced to put down. Cuthbert spent most of that night throwing up, but by then his actions on the field had earned him Wulfric's esteem, and by extension the esteem of all the men.

Cuthbert had also proven invaluable as a curator and archivist of the many and varied forms of misshapen wretch that Aethelred had taught himself to conjure. Many of the beasts had dispersed, in all directions, after the battle at Aylesbury, and they were now scattered far and wide throughout the kingdom, living and lurking in the shadows, masterless and wild. They had become the basis for a new folklore fast spreading throughout southern England: nightmarish stories told around campfires and to restless children about dark, malevolent, shapeless horrors that stalked their prey—animal and human alike—by night, taking whatever or whomever they could find and dragging their prey screaming into the darkness to be fed upon.

Wulfric's men had encountered more than a few of these feral types during their pursuit of Aethelred after Aylesbury, and after each kill Cuthbert took pains to catalogue it in his own bestiary, kept carefully in a leather-bound volume. He made detailed drawings of each species they came across, taking note of its behavioral characteristics, speed, strength, intelligence, and preferred method of slaying, thus making the next confrontation with a beast of the same type that much swifter and less likely to result in casualties. Cuthbert's work was as exhaustive and scholarly as it was useful in its practical application, and even Wulfric admitted to finding it darkly fascinating. It took him back to his boyhood, when his father would teach him to study and identify various forms of insect life. Now the insects were twice the size of a man and could kill you from twenty feet away, but the principle was the same.

Cuthbert arrived red faced and out of breath. He tried to speak but was too winded for words to come.

"Take a breath, boy!" barked Edgard. "A knee, if you must."

Cuthbert took a moment to regain his composure and catch his breath. "I'm sorry. Sir Wulfric, you have need of me?"

"A few nights ago you told me of another spell in Aethelred's scrolls that you had begun to translate before his escape," said Wulfric.

It took a moment for Cuthbert to recall the conversation. "Oh! You mean the scrying?"

"Yes. Can it be done?"

Cuthbert hesitated. "I'm not sure. My translation was incomplete, and—"

"But what you did translate, you remember precisely." By now, Wulfric had learned that Cuthbert's claim of a flawless memory was not unfounded.

Cuthbert nodded.

"Excuse me," Edgard interjected, "but what exactly are we talking about here?"

"From my understanding of the scrolls, scrying allows a person to see what is elsewhere," said Cuthbert. "The spell describes the use of a reflective medium such as polished metal or a pool of still water to project the image of a distant location exactly as it appears at that moment, like a window into that faraway place. I have done my own study on this, and I believe it may be possible to go further, to actually cast an immaterial projection of oneself into that place, and to explore it remotely, just as though one were actually there."

"And you can do this?" Wulfric asked, intrigued.

"In theory," said Cuthbert. "But in matters of magick, it is often a far cry between theory and practice."

"I need you to try," said Wulfric. "I need to know what lies in wait within the cathedral before I commit my men. That knowledge could be the difference between victory and defeat, or at the very least determine how many of us survive the day. Do you understand?"

Cuthbert was silent as the weight of what Wulfric was asking began to sink in. He began to wonder what he might have just talked himself into. He felt his stomach start to ravel itself into a knot. "I understand," he said finally, with as much calm as he could muster. "I will try."

"Good," said Wulfric, holding an expectant gaze on Cuthbert.

It took the young cleric a moment. "Oh! You mean now?"

"That would be preferable," Wulfric said with a thin smile. Cuthbert turned a shade paler.

"I . . . I will need a reflective surface of some kind," said the young priest. "Something glass or—"

Cuthbert flinched as Wulfric drew his broadsword, the flat of its blade glimmering in the sunlight that was beginning to peek through the gray cloud-filled sky.

"Will this suffice?"

Cuthbert regarded the sword and saw his own face looking back at him. Wulfric made the meticulous maintenance of his weapons and armor a point of pride; the blade was so finely polished it was practically a mirror.

"I believe it will," Cuthbert said. "If I may?"

Wulfric offered him the sword. On taking it in hand, Cuthbert almost toppled over—it was far heavier than he had imagined. *How does he even carry this damned thing around,* he thought to himself as he wrestled with it, *let alone swing it in anger?*

Wulfric and Edgard both took a step back and regarded Cuthbert with great curiosity as he laid the sword on the ground and sat cross-legged before it. He placed the fingertips of both hands on the blade, careful to stay far from the edge—he knew Wulfric kept it as sharp as he kept it shining—then closed his eyes and began to mutter the incantation under his breath. To Wulfric and Edgard it sounded no different from the words they'd heard him use many times before when placing the protective blessings on their armor; it was the same unintelligible, arcane tongue.

For several minutes they watched him sit, reciting the same lines over and over, seemingly to no effect, and then Edgard grew restless. He leaned toward Wulfric and whispered. "How much longer before we know if this is going to—"

Then he cut himself off. At that moment he saw something that beggared belief, even after all that he had seen in these past few months. Cuthbert seemed to somehow *shimmer*, becoming momentarily translucent, like gossamer, as though no longer fully there, before returning to a fully corporeal state. Both knights stared at him, wide-eyed.

"Did you—" Edgard began.

"Yes."

"What was that?"

"I don't know."

Cuthbert had now stopped reciting the words; he seemed to be in some kind of trance. Unmoving, like a statue. Wulfric found it disconcerting. The only time he had ever before seen such stillness was in dead men. He watched Cuthbert closely, looking for any sign that he was in fact still alive. At first, he could detect none, then he saw that the young priest was breathing, but so slowly and so shallowly that he barely seemed to be breathing at all. Still, Wulfric did not like this. Since he did not know how this was supposed to work, he had no way of knowing if something had gone wrong.

"Cuthbert?"

No response.

"Cuthbert!" Louder this time. Still, no response.

Wulfric had leaned toward Cuthbert to rouse him with a shake when the boy's eyes suddenly snapped open. But Cuthbert was not looking at Wulfric, or at Edgard, or at anything in his field of view that they could discern. His body was still there, but he seemed to be seeing something else entirely, something beyond their perception. And finally, he spoke, his voice low and measured.

"I am there."

For an hour, they watched Cuthbert sit there, motionless save for the occasional flinch or quiver, like someone in the midst of a powerfully vivid dream. *Or a nightmare*, Wulfric thought to himself. And yet Cuthbert's eyes remained open the whole time, blinking never once, staring into that faraway place. Occasionally he would shimmer, as before, and become momentarily transparent, as though he were as much in the other place as here before them. "Something is not right," said Edgard with rising concern. "We must wake him."

"Not yet," said Wulfric. He did not begin to understand the workings of this magick, but he knew enough to surmise that disturbing Cuthbert in his current state was just as likely to strand him in that other place as return him.

All changed when Cuthbert's flinches and twitches suddenly became something more—at first strange spasms, then violent convulsions. Wulfric's eyes widened in alarm as Cuthbert lashed his head from side to side, as if in the grip of some sudden terror. He cried out, kicking his legs as though trying to scramble away, but his feet found no purchase, the grass beneath them still wet with morning dew. And yet while the lower half of his body resisted, his fingertips remained firmly fixed to the mirrored blade of Wulfric's sword, unmoving, as though that half of his body were paralyzed by his connection to it.

"All right, enough," Wulfric said as Cuthbert continued to writhe and protest. He and Edgard moved in together, Edgard grabbing the boy as Wulfric went to separate him from the sword. It took all of Edgard's might to restrain Cuthbert enough for Wulfric to pull the sword free—but as Wulfric touched it, the world around him fell dark. He was no longer in a sunlit meadow but surrounded by dank walls lit by flickering torchlight, a narrow hallway extending into shadows and gloom. It was difficult to see; his vision was somehow distorted in this place, his surroundings indistinct and disorienting, as if viewed through thick glass. He could see clearly only what was directly in front of him, while all that on the periphery of his vision melted away into a blur.

He heard a low growling behind him and turned—slowly, for moving in this place was sluggish, akin to the motion within a dream. It took a moment for his vision to orient itself and focus on what was now in front of him: one of Aethelred's wretches, but unlike any he had seen in some while. Most of those that Wulfric's army had fought at Aylesbury and after retained at least some characteristics of the human men they had once been—mostly they walked upright, on hind legs. The thing before him now was more like the potbellied monstrosity he had first encountered, down in Alfred's dungeon. It sat low on the ground, its four clawed limbs extended on either side of a bulbous torso that resembled a giant lizard. Try as Wulfric might, he could not make out more through the distorted lens of his vision, save for the leathery, barbed tail that swished back and forth. There did not appear to be a head, at least none that Wulfric could see, just a gaping mouth where a head should have been, lined with razor-like teeth.

The beast scuttled toward him aggressively. Wulfric's retreat was like wading through knee-deep sand. He looked down and saw his sword in his hand, and he thought to slay the beast with it, but it felt so heavy he could barely raise it. Then he heard a voice, faint at first, so faint he thought it might be his own mind playing tricks. But it grew louder, unmistakably real, and recognizable as that of young Cuthbert.

Sir Wulfric! Let go! You must let go of the sword!

He tried to do as the voice bid, but his hand would not respond to his command. As the dire beast moved toward him again, to within striking distance, Wulfric focused all the mental capacity he could muster on his sword hand, and felt his grip slowly begin to weaken. And then the beast leapt at him and he stumbled backward, the foul stench of the monster's breath upon him—

Wulfric cried out as he felt himself hit the ground and looked up to see gray clouds drifting idly across the sky above. Edgard and Cuthbert hovered over him, looking down upon him with expressions of grave concern.

"What happened?" he asked, realizing then that he was breathing hard, his chest pounding. Edgard and Cuthbert both looked relieved as they saw Wulfric's eyes focus on one, and then the other.

"You should not have touched the sword," said Cuthbert. Wulfric looked and saw it lying in the grass, just beyond his reach. Cuthbert had removed one of his outer garments and thrown it over the blade. "I'm afraid it will have to be destroyed. The skill to disenchant it is beyond my ability. My apologies."

Wulfric sat up groggily. "I was . . . I was *there*," he said. His mind stumbled, recalling all that he had experienced in those last few moments.

"Remarkable, is it not?" replied Cuthbert with scholarly enthusiasm. "The clarity of the vision is almost—"

"What did you see?" demanded Edgard, and Cuthbert sobered instantly. "I saw what I had seen at Canterbury before," he said, and he looked to Wulfric. "When the archbishop first began his experiments."

Wulfric nodded. Now he understood why the farmlands and pastures surrounding Canterbury were eerily devoid of the animals that would usually be seen grazing there. He had assumed that they had been moved, or had fled in fear of whatever evil was brewing inside that cathedral. But he knew now what had become of them.

Wulfric sat astride Dolly, bedecked in her cavalry armor, with Edgard at his side, before the assembled ranks of his men on the hillside overlooking Canterbury. The time they had spent idling while Wulfric pondered had only sharpened their eagerness for this final battle; he could see it in their faces. And now that Wulfric knew what awaited them inside Aethelred's lair, they would have their wish.

"In his desperation, Aethelred has reverted to the most primitive form of his cursed magick," he announced. "He has gone back to whence he first began, transforming common animals into vile abominations that he hopes to use as a last line of defense. Whatever small measure of control he had over the men he once enslaved, he has even less over these beasts. They may fight savagely, but without discipline, courage, or loyalty. That is what separates us as soldiers of God's virtue, protected by his divine blessings, from the forsaken wretches in there." He thrust his sword arm in the direction of the cathedral. "Canterbury is home to our most sacred beliefs, yet has been besmirched by a foul, blasphemous presence. No longer. Today we cleanse that cathedral and return it to God's grace. Today we send the evil infesting it, along with the heretic who summoned it, back to the place from whence it came—*to the very depths of hell!*"

His men roared in unison, swords thrust aloft. As Wulfric turned his horse toward the cathedral, he and Edgard shared a last look, of the kind known well to soldiers who had seen battle.

"Good speech," Edgard said with a smile as he glanced back at the men assembled behind them. "Their blood is up."

"I only hope that no more of it than necessary is spilled today," replied Wulfric. "Now let us be done with it. I want to go home." And with that, he held his sword aloft, released a bellowing war cry, and spurred his horse toward Canterbury, with the thundering of three hundred hooves at his back.

SEVEN

Unlike the many Norse fortresses and strongholds to which Wulfric and Edgard had laid siege in their time, Canterbury was not designed to withstand an attack. Aethelred had made an attempt to barricade the outer doors with whatever materials he could find, but they gave with little effort, and Wulfric led the charge inside, into the cathedral's spacious outer cloister.

Once a place of tranquil reflection, the cloister now more closely resembled the many battlefields Wulfric had seen on campaign, or the sacked villages to which he had borne witness as a child. The ground was stained dark with dried blood and the lifeless bodies from which it had been spilled—the bloated, flyblown carcasses of some of Aethelred's contorted creatures that in their mindless savagery had taken to attacking and killing one another. Patches of ground were burned black from those beasts that belched fire. The whole place reeked of sulfur and bile and death, though there was little time to dwell on it. The many horrors that still lived within Canterbury's walls were rising from their slumber and moving to intercept the throng of mounted men now surging into the courtyard behind Wulfric.

Wulfric spurred Dolly on, into the fray. The first beast they encountered was trampled beneath Dolly's hooves, the second decapitated by a swing of Wulfric's sword. The blade he wielded now was not his favorite—that one had been rendered useless by the scrying—but he was no less lethal with it. The third beast attacked from outside his field of view—an oily tentacle coiled around the wrist of his right gauntlet and yanked him out of his saddle. His left foot was caught in its stirrup as he fell, and he hit the ground headfirst, hanging upside down on Dolly's side.

The tentacle released Wulfric's wrist and retracted, leaving a corroded ring around his gauntlet. As Wulfric struggled to free himself, he glimpsed, upside down, the beast that had dismounted him closing in. Even as it came closer, it was difficult to make out what exactly it was from this upended perspective. Wulfric still had hold of his sword, and he swiped wildly at the beast to keep it at bay, giving himself enough time to finally wrest his foot free from the tangled stirrup and right himself. As he rose and stood before the snarling beast, it occurred to him that it was no more recognizable right side up than it had been upside down. Its scaly, armored body was sinuous and lithe, and it moved like a serpent, except that it had four vaguely canine legs, an elongated nose, and sharply pointed ears. Its jointed tail curved upward and around behind it, like that of a scorpion. But where the stinger would have been, the tail instead bloomed open like the petals of a leathery flower to reveal within it the tentacle that had dismounted Wulfric. That tentacle slavered and writhed like a grotesquely distended tongue.

What had this horror once been? thought Wulfric. He studied it for traces of the familiar, some visual clue to its prior anatomy before Aethelred had desecrated it. *Some kind of dog? A wolf, perhaps?* It was difficult to tell. Even for someone familiar with Cuthbert's bestiary, there was always something new to chill the blood and shake one's faith in God. What manner of God, after all, would suffer such a blasphemy upon his earth?

The tentacle rattled like a cobra's tail and shot out at Wulfric once again, this time trying to snatch his sword from him. But Wulfric was faster; he sidestepped deftly and, with a downward stroke, sliced the tentacle clean in two. The serpentine beast shrieked as it retracted the bloody, flailing stump and, enraged, charged straight at Wulfric, jaws opening wide to expose rows of slobbering canine fangs. The beast's body lay low, no more than two feet off the ground, so as it came at Wulfric, he simply leapt atop it and, straddling it, plunged his sword down into its back, between the scales that ran along its spine. The beast shrieked ever louder and thrashed helplessly as Wulfric drove his sword deeper, skewering it to the ground. Still, it refused to die until Wulfric twisted the blade in place to open the wound wider and spill out its blood in a radiating pool beneath its quivering body.

When the beast was finally still, Wulfric withdrew his sword and turned to survey the scene. The battle was now fully joined, his men spread out across the courtyard and engaging all manner of misshapen beasts at close quarters. Watching as they hacked and bludgeoned their way through the monstrous herd, Wulfric grew satisfied that the fight out here was well in hand. Though they were outnumbered, it was clear that his men would carry the day—these lower, animalistic forms that Aethelred had conjured in his desperation were still fearsome, but less so than the humanoid varieties his men had become well accustomed to killing.

Wulfric headed toward the cathedral itself, where he knew he would find the fount of all this misery and death, and where he would finally put an end to it.

The wooden door was barred but gave with two slams of Wulfric's pauldron, and he entered into the cathedral's central nave. Sunlight shafted through the narrow slits of its windows and over the rows of pews that extended into darkness at the far end, where the raised altar was masked in shadow. His sword still drawn and at the ready, Wulfric trod carefully down the central aisle, his footsteps echoing off the stone slabs beneath. As he proceeded farther inward, the sounds of the battle outside receded, and he was suddenly aware of how quiet and still it had become. A church was supposed to be peaceful, but not like this. This was . . . not peace, just . . . nothingness.

There was an enveloping, almost suffocating sense that whatever a man might carry inside him, to armor him against despair
or to bring him solace or comfort, had somehow been left behind,
abandoned, upon entering this hall. It was the most unsettling sensation Wulfric had ever felt, and in that moment he knew exactly
what it was. The presence of true evil.

He moved carefully, aware that one of Aethelred's dire wretches
might be lurking between any of the rows of pews he passed. And
as he drew closer to the chancel, where the cathedral's altar stood,
and his eyes grew accustomed to the darkness there, he slowed.
Here he began to make out the shape of a cloaked figure, seated,
unmoving.

"Aethelred," he whispered to himself, so quietly that not even a
soul seated in the pew closest to him could have heard, and yet the
cloaked figure seated fifty feet away rose as though he had heard
his name.

"You will address me as Archbishop or Your Grace," said
Aethelred. He spoke softly, and yet when his voice reached Wulfric
it seemed to echo powerfully all around him, in a way that had
nothing to do with how sound normally carried in a place like this.
This, too, Wulfric knew, was something else, something wicked, at
work.

Aethelred took a step closer, into a beam of sunlight, and
Wulfric's suspicions were confirmed. Whatever dark magick the
archbishop had immersed himself in these past months had utterly
consumed him. His face had become pale and drawn, his frame
wizened to the point of skeletal frailty. And his eyes . . . his eyes
were worst of all, deeply jaundiced and shot through with blood.
He barely looked human. As Wulfric regarded him with revulsion
and dismay, he contemplated the final, bitter truth of the power
Aethelred had unlocked. Such was its malign influence that it radi-
ated not only outward, to make warped and pitiable creatures of
its intended victims, but also inward, to slowly, gradually, visit the
same fate upon any man who employed it.

While others might have hesitated out of sympathy for what appeared to be little more than a pathetic, afflicted old man, Wulfric knew better; he knew how much more dangerous Aethelred was than he appeared. Cuthbert had placed a fresh blessing of protection on his armor before he rode into battle, but still he took no chances; he made haste to close the distance between Aethelred and himself, to strike the corrupted priest down before he could summon one of his infernal spells. But to his surprise, the archbishop made no effort to defend himself; he did not raise a hand or mutter a word as Wulfric bounded up the steps to where he stood—not even when Wulfric grabbed him by the throat and forced him backward over the altar, his sword at the old man's throat.

This is too easy. Wulfric was briefly perturbed by the thought but set it aside to focus on his task. It was then that he hesitated, looking at the archbishop for the first time up close. Close enough to smell the sour stench of his breath, to see every line etched into his face. He realized it was not the yellowing, bloodshot appearance of Aethelred's eyes that he found troubling; it was the *way* the priest looked at him. He stared up at Wulfric, eyes wild and unblinking, as if he had journeyed into some unthinkable, nightmarish beyond and never fully returned.

Wulfric saw in that moment that Aethelred's magick had corrupted not only his body but his mind, had driven him to the depths of irrevocable madness. Killing him would be an act not only of justice, but of mercy.

And yet something stayed his hand. The edge of his sword was barely an inch from Aethelred's pulsing throat; it would be the work of slicing an apple to open up his flesh and watch the life bleed out of him. But there was something about the crazed, otherworldly look in the man's eyes. They bored into Wulfric, seeming almost to peer *within* him, into his very soul. He was the one holding this feeble and defenseless old man at swordpoint, so why did he feel so . . . vulnerable?

"So you are the one who led this war against me," said Aethelred from the altar. "Murdered my children, rent my family asunder. Sir Wulfric the Wild."

How does he know my name?

"Your children?" Wulfric responded with disgust. "Those innocent men and women you corrupted and enslaved?" But Aethelred seemed not to hear him, lost in his own demented reverie.

"No one understands vengeance better than God," the archbishop said finally. A vulpine grin spread across his face, revealing a mouthful of crooked and rotting teeth. "That is why he smiles upon its cause. I have grown weak, but I made sure to retain what little of my power remains, in hopes that you would be the first to find me. To get *close* enough. And now, here you are. Delivered unto me."

It was then that Wulfric noticed the parchment strewn across the altar next to Aethelred. Page upon page of handwritten scrawl in a language he could not comprehend, and did not at first recognize. And then he remembered where he had seen such writing before—in the transcriptions of Aethelred's scrolls that Cuthbert had made from memory in his effort to perfect his protective counterspells. Wulfric knew that the papers on the altar could not be the original scrolls, as Alfred had assured him they had all been destroyed. So what, then, were they? He saw then that the ink on the topmost sheet was fresh, saw the quill resting nearby. Wulfric grabbed the parchment with his free hand and held it up before Aethelred.

"What is this?" he demanded angrily. *"What is it?"*

Aethelred sneered, but did not answer. He no longer met Wulfric's eyes, but was looking at something lower, on his chest. The archbishop's gaze was focused on the silver scarab pendant that hung from Wulfric's neck.

"Perfect," whispered Aethelred with a broadening grin. And then, with surprising speed, he thrust his right hand upward and slammed it hard against Wulfric's breastplate, fingers splayed wide, palm covering the medallion and pressing it against Wulfric's armor. Wulfric grabbed Aethelred's wrist and tried to pry the hand free, but it would not budge; the seemingly decrepit old man was far stronger than he appeared.

Aethelred glared up at Wulfric with a withering, white-hot hatred. He pressed his hand harder against Wulfric's chest and began to mutter something under his breath. It was foreign and unintelligible to Wulfric, but he knew it immediately to be a magickal incantation. He felt his chest growing uncomfortably warm, and looked down to see that his breastplate had begun to glow beneath Aethelred's palm. To his horror, he realized that Aethelred was burning through his armor. The archbishop's hand had become brighter and hotter than a blacksmith's forge, and Wulfric's breastplate was turning molten around it as Aethelred pressed more firmly, his hand sinking into the hammered metal.

Wulfric cried out when he felt the flesh beneath his armor begin to burn. He could think of nothing else but to plunge his sword down, into Aethelred's throat. Blood bubbled up from the widening wound as the blade sank into it, but Aethelred still muttered in that infernal language, his voice now an empty hiss, spitting each word at Wulfric like it was venom and plunging his hand deeper, clean through Wulfric's melting armor and directly onto the flesh beneath.

Wulfric's cries echoed around the cathedral's stone walls. The burning was agony. In desperation, he retracted his sword and brought the blade back down lengthways across Aethelred's neck, pushing down, severing tendon and muscle until it cleaved clean through the archbishop's flesh and his head came off and rolled away, over the altar's edge and onto the stone floor.

Only then did the archbishop's strength finally leave him, allowing Wulfric to at last pry loose the hand from his chest. Aethelred's body fell away lifelessly and hit the floor in a crumpled heap. But although he had freed himself, Wulfric's breastplate was still white-hot and burning his skin. Dropping his sword, he tried desperately to unbuckle the armor, just as Edgard burst through the door at the far end of the nave, a force of men at his back, Cuthbert among them. Edgard saw Wulfric writhing in apparent distress and rushed to his aid, helping to unfasten the straps that held the breastplate in place before pulling it free—the metal so hot it burned his hands as he did so—and tossing it to the ground, smoke still rising from the molten gash in the shape of a handprint that Aethelred had left.

Wulfric's legs gave way beneath him and he slumped to the floor with the altar at his back, gasping. Edgard knelt before him and gave him water to drink as Cuthbert surveyed his wound. The tunic Wulfric wore beneath his breastplate had also been burned through, revealing a ghastly scar of blackened flesh in the center of his chest, as though he had been branded there with a hot iron. On closer inspection, Cuthbert noticed that the shape of the burn, like none that he had ever seen, uncannily resembled the shape of a scarab beetle.

"This burn is severe. It must be treated immediately," he said.

"I'll fetch someone," said Edgard, and he stood urgently to leave.

"No," replied Wulfric with as much strength as he still had. "It is but a burn. I'll live. See to the other wounded first."

Edgard nodded, then took a moment to survey the scene. The melted breastplate. The sheets of parchment strewn across the floor. Aethelred's crumpled body and, several feet from it, his head.

"What in God's name happened here?" he asked.

Wulfric just closed his eyes, exhausted. Even if he had possessed the strength to try to explain, he would have had no idea where to begin.

Wulfric stood in the cloister and watched Aethelred burn. His men had made a pyre of wood, hoisted the headless body atop it, and set it ablaze—soon there would be nothing left of the archbishop but ashes consigned to the wind. The head had already been burned, separately, its charred remains given to a rider to scatter a mile away. Wulfric was taking no chances with this man, even in death. As he watched the flames lick Aethelred's blackening body, his hand played across the dressing placed over the burn on his chest. The salve that had been applied did little to quiet the painful throbbing beneath. Worse, his scarab pendant, one of the few material things he valued, had been lost, melted into nothing; all that remained was the curiously shaped brand that Aethelred's hand had seared into his flesh.

Cuthbert emerged from the nave door. He clutched a sheaf of the parchments gathered from the altar inside and was studying them as he approached Wulfric. Each page seemed to cause him more puzzlement than the last. He looked up in time to see Wulfric draw his hand self-consciously away from the wound on his breast.

"Are you quite sure that's all right?" Cuthbert asked.

"It is nothing," said Wulfric, his attention fixed firmly on the papers Cuthbert held. "What have you learned?"

"It's curious," said Cuthbert as he sifted through the pages. "This is the language of the scrolls, but what I see here did not appear in any of them. I would remember. The archbishop was not simply transcribing what he already knew—this is his own original work. I believe he was attempting to further his understanding and command of the magick he had learned, to develop it to a higher, more advanced level."

"To what end?"

"That I cannot say, at least not without further study. Much of what he has written here is beyond my ability to comprehend. At best guess, I'd venture that after his defeat at Aylesbury, he began working on some way to improve the potency of his magick, in order to counteract my wards of protection or perhaps to create more powerful beasts. And he might have succeeded if we had not apprehended him when we did—this is advanced learning, far beyond anything that was set down in the original scrolls. After we return to Winchester, I will have more time to study this and perhaps learn what he—"

Wulfric took the parchments from Cuthbert's hands and tossed them onto the fire. Cuthbert looked on in shock as the flames took hungrily to them, the pages flaring brightly as they were consumed.

"Aethelred is dead," said Wulfric as he watched the blaze reduce the parchments to a flurry of blackened and glowing embers, to be carried away by the wind. "And the evil he brought forth dies with him." He turned and walked away, leaving Cuthbert gazing into the fire.

Their work was almost done. The last of Aethelred's abominations had been butchered and burned, and every inch of Canterbury Cathedral scoured for any that might still remain, lurking in the shadows. Of Aethelred himself, nothing was left but an unrecognizable heap of brittle and charred bone atop a mound of dying embers. All that remained was to see to the fallen, and in that they had been relatively fortunate. Of the seventy-six men who had stormed Canterbury, only five had been killed and another nine wounded.

Wulfric always insisted on seeing to the wounded personally; they were, after all, his responsibility. He had sought each of them out, recruited them, commanded them. Now it was his duty to tend to them.

He had done so already for all but one. He knelt before that one now, a man barely younger than Wulfric himself, who nevertheless seemed to Wulfric little more than a child. They all did; that was the commander's curse. He knew this man's face, recognized him as one of the many who had distinguished themselves at Aylesbury, following Wulfric into that hell-borne fray without fear or hesitation, fighting with courage, never yielding until the battle was won. As Wulfric looked upon the man now, he was ashamed to realize that he did not remember the soldier's name and was forced to ask.

"Osric," the man told him, though he was weak and found it difficult to speak. When Wulfric had first approached, Osric had tried to stand so he might salute his commander as befitting a soldier, but his wounded leg would not support him, and so he had to content himself with putting on the most valorous show he could while sitting on his arse, propped up against one of Canterbury's stone walls.

"You fought bravely today, Osric," said Wulfric, with a hand on the man's shoulder. "I am sorry it had to end this way."

"Not I," replied Osric, his voice raspy and meek. "I am glad that I got to see it through, to finish the good Lord's work . . . and to fight one more time by your side." Osric looked up with swelling pride, which only served to make Wulfric uncomfortable. It always did. This man was dying; he had given up his life for this cause. Yet the praise and the glory was placed on Wulfric, and it felt ill-deserved.

"Is there someone to whom I can convey a message?" Wulfric asked.

Osric shook his head. "Never married. A few women that might be pleased to hear I'm dead, but why give them the satisfaction?" He laughed a little, as did the men assembled around him. Even Wulfric managed a smile.

"I have one request," said Osric. "Bury me here, at Canterbury. I have no home to speak of. May as well be put to rest where I fell so that I might look down and remember the little good I did here, if nowhere else."

Wulfric nodded grimly, understanding all too well. He looked again at Osric's wound. Some kind of damned hog-like thing, already mortally wounded, had lashed out at Osric with a barbed claw as it lay dying, slashing open his left thigh. The wound was jagged and ugly but not particularly deep. Ordinarily, it would not be considered life threatening, nothing a competent physician could not treat, nothing that could not in time be healed. But this was no ordinary injury, as Wulfric and his men by now knew all too well. A wound inflicted by an abomination would never close, never heal, no matter how skillfully it was treated. Stitches would not take; no dressing could stanch the bleeding. A protracted and painful death was inevitable as blood loss slowly accumulated. It might take hours or days depending on the severity of the wound, but as Wulfric had come to learn, the outcome was always the same. It was no way for a soldier to die.

"Hold him," he said, and the men standing at Osric's side took him by the arms. Wulfric drew a dagger from his belt and with one swift and precise strike ended the man's life, as quickly and humanely as he knew how. He wiped the dagger clean and was about to resheath it when he realized he no longer had need of it. The war was over. Osric was the last poor soul under Wulfric's command that he would have to dispatch in such a manner. And he had no desire to carry around a souvenir of so grim a task. He tossed the dagger away, into the dirt, and looked to the two men still holding Osric's body.

"See to the burial," he said. "Find a suitable plot in the cemetery here and ensure that the grave is properly marked." The men nodded and carried Osric away. Wulfric turned, looking for Dolly, who was idling nearby with the other horses. It was the first sight that had brought him happiness all morning, and as he pulled himself up into her saddle, he found himself grateful for small mercies. He could not bring himself to imagine her killed, or worse still, wounded by one of Aethelred's creatures such that he would have to finish her himself. But at least one small part of this grim tale would have a happy end; they would ride home together.

Edgard cantered over to Wulfric's side on his own mount and the two watched the last of the twisted animal carcasses being put to the torch. "Not a bad morning, I'd say," Edgard offered, with the look of a man who might have enjoyed the day's slaughter a little too much.

"Nor a good one, either," said Wulfric. "I am only glad that it is over."

"Over? My friend, this will be over only after we have hunted down every one of Aethelred's monstrosities that remain. You and I talked about this. We both knew our task would not end with the death of the archbishop. After we return to Winchester, I suggest we take a day to resupply and rest, and then begin—"

"I am not going to Winchester," Wulfric interrupted. "I am going home. You are more than capable of commanding the Order without me."

They had discussed this many a time in the weeks since routing Aethelred's horde at Aylesbury—the need for a standing force of men to carry on the work that he and Edgard had begun. There remained the long and difficult task of hunting down each and every abomination that had fled from battle, hundreds of them now scattered throughout the land, a threat to every man, woman, and child in lower England. But Wulfric had never had any intention of commanding such a force. He had suggested founding the Order only so that someone else could complete the task in his stead, allowing him to go home to his family. And he knew that Edgard would relish such a duty, so he could delay going home to his.

Edgard looked at him, surprised. "You do not at least wish to deliver the news of our victory to the King yourself?"

"That honor I am happy to leave to you. I made a promise to my wife that I would not be gone a moment longer than necessary, and I intend to keep it. Give Alfred my regards, and ask him to please not call on me again. At least until my son is grown. He will understand."

Wulfric turned Dolly toward the gate and spurred her forward. A part of him, the part ever consumed by a sense of loyalty and duty, griped. Edgard was right that dozens of Aethelred's monsters still roamed free and would continue to pose a threat to innocent people throughout the kingdom until all were found and dealt with. But the greater part of him, the part that wanted nothing more than to be reunited with his beloved Cwen and to meet his newborn son for the first time, would not be argued with.

Aethelred is dead, the threat he posed vanquished, he told himself. *You have done everything that Alfred asked of you. You owe him nothing more. Now go home and be with your family. No one can say you have not earned it.*

The thought drove Wulfric to ride even faster. His home was little more than forty miles to the west. A new life awaited him there, a better life, and if he rode fast enough it could begin before sundown.

EIGHT

Wulfric made it home just before eventide. He had been mindful not to press Dolly too hard, but from the pace at which she ran even unbidden, one would think she, too, knew their destination and was just as impatient as Wulfric. Together they chased the setting sun until they arrived atop the selfsame hill from which Wulfric had taken his last look at his homestead before heading out to hunt Aethelred what seemed like a lifetime ago. The sunset painted all the valley below in gold, and there in the distance, Wulfric saw smoke rising from the chimney of his cottage. His humble home looked as it ever had, and yet to Wulfric it had never been quite so beautiful.

He rode Dolly down into the valley and across the fields that made up his small plot of farmland. In his absence, the soil had not been tilled or tended; he would have much work to do, and quickly, if he were to sow any crops in time for harvest. He smiled to himself, relishing the prospect of the sweat of honest labor, of dirtying his hands with something other than blood.

As Wulfric drew closer to his house, he saw her standing just outside it. Cwen was taking freshly washed clothes from a large wicker basket at her feet and pegging them to a line from which to dry. Wulfric gasped at the sight of her; he had almost forgotten how strikingly lovely she was. After long months away, seeing her now was like seeing her again for the first time. He reined Dolly to a halt and stayed there a while, admiring Cwen's beauty in the lambent sunlight.

Cwen caught sight of Wulfric when she turned to take a garment from her basket. She did not react instantly. Instead she finished with the washing, methodically hanging the last of it over the line to dry before walking to the front of the house to meet him. The sun was setting behind Wulfric, causing Cwen to shield her eyes as she approached.

Wulfric spurred Dolly forward, and as he drew closer, he saw for the first time that the great bulge in Cwen's belly that he had grown so accustomed to before he left was gone. Glancing at the washing line behind her, he noticed the tiny linen shirts that hung alongside the full-size dresses and skirts fluttering gently in the breeze. His son's clothes.

Wulfric dismounted, suddenly acutely aware of how uncertain he felt. In his zeal to return home, to arrive at this moment, he had never once thought to imagine what might await him. Four months ago, he had ridden away from his wife, leaving her to carry the burden of birthing and raising their first child without him at her side. He had broken his sacred vow to her, a vow little more than a year old, and had chosen the worst possible time at which to do it. She had cussed and cried and thrown everything at him that conceivably could be thrown—he still bore a mark on his forehead from that milk jug—and had told him that if he chose to leave he would not be welcomed home upon his return, if indeed she was even still there.

At the time, Wulfric had dismissed that threat as idle, blurted in anger in the heat of argument and to be regretted and withdrawn shortly after his departure. But now, as he stood before her, he was none so sure. He did find some small relief in seeing her here; she had at least not made good on that part of her threat. But as he looked at her now, her face expressionless and impossible to read, his stomach tightened. It began to dawn on him that the blissful reunion he had dreamed of for so long might in reality be something he had not prepared for.

She took a step toward him, to better see him in the fading light of day. Wulfric braced himself, too nervous to speak, and in any case not knowing quite what to say. It was a strange, unfamiliar feeling, this particular kind of trepidation. Wulfric was no stranger to fear, of course; no soldier was. He had come to know it well and in all its myriad guises, from mortal terror in the face of a crazed Norse berserker to the chill dread he had often felt in the presence of Aethelred's malformed horrors. In every case, he had known how to gird himself against that fear, to conquer it and thus his enemy. But this . . . the most abject terror in the face of almost-certain death somehow paled in comparison to how he felt now, caught in Cwen's inscrutable gaze, facing the sudden realization that the thing he cherished most in all the world might have slipped beyond his reach, lost forever, and by his own doing. He had never before felt so utterly disarmed, so helpless, so afraid.

His mind raced as he considered what approach to take. Contrition? Triumph? Should he have stopped on the way to pick flowers to offer her? Brought some of those elderberry scones she liked from the baker in the village? His heart sank lower still as it began to dawn on him that no words, no apology or gesture, might be sufficient to wipe away the wrong that he had done her.

He was still searching hopelessly for the right words when Cwen ended at least that part of his suffering by breaking the silence first.

"I knew it was you when I first saw you up there on the hilltop," she said.

What did that mean? Was that good? The words sounded good, but not their tone. If she was pleased to see him, why did she look at him like something the cat dragged in? Or was that just the way she was squinting against the sun? *Don't stand there like a dumb animal, you idiot. Say something!*

Wulfric glanced back at the hilltop, a good five hundred yards away. "Should I take it as a compliment that you recognized me from such a distance?" he asked, hoping to channel a little of the roguish charm that Cwen once admitted had made her fall for him in the first place. But she seemed unmoved.

"No," came her dispassionate reply. "It was Dolly I recognized, not you. I'd know that horse anywhere." She took a step closer, scrutinizing Wulfric more closely but without betraying any hint of what might lie within her. "What is that . . . thing?"

It took Wulfric a moment to realize that she was referring to something on his face. His hand came up to touch the thick, wiry beard he had grown while away. "You don't like it?" he asked as he self-consciously ran his fingers through it.

"It looks like a diseased animal crawled onto your face and died," she said. "It will have to go if you want back into this house, much less into my bed. So what is it to be?"

She placed her hands on her hips expectantly, as though awaiting his answer. But by now her cool facade was becoming more difficult to maintain; Wulfric detected the subtlest hint of a smile. She was toying with him—and the realization felt like a thousand-pound weight being lifted from his shoulders. He could breathe. But, just to be sure, he drew a knife from his belt, grabbed a bedraggled and bristly tuft of beard, and began sawing away at it. Cwen rushed to him with a broadening smile and moved the knife away.

"Later," she said, and she gazed lovingly into his eyes. "You can shave it later." And she flung her arms around him, pressing her body to his as tears flowed down her cheeks. Wulfric let the knife slip from his hand and returned the embrace, holding her more tightly than he ever had. A single tear rolled down his own face and disappeared into the matted jungle of his beard.

"I prayed every night for your safe return," she said between sobs.

"Every night?"

Cwen looked up at him and wiped away a tear, and there again was that impish curl of a smile. "Well, the first night I prayed you would fall from your horse and break your neck," she said. "But every night after that, safe return."

Wulfric smiled, more out of relief than good humor, and embraced her ever more tightly, not wanting to let go. "I feared that you would hate me," he said.

"Believe me, I tried. I learned I only hate the things that take you away from me." She looked at him again, this time without any trace of lightheartedness. "Tell me you are done," she said firmly, almost as a demand, one not open to negotiation. "Tell me that this was the last time. Swear it."

Wulfric cupped her perfect face in his hands. "I am done," he said, with sincerity and certitude. "This was the last time. I swear it."

Cwen melted. They kissed. And then she took him by the hand and, smiling warmly, began to lead him toward the house. "Come," she said. "There's someone I want you to meet."

It was dark inside the cottage, which was lit only by the failing sunlight arcing through a small window. But Wulfric saw it immediately, the little crib in the far corner with a woolen blanket within, its contours shifting gently as something beneath it stirred. Wulfric was drawn to it as though hypnotized, his hand slipping from Cwen's as she remained by the doorway, watching him with a smile. He approached the crib slowly, transfixed, until finally he stood over it and gazed down at the tiny, squirming bundle that lay there. He glanced back at Cwen, his eyes asking for permission. Smiling, she responded with an encouraging nod. *Go ahead.*

Gingerly, he reached into the crib. His hands were coarse, from a life spent handling all manner of tools and weapons, the instruments of life and death. He had never held anything so delicate, so precious as this. He trembled as his hands closed gently around the writhing blanket and lifted it carefully up and to his chest. He turned into the light and saw the child's face, no larger than his fist, eyes half-open, not long woken from sleep, so tiny and so perfectly formed it defied belief. Wulfric gazed down in awe as the child stretched and gave a wide-mouthed yawn, and his heart swelled. He had never in his life experienced a joy like it. And as he stood there, cradling his firstborn, he knew. All the horrors he had witnessed in his life, all the hardship and sorrow . . . if that was the road he had had to travel to arrive at this moment, to be rewarded with the priceless, perfect gift he held in his hands, then it was worth it ten times over and more.

Cwen arrived at his side, smiling warmly. "Here," she said as she gently adjusted the positioning of Wulfric's hands, showing him how to properly support the infant's head. "That's better."

Wulfric was still so overwhelmed that his words came haltingly; he stammered as he spoke. "What is his name?"

"I'd hoped to wait until your return so we might both decide," said Cwen. "But I like Beatrice. After my mother."

It took Wulfric a moment. Then he drew back the swaddling blanket and looked. Cwen regarded him with amusement as the realization sank in. Wulfric had not even considered it. Somewhere deep down he had been so sure it would be a boy. In his dreams, it was always a boy. All the names he had toyed with, spoken aloud as he and Dolly plowed his fields, to hear how they sounded, were boys' names.

Perhaps it had been a way to allay some of his trepidation about becoming a father; he had been the eldest of five brothers and knew at least a little about helping to raise boys. Sometimes in his dreams he would spar with his young son with wooden swords, teaching the boy to defend himself and his home should the need ever come—as Wulfric wished he himself had been able to when the Norse came for his family. That was one way he knew to be a father. But a girl was something else entirely. Girls were so much more *delicate*. What did he know that he could possibly pass on to a daughter?

Daughter. As it ran through Wulfric's mind, even the word itself sounded more unwieldy, more . . . complicated.

"Are you disappointed?" Cwen asked.

"No," said Wulfric, realizing in that moment that he was not, that it didn't matter. If anything, it only made the love he felt toward the child all the greater. She would need his protection more than a boy would have—and that he knew how to give. Beyond that, he had no idea how to be a father to a daughter. But once he had had no idea how to be a warrior, either. This might prove to be the greater test, Wulfric suspected, but he would meet it. He would learn. For now, just to be here with her, to hold her close like this, was enough.

I am a father. I have a daughter.

Yes, it was more than enough.

Wulfric's home sat on the outskirts of a small, close-knit farming village, and word of his return spread rapidly. When he had first come here to set up his home, many villagers were wary of him; they knew something of his bloody past despite his best efforts never to speak of it. But in time, all came to know him as a good neighbor, a good friend, and a man many found it hard to believe had ever raised a hand in anger. This was where he had met and fallen in love with Cwen. They were married within a month, and though the date had fallen at the height of harvest, not a single hand worked the fields that day; all were in attendance.

And together they now came again. The village square was bathed in torchlight as dusk turned to moonlit night and Wulfric's friends and neighbors gathered to welcome him home and congratulate him on his new fatherhood. Those who knew an instrument were hastily assembled so there might be music for dancing; food and wine were laid out in abundance; and after a conversation with Arnald, the village baker, Wulfric ensured that there were elderberry scones aplenty.

He danced with his wife long into the night, drinking in all the music and laughter and love that surrounded him. Such were the depths of gloom felt during the long days and nights hunting Aethelred that to be this happy again so suddenly was dizzying. It was such an intense and overwhelming feeling that he almost felt guilty. Did he really deserve to be this happy? What had he ever done to have earned such good fortune as this? Such a loving wife, so many good friends, so beautiful a child? It seemed wrong somehow to be rewarded for a life of bloodshed with such—

No. He pushed those thoughts from his mind. He would not allow himself to spoil this moment. He had never relished the slaughter, as so many others he knew did. He had done it only because it was necessary to protect his homeland, and he had asked for nothing in return. Whatever reward the fates sought to bestow upon him should not be cause for guilt. He had earned this, the life he had dreamed of, at long last. And he would not give it up. The promise he had made to Cwen he had made also to himself: he was done with blood, done with war, done with service to the King. If Alfred's messengers should ever call on him again, they would return only with a message of polite but firm refusal. This was his life now, for all the rest of his days. Home. Family. Peace.

Wulfric had not partaken of any wine—he wanted to remember this night clearly—but still he found himself feeling drunk and giddy as the festivities began to wane and Cwen led him back to their cottage. He was certain that for the first time in many weeks, a good night's sleep lay ahead—but not quite yet. In the darkness of their bedroom, Cwen pressed him against the wall, and her hot breath was close against his chest as she pulled apart his shirt and slipped her hands inside. Wulfric flinched when her fingertips played across his chest and found the coarse patch of scarred tissue where Aethelred had seared the scarab pendant into his flesh.

Cwen knew every one of Wulfric's battle scars—this one was new. But the story of it could wait; for now she simply gave thanks that her man had been returned to her with no worse a wound than this.

"I'll be gentle," she assured him.

"Why start now?" said Wulfric before clamping his mouth over hers and kissing her with all the passion of their first night together. Cwen's tongue danced with his as her hands slid lower and unbuckled his belt.

"What if we wake the baby?" Wulfric said as his heart pounded ever faster.

"I will be very disappointed if we don't," she whispered in his ear, and her hand reached inside his britches and closed around him.

An hour later, Wulfric and Cwen lay naked, tangled in one another, the sweat cooling on their bodies. But the restful slumber Wulfric had so long awaited, and that he was sure awaited him after so many sleepless nights in pursuit of Aethelred, never came. Instead, he was plagued by the most intense, most visceral, most horrifying nightmare he had ever experienced. And Wulfric was no stranger to night terrors; many times at war, he had woken in the small hours gripped by panic after the memory of some past encounter in battle had haunted him in the form of a horrific, blood-soaked dream. But this, this was something altogether more harrowing, more vivid.

In the dream, one of Aethelred's abominations came to Wulfric's village in the dead of night as those within slept. The vile creature moved from house to house, slaughtering men, women, and children in their beds. A woman woke to find it ripping her husband to pieces. It turned on her next and tore out her throat. Her screams roused nearby villagers, who ran from their homes with torches and pitchforks to find the beast emerging into the pale light of the moon, slavering and slick with the blood of its first victims.

For a moment they stood there, wide-eyed, frozen in place by the sheer, unbelievable horror of the thing. Then they rushed to attack it, only to be brutally savaged as it met them head-on, trampling them underfoot, shredding them with tooth and claw in a mindless fury. It was unstoppable. Axes and pitchforks glanced harmlessly off its scaly, armored hide. Fire did nothing but enrage it further.

When it was done ravaging its assailants, the abomination continued through the village, chasing down others who had been awoken by the panicked shouting and cries for help, and who now ran for their lives, to no avail. The beast was too fast for them; it ran down every one, goring them where they fell as they screamed and reached desperately for escape.

The horror of the nightmare was made greater by how acutely Wulfric experienced it. Every nauseating moment, every instant of terror was rendered with a clarity beyond that of any dream that had ever visited him before. Everything, except for the beast itself. Wulfric, too close to see its full form, only ever caught glimpses of it as it thrashed and flailed and murdered. A pincer. A claw. Six oily black legs that went *click-click-click* as the unseen thing scuttled from one victim to the next. And always the terrible, high-pitched shriek that it made each time it killed.

In other nightmares, Wulfric had always been able to will himself awake, to escape from the horror back into the waking world by telling himself it was only a dream, not real. Not this one. Try as he might, Wulfric could not make the nightmare end. He was imprisoned helplessly within it, unable to look away, as though his eyes were being held open by an unseen torturer forcing him to witness every moment. And now the beast was moving away from the center of the village, past the rent and broken bodies scattered upon the bloody ground, lurching toward the village's outskirts, toward the home where he and his wife and newborn daughter still slept, unaware. As the creature drew closer and Wulfric's dread deepened, he tried to focus his mind, summoning his every ounce of will to end this torment. *Wake up wake up wake up wake up . . .*

He woke. A great sense of relief washed over him as he realized he had finally escaped the dream's iron hold. But that relief fast gave way to a sickening sense of unease that lingered though the nightmare was over—an oppressive, almost suffocating feeling of dread. He rubbed his eyes, then raised his hand to the side of his head with a groan. His head pounded with a dull throb, as though he had just woken from a night of heavy drinking. But Wulfric had not touched a drop. The dream was so powerful, it seemed, so traumatic, that it had left behind some residual phantom pain.

More than anything, more than ever, Wulfric needed to be close to Cwen, to feel her comforting warmth against him. He turned, reaching for her in the dark. But she was not there. Wulfric's hand, searching blindly for his wife, found only a handful of straw. He sat up, and as his sight began to adjust to the dark, he saw that he was lying naked upon a bed of it. The whole place reeked of manure, and sulfur, and burned hay.

He was in a horse barn, lying atop a deep pile of pitch-black ash that was for some reason strewn atop the hay. He had apparently slept curled up in the center of this nest of cinders. It was the ash that stank of sulfur, and a fine coat of it covered Wulfric from head to toe, staining his skin the color of charcoal. When he tried to brush it away, he succeeded only in rubbing it deeper. And as he did, he noticed that something else was wrong. His wedding ring was missing. He had not removed it even once in the year that he had been married, but now, inexplicably, it was gone.

A single sliver of daylight cut through a gap in the barn door. Naked, Wulfric hauled himself slowly to his feet, crying out as he did so. It was not just his head—every muscle in his body, every bone, ached worse than the day after any battle he had ever fought. Hunched over in pain, Wulfric stumbled to the barn door and threw it open, squinting and raising his hand to shield his eyes from the sunlight that poured in from outside. Haltingly, he took a step forward, into the shade of an overhanging tree, and looked. And saw.

The bodies of slaughtered villagers lay all around him. Some bloodied and gored, their limbs broken and twisted into awkward, sickening shapes. Some slit open from gullet to gut, entrails spilled across the ground. Others little more than meat, trampled into the earth, or in pieces, scattered far and wide. The entire village, massacred. Wulfric staggered backward against the barn. His mind reeled. Was he still in the dream, his seeming to have woken just a cruel trick to prolong his torment? No, the maddening, frenzied sensation that defined the dream, the helpless paralysis he felt as it played out, was gone. He could move freely, look away from the horror before him if he wished.

But he did not. Steeling himself, regaining his bearings as best he was able, Wulfric walked among the dead, taking in every detail. A dizzying realization began to take hold; the body of every friend, every neighbor, lay exactly as they had fallen in his dream. There was Leland, Wulfric's closest neighbor and the first to come and shake his hand and welcome him home yesterday. He was facedown in the dirt, a pale and frozen ghost, his corpse bloated, innards strewn on the ground beneath him, spilled out just as the beast in the nightmare had gutted him with its demon talon. Not far from him was Arnald, the baker who had brought scones to the homecoming celebration and who in the dream had been among the first to assail the creature. It had set about him and those at his side with a flurry of flailing, scythe-like claws and torn them all limb from limb. Wulfric gazed upon the man's severed head, eyes wide and staring lifelessly at the sky, a grim mask preserving the terror that had gripped him at his moment of death. Just as in the nightmare.

Wulfric stood amidst the carnage, recognizing every grisly detail of it, and reached the inconceivable yet inescapable conclusion: the nightmarish visions that had come upon him as he slept had been no dream. What, then? Some form of premonition? But to what end, if it had come too late for him to prevent it from becoming reality? What did—

Cwen. The baby. Wulfric turned toward his cottage on the village's outskirts and ran. His every bone and muscle rang out in protest, as still his body ached from head to toe, but he did not slow. The dream—or whatever it had been—had ended before any harm had come to them, hadn't it? As best he could remember, it had, but much as with a dream, the memory of the vision was already growing foggy, specific details and moments becoming increasingly difficult to recall, until only the dreadful, uneasy sensation with which Wulfric had woken remained.

His cottage was the farthest from the center of the village—perhaps the creature had passed it by as it departed, perhaps it had been sated by the slaughter of so many others. But perhaps not. *Please, let them be alive. Please.* These were the thoughts still racing through Wulfric's mind as he flung open the door to his cottage and rushed inside.

It was as though the entire cottage had been painted red. What was left of Cwen was spattered and streaked across the walls and spilled on the floor, the residue of violence beyond imagining. Even the ceiling dripped with it. An ear, a finger, a torn and tousled mop of wheat-blonde hair stained blood red were the only identifiable pieces of her that remained. The barbarism required to do something like this was past anything Wulfric had ever seen, even from the most mindless and savage of Norse berserkers. Brutality like this was beyond the capacity of any man. But then, no man had done this. If it had been a man once, it had been twisted into something hideous and unrecognizable by Aethelred's foul magick.

In the corner was his daughter's crib, its wicker stained dark with Cwen's blood. Overcome, Wulfric stumbled toward it, hoping beyond hope that somehow the little one had been spared. But it was not to be. Inside, where the baby had slept, was now just so much flesh and blood and bone, butchered beyond recognition. Even the merest glance was more than Wulfric could bear. He wheeled away, staggered back outside into the light, and collapsed to the ground, unable to breathe. As he fought for breath, he looked up and saw that not even Dolly had survived. The horse's body lay on its side where Wulfric had hitched her to the post beside the house the night before, head severed and belly ripped open.

Finally, Wulfric's horror, confusion, and disbelief gave way to grief that hit him in an all-consuming wave. He cried out in anguish, his tears began to flow, and he descended into racking sobs so great his entire body convulsed. For an hour and more he wept, until he could do it no more. Then he sat in silent despair, to any who might observe him a hollowed-out, vacant husk of a man.

Inside, his mind was racing, desperately trying to comprehend the truth of what had transpired here. Where had he been when all this had happened? Why had the cries of the other villagers not woken him? And why had he awoken so far from where he had fallen asleep—in a horse barn, of all places? Even if he had the answer to all these questions, surely none of them could explain the nightmare and its dreadful portent. How could it possibly have—

It was then, as Wulfric gazed, lost in thought, at the ground outside his house, that he found his wedding ring. Except it was no longer a ring. Picking it up, he saw that the band had been snapped and bent grossly out of shape, into a mangled strip of gold. As he turned it over in his hands, trying to fathom what could possibly have torn it from his finger in so destructive a manner, he suddenly knew. Immediately, instinctively *he knew.*

It had not been a dream or a foreboding. Not an imagining of any kind. It had been *real,* all of it. Every other detail of his nightmarish vision had been all the more unsettling for its unwavering clarity, yet the beast itself was the one thing never fully seen by Wulfric. Because he had experienced it all through the beast's own eyes. Because he *was* the beast. Or somehow had been. He was human now, but his body, racked with pain and reeking of sulfur, told the truth. He felt, he now realized, as though something had burst from within him, splintering bone and tearing muscle and sinew as it broke violently free from its human cage. And then somehow, it was gone, leaving only the cage, made whole again.

Wulfric's hand drifted to his chest, to the scarab-shaped burn Aethelred had left him with the day before. The memory came rushing back to Wulfric now—the evil, knowing glare in the archbishop's eyes as he had muttered that final incantation, each unintelligible word laced with hatred, and the malevolent grin spreading across his face even as Wulfric's blade sank deeper and life left him. As though he knew this would not be the last of it; as though he knew that he would yet have his revenge.

Was it possible? To transform a man into a monster such as those the archbishop had conjured so many times before—and then back again? *He was attempting to further his understanding and command of the magick he had learned,* Cuthbert had said after studying the dead man's writings. *To develop it to a higher, more advanced level.* How it might have been done was beyond him, but Wulfric could not deny the torn and broken bodies all around him, everything his own agonized body was telling him, what his own mind was *screaming* at him. *He had done this.* Not some unknown monster. The monster was him.

This was Aethelred's revenge—to implant this curse within Wulfric so that it would take hold only after he had returned home to his loved ones. So that he would slaughter them all in a mindless fury, only to then be restored to his human form, his soul returned to him so that he could bear witness to the full horror of his own crime. So that he could be tortured by it for the rest of his days.

So that Aethelred, even from the fires of hell, could look upon his anguish and laugh.

Wulfric was still lost in his daze, trying to grasp the fullness of what he now knew to be true, when from the distance, beyond the hillside, came the sound of horses approaching. He panicked. What would it mean for him to be found here like this? Would anyone believe his story? Would he be taken for a sole survivor or a murderous lunatic? He did not know, nor even care, such were the depths of his despair. But what little presence of mind he still possessed told him that now was not the time to let his fate be decided by others. As the sound of the horses drew closer, he grabbed a woolen blanket and threw it around him, then stole away through the village, into the dense woodland that lay not far beyond, and was gone.

FIFTEEN YEARS LATER

NINE

The rain fell across the countryside in hard, driving sheets. It had been like this for weeks. The sky was the color of iron, the earth reduced to rain-sodden slop that buried each footstep up to the ankle and left wagons mired on even the best of roads. Farmers had brought what they could of their crops inside, where they themselves now waited, hoping that the rains might abate and the sun return in time to make something of the season. But for now most of southern England was a landscape of unrelenting gloom and desolation, even its busiest market towns and highways eerily deserted. Quiet permeated the land, with only the rainfall's monotonous, ever-present thrum, punctuated by the occasional rumble of distant thunder.

It was exactly as it should be, Wulfric thought to himself as he strode grimly across the moor, hunched over and leaning into the rain, blown hard against him by a freezing wind. Each step squelched as his foot sank into the swamp-like earth and again as he pulled it free. Hard going, but the roads these days were seldom better, and Wulfric wanted little to do with anyone he might encounter there. More than anything, he hated making excuses to those few who would take pity on him and offer him shelter. Even on a day like this he must refuse.

Wulfric slipped, then steadied himself as he scrambled down the shallow incline of the moor to meet a road that snaked through the valley. It was little more than a narrow footpath of gravel and mud, but the footing was slightly surer here, and Wulfric was tired. He looked left and then right to be sure there were no other travelers. Then he picked a direction, although it could not have mattered to him less, and continued on.

Though the going was far easier along the road than it had been on the marshlands, Wulfric moved at a slow, deliberate pace; the rain was still falling hard, and his heavy woolen cloak drank in the water, adding to its weight. But Wulfric did not grumble or complain. On the contrary. He knew he did not deserve fair weather, nor comfort, nor respite.

Soon he would need to find a place to sleep for the night. He had seen nothing but open country for most of the day, and he was beginning to regret leaving the relative safety and seclusion of the small copse where he had slept the night before. As it was within earshot of a well-traveled road, Wulfric had thought it less than ideal and had moved on at first light, hoping to find something better, but so far nothing had presented itself. He needed a wooded area, far from any town or thoroughfare. Somewhere with strong, deep-rooted trees. Somewhere—

"Hold, friend."

Wulfric stopped and looked up. He had been lost in thought, gazing only at the ground as he tramped through the mud. He saw now, in the mist up ahead, three men, and a small encampment by the side of the road. A few tents, some meager supplies, a campfire with a kettle suspended over it, although there was no way to keep an open flame in this weather.

There were few reasons to be out by the road on a day like this, Wulfric knew. Either you did not care, like him. Or you were desperate. Like them.

They were cutthroats of the lowest order. Even among scum there was a pecking order, and the best highwaymen claimed the broadest and busiest roads, the trade routes that gave up the richest pickings from farmers bringing their goods to market and other traveling merchants. That left the less-traveled footpaths and trails to dregs like this. These were the more dangerous. Out here on the back roads, it was rare to encounter anyone worth robbing, and so in lieu of money or goods, the lowlier thieves often took their satisfaction by beating, raping, or killing.

These were such men. Wulfric had met their type before. Once, his father had told him, centuries ago, during Roman rule, there had been law. Banditry and other crimes were effectively deterred by the harshest punishments, and there was little incentive to steal; under the Romans there was always something being built, and honest work not hard to come by. But decades of unrelenting Danish brutality had shattered and displaced entire communities, creating widespread poverty and engendering a new culture of anarchy and violence even among England's own. The three men standing before Wulfric now were born of that culture, as their fathers likely were before them. Their gaunt frames and animal eyes spoke of a hunger no man deserved, but one which far too many in these times knew. Wulfric's guess that it had been a week since any of them had eaten anything of substance was not far from the truth. There was another truth he did know—that men so hungry were capable of anything.

"This is a toll road," said the tallest of the three men as the others fanned out on either side of him, brandishing crude cudgels and sticks. "To pass, you have to pay the toll."

"I have nothing of value," said Wulfric. Though not entirely true, it would not be difficult to believe. As ragged as the three robbers were, Wulfric looked poorer still. They at least had shoes; though plastered with mud, Wulfric's feet were bare, his hands and face filthy with encrusted black grime.

"Then you don't pass," the tall man said.

Wulfric studied the men barring his way. They looked as tired and worn as he, with no appetite for a worthless struggle or violence for its own sake. But whatever passed for pride in men like these would not permit them to step aside either. Wulfric's choices, then, were simple and few. Turn back, or kill them. He could do either just as easily, but only one would leave intact the vow he had made to himself years ago.

He gave the tall man a humble nod and turned away, back the way he had come. What did it matter? Soon he would have to venture off the road again anyway, back into the wilderness, in hopes of at least putting some distance between himself and anywhere another person might be found before night fell. But as he turned, something made a sound beneath his cloak. A soft metallic clink, muffled beneath the sodden layers of wool, but the tall man heard it and started toward Wulfric, calling after him. "Not so fast!"

Wulfric halted with a sigh, knowing the sound had betrayed him. The three men promptly surrounded him. The tall one, the leader, came around to face him. He looked Wulfric up and down and saw it now, the strangeness about this man. He was too bulky under the cloak, oddly misshapen, and he had lumbered along as though encumbered by some unseen weight.

"What have you got under there?"

Wulfric said nothing. The tall man drew a dagger—little more than a sliver of sharpened iron, really—and dug it under Wulfric's chin. "I won't ask a second time. If you have nothing of value, show me."

"It is nothing of value to you," said Wulfric.

"I'll be the judge of that. Take off the cloak." The tall man shifted his weight and pushed the dagger's point a little closer, close enough to draw blood, though still Wulfric did not flinch or shy away from it. It unnerved the tall man a little; it was not natural.

"I should warn you I am naked under here," said Wulfric. "Perhaps it would be better, for all of us, to let me pass."

The other two men glanced at one another and chuckled, but a sharp look from the tall one put a stop to it. He had grown tired of this. He drew back the dagger from Wulfric's chin and plunged it deep into his belly. Wulfric let out a gasp of air and fell to his knees as the other men converged and set about him with their sticks and clubs, their own violence triggered by the sudden explosion of it from their leader. Wulfric remained still, making no attempt to deflect or shield himself from the blows that rained down upon him until finally he lay on his back, wallowing in the mud, welted, bloody, and semiconscious. Chests heaving from the exertion, his assailants stepped back and looked down upon him, bemused.

"Why don't he fight?" asked one of them. "What kind of a man don't even raise a hand to defend himself?"

"A coward," the other replied.

"A coward runs," said the first. "A coward . . . cowers! He did nothing! That is not right. That is not . . . human."

It bothered the tall man most of all. He had done much violence in his life, against all manner of men. Some fought back. Some tried to escape. Some begged for mercy. But never this. This one had simply knelt before them and taken the most savage of beatings without resistance or even complaint, almost as though it were a punishment he was glad to receive. Whatever his reason was, something told the tall man that he did not want to know it, that the explanation would be even more unsettling than what he had just witnessed.

He crouched in the mud beside Wulfric and began stripping him of his cloak. He untied the frayed cord of rope around Wulfric's waist and threw back the layers of sopping-wet wool, eyes widening at what he found beneath. Wulfric was naked save for the cloak, just as he had said, but his body was wrapped in a length of heavy iron chain slung across both shoulders, crisscrossing his chest, and encircling his waist like a saggy iron belt.

"What in God's name . . . ?" muttered one of the others. They all gazed down at the strange sight, none knowing what to make of it. But there was a reason the tall one was the leader. As the others tried to puzzle it out, he found one end of the chain and began to unravel it.

"I know an ironmonger in Ipswich who will pay well for this," he said. "Help me get it off him."

The notion that this bizarre episode might become a profitable venture after all bucked up the other men, and they moved without delay to help separate Wulfric from the chain. They rolled him over, face-first into the mud, as they unspooled the iron from around his waist and then his shoulders. They paused briefly as the unwinding of the chain revealed Wulfric's bare chest and the strange mark at its center.

"What is that? Some kind of a burn?" said one.

"Idiot," said another. "No burn looks like that. It's a tattoo, look at the shape of it. You can see it's supposed to be a beetle."

"Who would want a tattoo of a beetle?"

The tall one hissed at them both to get back to work. Soon they had the chain free, but seeing it all unwound, they realized there was much more to it than had at first appeared.

"There must be twenty-five, thirty feet of it," one of them said.

"It weighs a bloody ton," said the other as he tried to gather it up from where it snaked across the ground and haul it over his shoulder. "Ipswich is ten miles or more. Who's going to carry it?"

"We all will," said the tall man, picking up part of its length and motioning to the others to do the same. When they had managed to get it all up off the ground and had divided its weight equally among the three of them, they set off one behind the other with the chain draped over their shoulders. But it was heavier even than it looked and they staggered as they tried to walk it back to their encampment, just a few yards away. One man slipped and was dragged down into the mud under the weight.

"Bugger this," he said, as he threw the chain off him and clambered back to his feet. "It's too heavy! We'd be lucky to get this even a mile, let alone ten. And what about our gear?"

The tall man knew that he was right. Perhaps the three of them could haul it back to town, but not along with their camping gear, which was cumbersome enough. He glanced back at Wulfric and found himself wondering how one man could possibly have borne so heavy a load—and more perplexing, why he would be doing so, out here in the barrens.

The other two were still bickering with one another. The tall man shut them up and made them strike camp. With their gear on their backs, the three of them disappeared once more into the mist, leaving Wulfric in the road where he had fallen, motionless and naked, the rain washing away the blood that still seeped from his wounds.

It was some time before Wulfric came around. He rose slowly, with a pained groan as the bruises and welts all over his body hollered at him in unison. He was sitting upright before he realized he no longer felt the weight of the chain on his body. It was gone. Had the robbers taken it? The chain was the only thing he allowed himself to possess, the one thing in the world he truly needed. He looked around frantically, eyes trying to focus in the light of dusk, and exhaled in relief when he saw it lying on the ground a few feet away, where the thieves had abandoned it.

He felt a sharp pain in his abdomen as he stood and put his hand to it, remembering that he had been stabbed. It hurt, but it would heal; it mattered only if it would slow his search to find a safe place before night came. It was already getting dark.

Still unsteady on his feet, Wulfric walked over to the pile of chain lying in the mud and began to coil it around his body as he had done so many times before, around his waist and over his shoulders, until he carried its full weight. He glanced around for his cloak and found it balled up in the road a few feet from where he had risen. He shook off the excess mud and flung it around him before leaving the road and heading back into the heathlands. He rarely spoke to God these days, but as the skies darkened, he prayed he might yet find a single strong tree out here on this desolate moor before night came. He had far too much blood on his conscience already.

After walking for about half a mile, Wulfric found a small secluded wood on the far side of a hill that hid it from the road. It was perfect, and he gave thanks for not having to spend the night in the open. He had done so before when there was no better option, sleeping in some remote valley or field, and hoping. Yet sometimes an unfortunate traveler or some other hapless soul would stumble upon him, and Wulfric was powerless to prevent what would inevitably happen next. Every time, he punished himself for not being strong enough to stop it.

But for tonight, at least, he had found a place of safety, and just in time; as darkness began to fall, Wulfric could feel the tremors he had come to know all too well, the feeling of something beginning to stir beneath his skin. *Not much time.* He moved deeper into the wood and sought out the largest tree, a sturdy yew with a stout trunk and strong, deep roots. There he shrugged off his cloak and uncoiled the chain from his body until he stood naked once again. His body twitched and convulsed as he walked the chain around the girth of the tree, wrapping it once, then twice. *Quickly.*

Wulfric sat with his back against the tree and slipped the chain over his head and around his chest. On one end of the chain was a padlock, the key to which Wulfric kept on a loop of cord around his neck. Hands trembling, he turned the key in the lock, and the mechanism sprang loose. Pulling the chain around him, he hooked the padlock between two of its links and snapped it shut, then pushed his body against it to test the integrity of the binding. It was not an easy thing to do, chaining oneself to a tree, but Wulfric, through years of practice, night after night, had mastered it.

Satisfied that he was properly secured, he set the key on the ground beside him. And there he sat, shivering in the cold, waiting for the beast.

He would not wait long. Just moments after he shackled himself, Wulfric's tremors became convulsions, then worse. He cried out in pain as his entire body spasmed and seized. It had started in earnest, and what would follow would be agony, unbearable. He closed his eyes tight and bit down hard, trying to focus his mind, to divert it from the excruciating pain that was radiating out from the center of his chest and infiltrating every extremity. It was growing within him, the beast, pushing outward, violently, in every direction as it sought its escape. Wulfric's skin rippled and writhed, his arms and legs contorting at impossible angles, bones snapping with a sickening crunch as his back arched outward and he strained and thrashed wildly against the tree. Wulfric heard the iron chain groaning under the stress, and with his last coherent thought, he prayed that the many nights like this one had not weakened it. That it would hold him. Then he could tolerate the pain no more and finally, mercifully, he faded into blackness. His head lolled forward, and from the scarab-shaped scar at the center of his chest, his flesh tore open, an oily black pincer emerging from the widening wound and grasping wildly at the air. As it had countless times before, the monster that lay dormant within Wulfric by light of day was born once more into the darkness of night.

Wulfric awoke into the nightmare state that he shared with the beast.

He was conscious, after a fashion. It would be wrong to say that he and the beast shared a mind as they shared a body, for the beast itself was mindless. All it knew was hatred and death. It existed only to kill; that was its sole instinct, its sole purpose.

As the creature was trapped within the cage of Wulfric's body by day, so Wulfric was trapped within the body of the creature by night. An unholy symbiosis. Wulfric was fully aware, fully present, yet powerless to influence or control the senseless, savage thing that he became after dark. It was beyond maddening, the feeling of being nothing more than a marionette, forced to perform mindless violence by some maniacal puppeteer. Many times he had tried to overpower it, focusing his mind and mustering every ounce of willpower in a bid to stay the creature as it descended upon a defenseless village or caravan, but it was never enough. The beast's compulsion to slaughter and destroy was deep and primal; it could not be denied, try as Wulfric might. Time after time, he was an unwilling participant in the carnage, just as he had been that first night long ago when, in the form of the beast, he had murdered his friends and neighbors, his wife and newborn child.

Finally, having given up any hope of controlling the monster within him, Wulfric had hit upon the idea of the chain. If he could not restrain this vile thing while it possessed him, he would do so while it still slept. Lashed against a tree, the beast could writhe and flail and shriek all it wanted, but if the chain were strong enough, it could do no harm. So it would be tonight; the wretched thing emerged from its prison of flesh and bone hungry for blood, only to find itself immobile, imprisoned by the trap Wulfric had set for it.

Each night it awoke, the beast seemed surprised to find itself confined. As though it was born anew each time, with no memory of its prior incarnations. Each night it raged, as it did now, trying to break free of its iron bondage.

The first two chains Wulfric had had made, lighter and weaker than this one, had broken, no match for the creature's inhuman strength. The third chain, this chain, was more than twice as strong and had not once yielded. So long as he could safely tether himself each night, the beast within him could compel him to kill no more. But each night Wulfric suffered through its madness as it struggled relentlessly to break free—until the break of dawn, when finally the thing would release him, shrinking back into the dark place within him where it slumbered by day. Only then was he free to sleep for a few merciful hours, the only peace he knew.

It was still raining, though lighter than before, when a beam of daylight breaking through the leafed canopy of the forest fell on Wulfric's face. He woke to a familiar chorus of bodily aches and pains, his every muscle and bone screaming as though they had been torn apart and then somehow made whole again—which indeed they had. He had never understood exactly how his body remade itself each day after the beast had gone. It was some trick of Aethelred's infernal magick, a fiendishly cruel touch that forced Wulfric to endure this hell repeatedly, day after day, without end.

Though his body was racked with pain, the bruises from yesterday's assault were gone, as was the hole in his gut where the tall man had stuck him with the knife. That was the one small mercy of his nightly transformation from man to monster and back again; no wound, no matter how grave, lasted more than a day.

He had awoken, as he had every morning for the last fifteen years, amidst a deep pile of powdery, pitch-black ash reeking of sulfur. It surrounded him like a blanket of freshly fallen snow; it covered his naked body from head to toe, as though a flurry of it had settled on him overnight while he slept. Some residue of his transformation from beast into man, he presumed, although he had never been conscious to witness it and so could not be sure of what exactly happened during the restoration of his human form. All he knew was that the charcoal stains the ash left on him were hell to wash off, and he had stopped making any effort to do so. His hands and face, streaked and smeared with black grime, left him appearing monstrous even during his waking hours and repelled many who might otherwise stop to speak with a fellow traveler, and that suited Wulfric's purposes well enough.

He reached his hand into the pile of ashes by his side and groped around until he found the key he had left on the ground beneath. He pulled it out by its length of cord, blew away the ash that remained, and unlocked the chain, shrugging it loose. He stood, rising like some ghostly apparition, and brushed his hands through his hair and beard and all over his body to shake off excess ash before unwinding the chain from the tree and wrapping it once more around himself.

He examined the chain carefully as he did so, link by link, checking for any signs of wear or weakness. It was undamaged, though the tree had sustained severe injury, with deep gouges encircling the trunk where the chain had been wound, the bark stripped away like flayed skin. Wulfric had seen such marks before—rarely did the beast not leave behind some evidence of its violent efforts to break free of its bindings—but never so deep as these. Was the beast somehow growing in strength or in rage? Perhaps both? The thought chilled him on this already cold morning. He reached down to gather up his cloak and threw it on, tying it at the waist.

He considered staying. This was a good spot—remote, secluded, secure. Part of him did not want to give it up and run the risk of not finding another like it before nightfall. But he needed to eat, and the pickings here in the woodland were slim. A few nuts and berries would not be enough to quiet his growling belly. When had he last eaten a proper meal? He could not even remember. What he wouldn't give for a bowl of hot stew, a plate of roasted vegetables . . .

Despite the risk, he would venture out in search of food, but only so far. He would allow himself enough time to return here before sundown if he found no other safe harbor on his travels. He adjusted the chain under his cloak so that he might bear it a little more comfortably, then headed back toward the road. Over the years, he had learned to wear the chain like any other garment, but its weight never allowed him to forget that it was there. Nor should it. He had decided long ago that this was part of his penance, his punishment. To wander the earth alone, forever suffering in atonement for the atrocities he had not been strong enough to prevent himself from committing.

TEN

Indra was her name, and hardship was no stranger to her. She had lived without a home for ten months now, moving from place to place without a roof over her head except when she could afford to take lodgings, which was seldom. Most nights she slept beneath the open sky on the simple bedroll she carried on her back, along with her camping gear and the twin short swords she wore in crisscrossed scabbards. All in all, it was a heavy load, but she was young, and fit, and well trained. She strode briskly and purposefully, as though hardly burdened at all, marking each step with the planting of a strong wooden staff that she used to help her footing on uneven terrain . . . and for other purposes when necessary.

Living like this for the better part of a year had been hard, but she rarely complained. This trial had been of her own choosing; she had insisted upon it, in fact, over the stern objections of her father, who had always been so fiercely protective of her. In the end, he had been left with no choice but to relent. Once Indra was possessed by a notion, there could be no dissuading her. Many in the Order had laughed when she announced her intentions; in the fifteen years since its founding, no woman had accomplished, nor even dared try, what she had set out to do. She would show them all. She would not return home until her task was done, until she had proven her father wrong and earned the right to stand among them.

Still, she permitted herself a small grumble from time to time. Today she was exhausted and hungry and soaked through, and for all her grit, she was no closer to her goal than when she first set out. These past two months had been the hardest. It had rained incessantly, and food was harder to come by; though she knew how to live off the land, there had been precious little worth hunting in the past few days. There were rumors of some kind of wild beast roaming the countryside hereabouts, slaughtering deer and livestock. But that was why she was here. Perhaps here, at last, was the prey she had been searching for.

She stopped atop a small hill and waited. Venator would be back soon, and in this godforsaken weather, she wanted to be easy to find. He had left earlier in the day in search of food, and Indra hoped he would return having had better luck than she, though in truth she knew luck had little to do with it. Venator was a born hunter; if there was a time when he had returned without having made a kill, she could not remember it.

It was the one condition Indra's father had managed to persuade her to accept. *Venator goes with you.* He had thought this crusade of hers foolhardy and reckless, but since he could not talk her out of it, he wanted a protector to watch over her, and to bring him word if she ever needed his help. Indra had bristled at the idea that she might need the protection, or help, of another. She had not spent years practicing with sword and staff and fist for nothing and could more than capably take care of herself. But she liked Venator, had grown up with him, and knew he would be good company when the road was lonely, as it surely would be at times. And so she had agreed to take him as her traveling companion. She had been glad of it ever since.

There he was now. At first just a speck on the distant horizon, but Indra knew instinctively that it was him and smiled at the sight. She waved as he approached, marveling at his speed, and as he drew closer, she saw that he was carrying something, something almost as large as him. It had been a fruitful hunt. Of course, she expected nothing less. She had named him herself, and named him well. *Venator*, in Latin, meant "hunter."

Moments later, he was soaring overhead, wings spread majestically. She turned to follow him, looking up in wonder. *What a thing it must be to fly*, she thought to herself as Venator banked to the right and began to circle back around, effortlessly riding a current of air.

Indra often dreamed of flying. Once, years ago, she had shared this with a friend, who told her that the recurring dream was an expression of a desire to escape from her life as it was and to seek out some greater purpose, the answers to greater questions. Indra did not know what those questions might be, but her friend's words had stuck with her, nagged at her, and had played a part in bringing her to where she was now—if no closer to any answers. Her purpose, though, she was not uncertain about in the least. That had always been clear to her.

As Venator passed overhead once more, he released the thing he had been carrying, and it fell to the ground at Indra's feet. It was a salmon, a big, fat one, freshly plucked from the river. Indra's smile grew—this was Venator's best catch in some while. She extended her arm, crooked at the elbow, and Venator touched down gently upon it. She saw now that he carried a second, smaller fish in his beak. He displayed it proudly, for Indra to admire, then swallowed it down hungrily.

Venator hopped up onto Indra's shoulder when she crouched to pick up the salmon. It was heavier than it looked, ten pounds if it was an ounce. A fish that size at market would cost twice as much coin as Indra had ever carried. To someone who had been, of late, living off little but fruit and the occasional rodent, it was a wonder to behold. She would eat well tonight, better than she had in weeks.

"Good hunting," she said to the hawk as she reached up and ran her hand affectionately along his back, stroking his silken plumage. They were kindred spirits, she and Venator. They understood one another. They were, after all, both predators. He would never return from a hunt without a trophy to show for it. And neither would she.

That night, Indra camped on the hill and cooked the salmon for supper. She had feared having to eat it raw, but the rain abated long enough for her to spit-roast it over an open fire. If it had kept raining, she could have sought shelter in a wood and cooked the fish there, but she preferred to stay in the open by night, even if it meant getting drenched. Atop a hill, with good sight lines of all the surrounding area, it was more difficult for anyone—or anything— to approach her undetected. She had studied the Bestiary in the Order's library, read all its volumes from cover to cover so many times that she had committed all of it to memory. Many types of abomination saw better by night than during the day. And almost all were the color of oil, a deep, shimmering black that camouflaged them by night, making them difficult to spot until they were upon you—and by then you were as good as dead.

By night, abominations had many advantages, and Indra would not cede them any more by camping in a cloistered area that would only afford them more opportunity to approach her by stealth. And as well as they might see in the dark, Venator saw best of all. He often slept on Indra's shoulder by day while she walked so that he could keep watch by night; the eyes of a hawk were not synonymous with superb vision for nothing, and many times during her Trial they had proven a great asset.

Indra checked that the salmon was done and carved off a thick, succulent flake of pink meat with her pocketknife. She bit into it, and for a moment her eyes flickered; hunger might bias her, but it tasted heavenly, better than anything she had had even at her father's table, and rarely was anything less than the very best served there. But she had learned that it was most often in small, fleeting moments like this—the first bite of a favorite food, the touch of cool water on a hot day, the tranquility of a moonlit night—that something close to happiness could be found.

She had not been happy growing up, though she had been raised in a household surrounded by most everything a child could hope for, in a kingdom ravaged by poverty and privation. But she had from the beginning felt that something important was missing from her life. She was daughter to a wealthy lord, a widower who had raised her on his own—though mostly that meant delegating her daily care to nannies and other household servants. He rarely had time for her himself, even when he was home, which was less often than not. Mostly he was away, hunting or attending to important business of the Order.

Still, she knew that her father's presence was not the thing that was missing, the source of the emptiness that gnawed at her. Perhaps *missing* was not the right word. For as nebulous as the feeling was, Indra knew that it was something not absent, just somehow . . . misplaced. It was maddening, an itch she could never scratch, even though it bothered her constantly.

And then there was the other thing. The thing that had brought her here, had compelled her to walk away from a life of privilege and wealth in favor of the rigors of the Trial. Her father had always told her to put it behind her, to forget, but she could not. She knew she would never know peace until she had done the thing she had set out to do. Yet to the last, her father had tried to deter her, using every argument he could call to mind. *It's too dangerous. You're still just a child. Even if you somehow succeed, revenge will not bring you peace.* Indra often wondered if he would have counseled a son as he had her. She suspected not, and so she had set out, resolved to show him that vengeance was as much the province of women as of men. Perhaps more.

She cursed under her breath. It was an old mistake, dwelling on these things too long, and now her appetite was not what it was. She ate a little more of the salmon, for strength, then cut an extra piece and tossed it to Venator. She could finish the rest for breakfast tomorrow. Lying on her back, she gazed up at the infinite blanket of night above, looking to the sky to quiet her mind and usher her into sleep.

Suddenly she sat bolt upright. The sound that came echoing across the hills and valleys was beyond definition, a hideous, piercing shriek that rolled Indra's stomach and turned the skin on her arms and neck to gooseflesh. It was fleeting, the echo fast dissipating, gone as swiftly as it had come, leaving the night silent and still once more. And yet it left nothing unchanged. The air seemed colder in its wake, the sky darker and more menacing.

Indra had known trepidation and anxiety and unease, but she had never known fear, the true fear that coiled around your entire body like an ice-cold rope and left you paralyzed, unable to move though every fiber within you told you to flee. Now she wanted nothing more than to leap to her feet and run, though she knew there was nowhere—out here in the open—to run to. But she did not move. She stayed, rooted where she sat, listening, unable to do anything but. She turned her head, trying to place where the sound had come from. Near or far? Here or there? It had seemed to come from everywhere and nowhere. All she could be sure of was the terrible *wrongness* of it, a sound that belonged not in this world but in the conjurings of a nightmare.

No, no man could have made that sound, nor any beast of this earth. That sound was monstrous, as was the creature it had come from. An abomination, she was sure of it, though she had never seen nor heard one in the flesh before. Her father had sheltered her from that, had made sure that she was kept safe and far away when he and his men brought one back with them to study. He had intended to protect her from such horrors, things no innocent young girl should ever see, but had only made her more curious, more determined. She wanted to see one up close, to know how it looked and smelled and moved. More than anything, she wanted to watch one die, hear the sound it made when she drove a sword through its beating black heart and killed it.

And yet as that ungodly screech echoed through her mind, she found herself momentarily unsure of her wish to be that close. That deep, primal part of her mind whose sole function was to protect her from danger urgently wanted her away, far away from here. Then the cold rope around her slackened a little; she found that she could move and she rose to her feet, surveying her surroundings, though it was impossible to see anything in the blackness of the night. The urge to flee was almost overwhelming, a frightened companion tugging on her arm and whispering, *Let's just go.* Still, she resisted. She had not come this far only to cower and turn tail at the last. This was what she wanted, had wanted for as long as she could remember. To find such a beast as this, one of the last few that remained. An endangered species, soon to be all the more so because of her. *It is you who are the hunter, and it the prey*, she reminded herself. *It should be running from you.*

Venator flew to her side and alighted on her shoulder, as ever her protector. She stroked his feathers, which were ruffled; he was as unsettled by the sound as she. "It's all right," she said, in a vain effort to comfort them both. Then she sat back down, trying to relax, though her mind raced now more than ever. Yes, she was closer than she had ever been, and tomorrow would bring her closer still. Perhaps tomorrow, or the next day, would bring her face-to-face with this beast. Close enough to kill it, and watch it die.

She let Venator off her shoulder, and he resumed his watch over her as she lay back and closed her eyes. She feared that she would find little sleep tonight. Her chest was pounding. From excitement or from fear, she did not know.

ELEVEN

Stupid. Stupid!

Wulfric berated himself under his breath as he knelt by the river-bank, trying to wash away the ash. He knew he could not remove it all, nor usually would he try, but today he wanted as much of the beast's residue off him as was possible. Naked and shivering in the bitter cold, he plunged his hands into the flowing river, scrubbing at his arms and splashing the frigid water onto his face. *This is all your fault,* he told himself as the ash that stained his skin joined with the river and was carried away by the current. *You could have prevented this.*

Wulfric had long suspected it, but there was no longer any doubt: the beast was growing stronger. It had been for years, night after night, with each new incarnation, until finally, three nights ago, the chain had broken. Lashed as always against a sturdy tree, the beast had strained against its bonds until the iron, stretched beyond its tolerance, snapped. And the monster escaped, with Wulfric trapped within it, paralyzed in a waking nightmare, able only to watch in helpless dismay as the creature wandered the countryside looking for something to slaughter.

He had been lucky that first night; the surrounding woodland was empty, and though the beast wandered ravenously for miles, it had found nothing to feast upon. Wulfric woke a little after dawn on his bed of ashes and dust, cursing his luck but thankful at least that the night had passed without incident. He spent most of that day trying to find his way back to the tree so he could retrieve his chain and cloak—a difficult task since, as was often the case, he had only a vague, hazy recollection of the path the beast had taken in the dark. Long ago, in the nights before Wulfric had hit upon the idea of the chain, the beast had sometimes traveled farther than seemed possible with its lumbering gait, and the night the chain broke had been the same. By the time Wulfric found the tree with the broken chain around it, the sun was close to setting, and he thought himself lucky to have found it at all.

As his accursed fortune would have it, the link that had snapped was close to the center: where once he had one good chain, he now had two, each half the length and neither long enough to be of any use. He would need to find a smith to fix them together again, but the closest town was more than a day's walk. It would mean venturing perilously close to a populous area and spending the night there with no ability to safely bind himself. The beast, he knew from hard experience, would massacre every living soul within such a town if it should chance upon it in the night. Safer, he reckoned, to venture a little farther in another direction, toward a smaller, more sparsely populated village perhaps three days away. And so he gathered up the broken chain and started walking. The first night had passed without bloodshed somehow, and he hoped, if he was careful, he could survive a few more without doing harm.

He was wrong. The second night, though Wulfric had chosen the most remote, secluded spot he could find, the beast came upon a family of deer in a woodland clearing and tore them limb from limb, babes and all. The beast then moved on until it found a field of penned-in sheep. It clambered over the fence and descended upon the defenseless flock, hacking through them in a frenzy, chasing down the ones who tried to flee as they scrabbled desperately at the walls of their pen, until the last of them was silenced.

The next day, the day before this one, Wulfric happened upon a pit along his road through the forest. It was more than ten feet deep—a mass grave, he suspected, that for whatever reason had been dug but never filled. Hoping that while he could climb out of it, the beast would not be able, he lowered himself down at sunset. But the creature would not be confined. For a few minutes only it clawed angrily at the earthen walls of the pit before finding purchase and scrambling up and out. It bolted from the wood and into the open countryside, where before long it found a farmer's field where dozens of cows were sleeping—and worse, the farmer himself, keeping watch over his herd.

The farmer saw the vile black shape emerging from the darkness and into the pale moonlight that fell upon his field. He stood and watched, wide-eyed with horror and disbelief, as it lumbered toward his cattle; then he heard it shriek and the sound jolted him into action. He turned and ran.

And that was his undoing. The beast, focused on the herd, had not noticed the farmer until his sudden movement alerted it. Though the cattle were by far the easier and the fatter prey, the beast somehow instinctively knew what would be the greater evil. It stalked the man across the open field in the dead of night, watching him stumble and fall and get up again and keep running. It could have run the man down far more speedily, but instead toyed with him, allowing him to run and run until he was exhausted and his legs could carry him no farther. When he finally collapsed and rolled onto his back, gazing in terror at the beast as it closed the final yards between them, all Wulfric could do was look, through monstrous eyes, into the face of a man who knew he was about to die. As a soldier, Wulfric had seen many men face death. Not like this. This was a look of terror so raw, so pure, that death came almost as a relief. It was the kind of fear that could emerge only in the face of something as grotesque, as utterly *wrong*, as the thing that now possessed Wulfric. It surely would have been enough to inspire madness had death not immediately followed.

The beast stood over the fallen man and stabbed him in the belly with a long thorn-like claw, slowly, driving it deeper until it ran all the way through him. It watched for a moment as the man screamed and writhed in helpless agony, grasping at the barb that skewered him to the ground. Then it grabbed the farmer by one arm and one leg and simply pulled him apart, splitting him open at the center like an overripe fruit. That outpouring of blood, the blood of an innocent man that would forever be another stain on his conscience, was the last thing Wulfric remembered before waking the next morning. All because he was foolish enough to believe that he could have kept the unbound beast from killing for even a few short nights. *Stupid. Stupid!*

There was one small mercy. The beast had not traveled so far that night and even after backtracking to recover the chain and cloak, Wulfric was at last within daylight's walk of the small village he sought. If he made haste, he could be there by noon—time enough, he hoped, for the local blacksmith to repair and strengthen his broken chain so that he might secure himself before nightfall. Else he would have no option but to retreat back into the wilderness, as far as possible before sundown, and pray.

TWELVE

Indra arrived in the village a short while after noon. It had been some time since she had last passed through any kind of town, and she was grateful both for the touch of civilization after so many days of solitude and for the chance, perhaps, to gain some useful information.

It was not much of a place, a minor, nameless settlement that had sprung up at the crossing of two dirt roads in the hope of attracting passing travelers. Though it was still drizzling, the rain had relented enough for the local farmers and traders to have set out their stalls. There was one selling chickens and other meats, another with fruits and vegetables, and on the other side of the road, a blacksmith and a skinner.

Though it was the height of the day, none appeared to be doing much business. Perhaps because people did not yet trust this break in the weather or, as likely, due to the rampant poverty that still blighted much of the kingdom. There was a sign of that before her very eyes. A filthy beggar in a tattered cloak, his hands and face streaked black with grime, quarreling with the blacksmith over a matter of some pennies. Clearly the most pitiable fellow, yet the smith appeared to have no sympathy for him, and though Indra found so uncharitable an attitude contemptible, she knew it was not uncommon. In times as hard as these, few felt compelled to share the little they had.

She would have helped the poor man herself but for the fact that she had nothing of her own to give. Instead, she convinced herself that it was none of her concern. What interested her was the tavern on the other side of the crossroads. It was the kind of place locals came to trade gossip, and she needed to know if there was any truth to the stories she had heard.

The ramshackle structure of stone and thatch was too small to warrant a colorful name. Others she had passed in her travels had names like the Dancing Ogre, the Nag's Head, the Slaughtered Dane. This one was as anonymous as the hamlet it served. As she approached, Indra pondered what name might best suit it. The Pile of Bricks, perhaps.

Venator hopped from her shoulder and onto the single hitching post outside the tavern as she unbuckled her twin scabbards and slung them over a hook by the open doorway, where she could keep an eye on them. Many alehouses had rules about bringing weapons inside, beer and blades rarely proving a good pairing. And the sight of a woman with a sword—much less two—always seemed to make people uneasy. Her staff was less of a problem; people rarely realized it was a weapon until it was too late. Still, she propped it by the door.

"Enough!" barked the smith. "I will not be haggled with! Either pay what the work is worth or piss off somewhere else." He jerked his thumb over his shoulder for emphasis. "Good luck finding someone who'll do the job as well for less money."

Wulfric sighed. The smith was in a stronger bargaining position than even he realized; the only other man in the vicinity who did this kind of work was days away, and Wulfric would not suffer the beast to remain unbound for even one more night. This was his only option.

He had little money indeed and so had tried to bargain with half of it, but the smith had refused to lower his price. And so Wulfric reached into his cloak and retrieved the two coins that were all he had left. All together, it was still a shade under what the smith was asking, and he could only hope it would be enough.

He held up the two copper pieces. The blacksmith frowned and snatched them from his hand to inspect both sides carefully; counterfeit coinage was not uncommon. When the round ruddy-faced man bit down on both coins to prove their metal, Wulfric stayed silent; if the smith knew where he stashed those coins to keep them hidden from bandits, he would have refused to touch them even with a gloved hand.

The smith looked grudgingly at Wulfric for a moment before dropping the coins into the pocket of his stained leather apron. "Come back in an hour, perhaps two," he grunted, as he reached down for the two lumpen coils of iron that were piled at his feet and began to gather them up onto his anvil.

"It must be ready before sundown," said Wulfric.

The smith picked up a hammer from his tool bench. "At this price, you're lucky I'm doing it at all. Find somewhere else to wait while I work—I've had about as much of that smell as I can take."

Wulfric turned and ambled away. The smith gave him a parting scowl, then stoked his coals and went to work.

It was quiet inside the tavern. There were only a few tables, and all but one were empty. At the one table, two men sat opposite each other, while at the end of the bar sat an older man who by his demeanor appeared to have taken the morning's first cockcrow as the signal to start drinking. A thin bearded man was rinsing out mugs behind the bar and drying them with a cloth that looked dirtier than anything else in the place.

Indra noticed a tension in the air the moment she stepped inside. It was too quiet, the kind of uneasy silence that pervades not when people are simply saying nothing, but when they are making a concerted effort to pretend that there is nothing to be said. The old man polished off his drink as Indra pulled up a seat at the bar, and he waved his empty tankard at the barkeep. "Another one in there, Ymbert," he said, his slurred speech betraying just how far into his cups he was.

"I think you've had enough, Walt, don't you?" said the barkeep. From the table across the room, the two other drinkers were glaring. Indra got the distinct impression that whatever conversation they'd been having before she entered was neither a pleasant one nor one they were keen on continuing in the presence of a stranger. She made a show of minding her own business. Looking straight ahead, at the shelves of bottles and mugs behind the bar, she noticed the five-pointed star that had been carved into the wall behind them. The symbol looked old; it had been painted over more than once and then shelving had been erected over it. Many would have missed it, or mistook it for something else, but Indra had grown up with that symbol and would know it anywhere.

The old man started making a commotion, banging his tankard on the bar, so the barkeep reluctantly took it and refilled it. "That's the last you're getting," he warned, although the old man was already too busy drinking to pay attention. The barkeep shook his head and turned to Indra. "What'll it be?"

"Water," she replied, since she had no money for anything else. The barkeep gave her a look, but filled a mug from a flagon and placed it on the bar for her. He seemed to be waiting for her to drink it, and so she did, with him watching her all the while. She drank it down, not liking the way his eyes rested on her.

"Another?" the barkeep asked. Indra shook her head, so he took the mug away. "Sure you won't have something stronger? How about one on the house? Small payment in return for you prettying up the place on such a drab day. I—Oi! No you don't. Out!"

Indra flinched, startled. She turned in her seat to see the beggar from the blacksmith's stall standing in the doorway, a disheveled figure in his rain-soaked cloak, bearded face barely visible under its hood.

"Just want to sit for a while out of the rain," the man said before clearing his throat with a hollow, rasping cough.

"Less you're buying a drink to sit with, you're not doing it in here," said the barkeep, shooing the man away with his hand. "Go on, bugger off!"

The beggar let out a resigned sigh and turned away, about to head back out into the rain when Indra stopped him. "Wait!" she called out, then turned back to the barkeep. "I'll buy him a drink."

"What?" said the barkeep, genuinely confused.

"You offered me a drink on the house. I accept. Give it to him and let him sit."

The barkeep furrowed his brow. He looked at Indra, then at the beggar, then back to Indra again, as though trying to work out if he had just somehow been tricked. Finally he poured a mug of beer and placed it begrudgingly on the bar. Indra beckoned the beggar over, and for a moment he just stood there, unsure, as if conditioned to be wary of any display of kindness or generosity, before finally, cautiously, shuffling over to the bar.

As he drew up next to Indra, she tried not to react to the foul odor he brought with him. The barkeep was not so kind. "Sit by the door," he told the beggar. "I don't want you stinking the whole place out."

The beggar gave a grateful nod in Indra's direction as he took up the mug of beer, but was careful to avert his eyes and keep his head down. It was the kind of humility known only to the truly wretched. "Much obliged to you," he mumbled. Then he moved away and took a seat at the table closest to the door.

The barkeep, clearly irritated, took a rag and wiped the bar where the beggar's sleeve had briefly touched it. "Charitable soul, ain't ya?" he said to Indra in a derisive tone.

Indra wanted to just leave. She had felt vaguely uncomfortable from the moment she stepped into this place, and that feeling had only been growing steadily worse. Still, the words she had learned as a child rose up within her, unbidden, and she found herself saying them aloud without thinking.

"When you give a feast, do not invite your friends or your rich neighbors, in case they might invite you in return, and you would be repaid," she said, gazing down at her hands on the bar. "Invite the poor, the crippled, the lame and the blind. And you will be blessed, because they cannot repay you."

She looked up. The barkeep was eyeing her quizzically, as though she had started speaking in tongues. Indra felt very self-conscious. She had just given away a part of herself, a part that she usually kept carefully guarded. But something about the plight of the beggar had brought it out of her.

The barkeep's look of bewilderment turned to one of mirth. He looked to the table where the two men were drinking. "Ho! Bax, Roy! Did you hear this one? Give all your food to cripples and the blind because they can't pay you back. That's a new one on me!"

Neither man seemed particularly interested or amused, so the barkeep turned back to Indra. "What idiot taught you that?"

"Jesus Christ," slurred the old man at the end of the bar, and the barkeep's smile slackened. The two men at the table chuckled quietly to one another, deepening his sense that he had just been made to look a fool. He would usually be in no hurry to get a pretty young woman out of his pub, but he was beginning to lose patience with this one.

"That stool's for paying customers," he told Indra, in a tone far less convivial than it had been. "You've had your free drink, now either buy one or get out."

Indra imagined grabbing the man by the back of his head and bouncing his stupid face off the bar so hard it broke his nose. The image played vividly in her mind as she tried to suppress the urge to convert her mental picture into reality.

The barkeep placed both hands on the bar and leaned in a little closer. "'Course, if you've no money, there's always other ways to pay your way around here," he said. The little finger of the man's left hand lightly stroked the little finger of her right. Subtler than some of the crude advances to which she had been subjected, but enough to fill her stomach with ice and momentarily put her urge to hurt this man beyond her control.

The barkeep winced and released a quiet whimper that nobody but Indra was close enough to hear. He looked down at the bar, at where their fingers touched. Indra had entwined her little finger around his and was twisting it in such a way that every bone was brought close to breaking. The barkeep's knees buckled and might have given way but for his fear that his finger would snap under the strain.

Indra showed no sign of loosening her grip. In fact, she tightened it, compelling him to move closer. He was just inches from her face now, close enough for her to smell the onions on his breath as he gasped in pain and to see the rivulet of sweat running down his temple. It would be easy, so easy, to apply another ounce of pressure and leave him with a lasting and painful reminder of his disrespect. She looked into the man's panic-stricken eyes and thought of all the others who had insulted her or tried to take advantage. If she had succumbed to whim on each of those occasions, she would have left a trail of broken limbs from here to Canterbury. That was not the person she wanted to be. More than that, to react in such a way every time someone slighted her felt like a waste of good anger. The time would come when she would need it all.

She let him go. The barkeep stumbled backward, clutching his hand. Nothing was broken, but he would be nursing that finger for a day or two. She glanced over at the old man and the two at the table; their drinking continued undisturbed. The whole incident had happened so quickly and quietly that it appeared to have passed unnoticed. She did not think to look to the beggar by the door, who had been the one person to have seen it all and had quietly taken note.

"Thank you for the drink," she said, still trying to temper the wave of anger that had almost overwhelmed her and was only now beginning to subside. She noted furtive glances from the drinkers at the table as she turned and made for the door. They had made her feel unwelcome from the moment she had entered, and now they appeared glad to see her go.

She gave a nod to the beggar sitting at the table by the doorway as she passed, but got none in return. She did not think him impolite; men as lowly as he were invisible to most who passed, and so those people often became invisible in return.

When she stepped outside and took her swords from where they were hanging, she was relieved to have avoided undoing her small act of kindness with one of violence. But her blood was still up, the sound of her heartbeat thumping in her ears. She wanted to be away. Yet as she buckled her scabbards across her chest—

"All's I'm telling you's what I heard from Hewald, who saw it with his own eyes." It was the old man, in the overly loud manner of a drunk—loud enough for his voice to carry to the doorway and outside. "And Hewald's no liar! Torn in half, the poor bugger was!"

"Will you shut up about it?" said the fatter of the two men drinking at the table. "It's all you've gone on about all bloody morning!"

"It's an old wives' tale anyhow," said the other. "You do no one any favors spreading it around. Trade around here's bad enough as it is, and you want to saddle us with ghost stories besides."

The old man finished the last of his beer and slammed the tankard down sloppily. "You're none old enough to remember!" he exclaimed, with a wildly gesticulating arm that almost unbalanced him from his stool. "I am! Decade past, entire kingdom was rife with monsters! Roaming hither and yon, savaging all they came across, man, woman and child."

"Perhaps once, years ago," the fat man conceded. "But the Order did away with them. Everybody knows this."

"Ha!" The old man snorted, punctuating it neatly with a deep, resonant belch. "I've seen what those things left behind with my own eyes. Man and beast alike, ripped limb from limb. The same as we've seen these past two nights. I saw what happened over at Treacher's farm, saw it for myself!"

"We all saw it," said the fat man. "I still say it was a wolf what did for them sheep."

"Aye, wolves've been acting up lately," offered the other one. "Howling more'n usual and coming down out of the hills at night."

"A wolf's clever enough to know what you two don't," slurred the old man. "They know when one of them things is hereabouts—they can sense it! As for Treacher's flock, more'n a hundred head, butchered like that in their pen? No wolf, not a pack of 'em, could've done all that. Nor what was done to old Hagarth last night! Hewald saw what was left of him early this morn, told me all about it. Torn in two at the middle, like he'd been tied between two plow horses!"

"For crying out loud, Walt." The fat man grimaced as he put down his ale mug. "Enough."

"Ach, you'd rather stick your head in the ground until the truth of it's right in front of you. By then it'll be too late! I know what this is about, and it's not no beast that belongs on God's good earth. It's a demon, an—"

"Don't you say it, Walt!" The barkeep pointed a finger at him. "Not under my roof—it's bad luck!"

"An abomination," came a voice from the doorway, and all heads turned. There stood Indra, her twin swords securely belted onto her back. The men exchanged looks, uncomfortable.

"Little lady, you'd best be on your way," said the fat one. "And forget whatever you heard. Folklore's all it is."

Little lady. For a brief moment Indra imagined her hand at the fat man's throat. The image of it would have to be consolation enough. She had need of these men and what information they might possess. She stepped forward, trying to project an air of confidence and authority—not the easiest of tasks for a woman easily ten years the junior of the youngest man here. She reached into her tunic and produced a silver and gold medallion, holding it out for all to see. It bore an emblem in the shape of a five-pointed star similar to the one carved into the wall behind the bar, embossed with a relief of two swords crossed against the face of the sun, three Latin words engraved below: *Contra Omnia Monstra.*

The four men stared at her for a moment, nonplussed, before finally the barkeep spoke. "You're one of the Order?" he asked in a hushed tone.

"Yes," replied Indra, and that was a lie, or at least half of one. Technically she was not yet a paladin, a knight of the Order, but she would be soon enough. The medallion was her father's; she had taken it without his permission—just borrowing it for a while, she told herself—on the day she left home. She had hoped he would not notice it missing until it was too late to pursue her, and so it had proven. Or perhaps he had in fact finally chosen not to go after her; perhaps he had recognized that her task was already greater than that undertaken by any initiate before and that she would need every advantage.

It had been years since the time such a medallion was known throughout the land, but it still commanded respect. The four men were looking at Indra differently now, albeit with a degree of skepticism.

"But . . . you're a girl," said the fat man, mouthing the word *girl* as though it was as good a way of saying invalid or incompetent. Indra flexed her right hand and heard her knuckles crack. This was proving to be a robust exercise in managing her temper. About to say more, the fat man caught the eye of the barkeep, behind Indra, and decided to hold his tongue.

"How old are you?" asked the drunk at the bar, who did not care about causing offense. It was one of the perils of being drunk and one of the privileges of being old.

"I am old enough," she said without hesitation, and that, too, was a lie—though not by much, she told herself. Though she strove to be a truthful person, her ten months in the wide world had taught her that it was often necessary to embellish or bend the truth to convince people that she should be taken seriously. Through time and repetition, those lies had started to become truths in her own mind. They were a bulwark against her own fears and doubts and from the voice that sometimes visited on restless nights. A voice that sounded much like her father's, whispering, *You should not have come. You were driven to this not by courage or duty but by anger. You may be trained, but you are not ready. You are a foolish girl on a reckless quest, and you are going to die.*

She motioned to an empty chair at the table where the two men sat. They glanced at each other and shrugged, as good an invitation as she was going to get. She pulled out the chair and sat, noticing as she did so that the beggar who had been seated by the door was now gone.

"Thought the Order was all done with years ago," said the fat one.

"Few of us remain," said Indra. "As few abominations remain. But our work is not finished until the last of them has been slain. If one is here, I mean to hunt it and kill it."

"'I'?" said the old man. "Where are the rest of you? I remember when the knights of the Order used to come through here, years ago. Always mob-handed, a dozen or more at a time."

"As I said," replied Indra, "few of us remain. And what I do, I do best alone."

More glances were exchanged. "You've done this before, then?" asked the fat man. "Hunted these things, and killed them?"

"Yes," said Indra, and that was the biggest lie of all. The others had been easier to tell; this one did not come out as cleanly, and she worried that these men would see the brief crack in her facade. But the medallion and her practiced air of confidence had done their work, and now the men leaned in, becoming believers themselves, as though drawn into a compelling campfire story. Still, Indra sensed that some disquiet remained.

"It is not bad luck to speak of these things," she said. "It is refusing to speak of them, failing to heed these warnings, that leads to misfortune. I need you to tell me everything. Start with exactly what you have seen, and where."

THIRTEEN

For more than an hour they spoke and she listened. She learned every detail of the slaughter of the sheep in a farmer's field two nights ago and of the cattleman who had been so brutally killed on his own land just last night. She produced paper and had one of the men draw a map, as best he could, of the surrounding area and the two farms where the incidents had occurred. It suggested that whatever was committing these atrocities was moving in this direction. All three men ordered another drink when Indra made that observation. The barkeep poured one for himself.

She also learned of other things: strange behavior among the local dogs and other animals for the past several days, cowering and yelping and barking at things unseen; a god-awful screeching late at night that echoed across the countryside, waking children in their beds; and mutilated trees, their trunks scratched and scored deeply all around in ways that suggested someone or something had attacked them in a violent frenzy.

From her training, Indra knew that the first two omens were common signs of an abomination, and she had heard the screeching herself just last night. But the third sign puzzled her. She knew not why an abomination might attack or damage a tree and had certainly never heard of any such cases. Perhaps an animal flee-ing from the beast had, in a panic, tried to claw its way upward to safety? Even then, odd that it should happen in more than one place.

Still, though there were small anomalies, things that did not yet make sense to her, she knew that she was closer now to an abomination than she ever had been. For it was an abomination that had done these terrible things, she was sure of that, and its path was bringing it closer still. All that remained was for her to stalk it to close quarters and kill it.

From the demeanor of the men around her, it was clear they were in a greater state of unease than when she had found them— shaken by her warning that an abomination was near and not in the least reassured by her promise to vanquish it. That was all right, she told herself; they were not the first to underestimate her, and they would not be the last. That honor would fall to this beast, when she found it.

You are not ready.

She felt her heart beginning to thump harder and knew what that meant. Hurriedly, and with hands that had begun to tremble, she folded away the map that had been drawn for her and stood, thanking the men for their cooperation.

You didn't expect to be this afraid, did you? Now that it's close. Now that it's real.

It was becoming more difficult to take a breath, each one shallower than the last. She quickened her step as she made her way to the door. Yet though her mind was reeling, as she passed the table where the beggar had sat, she noticed that the ale in his mug was still full to the brim, untouched.

Return home, while you still can. There will be no shame in it. Better to admit to your father that he was right than make him grieve for you after this beast tears you limb from limb.

Dizzy now, she found her way to the doorway, and stumbled over the threshold into the open air. She steadied herself against the wall and closed her eyes, trying to calm herself and focus on her breathing. These sudden onsets of anxiety, the tightness in her chest and shortness of breath that made her feel as though she were drowning on dry land, came without warning, and at the most inopportune moments. But she had learned to better withstand them by turning her mind inward and telling herself, over and over, that the episode would soon pass. They always did, though some lasted longer than others.

The panic now began to subside. Her mind was quiet once more, her heart no longer a great drum pounding in her chest. She regained her breath and took a long, deep gulp of cold air, grateful for it and for the spattering of raindrops on her face. The raw touch of nature always calmed her, brought her back to earth.

Then she steeled herself once more. She would not allow her own fears or doubts to defeat her. Perhaps this beast she sought would. She was not so arrogant or naive as to deny that possibility. But first she would stand and face it with weapons drawn and fire in her eyes. And it would know why she had come.

She reached for her staff, which she had left propped by the door, and turned to head out, thinking of how best to prepare for the night's hunt, when she recognized the hooded beggar across the road, once again at the blacksmith's stall. He appeared to be in something of a hurry as he hoisted a great length of heavy iron chain up onto his shoulder, preparing, it seemed, to carry it away.

She stood and watched him a moment, her curiosity pulled in several directions at once. She had encountered many vagrants and vagabonds in her time, but none that had ever appeared to be in any kind of rush, nor any that would leave behind a free mug of ale. Why had he left so abruptly, without so much as touching his drink?

And that was to say nothing of the chain, which the man was inspecting carefully while wrapping the last of it around his waist and over his shoulder. How he could even carry such a load was a mystery all its own. While there was surely an explanation, for now the queer picture he posed was like a puzzle with a missing piece.

The kind of thing that had infuriated her as a child, and infuriated her still.

She was contemplating whether her small act of generosity in the tavern had earned her the right to ask the man a question or two, and was halfway to yes, when she saw three men, new arrivals, who seemed to recognize the hooded man and were talking animatedly among themselves as they approached him. Perhaps their exchange would satisfy her curiosity, which otherwise would gnaw at her for the rest of the day

——•◦⟫⟨◉⟩⟪◦•——

The blacksmith seemed to take offense at Wulfric's so-careful inspection. "That chain's stronger now than it ever was," he said, stabbing his finger at the point where he had joined the two pieces into one. "That's better work than you paid for, I'll tell you that."

Wulfric nodded; it was good work. Whether it was good enough, the night would soon tell, but not before he was far away from here. Being anywhere near a town was danger at the best of times, but having someone from the Order arrive and stir up suspicion was enough to make him hurry the smith along and leave all the quicker. There were still a few hours until sunset, and he would need that time to—

"Told you it was him!"

Wulfric looked over his shoulder and saw the three men standing in the crossroads. The bandits he had encountered along that slurry of a back road a few days ago, the ones who had beaten and tried to rob him. They were eyeing him aggressively now, the tall one most of all.

"Remember us?"

A little more than an hour ago, Wulfric had been gifted with a beer, his first in years—which he had been forced to leave unsupped. Now this. How quickly his luck seemed to turn these days, and only ever in one direction.

No doubt these three felt that theirs had changed for the better; back on that remote road, the chain had been too much for
them to carry, but here in town they could easily take it from him
and sell it, perhaps to the very smith who had just repaired it.
Wulfric despised the thought of breaking his vow. But he could
not, would not, allow the chain to be taken from him. Many more
people would die if he did.

"Take off the chain," said the tall man. He looked Wulfric hard
in the eye, trying to intimidate, but on stepping closer it was he
who had cause to be unnerved. Something was not right.

Not much of the beggar's face was visible behind the hood and
the tangled beard, and the streaks of black grime all over, but there
was enough to see that he showed no sign of injury. Just a few days
ago, he and his two cohorts had beaten this beggar half to death,
leaving him gasping in the mud with bruises, cuts, and welts that
would have, should have swollen and purpled over the days that
followed. And yet this beggar had not a mark on him. Were it not
for the chain, the tall man would not have believed it the same
wanderer. There was no explanation for how his wounds could
have healed so quickly.

More than that, there was something about this man, something in his eyes. Something that said, *Just walk away.*

But the tall man did not walk away. His companions, who
looked to him as their leader in large part because of the reputa-
tion he had cultivated as a hard man, were watching. What was he
to do? Back down from a confrontation he himself had initiated,
with a beggar so meek he had made no effort to even defend himself at their last encounter? No, despite his unease, he had to see
this through.

He shoved Wulfric hard in the shoulder, enough to push
him back a step, but Wulfric did not react. Frustrated, the tall
man hit Wulfric hard across the head with the flat of his hand.
Again, Wulfric seemed to do nothing in response; the sleeves of

his cloak were long and nobody saw him ball his hands into tight white-knuckled fists.

"Leave him alone."

The voice came from behind the tall man. He and the other two turned, and there stood Indra, a few yards away, glowering at them sternly.

"Fuck off," said the tall man, with a dismissive wave of his hand. But Indra took a step closer, seemingly undeterred.

"I said fuck off! Unless you want some of this." He brandished the cosh he carried, surprised to see this also fail to discourage her.

"This man has done nothing to you," Indra said. "Let him on his way, or answer to me."

That brought about a chuckle from the tall man, which spread rapidly to the other two, then grew into full-throated laughter. All the while Indra stood firm, steely eyed, until the three men realized that she was quite serious.

Their laughter waned, and the tall man moved toward her. It was for him as the leader to handle this; as well, he wanted an excuse to distance himself from the beggar, whose oddly quiet presence continued to trouble him. He looked Indra up and down with a crooked smile, and gestured to the pair of swords across her back. "Who are you carrying those for, little girl?"

Indra felt her jaw tighten. "They are my own," she said in as firm a tone as she was able, but it did nothing to dislodge the man's grin.

"It's good that there are two," he said. "So I can put one in each of the places the sun don't shine." That was all the cue his two companions needed to come forward and take up positions around Indra. The nearby merchants looked on, apparently happy for some free entertainment to break up the monotony of the day. The barkeep was at the tavern door, motioning keenly for his customers to come outside and watch.

Indra wanted to fight. Because she could use the practice, she told herself, but in truth she knew she was compelled by something worse than that. It was anger that had led her to confront these men, the same anger that had often drawn her into needless fights like this one. She reminded herself that she always regretted them afterward and that she owed it to herself—and to these men, however vile they might be—to try to resolve this without violence.

"I would prefer not to fight," she said, which was not easy, as her every fiber was screaming the opposite. "Let this man go, and—" She looked back to the blacksmith's stall and saw that the beggar was gone. It was his second abrupt disappearance in as many hours.

The three robbers saw the same and again laughed. "There's the thanks you get from a cadger like that," said the tall one. "He must be laughing all the way down the road, that some stranger'd volunteer to take his beating for him." All three men moved in a little closer, tightening the circle around Indra. They were emboldened now, mistaking her reluctance for fear.

So be it, thought Indra, trying to pretend that she was not secretly pleased. She planted her staff in the sodden earth so it stood upright freely and squared herself against the tall man.

He looked at her, puzzled. "Draw your swords, then."

"I hope I shan't have to," she said, and this was true. She would only punish herself more later if she put a lasting wound on any of these men unnecessarily. If this was to be practice, then let it be an exercise in the use of minimal force, an area in which she sorely needed improvement. *This might be useful after all.*

The tall man rapped his gnarled wooden club against his thigh excitedly, then charged at Indra, drawing his arm back to strike. As he came within range, he swung at her hard. Indra shifted her weight to one side, so imperceptibly that she barely seemed to have moved at all. But it was enough that the tall man found himself connecting with nothing but air. The unchecked force of his own wild swing threw him off-balance and sent him barreling past her until he pitched forward and landed face-first in the mud.

Now the second man attacked. This one had a pair of black-jacks, one attached to each wrist by a strap. He came at Indra fast, with a flurry of blows, but she deflected them all effortlessly, slowly moving backward as she glanced each one aside and allowing him to keep advancing while she waited patiently for her opening. Then Indra quickened her backward step, opening the distance between them just enough to invite the man to overextend himself. As he lunged at her, she dodged to one side and thrust the flat of her hand upward into his nose. He staggered dizzily for two steps before falling on his backside into a shallow puddle, nose bent badly out of shape and streaming blood. It was broken, Indra knew, but hardly for the first time, and if she had struck him any harder she would have killed him, so she had reason to be pleased with herself.

By now the tall man was back on his feet and angrily wiping away the mud on his face. He pulled a dagger from his waistband and came at her again, now joined by the third man, who was built like an ox and looked like he rarely needed to throw a second punch. But he was slow, and the tall man was angry, which made him sloppy. Indra easily ducked under the big man's lumbering first punch, then grabbed the tall one by the wrist as he thrust the dagger at her and twisted his arm, forcing him to drop the knife and double over. Perfect position for a sharp knee to the face. His head jerked backward and he went down a second time into the mud, this time flat on his back.

The big ox was still coming, hurling clumsy left and right hooks at her. Indra ducked and dodged, letting him wear himself out as she calculated her timing, then kicked him so hard between the legs that even the blacksmith watching from across the road felt it. The ox, with a wheezing gasp, slumped to his knees, and Indra pushed her boot into his chest, toppling him over so that now all three of her assailants languished, groaning in the mud.

Indra hoped that might be the end of it and sighed when the tall one got up again, barking at the others to do likewise. He was seething now. All of them were. They rose unsteadily to their feet, shaking off their injuries and rounding on her once again, faces red with rage. Then, all together, they charged.

Now she plucked her staff from where it was planted in the ground. She had never fought three opponents at once, and despite all the tales of heroic knights gracefully defeating multiple assailants in a melee, Indra suspected that the reality was a far messier and more difficult affair—that any three men, even three as unskilled as these, could present a challenge when taken all at once.

And so it proved. Armed with the staff, she whirled and darted, parrying one man's strike, then another's, then another's in rapid succession, but still they came at her. And hard though it was to keep them at bay, it was harder still for Indra to absorb so much of their anger and still contain her own. Finally, her fragile temper could take no more and something inside her snapped.

The fight came to an end in such a rush that the rapt audience of merchants and taverngoers would not later be able to agree on the exact sequence of events. But it was something like this: Indra let out a furious battle cry and surged forward in a fearsome whirlwind, first felling the big man with a blow to his skull so hard that he went down like a marionette whose strings had been cut; then the second man, the one with the blackjacks, who took an open-handed shot to the throat followed by a low sweep of Indra's staff that knocked him clean off his feet and sent him crashing onto his back, rolling and gasping for breath. The tall man actually managed to grab a fistful of Indra's hair and momentarily pull her off-balance before she brought her staff down on his arm with such force that all present heard the bone break. He instantly let go and collapsed in a heap, wailing and clutching his arm.

All three men were felled so quickly that Indra herself barely knew what had happened until it was done. She blinked and took a step back. She was breathing hard, less from the exertion than from the rage that had so suddenly and violently taken hold of her. She tried to take measured breaths, to calm down. But the sight of what she had done only made her more angry—at herself. She had shattered the tall man's forearm, she knew—not only because she had heard the sickening crunch when it happened but because it was now horribly and unnaturally crooked, with a jagged and bloody shard of bone protruding through his skin. It was more than any physician could put right; he would probably never use that arm again.

She was supposed to exercise restraint, self-control. She was supposed to avoid leaving any of them with a lasting injury. She was supposed to be better than this. As the three beaten men lay on the ground before her, she paced up and down, muttering angrily under her breath. Finally, she expelled a bellowing roar, spun around, and violently set about the first thing she saw, which was a large sack of carrots on the vegetable merchant's stall. Wildly, she pounded it with her bare fists, over and over, as she cried out, lost in her own fury, until the sack split apart and carrots spilled out into the mud. Only then did her rage at last subside, and she looked up to see the merchant staring at her, wide-eyed.

She took a deep breath and composed herself, trying to hide her embarrassment. "I'm sorry about that," she said, brushing aside a lock of hair that had fallen across her face. "I'm afraid I can't pay for the damage, but if—"

"That's quite all right, miss!" said the merchant, holding his palms out in front of him as he backed away a step. "Don't you worry about it at all."

Indra turned and saw the blacksmith and the skinner on the other side of the road gawping at her, openmouthed. Outside the tavern, the barkeep and his customers were doing the same. And all Indra felt now was a deep sense of shame, that her own stupid—what was it? pride? arrogance?—had led her to this ignoble public display of her inability to control her own anger. True strength lay not in conquering one's enemies but in conquering the foe that lay within. She had tried to prove that to herself, and had found herself wanting.

She placed two fingers to her lips and gave a short, shrill whistle. Venator flew from his perch outside the tavern onto her shoulder. Keeping her head low so as not to meet anyone's eye, she turned and marched away down the road. As she left the crossroads behind her, still quietly berating herself, she tried to find consolation in the knowledge that it could have been worse. If those men had been skilled fighters, she might have had to use her swords, and then there would have been real blood on her hands.

FOURTEEN

Indra walked faster than usual along the road, keen to get away from the crossroads behind her and all that had happened there. The short time she had spent in that little hamlet might have brought her closer to her prey, but it had also exposed and made raw all her frailties and left her more uncertain of herself than ever.

Such anxiety made little sense to her. In the face of actual danger, she never quavered. She had confronted and done battle with three armed brutes without fear or apprehension—in part, she knew, because her anger left little room for anything else. She hated her anger, but at least she understood it. Anger was simple and pure, a base element, like fire. She knew exactly where hers came from and how she planned to do away with it. There was no mystery. But these episodes of suffocating anxiety that crept up on her without warning or reason . . . they defied explanation and thus troubled her deeply.

What if it were a form of madness? On her travels, she had seen men in towns and by roadsides who rocked and gibbered and stared at things that were not there, their minds turned to porridge. Nothing could be done for them. A sickness of the mind was not like that of the body, which could often be diagnosed and remedied. A madman never got better, and no doctor knew of a cure for such a malady or even its cause. Was this how it started? Was that the fate that awaited her? Indra could think of nothing more terrifying than her own mind failing her. Yet the crippling spells of dizziness and trembling, the inability to breathe, as though being smothered, the vivid, uncontrollable thoughts and fantasies of her own impending death—

She halted, suddenly alert. Something had stirred in the woods ahead. For a moment she was unsure if the rustling sound had been a trick of her imagination, but Venator had heard it, too; his feathers bristled, his talons gripped Indra's shoulder more tightly than before. She stood a moment, listening. Nothing, just the soft whispering of the wind in the trees.

As the silence of the forest settled in around her, Indra turned to look back along the road—and there was no road. So consumed had she been by her own thoughts that somewhere along the way she had wandered from it without noticing. Now she had no idea where she was or in what direction she had been walking. She was lost.

There it was again; there was no mistaking it now. Something beyond the trees, not far from her, moving about in the under-growth. Too large to be anything but perhaps a deer. No, larger than that. What, then?

She stiffened. *The abomination.*

Could it be? In her self-absorption, she had almost forgotten why she was out here. She had been wandering through an area where an abomination might well be at large with her head down, brooding, oblivious to her surroundings, to anything that might be stalking her. Her failings back at the crossroads were bad enough; this one could have got her killed.

It might still.

But as she gathered her thoughts, it occurred to her that this was likely not an abomination. It was still hours before nightfall, and from her study of the Bestiary, she knew that most were noc-turnal. They hunted by night, their oily black hides near invisi-ble in the dark, and sought shelter in caves and burrows during the day to sleep. In her fantasies, played out a thousand times and

more, Indra imagined sneaking up on one as it slept and waking it
with a thrust of her sword—just long enough for it to see her face
in the broad daylight, for her to look into its eyes as she sank her
blade deeper, until all the life bled out.

No, whatever this was could not be an abomination. *Mostly
nocturnal.*

Mostly.

She looked again in the direction from which the sounds
had come. She saw nothing, no movement, but the trees were so
dense they might be hiding anything. Reaching over her shoulder,
she drew one of her swords and began to move carefully, quietly,
forward.

Wulfric had almost finished gathering wood for a fire. He had
decided to stop for the night, having traveled far and deep enough
into the woods that if the beast should break free when it woke
tonight, it was unlikely to find its way back to the crossroads and
the village there. But in truth, he knew there could be no guarantee
of that; as ever, all he could do was trust that the chain would hold.
He hoped the blacksmith's work was as good as his promise, and
that it had broken previously only because of a single flawed link,
weaker than the rest. The alternative did not bear thinking about.

He had debated venturing farther, as there was still time before
sunset, but he was tired. The sight of that star-shaped medallion
back in the village had caused him to take flight without even
thinking, a reflexive action, and had spurred him this far before it
had finally dawned on him: that girl could not possibly have been
of the Order. The Order was a shadow of what it had once been,
and even in years past, when its knights were hundreds strong,
they never traveled alone but in groups. And a female paladin?
A mere slip of a girl given a King's commission to hunt and kill
abominations? The thought was preposterous.

In fact, it seemed so glaringly obvious to Wulfric now that he chided himself for having needlessly left behind a perfectly good beer. True, the seal the girl carried had looked real enough, but it would not have been the first to be stolen or counterfeited. A decade ago, at the height of the scourge, the Order's paladins had been famed and given a hero's welcome in towns and villages up and down the land, their money no good anywhere. Even now, with their work all but done and little left to fear, that seal of silver and gold still meant something. It was a rare and valuable commodity on the black market.

Looking back, the biggest clue of all was that the girl had gone out of her way to help him. Paladins of the Order were not typical knights and did not engage in chivalry. Their first and only duty was to rid the land of abominations. They believed it a divine calling, to do battle with hell's own spawn, and thought all else beneath them. A paladin would never bother himself with such a mundane act as lending aid to a stranger—a beggar, what's more.

That episode still nagged at him. The gift of a drink was uncommon enough, and more charity than Wulfric had been accustomed to in many years, but to come to his defense against three armed men? He had never seen the like of it. It was not the question of why she would do such a commendable and foolhardy thing that ate at him, though it was riddle enough, but the fact that he had slipped away and allowed her to face those men alone. She had gone out on a limb for him, and he had rewarded her kindness and courage by abandoning her to her fate, to be beaten, and worse. What kind of a man had he become?

He grunted to himself and pushed the thought from his mind as he crouched by the small pyre he had made and began striking a rock against a shard of flint to light it. It was not for him to feel guilt over this. He had not asked for her help—she had made her own lot. He reminded himself that he already spent every waking moment of every day trying to protect others, doing all he could to keep them safe from the thing he became each night.

He looked again at the chain, gathered at the base of the tree, to which he would lash himself later. Again he found himself hoping that it was enough. That the beast had not grown stronger still. The night would tell, soon enough.

Indra was close enough now to see it: an indistinct form, difficult to make out through the dense thicket of bushes and trees. It was the motion of the thing that she had spotted, and she halted to watch it rooting about in the small clearing ahead. Dark and misshapen, at least as large as a man; she heard it grunt as it hunched over, lower to the ground.

She moved closer, her breath held in her chest, careful of every footfall. Now just a single line of trees separated them. She pressed her back against a tree and sidled slowly around it, then peeked into the clearing to see the dark shape standing only a few yards ahead of her, suddenly much closer than it had been.

Indra bolted backward in alarm, tripping over a tangle of roots. Venator squawked, flapping his wings to keep his balance on her shoulder as she stumbled and almost fell, but she thrust out her free hand and grabbed a branch to steady herself. Then she saw that the thing before her was no beast but a man in a rumpled, filthy hooded cloak that had disguised the shape beneath. It was the beggar she had tried to help back at the crossroads.

He stood unmoving, silently regarding her. She composed herself and stepped forward into the clearing, her sword still drawn but held at her side, ready if needed.

"What are you doing here, child?" asked the dark face behind the hood. The tone of his voice suggested not aggression, but caution. He was not afraid of her, but he was guarded, wary.

Indra's first instinct was to bristle angrily at being called a child, but now was not the time. "Looking for a place to make camp for the night," she said, glancing behind him at the flicker of the fire that was just beginning to take hold. "The same as you."

The beggar looked at her for a moment. "Look somewhere else," he said gruffly, then turned away and moved back toward his fire. Indra watched him, her curiosity about this strange man returning. She could see the heavy iron chain he had been carrying back at the crossroads resting in a pile at the base of an oak tree next to his campfire. Out here in the middle of nowhere. More and more of a puzzle. She had to know.

Wulfric sat down next to the fire. He looked up and saw, to his consternation, that the girl was still there, looking at him curiously.

"I said, look somewhere else!" he growled, his tone harsher than before. "This place is claimed." He waved his hand around in a wide circle to make sure she knew that he was referring not just to this little clearing but to the whole area around it. For her own protection, she was not welcome anywhere near here. Near him.

"I will," said Indra as she took a step closer, resheathing her sword over her back to show that she was no threat. "But I wonder if you might share your fire for a while first. It's been a long day."

Wulfric sighed irritably. "No. Go on now, on your way! I will not tell you again!" He rubbed his hands together and warmed them by the fire, staring into the flames as though she were already gone.

Indra could see that there would be no bargaining with the man. For a brief moment, she was annoyed by his ingratitude after the charity she had shown him earlier in the day. But true charity expected no recompense. To ask for something in return would only undermine the goodness of the original act. And so she quietly nodded and said, "I'm sorry to have troubled you."

Wulfric watched her walk away, back into the forest, and something tugged at him. The girl had done him a kindness, not once but twice, back at the crossroads. He had already wrestled with the guilt of leaving her in the lurch back there; here, perhaps, was his opportunity to show his gratitude, and he was turning it away? He looked up at the sky through the treetops. The sun was still some way from setting. And though the instinct that had guided him to protect others for fifteen years was telling him to let the girl go, he stood and called out after her.

"Wait."

She stopped, looked back. Wulfric motioned toward the fire. "For a short while only," he said. "You must be on your way before sundown."

She nodded and made her way back across the clearing toward him. The hawk she carried took flight from her shoulder and found a nearby branch overlooking the campfire as the girl laid down her staff. She waited for Wulfric to reseat himself, then sat before the fire across from him.

"Thank you," she said.

Wulfric said nothing in reply, just gazed into the fire.

"I am Indra," she offered cheerfully, clearly trying to appear friendly and open.

Wulfric offered only a quiet grunt of acknowledgment as he poked at the fire with a stub of branch. He had no intention of reciprocating.

There was an awkward pause before she tried again. "I wonder if—"

"No talking." Wulfric cut her off with a sharp look. "That is my condition. Sit and warm yourself if you wish, but remain quiet. If you cannot do that, go."

His tone made it clear there was to be no further discussion. Indra simply nodded and warmed her hands, sharing the simple comfort of the fire.

FIFTEEN

"Why did you help me?"

Indra looked up. Only now did she realize that the nameless beggar had been looking at her. She had become so entranced by the flickering and dancing of the flames that she had no idea how much time had passed since she sat down. All she knew was that she had felt a greater calm in that time than she could ever remember, a deep sense of serenity and well-being that was all but unknown in her young life. She wished it could have lasted forever.

"I thought we were not—"

"It is my condition, so my condition to break," said Wulfric. He paused for a moment, then, "You do not have to answer. Forget that I asked." He looked back into the fire. He appeared to Indra to regret having spoken. What could happen in a life, she wondered, to turn someone into this—a man seemingly afraid of even the most basic human contact?

"Why does any soul help another?" she replied. Was it wise to answer his question with a question? This conversation was new and fragile, and the man across from her was clearly unsure about having started it. If she appeared too clever or coy, he might retreat to silence, and there was much she still wanted to know.

"I'm a Christian," Indra said. "At least I try to be. It's my duty to help those in need." She took a branch from the ground and poked at the fire. "Besides, I don't like bullies."

He nodded, seeming satisfied by her answer but also perhaps a little surprised. "Not much Christian charity around nowadays," he observed, grim.

Indra nodded in agreement. These were dire times, and most folk had far too many troubles of their own to worry about others. But then, wasn't that when simple acts of selflessness were needed most? As she saw it, it was easy to give of oneself when it cost little or nothing to do so. It was in times like these, when generosity meant sacrifice, that one's true character was tested and revealed.

"What happened with the men at the crossroads?" Wulfric asked. The question had been eating at him since she arrived in the clearing. He had assumed they would leave her beaten or dead where she had challenged them. To see her here, unharmed, meant either she had somehow talked three belligerent cutthroats out of a fight that she herself had picked with them, or . . . No, there was no other explanation he could think of.

"I didn't want to fight them," Indra said, looking away, into the fire again. "Alas, I could not persuade them otherwise."

Wulfric looked hard at her, trying to divine something beyond her words. All he could sense from her was a strong unwillingness to speak of it further. This puzzled him. He had half expected her to tell some tale of how she had valorously defeated the three of them in mortal combat. In his time, he had seen plenty of that—braggarts and liars who spun elaborate yarns of daring and heroic feats of battle, woven entirely from their imaginations. With no one to refute her account, this girl could easily have done the same, perhaps to earn his gratitude and a longer stay by his fire.

Instead, she had responded in the manner of men who had actually done the deeds about which others falsely boasted. She had answered without answering, speaking only indirectly and with a tone of reluctance and humility that suggested she knew what violence really was—and that it was nothing to sing about, even in victory.

Was it possible? That this girl, little more than a hundred pounds soaking wet from the look of her, had fought those three thugs and bested them? Wulfric could not in any way imagine it, but everything suggested it was so. He had another question for her that might reveal more.

"How did you come by the seal?"

She looked up from the fire. "Excuse me?"

"The seal of the Order," Wulfric said. "I saw you with it at the tavern."

"I know what seal," said Indra, her tone now as quizzical as Wulfric's. "I don't understand what you mean, how did I come by it?"

"That seal is carried only by paladins, by knights of the Order."

"That is true," she replied flatly as she looked across the fire at him.

Wulfric regarded her a moment longer, wondering how far she was willing to go. *Fine, let us see,* he thought. "Or by those who have acquired one dishonestly."

Indra's eyes widened. "Is that what you are accusing me of?"

"Paladins never travel alone," Wulfric replied matter-of-factly. "They are none of them women, and certainly none of them children."

It was all Indra could do not to leap to her feet and kick burning embers at the man. Instead, she set her jaw and said, through clenched teeth, "I am not a child. I am an initiate."

"An initiate?" said Wulfric, bemused. "How old are you?"

"Eighteen," Indra snapped. It was the minimum age at which the Order would accept a new initiate, a paladin-in-training.

Wulfric scrutinized her, dubious. She looked to him younger than that, though what she seemed to lack in physical years she more than made up for with maturity and confidence, so who was he to say? But there was more that did not ring true.

"So, you are out here on your Trial?" he asked.

"Yes," said Indra. Any initiate, to be accepted into the Order as a full paladin, must complete the Trial: one full year spent in the open country, learning to survive in the wild, to live off the land, and most importantly, to hunt their prey. Before the year's end, the initiate was to return to the Order with the head of an abomination they had slain. Or not at all.

"Initiates are only accepted at eighteen, and must complete two years of training before they are ready for the Trial," said Wulfric. "And they never face it alone; always with a group of other initiates and an experienced officer to supervise them."

Silence. Only the crackling of the flames between them. Indra groped for a response, trying to project outward confidence while wondering how this man could possibly know so much about the Order's rules and practices. Enough to have led her into this trap. She could not know, of course, that Wulfric had played a part in creating those very rules, he and Edgard together, a decade and a half ago, while they were still hunting Aethelred and planning for what would come after. What seemed now to Wulfric like another life—someone else's life.

"My father is a senior officer of the Order," said Indra. "He recognized my potential at a young age and allowed me to be admitted early." The words spilled out in such a seamless blend of fact and fiction that even she had difficulty separating them.

"The Order is a far smaller force than it once was," she added, "and no longer accepts new initiates. Last year I was the only one, and so I was permitted to take my Trial alone." Though her story was laced with what were half-truths at best, it was true enough, and it irked her that this man did not seem to accept it as such. *Because I'm not a man. Because he thinks I'm some stupid girl telling stories.*

Wulfric was giving her more credence than she realized. Though her story seemed a stretch in places, he looked beyond the tale itself and at the teller. There was something to this girl, and the way she spoke and carried herself. Something he had not seen in many years. It takes a true warrior to recognize another, and though it beggared belief, Wulfric recognized one in the young girl sitting across the fire from him now.

The realization brought with it concern. If she truly was of the Order, why was she here now? Was it coincidence that she had found him, or something else? Could it be that the Order knew of him, of the abomination that hid by day within the body of a man?

Thinking on it, he had reason enough to believe so. He must tread carefully.

"How many months into your Trial are you?" he asked.

"Ten," Indra replied. There was no point in lying about that. In two more months, if she had not returned with her trophy, she would never be accepted into the Order.

Though the prospect of that stung, acceptance mattered far less to Indra than the trophy itself. That single kill was all she had ever wanted. She would scour the land for the rest of her days if need be, with the Order's authority or not, until she found an abomination and slew it. Then, perhaps, she could find some kind of lasting peace.

"Not much left to hunt anymore," said Wulfric, pulling Indra once more from her private thoughts. He was right; the Order had done its job well. It had been some years since the last true sighting of an abomination. Long enough now that tales of them had begun to pass into folklore. For all Wulfric knew, he might be the last that remained.

"No," said Indra. "Very few. But I think I may be close to one now."

Wulfric glanced furtively up at her from the fire. What did she mean by that? Was she testing him to see how he would react? But as he studied her expression, he saw no hint of insinuation or accusation. She was not even looking at him now but gazing once more into the flames; if it had been a test, she would surely be watching closely to measure his reaction.

"Oh?" he offered, as casually as he was able.

"There are reports of sheep slaughtered in a field not far from here, two nights ago, and of a farmer savaged and killed just last night," Indra said. Wulfric relaxed a little. He had read more into her words than she had intended. Though he knew now that it was indeed him she was hunting, she did not know it herself.

"Some of the locals don't want to believe it, but I am trained to know the signs when I see them, and I see them here," she said. "An abomination is at large somewhere in this vicinity." Her eyes met Wulfric's. "You should be watchful, especially at night. These beasts are nocturnal."

"Mostly," said Wulfric, and his eyes went back to the fire, and now it was Indra's turn to stare at him and wonder exactly how much he knew. Abominations—and, with them, the Order—had been all but absent from the land for enough years now that few commoners still knew the lore. Those who did were usually older, old enough to remember the time when abominations roamed wild and free across the land, killing all they came across, and the Order's paladins thundered from town to town on armored horse-back in pursuit.

But as she studied the man across the fire from her more carefully, Indra began to think he was perhaps not as old as his appearance first suggested. His wild, bedraggled beard and face caked with black grime, and that haunted look in his eyes—more than anything, those *eyes*—gave the impression of a man far older than he actually was. Looking more closely at him now, behind his mask of dirt and matted hair, she saw a man likely not much older than thirty.

That meant he would have been little older than she when those things about which he seemed to possess so much exper-tise were last common knowledge. It was not beyond reason, but she now harbored a strong suspicion that there was more to this strange wanderer than he had yet told her. In fact, now that she thought of it, he had told her almost nothing at all, not even his name. And she had answered all of his questions, hadn't she? *Quid pro quo.*

Her eyes went to the iron chain at the foot of the tree just behind Wulfric. "I was wondering," she began, hoping to start with something innocuous, and yet so curious. "What is the chain for?"

His eyes flared so brightly that the flames before him almost seemed to flare with them. The folds of his crumpled cloak fell away as he rose to his full height, his shadow looming over Indra where she sat.

The sky had darkened, the sun far lower than it had been, hidden now behind the maze of treetops. There was still at least an hour before dusk and the first stirrings of the beast, Wulfric knew, but more time had passed than he had realized. Certainly more than he had allowed for when he permitted the girl to sit. What had he been thinking?

He had intended to let the girl stay only a brief while, just long enough to assuage his guilt, before sending her on her way again, but his curiosity about her had got the better of him. Even more, the simple pleasure of conversation, of civilized human interaction, lost to him for so long, had led him to forget all the walls he had spent years painstakingly building around himself.

It occurred to him that he had spent more time in the company of this girl than he had with any other soul in all the fifteen years before. How had she beguiled him so, that he had lost all sense of time, all sense of himself?

No matter how. Enough was enough. He had shown her his gratitude, had satisfied his obligation to her, but night was coming, and she needed to be away from here—for her own good more than his. He kicked dirt onto the fire to snuff it out and pointed into the woods from whence Indra had first appeared. "It is time for you to go," he said.

Indra stood. "I'm sorry, if it was something I—"

"It is nothing you said. I agreed that you might stay a short while. It has been that and more. I thank you for your kindnesses at the crossroads and wish you well. Now go."

Indra could see that no words would move him. "Thank you for the fire, and for the conversation," she said. "I'm grateful for it."

"As am I," replied Wulfric, and Indra could see in those hollow, ancient eyes of his that he meant it sincerely. This was now a riddle even greater than that of the chain; she could see that he was genuinely sorry to see her go, yet here he was, turning her away. She would have asked him why if she had thought it would do any good.

"Venator, to me." The hawk leapt from the branch of the tree nearby and fluttered onto her shoulder. Then she saw that Wulfric was now looking beyond her, to the tree line where the clearing ended and the forest beyond it began. She turned to see what had so suddenly caught his attention.

Five men stood at the edge of the clearing, five more emerging from the darkness of the forest to join them. Indra and Wulfric did not recognize most of them, but they both recognized the three who stood at the head of the group. The big barrel-chested one with the broken nose. The one with the blackjacks strapped to his wrists. And the tall one with his arm in a bloodstained sling, pointing at them now with his one good arm.

"Them!" he hissed as he glared at Wulfric and Indra murderously. "That's them, right there."

SIXTEEN

All ten men were armed. Clubs, sticks, knives. One had a sword, the blade worn and chipped, but effective enough. Indra did not know where these seven new men had come from, but from the look of them they were all cut from the same cloth—all born to the same low, cold life of villainy.

The tall one staggered forward a step, and Indra saw that he was drunk. Not just him, but all of them, to varying degrees, judging by their ruddy faces and the way some of them swayed gently where they stood. She reckoned that the three she had trounced at the crossroads had retired to the tavern to nurse their wounds and their pride, and recruited these others as they drifted in for a drink throughout the waning day, and she wondered what kind of story had been told. Certainly not the truth, which would have only made the ringleaders a laughingstock. No, the tall one, the mouth, had concocted some cock-and-bull story, and the ale had done the rest. Now here they were, filled with false courage and spoiling for revenge.

This was both good and bad, Indra thought. Good because the drink would make them even slower and sloppier than they had been at their best. She knew the first three possessed little talent for close combat, and she estimated the others to be no better. The problem was that she might actually have to fight all ten of them.

Were they sober, it would be easier; make a quick example of the first few, and the others likely would see sense and flee. Most men, when push came to shove, were cowards. But alcohol had a way of separating men from their senses and suspending cowardice just long enough to make them truly dangerous. One against ten, even ten unskilled drunks, was odds enough to give Indra pause.

One of the new men, who carried what looked like a fish knife, came unsteadily forward to get a closer look at Indra and her companion. He let out a sonorous belch. "This?" he said, waving his knife hand in their direction. "This is who beat you up and robbed you? An old man and a little girl?" The others snickered drunkenly. Only the original three remained unamused.

"I told you! They jumped us while we were sleeping!" the tall one insisted, trying to stave off the embarrassment. "And right there's the iron they took from us!" He pointed to the base of the oak tree where the chain Indra had been so curious about sat in a misshapen spool. "An even split when we sell it, like I said."

"I can see why you'd need to come mob-handed to get it back," said Fish Knife, not yet satisfied that he'd had his fun. "A formidable pair, these two. Just look at 'em! Was it the young girl broke your arm, Pick? I imagine the stink from the old beggar felled the other two of you."

Now the other newcomers were laughing raucously, which only enraged the tall man further. As they bickered among themselves, Indra took a backward step, closer to Wulfric.

"Can you fight?" she asked.

"Yes," he said. "But I will not."

She glanced at him. "What?"

"Long ago," he said, "I took a vow to never again do violence against another."

"How lovely for you. You do understand that these men mean us harm?"

"Yes. You should run."

"And you?"

He gave no answer; simply stood there. Indra shook her head, exasperated. So he was a madman after all, just another vagrant without the sense to care even for his own life. And she was going to have to do this all herself. Run? The very thought made the anger start to rise up from the pit of her stomach like bile. She had never run from danger; she had spent her entire life running toward it.

She looked down and saw her staff where she had laid it to rest in the grass. She hooked the toe of her boot under it and with a flick of her foot brought it up to meet her hand. The band of ten appeared to have settled their differences, and the tall one turned away from the others and back toward Indra, standing before him, defiant. She raised her voice, loud enough to address them all.

"For whatever it's worth, this man is lying to you," she said, gesturing with her staff at the tall man. "We never robbed him— the chain was never his. You've been brought here under false pretenses. You'd do best to turn around and go back to town."

"Or what?" growled Fish Knife. As Indra suspected, there would be no way to talk these men down. The more she tried to reason with them, the more riled up they would get. Better to just get the thing over with.

"Or I'll show you how these three morons really got hurt."

Two steps behind her, Wulfric again found himself deeply conflicted. Never once had he broken his oath, an oath taken long ago and forged by the fire of his will over the past fifteen years: though he could not always protect others from the violence done by the beast within him, he would at least ensure that as a human he never harmed another, not even to defend himself. The beatings he sometimes took as a consequence were part of his penance. But his years of isolation had forestalled the question—was he prepared to stand by and let violence be done to another? An innocent endangered only because she had come to his aid?

Another problem, more practical, also now occurred to him. The chain. They were not so far from town yet, and there were now more than enough of these ruffians to carry it. He could not lose it now, not this close to dark. Many more than just these ten would die if he did.

And the girl.

There were precious few like her left in the world, who would risk their own life to save that of a stranger. His conscience would not allow so rare a soul to be snuffed out by these, the worst of men. He had come to think of all forms of violence as evil, but the greater evil would be to stand idly by and allow darkness to swallow up this small, bright point of light.

Indra sensed movement behind her and glanced over to see Wulfric now standing at her side, his gaze intent on the men confronting them.

"Give me a sword," he said.

"I thought you didn't fight."

"Would you prefer to face them alone?"

Indra thought for a moment. Perhaps now wasn't the best time to question his sudden change of heart. She shifted at the waist, turning to offer him his choice of the two swords sheathed across her back. He hesitated for a moment, then reached up, almost gingerly, and pulled one free.

Wulfric flexed his fingers tight around the hilt. He could tell by the sword's weight and balance that it was quality, not the weapon of an amateur. It felt light to him; it had likely been custom-made for the girl, who was smaller and more agile than he. But though it was not a sword he would have chosen for himself, it felt familiar in his hand, so much so that it unsettled him. This was the first time in more than fifteen years that he had held any form of weapon, and yet the sword felt like an extension of an arm that had only been numb a while and had now regained full feeling. He hated how natural it felt.

The ten men looked at him, amused. The sight of this filthy, disheveled old man wielding a sword was ludicrous. He looked like he was fearful he might cut himself.

"Hold up," said Fish Knife, grinning and mockingly waving the others back. "The old fella wants a piece of us now as well."

Wulfric raised the sword and pointed it at the men. "Leave here," he said. "Or die here."

He did not bellow it, barely raised his voice at all. Just enough to be heard clearly and no misunderstanding. But something in his tone gave each man pause. They might actually have thought twice and walked away but for Fish Knife, who was too drunk and riled to be deterred, and who now ran headlong at Indra with his dull little blade.

Indra spun and caught him hard on the side of his face with her staff and he went down, rolling in the grass and clutching his cheek. The sight of the fallen man spurred the others to charge in, all at once. Indra and Wulfric stepped away from one another to each give the other room and went to work.

The one with the blackjacks was the first to die. Wulfric brought his sword up and caught him across the neck with the tip of the blade, opening up his throat. As his body fell away, two more men came at Wulfric. One was met with an elbow to the jaw that shattered it and knocked out most of his front teeth; the other took a wild swing at Wulfric with a gnarled club. Wulfric ducked and thrust his sword upward, beneath the man's extended arm and deep into his armpit, until its point burst through the far side of the man's neck. The man made a quiet gurgling sound, then fell limply to the ground as Wulfric withdrew the sword.

Indra had felled two men with her staff and was parrying a flurry of wild attacks from a third. She was a half step slower than usual, having positioned herself to watch Wulfric from the corner of her eye as she fought.

It was astonishing. Not so much that he could in fact defend himself—although that was surprise enough—but more the brutal efficiency of it. The first man had gone down so fast that at first Indra had thought he tripped, only noticing that his throat was slit wide open when he hit the ground. She had never even seen Wulfric's deft flourish of the sword.

The second had died in no manner that she had ever seen: a lethal riposte that should not have been possible from that position. And he was as merciless as he was skilled. Indra had spent years learning how to defend herself without killing, using lethal force only when necessary, but this man apparently knew no other way. For a man who just moments ago had proclaimed a vow of peace, he—

Nnff. Indra felt a sudden pain in her ribs. Momentarily distracted, she had allowed the man she was fighting to land a blow, which took the breath out of her and sent her reeling backward. Another man seized on the opening and came at her, and this one was more skilled than he looked, jabbing and thrusting with a thin needle-like knife, vicious and fast. She parried, but with the first man still coming at her with his club, it was all she could do to keep them both at bay. She could no longer afford to fight by half measures. If she wanted to stay alive, she had to let her anger in.

She let loose a roar and drew her sword. As the man with the knife swiped at her, she dodged and took his hand off with one clean blow. He cried out and stumbled toward her, blood pouring from his wrist, and she thrust her sword forward, deep into his gut. As she ran him through, the man with the club came at her with a crude overhead swing. It would have been easy to glance aside, but that the man with her sword through him was clutching her wrist with his one remaining hand, still alive, still screaming. She could not pull the sword free.

Straining, Indra swung around to put him between her and her other attacker, so that as the club came down it struck the skewered man sharply across the head. Mercifully, he stopped screaming and released her wrist. As soon as his body slackened and slipped free of her blade, Indra lunged at the other man, piercing him just above the groin. He shrieked, then toppled face-first to the ground, writhing, as she withdrew.

Wulfric was fighting with another man now, a big man who seemed to be pressing him, at least for the moment. Indra was about to go to his aid when she felt something hit her hard in the chest. The ground left her feet and suddenly she was on her back, a man with a bloody, toothless mouth and a horribly crooked jaw on top of her, pounding her with his fists. He managed to bloody her nose before she could raise her sword up and jam it against the underside of his unhinged jaw. She drove upward with both hands and heard a crunch when it would go no farther. The man's eyes rolled back and he went limp and slumped forward onto her.

She rolled him off hastily and clambered back to her feet, pulling the sword free and looking up in time to see Wulfric split the head of the man he was fighting into two pieces. Three men dead at his feet now, with yet another man coming at him, flailing this way and that with some kind of crude mace.

One of the men Indra had knocked down was clutching at her thigh, trying to pull himself up or her down. She bashed the pommel of her sword against his head and he went back down, quiet again. Then she felt something cold and sharp against the back of her head and suddenly the world was spinning away from her. She stumbled, dizzy, and the ground rose up to meet her.

She felt herself hit the ground, and for a moment it was almost peaceful there, with the cold wet grass against her cheek. Then she was pulled up from behind, with arms hooked around her elbows to keep them pinned behind her back. When she was hauled to her feet, there was the tall man, with a malevolent grin, a bloodstained hunk of rock held in his one good fist. He dropped it and bent over to pick up Indra's sword instead. She had lost it when she hit the ground, and now he had it, the pig.

This pig had her sword.

She was still dazed, her vision blurry, and separated enough from her senses that her anger now had free rein. Otherwise she would surely have known better than to spit in the face of a man who held a sword against her while she was pinned. But that is what she did, her thick gob of phlegm hitting the tall man between his nose and his top lip. He stood there for a moment, frozen in disbelief, and in her delirium, Indra laughed.

Her laughter brought back the tall man's anger, and he wiped the spit away with his forearm, then brought the tip of her own sword up to her throat.

Indra thrust her head back sharply and caught the man who was holding her from behind square in the nose. Fish Knife released her and stumbled backward, clutching his face. Free to stand on her own, Indra realized how unsteady on her feet she still was. Drunkenly, she made a grab for her sword, and as she and the tall man struggled, she saw Wulfric kill the man he had been fighting.

As the body in front of him collapsed to the ground, Wulfric looked over to see Indra in trouble, wrestling with the tall man for control of her sword. He did not see the man that Indra had knocked to the ground during the first throes of the melee, the one with the chipped sword, getting to his feet. Indra saw it, saw the man coming up behind Wulfric and drawing back his blade to strike. She opened her mouth to call out a warning and realized that she still did not know his name, this strange man who knew too much about the Order, who claimed to have renounced violence, and who then killed four men with more brutality and skill than she had ever seen.

Time seemed to slow and sound to fall away into silence. Indra heard herself call out, "Behind you!" and saw Wulfric turn, but too late. The man with the sword swung it hard and well and caught Wulfric exactly where he had aimed, at the base of his neck. Wulfric's head separated cleanly from his body as the blade passed through, blood pulsing from his stump of a neck. Indra screamed but heard nothing, her world now a silent nightmare. Wulfric's headless body seemed to take a faltering half step forward before slumping to its knees and toppling to the ground a few feet from where his head had come to rest.

Indra looked down in horror as Wulfric's body twitched once, then again, and was still. Her stomach rolled over, sickened. Then she felt another sharp blow to the back of her head, and this time the world went away completely.

SEVENTEEN

Indra did not know how long she had been unconscious, only that it was darker than before when she groggily came around. The day's light had waned to its last ebbs, soon to give way to the onset of night.

She blinked, trying to clear her blurred vision, and looked around. She was still in the clearing, not far from where she had fallen. Her arms and shoulders ached, and the back of her head stung where she had been twice struck. She could feel that some of her hair was stuck to the side of her face, matted with her own dried blood. She tried to reach up and brush it away, only to realize why her shoulders ached. Her arms were pulled behind her and bound at the wrists. She looked around, as much as her limited movement would allow, and saw that she was seated on the ground at the base of a tree, and secured fast to it by a rope that wrapped around her torso. Whoever had done the tying had done it well; try as she might, she could barely move. She tried to get her feet under her, push herself up so that at least she would be standing, but even that was beyond her. She slumped back down, frustrated.

The bodies were still there, of the thugs that she and the man who had fought alongside her had killed in the melee. Indra had never fought in or seen a real battle, a military battle, like the ones her father had fought during the wars against the Norse, but from the stories he told she could imagine that this is what the aftermath looked like. Bodies splayed across the ground, bloodied and cleaved, so still it hardly seemed possible that there had ever been life in them at all.

And though she could hardly bear to look, she saw that he was still there, too. She glanced over just long enough to see the body lying on the ground, the head a few feet away, the ground stained dark with drying blood. Like the other bodies, his head, drained of all life, barely looked real: a pale, waxy imitation of what it had once been. His eyes were open wide in a ghastly stare that would remain until flesh rotted from bone, though mercifully that stare was directed not at Indra but up at the darkening sky. She looked away.

She had seen dead men before. This one had been a stranger to her; they had met that same day and had shared a campfire for a short while, nothing more. But though she barely knew him, she felt almost overwhelmingly sad to see his body bled out and lifeless on the ground. She tried to tell herself it was merely the vexation of knowing that the many riddles about him would now never be solved. But deep down she knew it was more than just her unsatisfied curiosity. The deep, iron-heavy sorrow came from knowing that he had been a good man.

She hadn't needed to know him long to be sure of that; somehow she had known it instinctively. In their short time together she had glimpsed a life that had conspired against a decent man, a life of wretched indigence and isolation. To see that life end undeservedly as well, simply because he had stood by her side against a gang of drunken bullies—where was the justice in that, or in any of it? Where was God?

It was a question she had once asked her father when studying history as a child. *God always delivers justice to those deserving, in one way or another*, he had told her. But glancing again, in spite of herself, at that headless body, in that pitiful, filthy sackcloth robe, it seemed to her now that it was just another one of her father's lies. If God was real, all he ever did was look on with callous indifference.

The only justice she could ever rely on was that which she made for herself.

She heard voices. They came from behind her, where she could not see, but she recognized them.

"Two of my best friends she killed, their bodies still warm right over there! And you want to do nothing about it!" It was Fish Knife. He sounded less drunk than before, and far angrier.

"Use your head!" This voice belonged to the tall one, the one who had started it all back at the crossroads. Pick, someone had called him. "It's better this way. I know a man—"

"Oh, you know a man, you know a man. You always know a man! You talk and you talk and that's all you ever fucking do! Blood demands blood, that's the law we live by!"

"Listen to me. Listen! She's a young girl, not bad to look at. Unharmed, the man I know will pay well for her. Believe me, whatever the iron is worth, she'd be at least double! Or we can do it your way and kill her, and your friends *and* mine will have died for a lot less."

There was a pause.

"Double?"

"At least."

Footsteps approached. Fish Knife came into view, followed by Pick and Broken Nose. The only three of the original ten to have survived. Fish Knife looked down at her. He was carrying one of her swords, while Pick had the other.

"Look, she's awake." He kicked her in the thigh, just enough to hurt.

"Unharmed, I said!" Pick protested, shoving Fish Knife in the shoulder. "Do you want to earn out of this or not?"

Fish Knife seemed to care little. He looked down on Indra, bound and helpless. "Maybe there's a way we can all be happy," he said. "I want her dead. You want her unharmed. What if we deliver her to this man of yours somewhere in the middle?" He cracked his knuckles. "We don't kill her, just give her a proper going-over.

Enough that she'll remember it for a good long while. Won't leave nothing permanent."

"She's banged up enough as it is," Pick said. "You make it much worse, it'll take her price down by half, at least."

Fish Knife glared at Pick, the look in his eyes and the ice-cold tone of his voice both conveying the strong impression that he had reached the limits of his willingness to bargain. "Then half it'll have to be."

Pick put up his hands in a gesture of surrender and gave a sigh of frustrated resignation. "Have it your way. But mark my words, this is why we never improve our station in life."

Pick turned and walked away, grumbling, and Fish Knife crouched down before Indra, looked her square in the eye. "You killed two of my friends, including one of my best," he said. "Now, I'm going to sit over there, make a fire and have my supper. And then I'm going to come back here and show you how unhappy I am. You're not going to enjoy it." He leaned in close, close enough for Indra to see the brown and black of his rotten teeth and smell the ale on his breath. She grimaced, but did not look away. "Something for you to think about while I'm eating."

In that moment, Indra wanted nothing more than to tell him that in the confusion of the melee, he had been mistaken: she had in fact killed three of his drunken idiot friends, not two.

She thought better of it. She stared back at him with a numb, expressionless look, unwilling to give the man the satisfaction of seeing the fear beginning to settle in her gut.

Fish Knife stood, dusted himself off, and turned to take in the clearing. Pick and Broken Nose stood nearby, sharing a skin of ale brought with them to keep their courage up.

"I'll get a fire started," Fish Knife said. He snatched the ale skin from Broken Nose's hands and took a long draw from it. "We can eat and rest here tonight, go back in the morning."

"We might need more help to carry that chain back," said Pick. "Three of us tried before. It's heavier than it looks. And my arm's broken."

"The girl will help, if she knows what's good for her," said Fish Knife as he began building a fire. "And if we need more, you'll walk to town and fetch some help back here. God's mercy, do I have to think of everything?" He glanced at the bodies strewn about. "Here, make yourselves useful—get rid of these lot."

Pick blinked. "What?"

"I don't want 'em around me when I'm eating. Puts me right off my food."

"What are we supposed to do with them? We can't bury them out here!"

"Who said anything about bury? I just don't want to have to look at 'em. Drag 'em into the woods there."

Pick and Broken Nose exchanged a look. Pick gestured to the makeshift sling cradling his broken arm and shrugged. With a sigh, Broken Nose trudged over to the nearest body, grabbed it by the ankle, and began dragging it toward the trees, the dead man's arms trailing in the dirt behind him. By the time the campfire was good and blazing, all seven of their dead had been removed from the clearing and deposited in the darkness beyond the tree line. Only Wulfric's body remained.

Broken Nose grabbed the headless corpse by a wrist and, with some effort, pulled him toward the trees. He was heavier than he looked. Pick warmed his hands by the fire and watched as Broken Nose disappeared into the darkness of the forest with the body and returned without it moments later, wiping his hands. He walked over to the fire and planted himself on his backside beside the others. Fish Knife produced a hunk of bread, halfway stale, and tore off a piece for Broken Nose, which the big man set about hungrily. Pick held out a hand for his share, but Fish Knife glanced over to where Wulfric's head was still staring blankly up at the evening sky, surrounded by a pool of half-dried blood. Pick grimaced, but Fish Knife just tore off a piece of bread for himself, and wolfed it down.

"You always were a lazy fucker, Pick," he said. "You want your share, do your share. Don't tell me you can't manage that, even with one arm."

Pick let out an exaggerated sigh and got to his feet. As he made his way over to where the head lay on the ground, he cursed himself for bringing Ron into this. This had been his idea, his plan— Ron and his crew of drunks were just hired help. And now here he was, taking orders. It had been this way for years, whenever they banded together. Ron always knowing better, taking charge, belittling him. Well, he vowed, no longer. Once the chain and the girl had been sold off and their pockets filled, he'd slit Ron's throat with his own stupid fish knife and take his share for himself. Pick knew well the credo of honor among thieves; he had just never subscribed to it himself. As Ron, the bully, the usurper, would soon learn to his profound disadvantage.

He arrived at the head and hesitated. He did not have the stomach for things like this. The worst thing he had seen before today was a leg crushed from the knee down by the wheel of a wagon in an accident. He knew, of course, that the man was dead and that his eyes, while open, were just staring lifelessly up at the sky, but as he looked down, it seemed as though the head was gazing directly back at him.

Just get it over with. He reached down and grabbed a tuft of hair and lifted it from the ground, surprised by how heavy it was. He made his way to the trees where Broken Nose had dumped the rest of the bodies. There he stopped. He peered into the dense, impenetrable black of the forest beyond and found himself unable to take another step. He did not want to venture into that darkness, where dead men waited. And so he swung back his arm and flung the head into the trees and watched it disappear into the dark. He heard the rustle of branches and the soft thud of the head landing on the ground, then turned back and sat by the fire. Fish Knife tossed him what remained of the bread with an amused sneer.

"What did you think?" he asked with a nod toward the forest. "The dead were going to rise up and get you?"

Pick looked away, embarrassed. "It's done, isn't it? Leave me be." He tore off a piece of the bread and began to eat. Fish Knife chuckled and looked across the fire at Broken Nose. "Worried about ghosts and ghouls, this one," he said. Broken Nose said nothing, as was his custom. Fish Knife gave a snort and supped the last of the ale from the skin. He glanced over to where the girl was bound and saw that her head had lolled forward, her long brown hair covering her face. Asleep. But not for long. He would wait for his food to settle, then go over there and pay her the visit she'd been promised. He lay back on the ground and gazed up at the blanket of stars becoming visible as the sky turned to night.

Over by the tree, Indra worked. Her head was down, eyes closed—but she was far from asleep. The illusion of it might lure her captors into paying her less attention, but more than that, she could not bear to look at them, and keeping her eyes closed helped her concentrate on the task at hand. She had found just enough leeway in the bindings at her wrists to bend her hands around and begin to pick away at the knot with her fingernails. She had made little progress so far, but if she just kept trying . . .

She had to try. She would not be a prize, a trophy, to these men. She would die fighting before it came to that. But so much better that *they* should die. Once her hands were free, she could take them by surprise when they approached, grab a weapon, and then anything was possible. If she could only get this damn knot to give just a little . . .

EIGHTEEN

The sky was black now, and the forest around them was still. Fish Knife was still on his back, gazing lazily up at the moon. Broken Nose, snoring quietly, appeared to have fallen asleep where he sat. Only Pick remained fully alert. His attention was fixed on the tree line, where the clearing ended and the darkness of the forest began.

Something was not right. He found himself again and again peering toward the trees where the dead men had been disposed of, sensing sounds and shadows that he only half believed were real. And yet—

Suddenly he stood bolt upright. No trick of the mind could account for that: something had moved, in the darkness beyond the trees, something large disturbing the dense carpet of bracken and undergrowth that made the forest floor. He stood there, frozen, for what seemed an eternity, watching, listening for any other sign of movement in the trees.

Fish Knife turned his head and belched. "What's the matter with you?"

"Did you hear that?" Pick replied without looking away from the trees.

Fish Knife listened for a moment. "Don't hear anything."

It was then that Pick realized the source of the strange, unsettling sensation that had been plaguing him. As he listened now to everything around him, he heard precisely nothing. He had spent the night in the woods enough times to know that there was always something to hear. A forest was alive with countless creatures, many that came out only at night, which created an ever-present tapestry of sound even in the small hours. It was those sounds, the sense of being surrounded by a thousand living things great and small, that offered comfort on nights like these, deep in the woods. No matter how dark the forest might be, you were never in it alone.

Now there was nothing. Not the cooing of nighttime birds nor the scampering of woodland critters nor even the chirp of insects. There was only silence—a perfect, unbroken stillness that enshrouded everything. They were alone. Pick could not imagine how a place usually so teeming with life could suddenly be so entirely devoid of it, only that it would take something truly abnormal, truly terrifying, to cause every living thing to flee.

Now it was Fish Knife's turn to rise to his feet. Broken Nose, roused from his slumber, turned groggily toward the trees at which the two other men were looking warily.

"All right, I heard it that time," said Fish Knife. "I think I saw something as well."

Pick nodded. They had both seen it. A black, formless shape, at least as big as a man, had shifted in the darkness ahead. In the trees, where the moonlight did not penetrate, it was already black as pitch, and Pick found himself wondering how it was that anything could appear even darker.

Fish Knife stepped forward, still keeping some distance from the trees. "We see you out there," he called out. "There's five of us, and we're all armed. You see the dead men out there? Those are the last that tried us. Turn around and go."

For a moment, their answer was silence. And then there came a great rumble from the darkness, and a deep, guttural growl that echoed through the forest, powerful enough that the three men felt the vibrations in the earth beneath their feet. The trees shook, the tops swaying in the night air, and a flurry of leaves fell to the ground.

"All right," said Fish Knife as he backed up a step. "What the hell is that?"

Across the clearing, at the tree where she was bound, Indra tried not to react, lest she draw attention to herself. Keeping her head hung low, she glanced up and through the strands of matted hair hanging over her face saw the attention of her three captors fixed firmly on the trees, away from her. Perhaps now was her chance. The knot she had been picking at had begun to loosen—not yet nearly enough, but with the three of them distracted she could allow herself to struggle more openly against her bonds.

She was motivated now as much by what might be lurking in the woods as by her desire to free herself from these men. Whatever it was that had so unsettled them had the same effect on her. She knew how to travel a forest safely, how to identify everything that lived there by sight, sound, and smell. Whatever was out there in the darkness was not any of those things—which left only one dreaded possibility. That she could spend her entire life dreaming of this moment, training to finally face an abomination, only for it to arrive with her bound and helpless . . .

No, she would not allow it. She wrestled with all her might against the rope that tied her; her captors were too petrified to notice or perhaps even to care. Then, as she twisted her wrist, the rope slackened a little more, and then one hand was free. From there, the rest was easy.

"A bear?" Pick wondered.

"No bears in these parts," said Fish Knife, although he had briefly considered the same. What else could be that large? He nudged Broken Nose with his elbow, never taking his eyes from the trees where the thing was moving. "Go and have a look."

Broken Nose shook his head emphatically.

"I think we should just go," said Pick. "I mean, right now, we should go."

"And come away from this with nothing? I don't think so."

"We can come back for the chain tomorrow."

"I'm not leaving it here for someone else to find!"

"Even if someone did, we still have the—" For the first time he looked away from the trees, only to see that the girl was gone, the rope that had bound her left in a loose spool around the base of the tree.

"Fuck."

Another deep, ominous growl brought them all back to attention.

"We'll all go," said Fish Knife, girding himself. Reluctantly, the two others nodded agreement. Pick and Fish Knife each had one of the girl's swords, Broken Nose his gnarled club. Together, they approached the edge of the clearing, the sounds of the beast beyond, grunting and rooting around in the darkness, growing louder as they drew closer. They were close enough now that they could not only hear the thing but smell it, too. It brought them all to a stop, just a few feet from the trees, as the rank odor overpowered them. Pick raised a sleeve over his nose and mouth; Broken Nose retched with the stench in his throat.

"What in God's name is that stink?" Pick said, his voice muffled through his sleeve.

"Sulfur," said Fish Knife, who in his youth had apprenticed for an alchemist before his life took him down a less noble path. "Brimstone."

Broken Nose squinted and leaned in closer. "I think—" he said, and then something dark and wet shot out from the forest and coiled around his waist and yanked him into the darkness, limbs flailing.

Fish Knife and Pick sprang backward. Broken Nose's shrieks rose in pitch, turning from those of terror to those of agony, and were joined by the wet, sickening sounds of rending flesh and splintering bone and the ravenous, unnatural snarling of the thing that had him.

The screaming stopped.

After a moment of unnerving quiet, two torn and bloody hunks of meat were flung from the darkness, landing on the ground before Fish Knife and Pick—the two halves of what remained of Broken Nose, one leg and both arms gone at the knee and elbows, blood and bowels oozing into the dirt.

The trees shook. And now the beast came forth, out of the dark, into the clearing and the pale light of the moon. It shook its head and made a gruff, guttural snort, its hot breath fogging in the cool night air.

Fish Knife and Pick stood before it, wide-eyed, mouths agape in silent, paralytic terror. It was at least three times their size and resembled nothing so much as a giant, grotesquely malformed beetle. It moved with a lumbering scuttle on three sets of barbed and bone-like legs, its body encased in an armored carapace that looked like a gigantic, oil-black walnut shell. It peered down at the two men with a cluster of a dozen globular, irregularly sized eyes, which glimmered in the moonlight. Beneath those eyes, a pair of jagged, claw-like mandibles scissored back and forth, slick with saliva and blood.

For a moment the beast stood there, regarding the two men frozen in fear before it. And then it opened its jaw wide, revealing a black chasm lined with densely packed rows of long needle-like teeth, and let out a long breathless hiss, a sound so hideous that Pick instinctively turned and fled. Running faster than he ever had, he covered perhaps ten feet of ground before the monster's long glistening tongue lashed out and ensnared his leg like a toad catching an insect. Pick fell to the ground, dropped his sword, and screamed and clawed at the earth with his one good arm as the tongue retracted, dragging him toward the beast's maw. As he was brought yammering before the creature, it lowered its head and took him between its mandibles, then tossed him into the air and caught him between its jaws.

Fish Knife saw his chance, with the creature distracted as it fed, and ran for his life. He made it across the clearing in galloping strides, glancing behind him as he approached the trees to see, to his relief, that the creature was not following. Then he was brought suddenly to a hard stop, something cold against his chest, and found himself face-to-face with the girl, emerging from the shadows.

He looked down and saw the hilt of the sword Pick had taken from her square against his chest, surrounded by a blossoming saturation of blood on his shirt. He could not see the blade, as it had run clean through him—or, rather, he had run clean through it. The girl had simply stepped out from hiding as he ran full pelt, his eyes behind him, and offered the blade to meet him. His own forward motion had done the work of a thrust.

Indra watched the man closely as the realization of his imminent death set in. She did not enjoy the suffering of others, but she allowed herself the satisfaction of this one moment—if not for her, then for the innocent man they had murdered only for trying to protect her. Then, as Fish Knife's eyes rolled back and the life left him, she drew back the sword and let him collapse to a heap on the ground. She bent down to pry her other sword from his lifeless grip and, reunited now with both of them, marched forward to face the monster.

NINETEEN

Indra had not considered running away, as the two cowards had tried to, though she had had far better opportunity. Free from her bindings, she had watched from the seclusion of the trees on the far side of the clearing as the creature killed one man then emerged from the forest to kill another.

The sheer size and monstrosity of the thing gave Indra pause; even after all her studies of the Bestiary and all the tales she had heard, nothing could have prepared her for the ice-cold horror of seeing an abomination in the flesh. But she had not dedicated her life to this task only to run away at the last. All she needed were her swords, and now she had them both. She strode across the clearing, past the sputtering campfire, as the great black beast with its slavering tongue devoured what was left of Pick. It did not notice her until she drew closer, shoulders back, a sword held firmly at each side, marching right toward it with steely determination.

She stopped a handful of paces in front of the monster, her hands closing around the grips of her twin swords so tightly that her knuckles began to whiten. If the beast was three times the size of the men it had killed, it was at least four times hers, and the way it moved suggested that it weighed even more. She was dwarfed before it, and the shadow it cast against the moonlight swallowed her entirely.

For a brief moment, the absurdity of it all came crashing down upon her—she was a tiny girl before this behemoth, a thing shaped and brought into the world for the sole purpose of killing—and she felt herself tremble before reminding herself that it was she who held the advantage. The beast was mindless, no more than a dumb animal, while she was trained to be a finely honed weapon. She, too, had a singular purpose. And she, too, had been shaped to kill. She looked up at the beast, glaring into its cluster of black, soulless eyes with fierce resolve.

"Come on," she growled.

The abomination cocked its head at her, as though confused. It had likely never encountered a human whose reaction had been anything other than to flee in terror. It made a strange chittering sound, its mandibles scissoring open and closed as it regarded her.

Indra was fast growing frustrated. In her daydreams of how her confrontation with an abomination would one day play out, she had imagined every possible scenario, and none of them had ever gone like this.

"Come *on!*" she barked, her tone unmistakably a challenge, and to make sure of it she clashed the blades of her swords together hard enough that it drew a spark. Something seemed to work, for the beast suddenly reared up, its thorn-tipped front legs thrashing wildly, and let loose a shrill, piercing screech. Instinctively, Indra backed away as the monster towered over her and the full size of it became terrifyingly apparent.

The thing attacked. Its insect tongue shot out at her, making a grab for her arm, but Indra rolled away to one side and was up again, eyes locked on her enemy. It lunged, with an outstretched front leg, razored claw scything through the air—a swipe that would surely have taken Indra's head clean from her shoulders had she not ducked so swiftly and batted it away with the flat of her sword.

The beast hesitated, grunted, seemingly surprised that the girl could move so quickly. Indra saw it in its unblinking eyes and was emboldened. *Yes, that's right. I'm not just another of your helpless victims. This one is going to fight back. This time, you're the prey.*

The creature scuttled sideward, circling Indra, still apparently sizing up this strangely adept and unafraid opponent. She matched it step for step; the two circled each other now, a dance. Indra used every moment to observe the beast intently, watching the way it moved, how it shifted its weight, where it was fast and where it was slow. Her eyes darted over its anatomy, looking for any soft and fleshy spot where a sword might find its way in. Where was the heart on a thing like this? Was its brain even in its head? Sometimes it wasn't. One thing Indra had learned from countless hours studying the Bestiary was that no two abominations were ever exactly the same anatomically. There were commonalities among those of similar type, but the one before her now was of no type that she had ever seen. How could she—

It charged, thundering at her like a giant bull. And now it was Indra's turn to learn how deceptively fast the thing could be as it sprang from a standing start. Indra flung herself to one side to get clear of its path, but not fast enough; the beast's armored shell sideswiped her as it passed. The force of the impact lifted her off the ground and tossed her several feet through the air before she landed in a tangle of limbs in the dirt. She had lost hold of one of her swords as she fell, but recovered it even as she hauled herself up, staggering for a moment as she regained her footing. Though she had escaped a trampling that would surely have killed her, even the glancing blow from the monster had hit her with the force of a runaway wagon. Her side ached, and she touched her hand to her rib cage, wondering if something might have broken.

The beast halted and turned back around. Indra noticed that it did so slowly and not with ease, its legs moving awkwardly beneath it to rotate its body in place so that it faced her once more. There was an advantage: the beast was fast and powerful at full charge, and it could scuttle sideways easily enough, but it could not quickly turn itself around. It was something she could use. If she could get behind it . . .

The beast came at her again, but seemed to have learned a lesson and did not commit to another thunderous charge. Instead, it got within striking distance and lashed out at her with a claw. Indra deflected it with her sword and skipped to the side, trying now to circle the thing at close range.

As she'd hoped, the beast could not turn swiftly enough to keep facing her, and Indra was gifted a free window of attack. She drew back her sword and brought it down with all her might; the impact drew sparks, but the blade bounced harmlessly off the beast's carapace without leaving so much as a scratch. She might as well have tried to cut into a boulder.

As the jarring force of the impact reverberated along her arm, the beast continued to turn toward her, and though it was not well enough aligned for a frontal attack, it lashed outward with a mandible and struck her, backhanded, at her right shoulder. Indra cried out and dropped the sword she had been holding in her right hand. No time to retrieve it; she was forced to back away as the beast faced her again, and pressed its attack. Its tongue shot out and coiled itself around her left wrist. Indra tried to wrest free, but the thing was too strong, yanking her arm ahead of her as it began to reel her in.

Indra passed her sword from her ensnared hand to her free one, but when she tried to raise it to cut herself free, she was greeted with a sharp bolt of excruciating pain up her right arm. Something in her shoulder had been badly hurt by that backhanded blow; her arm would not move without causing agony. But as the beast pulled her closer to its gaping mouth, she knew she had no choice. Wailing from the white-hot flare of pain, she brought the sword down, with as much force as she could. It was not enough to sever the tongue, but it made a deep cut that spat black blood and caused the beast to let out a wounded screech and release her.

As Indra retreated, she heard something that sounded like bacon frying in a pan. She looked down to see that the beast's saliva was burning its way through her leather gauntlet. Her right arm was useless, so she tore open the gauntlet's binding with her teeth and shook it off. It fell to the ground, sizzling, as the acid ate clean through it. The beast was still shrieking and stamping its feet in a rage, its lacerated tongue retracted into its mouth. Indra clutched her hand to her shoulder and winced from the pain she felt there. She was quite sure that it was dislocated, the arm now useless. So they were both injured now. The difference was that she was growing tired and less able to fight, while the minor wound the beast had sustained seemed to have served only to enrage it further.

She would not run; she would never run. Nor could she continue to fight like this much longer. She had already lost one sword arm, and the beast was too resilient, too powerful. Her only chance now was to gamble all on a last-ditch attack, to force this thing onto the unfamiliar ground of defending itself and hopefully land a mortal blow—or die in the attempt. She was not a fool; in all her years of dreaming and training and preparing for this moment, she had always known that her own death was the more likely outcome. Whenever that unwelcome inner voice arose to taunt her with the thought of it, she would become crippled by suffocating panic. But now that she faced the reality, she did so unafraid. If she were to die, it would be fighting to the last, in the service of the quest to which she had devoted her life. Even as she died, the monster would see not fear but defiance in her eyes. She would know, and it would know, that she was not a victim.

She charged, her body sidelong so as to keep her injured shoulder to the rear, with her good sword arm aloft and shouting a war cry so fearsome that even the beast seemed taken aback by it. It froze briefly as she stormed toward it, then opened its mouth wide, let loose its own roar, and charged to meet her.

As the two converged at the center of the clearing, Indra dropped to the ground and slid beneath the beast and raised up her sword, the blade scraping along its underside as it thundered over her. She heard it cry out, then she scrambled back to her feet after it passed and watched as it tried to turn itself back about. It was limping now, lopsided, and she could see black blood trickling from beneath it into the patchy grass. She looked at her sword and saw its blade dripping with the stuff. As she'd hoped, she had pierced something in the beast's soft, unarmored belly. Now it was truly hurt—not nearly enough to kill it, but enough to hobble it, to bring it real pain, to diminish its ability to fight. Now, perhaps—

Its tongue lashed out at her again. Indra, taken by surprise that the beast could counter so quickly after such a grievous wound, could only dodge, throwing herself sideways to the ground and crushing her injured shoulder against it. She wailed and promptly rolled onto her back to relieve the pain.

The beast staggered slowly toward her, trailing blood behind it.

Though she was reeling, her vision obscured by a haze of bright, shimmering points of light that flared with every fresh stab of pain from her shoulder, she looked across the ground to her other sword, lying where she had dropped it. Somehow she had still held on to the one. If she had both again . . .

She reached out; the hilt was less than a foot from her fingertips. She clawed at the ground and dragged herself closer, but as she came within reach, closed her hand around it, she felt a blow to her stomach like a kick from a horse. The world spiraled around her and she gasped for breath as she tried to sit up. She tried to orient herself but could see only the scattered stars above. Then even they disappeared as the great black mass of the beast appeared and stood over her.

A clawed limb pressed down on her wrist and squeezed until she was forced to open her hand and release the one sword she still held. Now she was unarmed and helpless, pinned beneath the monster as it settled into position over her to ensure she had no chance of escape.

She groped for her other sword with her injured arm, but it was hopeless, and to be sure, the monster flung it across the clearing with a swipe of its leg. Then it leaned in close, close enough for Indra to feel its hot breath on her face.

So this was how she died.

The certainty of it came almost as a relief; she realized now that the fear of death lay only in the anticipation of when and how it might come. Once it was settled, inevitable, all that remained was to accept it and die well. And so she let herself go, slackened her body, refused to give the beast the satisfaction of a struggle or the slightest hint of desperation or fear.

It leaned in closer still, mere inches from her now. She looked up into its hideous cluster of wet, bulbous eyes and saw herself reflected a dozen times in them. It was oddly beautiful, she thought, to see herself that way, each of her reflections a different size, each one a perfectly convex distortion, like an array of spherical black mirrors. More than anything, she was satisfied to see in herself no trace of fear. The certainty of her death had brought upon her a warm, comforting sense of tranquility. The very concept of fear now seemed to her like a foreign thing, absurd even. Though her life did not flash before her as she'd heard others speak of, she found herself thinking back to all the times she had allowed fear or trepidation to slow or thwart her ambitions or had seen it happen to others. *What a terrible waste it is to be afraid*, she thought.

The beast pressed down harder on her arm with its claw— Indra could not help but gasp from the pain—and opened its mouth wide with a breathless hiss, exposing rows of needle-teeth, saliva running down them in long beaded threads. Indra closed her eyes, bracing herself for the end . . . and then the beast's mouth closed again.

Indra opened her eyes to see its vile face still encompassing her vision, still so close that she could feel the thick, coarse hairs that protruded from it brushing against her skin. Its mandibles twitched and it made a sound like a truffling pig as it sniffed at her, then drew back its head and shook it as though disoriented, confused. It snapped at the air with tooth and claw, its head now gyrating wildly, beset by some maddening sensation beyond Indra's own perception. And then it reared up with a tortured roar, removing the claw that had pinned her to the ground, and setting her free as it withdrew, yowling in distress and gnashing its teeth.

Indra found strength in her legs and scrambled backward across the ground, planting her good hand and pulling herself unsteadily to her feet, all the while watching the beast. It stamped its feet and lashed out blindly, fighting some unseen enemy through a haze of bewilderment and undirected rage. And then, with a final bellowing howl so filled with torment that for a brief moment Indra actually pitied it, the beast turned and took flight, still limping and bleeding as it crashed headlong into the forest. Indra stood and watched the trees shake and branches snap as the beast once more became a shadow in the darkness, the sound of its retreat growing fainter and fainter until finally it was gone.

Indra stood there for a moment at the center of the clearing, the perfect stillness of the forest returning to settle in around her. All that remained was the sound of her labored breathing as her chest heaved inward and out. And just as quickly as the outer calm returned, the inner one that had allowed Indra to face her own death free from fear drained away, replaced by an overwhelming sense of panic that sank deep into every pore. Without thought or reason she turned and fled, as fast as her bruised and aching body could manage. She bounded into the dense forest of trees without breaking stride, branches whipping at her and scratching at her face but slowing her not at all as her heart pounded deafeningly in her chest and she ran and ran and ran.

TWENTY

Wulfric woke as he did every morning, naked and half-buried in a heap of smoldering black ash that reeked of sulfur. He sat up with a groan, every muscle in his body aching, every bone ringing out like a struck tuning fork. It was just past dawn, the forest still shrouded in early-morning mist, sunlight shafting through the trees in a dull gray haze.

It was bitterly cold, but at least it was dry. Wulfric raked his fingers through his hair to shake loose the ash, then, bracing himself for the pain, rose to his feet and brushed as much as he could from his body, flakes of ash falling like fluttering snow to be carried away by the wind.

He looked around, trying to gain his bearings. He needed to find his way back to the clearing and recover his chain. He hoped he would find his cloak there, too; roaming the countryside naked in this cold weather neither appealed nor suited his intention to draw minimal attention to himself. But the chain was important most of all. The beast had been allowed too many nights of freedom—though last night could not be helped—and he would not allow it another.

His stomach gurgled and growled. He was hungry. Just another small but punishing detail of Aethelred's hateful curse: even when the beast fed, as it had last night, Wulfric always awoke feeling starved. But there would be time enough to forage for food once he was clothed and able to shackle himself once more.

He touched his hand to his stomach in a vain attempt to quiet it and noticed that the skin was rough and sore to the touch. He looked down and saw a long, jagged scar that ran from just above his genitals to his sternum. Evidence of an apparently deep and grievous wound, it looked relatively fresh but already well on its way to healing. Wulfric could not understand it. He did not recall sustaining any such wound, and even if he had, his body was remade whole each morning after the beast was gone.

Could his memory be failing him? Certainly his recollection of the waking nightmare he shared with the beast was muddled and hazy, more so than usual. He remembered, clearly enough, killing the two men, or at least watching helplessly as the beast within which his consciousness was imprisoned killed them. That distinction mattered little to him; he held himself responsible for each and every death all the same. He did not remember what became of the third man, but he remembered the girl striding toward the beast, as no one had ever done, standing before it defiantly and clashing her swords together. Goading it to fight her.

He found himself questioning whether that had really happened or if it was some lie of his hazy, half-remembered dreamstate. All he knew for sure was that everything after was a blur, a flurry of disjointed images and confusing sensations. He touched his belly again, recalling a sharp pain there, though from what he could not remember. He remembered feeling the searing fury and bloodlust of the beast's consciousness, as he always did, and summoning all his will in a desperate attempt to suppress it, even though he had proven time after time that all his efforts to stay the beast were useless.

But somewhere amidst that nightmarish cacophony, there had been . . . something. Some emotion that seemed to him now more vague and dream-like than all that surrounded it, so distant he could not place it. Yet in the moment, he had felt it more keenly than all else, and for the briefest instant it had armored him, made him immune to the beast's vile hatred and rage.

It was a strangely familiar sensation, and he struggled now to remember why that was so. It was—

He shook the thought away; it was confusing him, and besides, it mattered not. What mattered was that the girl was most certainly dead. None had come into such close contact with the beast and lived; the only variable was the manner in which they died. Sometimes it was mercifully quick; other times the beast was spiteful and would watch its victims suffer. Wulfric hoped that in the girl's case it had been the former. Though foolhardy and far too sure of herself in a world as dangerous as this, she was noble and good-hearted, and he had liked her. He despised himself anew for failing to find the strength to save her. Just one more soul for him to carry the rest of his days, a greater burden than the chain would ever be.

The chain. He could waste no more time in finding it.

The beast's footprints trampled into the forest floor provided all he needed to find his way back to the clearing. But, spotted along the forest floor and upon the leaves of ferns and other plants thereabouts was also a trail of blood as black as pitch. Wulfric touched his hand to a patch of it and brought it up to examine the rank, viscous fluid that stretched between his fingers like an oily spiderweb.

He had never seen the beast's blood before, but he had seen the blood of many like it—there could be no mistaking it. Wulfric wondered how the beast could possibly have been wounded, trying to recall but remembering nothing. And then he felt his stomach again, and realized where his scar had come from. It seemed that the beast's wound, however it might have been sustained, had somehow affected more than just the beast itself. Somehow it had carried over to him.

There was much to think about. He walked on, absentmindedly bringing his hand up beneath his chin and feeling around his neck where the sword had passed through it, decapitating him. He rolled his head from side to side as though trying to work out a crick. There was no scar, no sign of a wound, but that part of him ached most of all.

Indra was trying to make headway through a particularly wild and overgrown area of bracken.

Last night she had run without stopping or even slowing for a mile or more before her panic finally subsided and she slumped, exhausted, at the base of a tree and fell asleep. When she woke, she realized that she was completely lost. And as much as she hated the idea of returning to the clearing and all that had transpired there, she needed to recover her swords. She felt naked without them. Just making her way through this godforsaken forest would be so much easier with a blade to hack out a path, but she also expected that the abomination was still close by. She had wounded it—not enough to kill it but perhaps enough to keep it from fleeing very far. Why it had not killed her when it had the chance she could not fathom, but she was certain that she could not count on being so lucky a second time. If she came upon it again, she needed to be armed and ready.

When—not if, she corrected herself, for nothing about their first encounter had deterred her from her mission. If anything, she was more emboldened than ever. The beast had beaten her, yes, but she had been far from her best at the time, already injured and dazed from fighting those drunken brutes. Things would be different next time. The beast was wounded now, and she had learned much about it. She knew now how it moved, how it attacked, where it was vulnerable, how to make it bleed. Next time, the odds would be in her favor.

But first she needed her weapons, and she had no idea where to find them. The forest looked quite different in the daylight, and she had fled from the clearing in such a panic that she had no idea of her way back. She had been wandering for more than an hour and, for all she knew, was no closer than when she had begun.

She stopped to take a breath and also to gather herself, for she could feel herself growing frustrated with her lack of progress. Part of what was slowing her down, she knew, was her injury. She had been woken by the powerful, throbbing ache in her shoulder, and when she tested the arm was rewarded with a sharp pain that felt like being stabbed with a hot needle. If anything, it hurt worse than the night before; there was no doubt that the shoulder was out of joint and would have to be reset if she wanted use of the arm again.

That, she knew well enough how to do, from watching the procedure performed on initiates who had been injured in combat training, but she had been putting it off. She had been told by those who had endured it that getting the shoulder back into its socket hurt even worse than the initial injury, which at this moment she found difficult to imagine. It was that thought that had kept her from facing what needed to be done, but the persistent, painful ache had been growing steadily worse, as had her frustration at having to make her way through the forest's dense undergrowth one-handed. She could postpone no longer.

She found a tree, stout and strong. When she had seen it done in the training courtyard back home, it had been against a wooden post, but out here this would have to do. She stood facing the tree, her stance slightly askew, and lined up her lame shoulder against it. Rotating at the waist, she brought her shoulder slowly back then forward to touch gently against the bark of the tree—a practice arc to ensure she would make good contact. Still she hesitated. What if she was remembering this wrong? What if there were some subtle trick to it that she was missing? It had been so long ago when she had seen it done, and not up close but from several yards away. If she did this incorrectly, she might make the injury worse and damage her arm permanently.

She sighed, knowing she had no other option. She looked to the ground, found a stub of broken branch, and placed it between her teeth, biting down hard. Another moment's pause, then finally she drew back her shoulder and with all her might slammed it against the tree. As the pain shot through her, she bit down on the branch so hard that it splintered between her teeth.

Indra staggered backward, spitting out the broken branch and, finally, letting out a cry that shook the birds from the treetops overhead. Her eyes watered as she leaned forward, breathing heavily and wondering if she might vomit. But the nausea passed quickly, and as the pain too began to subside, Indra tried flexing her arm and found to her great relief that she could move it almost normally, and with only a dull ache. It had worked. She arched her back and looked up at the sky between the wavering treetops, taking a moment to relish this small victory, and to spit out the couple of small remnants of splintered wood still on her tongue.

Now what? She turned, taking in the forest surrounding her. She was just as lost as before, each direction looking just the same.

When she heard the creaking of a branch behind her, she spun, suddenly on guard. The forest was perfectly still. Her first thought was of the abomination, though she was quite sure that a beast of its size and weight could not stalk her undetected across terrain like this. But that was not the only predator that might be found deep in these woods. She would not feel safe again until she was armed. At this rate, it could be dark again before she—

She heard another sound, from above, and looked up. It was Venator, perched on a tree above her. He flapped his wings against the sunlight and Indra smiled for the first time in days. She could not remember ever seeing such a happy sight. Keenly, she raised her forearm for him to land on and called to him.

The hawk took off from the tree but flew right over her, alighting on another tree a short distance away. He looked back at her and uttered a caw that Indra had learned to identify. He wanted her to follow him. She might have been lost in this wilderness, but Venator would never be. He knew the way back.

The hawk spread his wings and took flight again, sailing away between the trees. With renewed energy in her stride, Indra went after him.

Wulfric arrived back at the clearing after following the trail of blood and trampled foliage for about half a mile. The beast, it seemed, had not traveled far before succumbing to the sleep that would disappear it from the world for another day. Perhaps it had been slowed by its wound, Wulfric considered, only to wonder again who or what could possibly have inflicted such an injury. In fifteen years of nightly horrors, Wulfric had seen the beast scythe its way through countless men and women. Some had died helplessly, while others had tried, hopelessly, to defend themselves. Some had even been armed, but not once could Wulfric recall the beast sustaining so much as a scratch. Over time he had come to wonder whether it even could be hurt. Years of experience had caused him to conclude that it could not, but as he had followed the trail of the beast's blood, for the first time he found cause to believe otherwise. What that might mean, for the beast, and for him . . .

He thought on it no longer; now was not the time for flights of fancy. He was accustomed to thinking only from one nightfall to the next. His one thought each and every day was to ensure that the beast was secured each and every night. For that he needed the chain.

In the clearing, the pools of blood that had dried into the grass where last night the bodies of the dead had fallen were a grim reminder not just of those the beast had killed, but of those whose lives Wulfric himself had taken willingly, by his own hand. A solemn vow broken after fifteen years. This thought, too, he pushed from his mind. The chain. The chain was all that mattered.

He exhaled, a sigh of relief. There it was, in a coil near the ashes of last night's campfire, just where he had left it. He made his way over to it at a keen jog and knelt to examine it more closely, further relieved to see that it was untouched and intact. Only now, with the day's most pressing concern lifted from his mind, did he allow himself to care about the fact that he was still, from top to toe, naked, his body covered only in the grimy black residue of the beast.

He stood again and looked for his cloak, but it was nowhere to be seen. Nor, it occurred to him now, were the bodies of most of the men who had died here last night. There was one nearby, the one who had threatened the girl. He was bled out from a sword wound clean through the center of him. Farther across the clearing was what remained of the big barrel-chested one, torn in two, entrails spilling from each ragged and bloody half of him, a feast for the carrion birds that would come down out of the trees to peck at them. But of the others there was no sign. Wulfric wondered what could have become of them until he noticed the trailing marks in the earth leading from the patches of blood where the dead had fallen and into the trees. Someone had dragged their bodies from here to there. Why, he could not fathom, but he knew now where he might find his cloak.

He followed the trail to the tree line and a few yards beyond, where he found the bodies of the missing men dumped among the bushes. Assuming that his body had been dragged out here similarly, he hunted for his cloak, glancing at the faces of the dead men as he searched, separating those he had killed from those the girl had, and thinking of how surprised he had been by her prowess in battle. Perhaps his own prejudice had led him to not expect much from a mere girl, in spite of the way she spoke and carried herself. Yet for all the courage she had shown, she had the skill to match. She was nimble and fast and precise, and more than anything, she had a true killer's instinct, much like his own before he had renounced the sword.

There had been no sign of her body in the clearing with the others, only her twin swords on the ground. The beast must have devoured her whole. The thought of that made him ache with sorrow. The knowledge that she was an Order initiate, who had by her own choosing sought out the beast, lessened it none. He tried to remember her name, for he was sure she had told him, and he hated himself that he could not. He was not sure why, only that he knew she deserved better than to be just another of the beast's—of *his*—nameless victims.

He found his cloak lying in the undergrowth. He picked it up and brushed away the loose dirt and leaves. It was damp from being left overnight on the wet ground, but would dry. The larger problem, Wulfric saw as he examined it, was that it was more tattered and torn than ever. A deep split ran along one side, no doubt caused by the beast's emergence from Wulfric's headless body while the cloak was still on it. That would have to be mended, which meant another town or village, another favor to beg. For now, he would make the best of it. He threw the cloak around himself, then made his way back through the trees to the clearing to begin the laborious task of wrapping his body in iron.

He was crouched beside the heap of coiled chain and starting to unravel it when he heard behind him the snapping of a twig and swung in its direction. A short distance away, at the edge of the clearing, stood the girl, just emerged from the trees. As Wulfric looked upon her, her name suddenly came rushing back to him. *Indra*.

She did not speak, nor move an inch. She simply stood, perfectly still, staring at him as though he were a ghost.

TWENTY-ONE

For the longest while, there was only the sound of a gentle breeze whispering through the treetops. Wulfric was as surprised to see Indra as she clearly was to see him. How could she have survived the beast? There was no scenario he could imagine in which it was possible. She could not have fought it off, nor escaped it; no one who had been so close ever had.

Slowly, Wulfric rose from his crouch, and that spurred Indra from the spot where she was rooted. She bolted to her left, to where one of her swords rested in the patchy grass, grabbed it up and held it defensively outward at Wulfric, though he was unarmed and thirty feet away.

Wulfric raised his palms slightly to stay her and indicate that he was not a threat, but Indra did not seem at all reassured. As Wulfric studied her more closely, he noticed that her sword arm was trembling. Another moment passed before she gulped down a breath and broke the silence between them.

"How are you alive?"

Wulfric hesitated, unsure what to say. The girl had seen him beheaded right in front of her, he realized. In all the chaos and confusion of the night, he had forgotten that small detail. Now he understood why she was looking at him so. To her, he was a ghost, a dead man somehow still walking the earth. It demanded an explanation, and he had none to give.

"Why would I not be?" he said, feigning confusion.

Indra shook the sword at him angrily. "You were killed last night! I saw it with my own eyes!"

Wulfric made a show of finding that amusing, a half laugh. "I think your eyes must have deceived you. If I had been killed, I am sure I would remember it." Deceit was his only option. The girl seemed sensible enough; perhaps she could be persuaded that what she saw now was more reliable than her memory of last night, since the alternative defied all reason.

"I know what I saw!" Indra said. "It happened not five feet from where I stood! I saw you beheaded, and then one of them dragged your body into the trees over there. *How are you alive?*"

Wulfric had no choice but to play this out. "All evidence to the contrary, as here I stand," he said calmly. "In the chaos and confusion of battle, the truth of events can easily be lost. What we saw is often not what we think we saw." Wulfric noticed the patch of dried, matted blood in Indra's hair and saw an opportunity to bolster his lie. "Did you by any chance take a blow to the head last night?"

That gave Indra pause. For the first time, her eyes left Wulfric, glancing away. Perhaps she was beginning to question herself. Wulfric saw the opening and pressed. "Which is the more rational explanation? That I was killed and have miraculously risen from the dead? Or that you are simply confused?"

Her eyes returned to Wulfric, now tempered by a hint of doubt. "All right then," she said. "You tell me. What did happen?"

"As I recall, I, too, took a blow to the head," he said, making up the tale as he went. "I was coming to your aid, then I was hit from behind and all went black. That is the last thing I remember. I woke up over there, in the trees, surrounded by the bodies of the men we killed. You are gifted with a sword, by the way. Truly, I was impressed." If there was one thing that Wulfric remembered from his former life, it was that flattery was often a useful tactic when in trouble with a woman.

Indra lowered the point of her sword from chest to waist height—still on her guard, just not quite so much as before. Wulfric saw her struggle to reconcile what her senses and her memory were telling her, both equally clear and yet at odds with one another. It pained him to use her own sense of reason against her, but he could not tell her the truth. He needed her to believe the lie so that he could be rid of her, for both their sakes.

"I am relieved to see you alive," he said, only the second true thing he had told her this morning. "But it will take some time for you to recover from what happened last night. Not just physically— I have seen this many times. The fog of war plays tricks with our emotions and our memory. But in time your mind will clear and you will remember things as they were."

Though still unsettled, Indra composed herself. "I remember the abomination clearly enough," she said. "And I have the scars to prove it. You are lucky it didn't tear you to pieces as it did the others."

Wulfric realized there was an opportunity now to get answers of his own, but carefully.

"An abomination was here?" he asked, feigning disbelief as best he could.

Indra nodded. "The one I have been hunting. It came from the trees over there and killed two of those men," she said, pointing. "See there, what remains of them."

"And what did you do?" asked Wulfric. He knew part of it, of course—that she had foolhardily approached and challenged the beast—but he desperately needed to know the rest. How could she possibly have survived? To him, seeing her alive defied any rational explanation—much as seeing Wulfric alive had done to Indra.

"I did battle with it," she said. "It almost killed me, but I wounded it and it fled, back into the forest."

This time Wulfric did not have to feign disbelief. It wrote itself all over his face, and Indra saw it.

"What?" she said, indignant.

"Forgive me, but I have never heard of anyone surviving such an encounter," he said.

"You forget, sir, that I am not *anyone*. I am an initiate of the Order, trained to fight and kill abominations."

It was true that she could fight, and fight well. Wulfric had seen that for himself. But still, that she could have survived alone against a beast that Wulfric had seen kill so many was impossible. He stepped forward, looking at her hard. "What really happened? How did you get away? Tell me the truth, girl."

His tone, now gravely serious, perhaps betrayed too much of Wulfric's own interest in the matter, but Indra did not notice. All she heard was the insult, and to her, none could be worse. Her nostrils flared, and now she took a marching stride toward Wulfric. "*Get away?* You think I *fled* from it? How dare you! Do you think I'm a coward?"

"I think you are not telling the whole truth. It is not possible that you could have fought such a beast as that and survived."

"And what makes you such an expert?" she spat back, and because he could not tell her the truth, Wulfric had no answer.

Not content with having silenced him, Indra was determined to prove herself. She lifted up her jerkin on her right side, exposing her bare ribs. Her flesh looked painfully bruised, an ugly mottle of purple and brown. "See here, where it charged at me and nearly broke my ribs!"

"You could have sustained that in the battle with those thugs," said Wulfric, which only made Indra more determined. She scanned the ground around her. When she saw what she was looking for, she marched over and picked it up.

"See here, where the thing wrapped its vile tongue around my wrist!" She handed Wulfric the rotted leather gauntlet, which still smelled vaguely of sulfur. "If you know anything of abominations, as you claim to, then you know that their spittle is like acid. I had to tear this off before it burned through to my skin." Indra left Wulfric to study the ruined gauntlet and turned around again, looking for something else. She spotted it a few yards away and went hurriedly to retrieve it.

"Here!" She bent over to pick the thing up from the grass and Wulfric saw that it was her other sword, stained with a thick, oily substance that he recognized as the beast's blood. Indra held up the blade to show him. "The black blood of an abomination! Do you smell the sulfur? There is no mistaking it. And over there, the trail it left as it fled, bleeding from the wound I gave it!"

Wulfric did not need to look; it was the same trail that had led him back here. In fact, the realization finally dawned on him that she was telling the truth. She really had fought the beast and survived, and more than that, she had actually hurt it, wounded it. Wounded *him*.

"Why are you looking at me like that?" said Indra, no doubt unnerved by Wulfric's suddenly dumbfounded expression. For his mind reeled with the repercussions of something that he had thought impossible. And with the seed of an idea—for the first time in so many years, a glimmer of hope, so faint he dare not nurture it, and yet he did so all the same, for the promise of what might, just might, be possible was so alluring he could not resist. *Peace. Freedom.* Things that felt so distant, so ancient, that he barely remembered them, had long ago given up any thought of ever reclaiming them.

But now . . . what if it were possible? What if he could—

"Hello?"

Indra's voice snapped Wulfric from his reverie. "I'm sorry," he said, returning to the moment. "What?"

"You were looking at me strangely," said Indra, regarding him warily. Wulfric noticed that her grip had tightened around the hilt of her sword, stained with the beast's blood. His blood.

"You wounded the beast," he said, his tone hushed, as though the truth of it were so fragile he dared not speak it aloud. "Made it bleed."

Indra relaxed a little. "I'm glad we have that settled. I don't like to be thought a liar, worse still a coward." She wiped the blood from her blade with a rag from her pocket then returned both swords to the scabbards crossed against her back.

Wulfric so wanted to believe, but he would not gamble his hopes, nascent though they were, on anything less than surety. "Where exactly did you cut the beast?" he asked.

"It charged at me, tried to trample me," said Indra. "I slid beneath it and raised up my sword as it passed over me, cutting it along its belly." Dramatically, she mimed the act of raising the sword overhead. Wulfric's hand instinctively began to move toward his own stomach, to the long scar there beneath his cloak. His wound and the beast's were one and the same. He was not yet certain that it meant what he hoped it did, but . . .

He needed this girl.

"I would advise you not to stay here," Indra said as she scanned the trees watchfully. "Wounded, the beast will not have fled far and is likely still about. Go back to town. You'll be safer there."

"And you?" said Wulfric. Moments ago he'd been anxious to be rid of her. Now more than anything he needed her to stay. All his new hopes depended on it.

"I mean to finish what I began. I will return home when the beast is slain, and not before. But you must be on your way. I bid you well."

She turned and headed toward the trees, leaving Wulfric to think. This would not do. Yes, the girl was skilled, and she had fought the beast and made it bleed, but her partial victory was surely a fluke, and one that would likely not be repeated. He needed the odds at their next encounter to be far better. He did not relish what he would have to do but could think of no better option.

"Wait!"

She stopped and looked back, her brow furrowing at the sight of him following along behind her. "I said, you must—"

"Is it wise to go after the beast again so soon?" said Wulfric, in a cautionary tone.

Indra's expression suggested that she did not appreciate her tactics being called into question. "Wiser than allowing it time to rest and lick its wounds. My best chance is to follow its trail now, while it is still bleeding and hurt."

Wulfric could not tell her—not yet—that setting out by day would be useless, that the blood trail would lead her nowhere, as the beast she sought was slumbering invisibly within him. Or that by the time it emerged again tonight, its wound would most likely be gone, and it reborn whole again and back to its full strength. He would need another tack to delay her, at least for the moment. Because though it would need to be dealt out carefully, his best course now was the truth.

"What of your wounds?" he said. "Your ribs are bruised and will slow you in a battle, and you cannot hope to fight effectively until you have full use of that shoulder you dislocated." He pointed. "You made a good job of setting it, but it will not be as it was for at least another day."

Indra's hand went to her shoulder. The hitch in her movement was barely perceptible, yet Wulfric had noticed that she had had some small difficulty extending her arm over her back to replace her sword in its scabbard.

"I cannot afford a day," she said.

"A few hours, then," he said. "Stay awhile and allow me to thank you."

"For what?"

"For my rudeness at the fireside last night, and for your kindness back at the crossroads. And if I was unconscious when the beast came, then you surely saved my life by driving it away."

"That is my job. I require no thanks for doing it."

"My honor demands otherwise," Wulfric said. "Please, take pity on an old man and lend him some company."

It seemed to Indra an odd thing to say. He did not look that old to her, although it was difficult to be sure behind the matted beard and caked-on grime that covered his face. But then, everything about him was odd, this strange, disheveled man who spoke of honor and wielded a sword more skillfully even than her father, a master knight. Who seemed to know so much about so many things, and who carried a heavy iron chain for reasons that still eluded her. There was nothing about him that did not baffle or intrigue her in some way.

And he was right about her shoulder. It was not yet fully mended and did not have as much ease and freedom of motion as she would need when next she faced the beast. Relenting, she let out a sigh. "One hour, no more. On one condition."

Wulfric smiled, and Indra realized it was the first time she had seen him do so.

"Name it," he said.

She glanced over to the coil of heavy iron on the ground behind Wulfric. "You must tell me why you carry the chain," she said, wondering how he would react. The last time she had asked about it, he had suddenly grown angry and ordered her away.

Wulfric hesitated for a moment before agreeing with a nod. He motioned for her to sit and began gathering wood for a fire. Indra watched him as he went back and forth, seemingly deep in thought, and wondered what was occupying him so.

Wulfric wondered how he would go about telling her the truth.

She had asked about the chain, so perhaps that would be a good place to start. Or better to start at the beginning, with the story of who he once was and how he had become this monstrous, tortured shadow of himself? However the story was to be told, it would require great care if he were to enlist her help.

But more than anything, he hoped. He knew it was dangerous to do so. There were so many ways in which his plan might fail. To raise his hopes after having given up on them so long ago . . . But he could not stop thinking of it. The long scar on his belly seemed to burn as his pulse quickened with excitement:

If the beast can bleed, then it can die. And so can I.

TWENTY-TWO

Together they shared the labors of lunch, Indra skinning and cleaning the rabbit that Venator dropped at her feet after a short hunt, and Wulfric roasting it over the fire he had made. They ate in silence, Indra waiting patiently for Wulfric to tell her about the chain. But as the meal went on, he appeared no closer to doing so. He seemed to be lost in thought, much as he had been the night before, and he gazed absently into the fire as he ate. Indra was hesitant to press him; she had seen enough to deduce that the chain held a special, private significance for him. But she would not leave his fireside again without an answer to this riddle.

"It just occurred to me," she said casually as she licked warm grease from her fingers, "you never told me your name."

Wulfric glanced up from the fire to see Indra looking at him expectantly. It was an innocuous-enough question, after all. Still, he found himself unable to summon the word to his lips. It had been fifteen years since last he had uttered it, in part because he no longer thought of himself as that person. He was something else now, something not worthy of the name his mother and father had given him. To even think it now reminded him of all that he had lost, all that the beast within him had destroyed. Would saying it aloud make him feel the pain of those memories all the more keenly?

Perhaps, but then, what choice did he have? Eventually he would have to tell the girl more, much more, than just his name. He would have to tell her the whole truth if his plan were to succeed. He had been wondering where in all of it to start as he ate the rabbit that the girl's hawk had caught, and he saw now that perhaps this would be the simplest place, with the name of the man he had once been.

"Wulfric," he said finally. He took a breath and tossed a bone onto the fire. It felt strange to hear himself say it, though not as painful as he had feared. The girl appeared to react as though the name sounded somehow odd to her, but made little else of it.

"How did you come to live this way?" Indra asked. She hoped to learn not just the story of the great chain the man carried, but of the man himself. Everything about him was an enigma. He was more erudite and mannered than any vagrant she had ever encountered. Were it not for his appearance, she might have taken him for a nobleman. Perhaps one who had somehow fallen from grace, she surmised, though even now, in his wretched state, there was more grace about him than most true nobles she had known, including her own father.

Wulfric sighed, tossed away the last of the rabbit carcass he had been picking at, and finally looked her squarely in the eye. Indra had always read people well, and what she saw now, to her satisfaction, was a man who had resigned himself, albeit reluctantly, to tell her his story. At last. Eagerly, she leaned forward.

"Once, long ago, I was a soldier," he began. "In the service of King Alfred. I . . ." He faltered, unsure how to continue. Or perhaps loath to; it was difficult for Indra to tell. He looked back to the fire, turning inward again, some deep and long-nursed conflict roiling within him. Suddenly he sprang to his feet, so swiftly it startled her, then paced back and forth, his head bowed in tortured contemplation. Eventually he turned to face her. "I am sorry," he said with a look of genuine remorse. "This is more difficult than I had

imagined." And Indra saw now that there was more than just contrition in his eyes. There was shame.

She rose to her feet. "Whatever you may have done," she said,
"I will not judge you for it."

Wulfric grunted and made a face that might have been a dark
half smile, beneath the grime and tangled beard. "An easy promise
to make prior to hearing the confession," he said.

"Then let me hear it." She stepped closer to him and placed a
hand compassionately on his arm. Then she winced at the dull but
powerful ache blossoming in her injured shoulder.

"Your shoulder still pains you," said Wulfric, seizing on the
opportunity to talk of something, anything, else.

Indra placed her other hand on her shoulder. "It's nothing,"
she said, but she could not disguise the discomfort.

Wulfric took her by the arm. "Here, let me show you."

Indra's natural instinct at being grabbed by any man would
have been to break the hold, and perhaps the man's arm with it,
and pull away, but for reasons passing her understanding, she did
not. She stood still, subdued by the intensity of Wulfric's gaze. Still,
"You promised to tell me," she began, haltingly.

"There will be time enough for stories after. Move your hand
away."

She hesitated, so Wulfric reached up and pried her hand from
her shoulder, then clapped his own firmly over it, though he did
not hurt her. "Be still," he said as he gripped her shoulder, squeez-
ing it in several places, feeling every muscle and sinew. "Mmm,"
he murmured with a knowing nod. Then he released her arm and
stepped back.

Widening his stance, Wulfric reached over his shoulder with
one arm then raised his other up behind his back and held it by
the wrist. Indra watched with puzzled amusement as he contorted
himself.

"Like so," he said, and only then did she realize that he meant
for her to mimic him. Self-consciously she did so, reaching over

her back as Wulfric nodded his approval. Her shoulder cried out in pain, more than it had since she had reset it, and she might have quit but that Wulfric hurried forward and kept her at it, helping to ease her arm into place.

"Are you sure you know what you're doing?" she said as she grimaced through the pain. "It hurts worse than before!"

"Which would you prefer," said Wulfric. "Pain now, or a feeble sword arm later? Trust me." And though her shoulder burned, she allowed him to guide her arm back far enough for her other hand to reach behind her and grab it by the wrist. When she had done so, Wulfric stepped back.

"Good. Now slowly pull down, as far as you are able, ten times."

She did so, trying to ignore the pain and the feeling that she must look as absurd as Wulfric had when he demonstrated the position. When she was done, she released her wrist and gasped with relief as she brought her arm back to her side.

"How does it feel now?" asked Wulfric.

Indra tried flexing and rolling her shoulder again and was surprised to discover that the discomfort, while still present, was a faint shadow of what she had felt just moments before the exercise.

"Better," she said, with amazement. "Much better."

Wulfric nodded and gave as much of a smile as the man appeared capable. "Repeat that exercise every hour, and by tonight the pain will be gone and your arm will be as strong as it ever was. If you—" He halted, suddenly aware that the look of pleasant surprise on Indra's face had turned to something that looked more like shock. She was no longer looking directly into his eyes but lower, at the center of his body.

"You did not have that scar yesterday," she said.

Wulfric looked down and saw that his cloak had fallen open along the split in its side as he had stretched to adjust Indra's arm. It was still loosely belted at the waist, but his torso was exposed upward of that point. Though his flesh was discolored gray from the ash that clung to it, the dark scar that ran from beneath his belt and along the center of his stomach to the top of his ribcage was clearly visible. He opened his mouth to speak, unsure what he planned to say, but Indra cut him off.

"Last night as we ate, you adjusted your cloak, and I saw that you had many scars—but not that one. Nor did you sustain it last night in battle." Her eyes narrowed. "And what . . . is *that*?"

She marched forward, looking closer. The black burn mark in the center of his chest had not been clearly visible the night before, amidst the firelight, but now, in the broad light of day, it could not be more prominent. It was like an emblem seared into his flesh, a human cattle brand in the unmistakable form of—she looked closer to be absolutely sure—a *beetle*.

Her eyes widened in alarm and she bolted backward, almost stumbling, so sudden was her retreat. She reached back and unsheathed one of her swords, holding it toward Wulfric. As she stared at him in horror, he could see the realization dawn.

"The mark of the beast is on you," she said through gritted teeth. "So is its stink. I thought the sulfur I smelled came only from my blade where I wounded it . . . but it's coming from you!"

Wulfric pulled his cloak around him and refastened his belt. He felt a sense almost of relief as he stood there, content to let the girl arrive at the truth by her own deduction. This, surely, was better than having to find a way to tell her himself. The challenge now was to keep her calm, to talk some sense into her and keep her from doing something rash, as she seemed heavily inclined to do.

"You should put down the sword," he said calmly. He took one careful step toward her, palms raised. "I mean you no harm."

"Come no closer, I warn you!" she spat back. "Or I will be the one to harm you!"

"What do you propose to do?" said Wulfric dryly. "Cut off my head? As you have already seen, it takes more than that."

Indra's face was hot, her chest heaving as she struggled to contain the sense of alarm welling up within her. Alarm that, if not properly managed, could quickly grow into debilitating panic. She centered herself, pushing it down deep, doing everything she knew to keep herself in the present moment. And, as she often did, she relied upon the one honest emotion from which she could always draw strength when she needed it most: anger. She spat on the ground and looked back at Wulfric fiercely. "I should have known better, known to trust my own senses, my own memory, for never once have they failed me. But you were so very persuasive, weren't you? An expert liar, just as the legend says!"

Wulfric furrowed his brow, puzzled. "Oh, yes," Indra went on, "I have heard the stories, from others in the Order, of an abomination unlike any other, one that takes the form of a man by day and shows its true self only by night. One that lies and deceives in order to hide among men, only to slaughter them when they are least suspecting. I always dismissed it as a myth, told to new initiates to frighten them, but now I see it is the truth! Was that your plan? To delay me here long enough that you might kill me after nightfall? Speak the truth, beast, if you can!"

For a moment, Wulfric just looked at Indra in silence, caught in her steely glare. Then, to both their surprise, he began to laugh. It was little more than a chuckle, but it served to inflame Indra's anger further. She stepped toward him, sword arm outstretched. "Mock me at your peril," she hissed.

Wulfric saw that his involuntary outburst had only worsened matters and stifled it, turning his attention to the point of Indra's sword, which was now less than a foot from his nose.

"I did not mean to offend," he said. "And unless you wish to, I suggest you remove that sword from the vicinity of my face."

His tone might have caused a lesser man to drop his sword and flee, but did nothing to cow Indra. If anything, her sword arm stiffened. "No wonder you know so much about abominations and the Order. How many of my brothers-in-arms have you killed? How many innocent men, women, and children? Oh, what a prize your head will make! You—"

What happened next was too fast for Indra to fully perceive. There was a sudden blur of movement from Wulfric, and almost instantaneously she felt something hard as a wooden club come down on her sword arm. She cried out and drew it back, clutching her wrist, which now rang with such pain that she feared it was broken.

Instinctively, she sprang backward, away from Wulfric. The sword she had held in her hand not a blink of an eye ago was now in his. She hastily drew her other blade, and held it outward against the one he had taken from her. For a moment, the two stood like that, sword lengths apart, Indra on guard to defend herself against an attack.

"You are good, child, but not that good," said Wulfric wearily. "If I wanted to kill you, I would not need to take the form of a beast to do it." He lowered the sword, then tossed it toward her, the blade sticking into the earth at Indra's feet. She snatched it up, realizing as she did so that the pain in her wrist had already begun to subside. Wulfric now stood before her unarmed, having given up the sword as readily as he had taken it.

"Your arm will hurt for a while, but it is not injured," he said. "As I said, I have no wish to harm you."

"Another trick," she spat back defiantly. "Another lie!"

Wulfric just shook his head. "I swear, I have never encountered a person possessed of such intelligence and yet so disinclined to use it. Think, girl! If I meant to kill you, would I have helped mend your shoulder? Or tried to send you away from my fire? Or fought by your side?"

Indra's eyes betrayed a flicker of doubt. "Perhaps not as a man, but in the form of the beast, your intention to kill me last night was more than apparent."

Wulfric nodded. "True, but there was little I could do to prevent that. As I recall, you were the one who picked that particular fight. Marching up to the beast full of piss and vinegar and goading it into battle. Or do I remember wrongly?"

Another flicker of doubt, again quickly quashed. "So you admit it. You and the abomination are one and the same! Shape-shifter!"

"I admit it," said Wulfric. "But the truth of the tale is not as you have been told. There is more to it than you know. The chain, over there, is part of it. I had begun to tell you this before you leapt to your own half-founded conclusions. I still will tell you the whole truth, if you will agree to listen."

Though Indra's sword did not lower, Wulfric could see that his words were taking hold. There was more doubt than certainty now, though still enough of the latter to keep her cautious.

"Indra, I have not known you long, but long enough to see how prone you are to anger, how quickly that red mist descends and clouds your judgment. I would guess that it has steered you down the wrong path more often than you would like. Do not make that mistake now. I ask you to look beyond your anger for a moment and ask yourself what you really believe. If I am really your enemy."

He watched her carefully, hoping that he had not missed his guess about her. He was within striking distance of her blade, and he doubted that he could rely on the same trick to disarm her again. That had been enough of a gambit the first time. The truth was, she was better with those swords than he had admitted—among the best he had ever seen.

Finally, after what seemed like an interminable moment, Indra lowered the point of her sword a fraction—not enough to give up her defensive advantage, but enough to indicate a glimmer of trust. "If you try to deceive me, or trick me in any way . . ."

"I will not. I swear it," said Wulfric. "In fact, I believe I can help you."

"Help me? How?"

"You must slay an abomination and return to the Order with its head as proof of the deed, yes? I can help you do that. And I ask only one small favor in return."

Indra's eyes narrowed in suspicion, some inner sense clearly telling her that she would not like this bargain, tempting as it sounded. "What kind of favor?"

Wulfric turned and went back to the campfire, which had begun to die. He picked up a gnarled hunk of branch and stoked the embers with it before throwing it onto the fire. He sat back down, cross-legged, and warmed the palms of his hands as the flames rose up around the fresh wood, causing it to crackle and spit. Only then did he look back at her.

"I want you to kill me."

TWENTY-THREE

As the day wore on, Wulfric told Indra his tale, though not all of it. Some details, he discovered in the course of the telling, were too painful to recollect, much less recount, and, he reasoned, were not necessary to convey to the girl what he needed her to know and understand. Indra stood—still not trusting enough to sit—and listened as Wulfric sat by the fire and told her of his time as a young soldier in the service of Alfred the Great—though not how he had once saved his King's life and gained a knighthood as well as Alfred's undying gratitude and friendship. Such details, true though they were, seemed boastful, and this was not a story in which to take pride.

He told her that as part of his military service, he had enlisted in a newly founded order charged with hunting down the mad Archbishop Aethelred, and his demonic horde—but not that the King had commissioned him personally to found it and recruit its members; that, too, seemed prideful. He told her of the bitter final battle with Aethelred and of the special, most hateful curse the archbishop had placed upon him as his wizened hand burned the beetle medallion into Wulfric's flesh, though he took no credit for killing Aethelred and ending his reign of chaos and terror.

And he told her that he had sent himself into exile after realizing what he had then become. He could not bring himself to share the details of how he had first come to realize it. The memory of that day, so long ago now, that he woke in a barn covered in ash to discover that he had slaughtered every man, woman, and child in his home village, including his own beloved wife and newborn child, was simply too agonizing to revisit.

Indra took in every word, sometimes standing still, other times pacing back and forth, but never once taking her eye off the storyteller—at first because she still did not trust him and was watching like a hawk for any sudden move or sign of deception, but by the end because the tale, incredible and tragic as it was, so commanded her attention. And when the telling was done, she finally sat, slumping to the ground by the fire in a way that Wulfric took as a further indication of trust but was borne more out of exhaustion, the tale having taken as much of a toll on the listener as it had the teller.

For a while the two sat like that, on opposite sides of the fire, in silence. For what was there to be said? Wulfric went back to staring into the dancing flames, and the sorrowful look in his eyes seemed all the greater now that Indra knew the truth behind it. For her part she remained silent, not because she could think of nothing to say but because she had so many questions that she barely knew where to start. Finally, she arrived back at where this had all begun.

"The chain . . ."

Wulfric glanced over at it, the misshapen spool of gray iron taking on a golden hue in the failing light of late afternoon. "The only way I am able to restrain the beast when it emerges," he said. "Before the end of each day, I must shackle myself so that when the change comes upon me at nightfall, it can harm no one."

"When you become this beast, you can't control yourself?"

Wulfric shook his head grimly. "Oh, how I have tried. But I am never strong enough. When the beast wakes, it is as though I am paralyzed within it, aware of its actions but powerless to influence them. And so, the chain is all I have."

Indra thought on this for a moment. "You speak of the beast as though you and it are not one and the same, but as though it is a separate being, with its own mind, independent of yours."

Wulfric spat into the fire, waved his hand dismissively. "To describe that thing as having a mind is to give it entirely too much credit. It has its own consciousness, for I can sense it alongside my own, but it does not think or reason as you and I understand those things. It is driven by something lower, lower even than animal instinct. A desire, an urge to inflict suffering and death so profound that while I can feel it, I cannot describe it. I cannot . . ." Wulfric trailed off. Indra watched as he took a moment to compose himself, to push down whatever dark feeling was welling up within him. "In truth, where the beast ends and I begin, I do not know. All I know is that its will is more powerful than my own."

"So you are conscious, even as it is conscious," said Indra, realizing as she spoke that she did so now in a tone more hushed than before, as though to speak of the beast too loudly might somehow awaken it. "Everything it experiences . . . you experience?"

"Sometimes more than others," said Wulfric. "There have been times when I have seen the faces of the people it has killed with perfect clarity, heard every scream, even tasted the blood as the monster feasts. Other times I experience it only as a kind of nightmare, vague images and sensations, a kind of madness I cannot comprehend. Often, before the chain, I would wake with no recollection of the carnage the beast had wrought the night before, only a sickening sensation in my gut and whatever bloody evidence it had left behind." Wulfric motioned across the clearing to where the remains of the thugs that the beast had slaughtered last night were still splayed across the bloodstained earth, and Indra shuddered.

A quiet moment passed as she thought on how to phrase her next question, one that had been begging to be asked for some time. She leaned closer. "Forgive me, but . . . how exactly does it work? The change, from man to beast, and back again?"

Wulfric shrugged. "Sometime after nightfall I begin to experience convulsions, spasms that contort my body. They grow ever more violent until at last I lose consciousness. Then there is pain and blindness, and then the madness, the nightmare, descends and I am within the beast. I awake sometime after dawn, covered in sulfuric ash—the remnants, I presume, of the transformation back to my human self. What any of this looks like I cannot say, for I have never witnessed it, nor have any others lived to tell the tale." And with that, he looked up at the sky and stood. "You will be the first."

Indra leapt to her feet, her defensive instincts not yet fully quieted, though she did not reach for a sword. "What do you mean?"

Wulfric ambled over to where the coil of iron chain sat and began slowly to unwind it. "For a long time, I believed that I could not die. That first year of the curse, I tried. Every way you could imagine. I tied myself to a heavy stone and let myself sink to the bottom of a deep lake, where I drowned. I talked my way into fights with violent men and let them cut my throat. Once, I walked all the way to the sea and threw myself from the tallest cliff, to be dashed against the rocks below. Each time I was reborn within the beast that very night. There was a time, long ago, when some people who had discovered what I was burned me at the stake in their village square. The next morning, I was alive and they were all dead, slaughtered in the night by the beast risen from my ashes. After that, I came to understand that my inability to die, or at least to stay dead, was part of my penance, that I must carry this curse with me for all eternity. But you have shown me otherwise."

The sinking feeling that had begun to creep up on Indra deepened. "How have I done that?"

Wulfric continued to unravel the chain, inspecting each link as he did so for any sign of a kink or flaw. A daily ritual.

"As a man, I know that I cannot be killed, and for a long time I believed that the beast could not either, for all those who have tried have failed. And there have been many. Skilled men, armed men, none of whom ever so much as scratched its hide. Until you did this to it." He set down the chain and turned to face her, opening his cloak to the scar that snaked upward from navel to nipple. "You proved that the beast can be hurt, that it can bleed as any abomination bleeds, and more—that whatever is done to it is done to me. If the beast's wound is also my wound, then perhaps its death is also my death. Do you understand?"

Indra shook her head. She understood it well enough, but she did not want to accept it. "You cannot be sure that it would work," she offered meekly.

"Perhaps not," said Wulfric, returning to the chain. "But it is in both our interests to try. I have no desire to live this cursed existence for even one more day if there is indeed a way to escape from it. And for you—once dead, the beast's corpse is yours to do with as you wish. Cut off its head and return it to the Order. Claim your prize. Tell them whatever heroic tale you care to. It matters not to me."

He took the chain and began to drag it toward a nearby tree. "It will be night soon," he said. "I will chain myself, which I must do whether you agree to this bargain or not. When the beast emerges, it will still be a danger—do not underestimate it even when imprisoned. But its underside is vulnerable, as you have so ably shown, and shackled against the tree, it will be exposed. I believe you are more than equal to the task. Do we have an agreement?"

Indra had dreamed of slaying an abomination her whole life. Not once had she imagined it might be like this. Never anything like this. To have her prey served up to her for the killing like a rat caught in a trap—where was the honor in that?

But then hadn't she already earned honor enough? Though she said nothing, she was offended by Wulfric's suggestion that she manufacture some story of false heroism. She knew that she had shown plenty of the real sort when she willingly faced the beast and proved herself against it in mortal combat. She had made it bleed, shown it that she was not just another helpless, terrified, screaming victim.

Something about that encounter nagged at her, but she set it aside and told herself something else: *This isn't about honor. It's about revenge. Take it however you can.*

She gave Wulfric a nod. Satisfied, he began the work of walking the chain around the tree to wrap it in iron. As he did so, Indra looked up at the clouds forming in the darkening sky and asked herself how she could be getting everything she had ever wished for and yet still feel such uncertainty. Such dread.

Indra watched in grim fascination as Wulfric went about his task, observing the care and detail with which he performed it—the mark of a man who knew the importance of a job well-done and who had perfected it through years of practice. He made only one deviation from his normal routine; he did not remove his cloak, partly to spare Indra's blushes, but mostly because he hoped never to need it again. If she did her job as agreed, Wulfric and the beast would die as one, and he would no longer have any use for earthly possessions.

At first she had watched him closely, from a distance of a few feet, but Wulfric had told her to move farther back and pointed to a large rock several yards away. The beast, he reminded her, might not be able to move while shackled, but it could still lash out with a tongue or an outstretched claw or a gob of lethal saliva. And so she witnessed the last of the ritual from there, her back resting against the smooth rock, knees drawn up to her chest to protect against the cold that the onset of night was ushering in, and Venator perched watchfully over her. She watched as he sat at the base of the tree and brought the chain over his head and around his chest, using both arms to wind it tighter around him. She noticed that he left enough slack to account for the greater size of the beast. As a man, he might be able to wriggle loose from his own bonds; the beast would find itself bound tightly in iron.

One final touch. Wulfric slipped a padlock between two links to fasten the chain around him, then turned the key to secure it. He set the key down on the ground nearby, but after regarding it for a moment, picked it up again and tossed it away, out of his reach. Indra realized that he intended never to need it again.

The time after that passed strangely. Dusk turned to night, and the darkness seemed to amplify the silence between her and Wulfric as the two of them sat, some distance apart, her watching him closely and him gazing off into the forest. There was a serenity about him she had not seen until now, his mind already in some faraway other place, a place he hoped his soul would soon follow. She asked him if he wanted to talk; just to break the silence, she said. In truth, she wondered if he might have any final words, anything he wished to unburden himself of before he died—before she ended his life. But she could not bring herself to say it that way.

Wulfric seemed to discern her meaning anyway, but said no, all he wanted to do now was sleep. To really, at last, sleep, the way he remembered from long ago, and to never wake. And he thanked her, which took her by surprise.

"For what?" she asked.

"For freeing me," he said. "I had given up hope long ago, but when I first saw you, something within me told me that you offered it. I cannot explain it. I knew, somehow, that you were a merciful soul, that you would do me a great kindness. Know that I am grateful for it."

Indra looked away, suddenly feeling ashamed, unworthy. "What mercy or kindness there is in ending a man's life, I fail to see," she said.

"If you had lived mine," he said, in a voice so weary that it had become little more than a whisper, "you would know."

For a while Indra kept her eyes off him, watching instead the subtle movements of leaves in the wind, listening to the gentle sounds they made as the night air wafted between them. Anything to avoid looking at the man she had pledged to kill. *Not a man*, she reminded herself. *An abomination, just not in the form you expected. But like any other, one that has killed countless innocents, and will kill many more if you do not see this through.*

Finally, she looked back at the tree where Wulfric sat. As the last of the day's light had faded, he had been partially hidden by the broad shadow cast by the tree's boughs, but now the darkness of night had moved in and consumed the rest of him. Now he was just a black shape set against what little pale moonlight penetrated the canopy of leaves above him. Unmoving.

"Wulfric?"

He did not answer. Indra slid her back up along the smooth stone she rested against until she had risen to her feet. Warily, she peered into the darkness beneath the tree. As her eyes slowly adjusted to the night, she was able to see that Wulfric had slumped forward against the chain. His head hung low against his chest, a mop of tangled hair obscuring his face. So still he barely seemed to breathe.

"Wulfric?"

Still nothing. She took a step closer. Venator, from his perch on the rock behind her, squawked and flapped his wings, a warning. Indra silenced him with a wave of her hand and took another step, close enough now that the beast might be able to reach her, but Wulfric was not yet a beast, still just a man. She found herself wondering how quickly the transformation occurred. Could the monster burst out from within suddenly, without warning, and catch her by surprise? She doubted it, while admitting that the things she had seen since first meeting this man gave her little cause to doubt that anything was possible.

She was aware that her curiosity might be endangering her and kept a close eye on the distance that separated her from him— from it. Satisfied that it was still sufficient for her to react speedily should the need arise, she took one more step closer. It was then, as her foot touched down gently on the soft earth, that Wulfric's head suddenly snapped back, fully upright against the trunk of the tree, his eyes wide open.

Indra sprang backward. Her face flushed red as a hot jolt shot through her, radiating outward into every muscle and sinew—her body arming her to either fight or flee. But she did neither, rooted to the spot and fixated on the man bound to the tree before her.

Moments ago, she could not bring herself to look at him. Now she could not look away. The position of the moon had changed; now its light shafted through the gaps in the canopy of leaves and fell directly upon Wulfric. In that pale swath of light, Indra saw that though his eyes were open, it was no longer him. The warmth, the spark, the life she had come to recognize in those eyes, was gone. These—and she had seen enough to know—were the eyes of a dead man. And yet still he moved, a puppet now controlled by some wild and inhuman force within him.

His body began to shudder and twitch, not greatly at first, but soon he was writhing and thrashing uncontrollably, only the chain around him holding him in place. Indra had once seen a man in the throes of a convulsive fit, his entire body racked by spasms so violent it took three others to hold him down while his back contorted to the point of almost breaking. This was worse.

The thing that had been Wulfric opened wide his mouth and let out a tortured howl that shook the birds from the trees above, scattering them into the night, and made Indra shudder with a sudden chill. It was Wulfric's voice, but it was also something else: a base, guttural sound that did not belong to this world— the sound of whatever now possessed him. Indra reached over her back for a sword, her heart jumping when her hand groped for it but found nothing there. Suddenly she remembered that she had unsheathed her swords and propped them against the rock so that she could rest her back against it. *Stupid!* She darted back to the stone, grabbed both swords, and gripped them tight, the feeling of the hilts' leather bindings in her hands instantly reassuring.

Venator was dancing atop the stone as if it were a hot stove, flapping his ruffled feathers and screeching like Indra had never heard. She looked back to the tree and saw the worst thing she had ever seen in her young life.

Wulfric's body had begun to split open like an overripe fruit as something inside him pushed violently outward, fighting to escape. The tearing began at the center of his chest, where the beetle-shaped scar was burned into his flesh, and proceeded downward to his navel. Wulfric's eyes rolled over white and his head sagged to his chest as the two sides of his body were pulled apart from within. What issued forth was not blood but slimy, glistening black viscera that bubbled and oozed as it spewed from the widening gash. Indra stepped back, aghast, as a grasping claw, dripping with the oily black muck, appeared from within Wulfric's open chest and felt around blindly before finding the forest floor. Then another clawed, elongated leg followed. By now, there was almost nothing human left of Wulfric, or at least nothing visible; what flesh of his still remained was covered with the seeping black slime, and it was impossible to tell where he ended and the beast began.

Its two front legs found their footing, allowing more of it to clamber out from within. As the beast's head emerged, Indra recognized the hideous cluster of bulbous eyes, the awful chittering mandibles, those great needle-toothed jaws. It reared its head upward, its mouth yawning wide and drooling thick saliva as it breathed in the night air. As the rest of its body emerged, the elongated legs unfurling at their joints, the plates of its armored carapace spreading outward, Indra marveled in horror at the black magick that allowed this monstrosity to somehow be birthed from a vessel so much smaller. For that was what she had witnessed, she realized. An infernal, violent birth, a parasite born in darkness, killing its host so that it might live.

When the beast had fully emerged and nothing of Wulfric remained, it tried to move forward—and found that it could not. The chains that had hung slack around Wulfric's chest were now stretched taut around the increased girth of the beast. It looked down in confusion, its gnarled limbs clawing at the chain with growing frustration, but to no avail. Now its entire body flailed against its confinement, the chain twisting and pulling against the trunk of the tree so violently that it gouged deep into the bark. Leaves fell to the ground like rain as the boughs above shook.

Indra stood in a defensive posture, both swords at the ready in case the beast should break free, but both the chain and the tree held fast. She watched it for a while longer, waiting for the beast to tire or quit and realize the futility of its struggle, but it never did. If anything, it seemed to grow wilder and more violent the more it tried—and failed—to get free, its frustration ever building, its rage without end.

Now is your chance, said the voice within her. *Do it!*

The way the beast's back was lashed against the tree left its soft, pulsing underbelly exposed, like a tortoise turned on its shell. While a blow anywhere else might glance uselessly off its stone-thick armored plating, underneath, it could bleed. She had done it once already; now it would be easier. Though its clawed legs struck at the air and it continued to struggle against its bonds, it remained a static target. She could dart and dodge before it, striking at will, bleeding it one thrust of her sword at a time until it was dead.

And yet something stayed her. She moved only a few steps toward the beast before finding herself rooted to the spot again, her swords at her sides.

The sound of her approach alerted the beast to her presence, and the sight of her enraged it further. It howled and hissed as it strained against the chain, desperate to be free, to kill. It lashed out at her with outstretched claws, but she was still yards out of range. It spat its acidic venom at her, but Indra had learned to recognize the chewing motion that preceded the spitting and dodged easily, the gobs of sputum burning into the bark of the trees behind her.

She knew that killing it would not be difficult. She knew that she would be doing the world a service by sending it back to the infernal pit from which it had been so wrongly summoned. She knew that her father, on seeing what she had done, would be forced to admit that he was wrong. And she knew that she would at last find retribution. But it was no longer so simple a matter as slaying a monster, as she had always imagined. For she could not escape the knowledge that the hateful, murderous thing that thrashed and howled before her was not only a monster but also a human soul. Somewhere within that black, soulless shell there was still an innocent man, a good man. A man as much the victim of an abomination as any who had been killed by one. Perhaps more.

As the beast continued to screech and writhe and claw at the air, straining with all its rage to reach her, Indra returned her swords to their scabbards, then turned away and walked back to the rock, where she sat. From her tunic she retrieved a small piece of parchment and a piece of sharpened reed, which she used to scratch out a short note. It was something she had hoped never to do, but this situation was far beyond anything for which she had prepared herself, and she needed the counsel of those with expertise greater than her own.

When the note was done, she rolled it up as small as she could make it and attached it to Venator's leg. "Home," she said, then watched as he took flight, disappearing into the night sky.

She sat back down and began to rummage through the small pack on her belt for the needle and spool of strong thread that she kept for repairs to her leather armor. She would have need of them come the morning.

TWENTY-FOUR

As the early-morning clouds parted, dappled sunlight broke through the treetops and fell upon Wulfric's face, sparking him awake. He sat up with a groan. Some days, the lingering after-effects of his transformation were worse than others. Today, the hangover, as he sometimes thought of it, was a bad one. His head pounded, the bright light from above only making it worse. His stomach ached with a hunger as if he had not eaten in days, though he knew that he had, just last night. More than anything, he was disoriented, his vision blurred, and the world around him seemed to rock back and forth like a boat on an uneven sea. It would be some time, he knew, before he would recover fully.

Even so, his faculties were present enough to know that something was wrong. From the moment of his waking he had sensed a strangeness. As he slowly grew more aware, he realized that it was an absence that puzzled him. Several absences.

First, there was no chain around him; he had woken not shackled upright to a tree, as was normal, but free and on the ground. What else? He had long grown accustomed to waking to the stench of sulfur, but this morning he could barely smell it at all. It was only as he sat up, his vision slowly focusing and adapting to the light, that he saw why. He had not woken covered in and surrounded by a thick layer of ashes, as he had every day for years. The gray patina of grime that usually coated every inch of him had been largely washed away, and his skin was bright pink and clean—which seemed to Wulfric unnatural, so long had it been since he last saw himself so. And he was not naked, but dressed in his tattered hooded cloak.

None of this was normal. None of it was right.

Slowly, he pulled himself to his feet, letting out a pained groan as at least one familiar thing made itself known: every muscle and joint in his body ached when called upon to do anything. Still dizzy, he stumbled and almost fell, steadying himself against a nearby tree. He noticed the splintered grooves gouged into its bark, looked down, and saw the iron chain sitting loosely around its base, unlocked. Then, at last, he realized the thing that from the first had seemed to him strangest of all, the thing he had least expected upon waking. It was the fact that he had woken at all, that he was still alive.

"Good morning," came a voice from behind him. He spun around, more quickly than was wise given his poor state of balance, and staggered awkwardly before regaining his footing. Then he saw Indra, sitting not far away, casually skinning a small animal. She smiled at him, which he returned with a look of bewilderment.

"How am I alive?" he asked. He spoke hoarsely, his throat dry as a bone, as he always woke not only starved but parched as well.

"I'm making breakfast," she said. She held the dead animal up by its hind legs and yanked its skin down over its head to expose its flesh. "Could you make a fire?"

Wulfric marched closer to her, his footing steadier now. "Do not toy with me! I am supposed to be dead!"

"All evidence to the contrary," she said as she set down the animal and wiped her hands on a rag.

The sky above her darkened, and she looked up to see that Wulfric had moved closer still, his shadow falling over her as he looked down upon her, his look of puzzlement now turning into something bordering on anger. She wondered for a moment if she might have to reach for a sword, but saw that Wulfric was trying to calm himself.

"We had an agreement," he said in a more measured tone. "You agreed to—"

"I know very well what I agreed to!" she said, jumping suddenly to her feet, her own composure slipping away. "But it was easier said than done."

Wulfric turned away, shaking his head in vexation. "I could not have made it easier for you. I offered up the beast to you shackled and helpless, told you how and where to strike . . . Tell me, what more should I have done?"

Indra thought quietly on this for a moment as Wulfric paced bearishly up and down the clearing. Finally, "You should not have thanked me."

He stopped, looked at her. "What?"

"You thanked me. That was the last thing you did before you . . . before you became that thing. Perhaps if you hadn't, it would have been easier for me to forget that even after the beast emerged, there was still a good and decent man trapped somewhere deep within it."

Wulfric looked at her in dismay. "I thanked you not out of any goodness or decency but out of relief! Because I believed that you might finally be able to grant me the release I have longed for. What a fool I was."

"I'm sorry," said Indra. "I came out here to kill an abomination, but not like this. I could not take its life if it meant also taking the life of an innocent man."

Wulfric snorted disdainfully. "If you knew me better, you would not think me so innocent."

"It's not for me to judge you," said Indra.

"Quite right! It is not!" spat Wulfric, stabbing a finger at her accusingly. "Then who are you to judge me innocent, or decent, or good? What do you know of me? Nothing! You know nothing!"

"I know that nothing you might have done could possibly warrant such a punishment as this, even if that is what you believe it is." She hesitated to ask the question, but her curiosity would not let it rest. "What did you mean when you said that this curse was part of your penance? Penance for what?"

Wulfric shifted awkwardly and turned away from her. "What does it matter to you? You have already decided that you will not help me."

"You're wrong," she said. "I want to help you. But I have to believe there is a better way. Some way other than death."

"Death is all that I deserve," he said, his back still turned to her.

"I don't believe that either," she said. "No man is beyond redemption, beyond forgiveness."

He faced her, and Indra saw there were tears welling in his eyes.

"Even if that were true, I am not just a man. Am I?"

"You're not just a monster either," she said, and she tried to reach out and place a hand on Wulfric's arm in reassurance, but he shifted a half step away from her.

"When those men came here two nights ago, more were slain by my own hand than by the beast," he told her. "In my life as a man, I willingly, knowingly killed more than that mindless creature ever has. And it has killed many. And so I ask you, which of us is the real monster?"

There was a moment of silence before Indra spoke. "These men you killed . . . that was as a soldier, in war, yes?"

Wulfric waved a dismissive hand at her. "Many men have used that excuse to justify what they enjoyed doing."

"Perhaps so," said Indra, scrutinizing him. "But not you. I don't think you enjoyed it at all. I've known men like that, and I can tell that you are not one of them. If I am wrong, tell me."

Wulfric grimaced and gave an awkward shrug, again signaling his reluctance to talk more on the subject. He shuffled back and forth for a moment, indecisive. Then he wheeled around and looked at Indra intently. "I ask you one more time. Will you help me or not? If not, be gone and leave me be."

Indra drew back her shoulders and stood tall before him, uncowed. "If you mean will I slaughter the beast, and you with it, the answer is, and will always be, no. Nor will I be gone. I am sworn to protect mankind from the scourge Aethelred set upon this land, and you are as much its victim as any other. I believe it was no accident that we found one another. I believe I was sent here to help you."

Wulfric looked at Indra strangely, then startled her as he flung his hands into the air and looked skyward. "Lord!" he cried out in exasperation. "Am I not cursed enough that now you afflict me with this? This stubborn carbuncle?"

Indra folded her arms across her chest, unamused. "You mock me."

Wulfric looked down from the sky. "I do not mock your intentions; they are honorable enough. Only your naiveté. Tell me! Tell me how you can possibly hope to help me."

"Perhaps we should start small," she said as she unhooked a small skin of water from her belt and offered it to Wulfric. "You look thirsty."

Wulfric regarded the water skin gingerly. He was loath to accept any offer of assistance or friendship from the girl, lest it encourage her. But then, she seemed to need little encouragement anyway. And he was so thirsty. After a moment's hesitation, he snatched it from her, threw it back, and gulped it dry. When he was done, he wiped his mouth with his sleeve, and as he offered the empty skin back to Indra, he saw a hint of a satisfied smile on her face.

"This means nothing," he said.

She took the empty skin from him. "If you will not accept my help, at least for now accept my companionship. You're welcome to join me for breakfast. Unless, of course, you have more pressing things to do today."

Wulfric frowned at her. "Now you mock me."

"No more than you deserve," Indra said before walking back to her campsite, where she sat, took up the skinned animal, drew a small knife, and slit it open along its belly to clean it. Wulfric watched her as she went about her work, efficient and skilled, and tried to gather his thoughts, which the girl had done such a good job of scrambling. He wanted so much to take his chain and be on his way, to leave the girl far behind him. No good could come of keeping her near. Why, then, were his feet carrying him toward her, rather than away?

He knelt opposite her and began gathering nearby tinder for a fire. Still he did not understand why he was doing this, why he was even still here with her. He had walked with kings, fought the fiercest barbarians from across the sea, and slain monsters unimaginable. So why did this upstart girl, barely half his size and a fraction of his age, confound him so? Had she been like so many others he had met on his travels, had she beaten him or tried to kill him or run him off, he would have known precisely how to react. He would—

It was then that he realized. The girl seemed so strange, so confusing to him, because she spoke a language he had all but forgotten. Sympathy. Tolerance. Compassion. He was in territory so long unexplored that it felt wholly unfamiliar, yet the compulsion to rediscover it was like some ancient, bone-deep ache, something more powerful than every instinct that was telling him to flee.

He sparked a flint and got a fire going, then adjusted his cloak so that he might sit properly on the ground. Indra did not acknowledge the gesture, but continued quietly about her work. And so Wulfric continued about his, throwing more wood onto the fire to help it grow. He was so consumed with his own muddled thoughts that he did not think to ask the girl where her hawk was, nor even notice that it was gone.

TWENTY-FIVE

Venator arrived at his destination before Wulfric had even woken, having flown through the night. It was a long journey, but so much faster as the bird flies, and Venator was fast indeed, by both breeding and training.

What had once been Canterbury Cathedral had changed much in the years since it was last the seat of an archbishop. Aethelred's foul experiments there and its subsequent infestation had led King Alfred to declare it no longer a holy place, no longer fit for its original purpose. Instead he had given it over to the newly established Order to use as it set about its task of hunting down the hundreds of abominations that had scattered across England, a danger to men, women, and children everywhere. Befitting its new role as a military garrison, the cathedral had been heavily modified, with ramparts and other fortifications erected alongside the church's ancient spires.

Venator alighted atop one of the cathedral-fortress's towering bulwarks and strutted back and forth along the parapet, screeching and flapping his wings. Eventually the hawk's loud, persistent squawking roused a guardsman from his bed in a nearby barrack. He emerged from an arched door onto the rooftop walkway, still only half-awake and struggling to fasten his breeches, but when he saw that this was no troublesome crow, he became fully alert in a snap. As the hawk continued to strut and flap, he approached the parapet to get a closer look.

There could be no mistaking this bird's plumage or the piercing look in its amber eyes. The Order kept many birds of prey, but no other like this one.

Venator.

A second guardsman emerged, naked save for a rough woolen blanket thrown around his shoulders. Rubbing the sleep from his eyes, he fumbled drowsily with a crossbow. "Fucking crow," he mumbled. "I'll have it for breakfast!"

"That's no crow," the first man said, and when the second looked up he let the arrow slip from his hand and clatter onto the stone flags. "Bloody hell," he said, suddenly wide awake.

"Go and fetch the lord marshal," said the first man.

"The sun's barely up. He'll still be asleep."

The first man snapped around to face the other. Perhaps this fool had forgotten the standing orders given to every man by Lord Edgard when his daughter had left nigh on a year ago, but he had not. "Then wake him up. Now!"

Edgard sat up in bed groggily, stirred from sleep by the urgent hammering at his door. One of his men, shouting between bouts of thumping his fist against the door, voice muffled through the stout oak. He had been having an excellent dream, and to be snatched away from it brought him back to the waking world in a foul mood. When he saw that it was barely even dawn, he swung his feet out of bed onto the cold stone floor and rose, stretching as the hammering outside the door continued, and contemplating various ways in which to make the life of whoever was doing it thoroughly miserable.

"Enter!"

The door flew open and a guardsman rushed in. Edgard looked him up and down curiously. In his haste, the man had not thought to dress and was still naked save for a blanket wrapped around him, an unloaded crossbow in his hand. Edgard paused for a moment to take in the full absurdity of it before he spoke.

"All I can say is, this had better be very, *very* good."

The man did not hesitate. "Venator has returned."

Every muscle in Edgard's body tensed, and he felt hot blood surge through him. "When? Where?"

"Just now, up on the west rampart."

Edgard dressed faster than he ever had, throwing a cloak around him as he made for the door.

"Show me."

The guardsman led Edgard through the fortress's halls, while gathering up the blanket that dragged around his bare feet so he would not trip. It was a comical sight, and on another day Edgard might have taken some amusement in it, but he could think of nothing now but the hawk's arrival and what it might mean.

On the one hand, there was cause for relief, as it meant that his daughter was surely still alive—a prospect that, after ten long months, had begun to feel depressingly grim. By the sixth month, with still no word—though he had expressly told her to send back the hawk with regular news, even if just of her continued well-being—he had begun to fear the worst. He had considered sending parties out after her. But he was certain that if he did such a thing, and they were to find her alive, she would never speak to him again.

It would not take much, he knew, to push her to that. She was too damn stubborn and proud—some, himself included, might say arrogant—to accept assistance, and she would be mortally insulted by the suggestion that he might think her in need of rescue.

That, and she hated him well enough already. In a strange way, that had come as some solace to Edgard during Indra's months away; he knew that the lack of communication was more likely due to her being unwilling than being unable.

On the other hand, her pride and her obstinacy meant also that she would not write unless she were truly in dire need, perhaps in fear for her life, and it would be a grave situation indeed that Indra would admit was too much for her to cope with alone. Oh, she could handle herself more than ably; there was no shortage of initiates, full paladins even, who would reluctantly testify to that after trying to bring her down a peg in the sparring circle. Some of them still bore the bruises. Still, sooner or later, out in the wide world, she was bound to get herself into a fight beyond even her abilities.

Before she left on her Trial, Edgard had told her that if she did not return, it would likely be her own hubris that was the cause. That, or her damn anger, which she never had learned to properly control. Where she got that from, God himself only knew. Her father, he supposed.

They walked briskly past the colonnades of the old cathedral's central cloister, long since converted into an outdoor training yard. King Alfred had at first balked at the suggestion that the vacant cathedral be converted into the Order's base of operations—turning a house of God into a house of war—but Edgard had convinced him. *God or war, is one any better than the other these days?* he had argued. *Which one has claimed more lives—who can say?*

Alfred had reluctantly consented, and the transformed cathedral had been a fine place when the work was completed, fit to house any fighting force in the world. Alfred, in his day, had supported the Order well, as he held himself responsible for the menace he had allowed Aethelred to unleash. He had spared no expense as Edgard built the Order into a force of, at its peak, almost a thousand men. The King, determined already to eradicate every trace of Aethelred's scourge, had become even more so upon the news of Wulfric's death. His closest friend, slaughtered by an abomination along with his family and neighbors as they celebrated his homecoming—Alfred had felt responsible for that, too. *Whatever you need, you shall have it,* he had told Edgard when he placed him in charge of the Order. *Until the very last of them is dead.*

But that was long ago, and the cathedral was now badly in need of repair. In the years since Alfred's death, his son and successor, Edward the Elder, had not looked so favorably upon the Order. Perhaps Edgard and his men had done their work too well; by the time of Edward's succession to the throne, much of the scourge had been hunted down and killed. Only a few remained and those were rarely seen; already the very existence of abominations had begun to fall into the realm of myth.

And so the new King had come to view the Order as largely redundant and a drain on crown resources that were sorely needed elsewhere. For all the good work his father had done to maintain peace with the Norse, Edward had made a vow to reclaim all of England from those who had settled there and was spending to build an army fit for the task. That left precious little for the Order, which Edward saw as his father's folly. Edgard had managed to convince the King to continue granting them a small stipend so that they might finish their work. But the fact was that the Order was a shadow of its former self: barely a hundred men, with scarcely the gold to keep them quartered and fed.

More men left by the day, tempted by better pay and conditions in Edward's vast new army, and it had been more than a year since they had taken on a new initiate, Indra notwithstanding. Soon there would be nothing of the Order left. Edward had made known his plans to disband it and give the cathedral back to the church.

The thought of what life might hold for him after that had kept Edgard awake many a night. He could always go back to war, but he found men to be far less satisfying prey than the monsters he had grown accustomed to hunting. All he knew now was that hunt, the greatest of all games—and the glory that came with it. But the glory was all but gone, as the game itself soon would be.

Yes, times were grim. But still Edgard was buoyed as he followed the guardsman up the spiral staircase that led to the west rampart, taking the steps two at a time. His daughter might despise him, and perhaps rightly so, but she was alive. And she was speaking to him.

——•◉❀◉•——

Venator flew from the parapet to Edgard's forearm when he arrived. The bird had been trained well; had anyone else tried to remove the message from around its leg, they would be mourning the loss of a finger or more. Even though he was the intended recipient, Edgard made careful work of loosening the copper anklet and retrieving the scroll from within, while keeping one eye on that hooked beak, sharp as a dagger.

As Edgard unfurled the parchment and began to read, Venator hopped from his arm and perched on the wall nearby. The sun was rising now, its light creeping over the land, casting all beneath it in warm gold. It was a sight to see, though none but Venator saw it. The two guardsmen were watching Edgard as he read, and they grew uneasy as they saw their commander's hopeful expression begin to fade. His face slackened, then he tightened his jaw and the color drained from his cheeks.

Edgard rolled the small piece of parchment up, slowly and carefully. His expression was blank, impossible to read. The guardsmen waited for some command that might indicate what had perturbed him so, but none came. Instead, Edgard whipped around to the arched doorway and made his way hastily down the stairs, cape billowing behind him. The two guardsmen exchanged a look. "My lord?" one called after him.

Edgard was already out of sight, but his voice echoed back up the spiral staircase. "See that the hawk is well fed and well rested! It goes back out in one hour."

— —•◦⦂◉⦂◦•— —

The part of the old cathedral where Edgard was headed was on the other side of the building from the western rampart. And though it had been a long time since he'd had cause to run for anything, he ran now, as fast as he ever had though he was far from the young man he once was. He sprinted clear across the training yard and into the cathedral's nave, which now served as a vast storage room for rations, supplies, and equipment. It was mostly empty these days, its stores slowly dwindling as the means to replenish those that were consumed grew less month by month.

Edgard made his way down the aisle toward the altar, then down another winding staircase into the cathedral's underground. It was cooler down here, and dank and dark. Edgard had to light a torch to find his way along the hallway, its flame casting long shadows on the old stone walls. He passed several doorways and arrived at the one at the hallway's end. The room beyond had once functioned as the cathedral's library and archive but, like the rest of the church, had been converted to another use when the Order had taken possession. It was still a library of sorts, only now a library of things that should never have existed.

Edgard threw open the door to the chamber and swept inside, not bothering to knock. Though the hour was still early, his arcane advisor would already be up and working. The man barely slept at all.

And there he was, at his desk at the far end of his dimly lit study, head down, so absorbed in his work that he had not even noticed Edgard's strident entrance. It was only as Edgard marched toward him that Cuthbert saw the shadows cast on the wall by the torch he carried and looked up to see the knight approaching. He leapt to his feet, as rank and respect demanded, but his attention was more on the flame of the torch than the man who carried it.

"My lord," said Cuthbert. "Please, no firelight in here." His desk was littered with densely written parchments that he began to shuffle together and draw toward him protectively. The two men were surrounded by books and papers, on every table and surface, even piled on the floor; the room's long black shadows suggested even more hidden in the darkness.

On the shelves behind Cuthbert was the heart of it all: the Bestiary. A project he had begun on a sheaf of paper fifteen years ago, in the years since, it had grown in size to a dozen thick leather-bound volumes cataloguing every species of abomination ever encountered by the Order, complete with detailed drawings of which Cuthbert was particularly proud. In each case, the beast's description, behavioral traits, habits, mode of attack, and—most crucially—vulnerabilities, were recorded in painstaking detail. A zoology of hell. Priceless knowledge that could easily be destroyed by an errant spark from an open flame.

Edgard sighed—*This man and his obsessive habits*—and blew out the torch, casting the room into near total darkness, save for a strange green light that was glowing dimly inside a glass reading lamp on Cuthbert's desk. Cuthbert turned a knob on the lamp's brass base and the green flame within flared brighter, though it did not flicker or dance in the manner of any fire known to science. It was brighter and more steady, and cast the room in an ethereal, viridescent glow. Only now did Cuthbert notice the grave look on his master's face. He made to ask him the cause, but Edgard beat him to it:

"Indra is alive."

"Blessed be!" said Cuthbert, smiling wide. His relief at the news was palpable, and so he wondered why Edgard did not appear to share it. "Has she returned?"

"No, but she sent a message." Edgard handed him the scroll. "Read it."

Cuthbert unrolled the parchment, his eyes darting swiftly over it. It took little more than a moment for his jaw to fall open. He looked up at Edgard in astonishment.

"Loath as I am to admit it," said Edgard, "it would appear that you may have been right."

You knew I was, from the first day I told you, Cuthbert thought but did not say. *You just chose to ignore me.*

"What do you propose to do?" he asked aloud.

"I propose to do as she asks," said Edgard. "We ride out to meet her as soon as my men have made ready."

Edgard sensed Cuthbert's hesitation. It had been a long time since the scrawny little priest had been in the field, and he had never been much suited for it in the first place. Though one had to admit the man had toughened up considerably in the years since Wulfric had first introduced them. A career spent hunting abominations would do that to you, after all.

Cuthbert had not aged well during those years, though Edgard had to concede that neither had he. A career spent hunting abominations would do that, too. But something in those pale, sunken eyes of his suggested Cuthbert had got the worst of it. Perhaps it was not the abominations themselves but the close and prolonged exposure to Aethelred's magick that had done it.

Recognizing that Cuthbert had perhaps missed his true calling when he entered the priesthood, Edgard had made him a permanent civilian member of the Order upon its founding and set him to the task of furthering the arcane work that Aethelred had begun in hopes of finding new, more constructive uses for it. He had found many such uses, though most were little more than curious novelties. The unburning lamp on his desk was one of the better ones.

Though Cuthbert was indeed hesitant, Edgard was mistaken as to its cause: "I mean, what do you propose to do once we get out there?" the priest said. "Indra is asking for your help."

Edgard smirked as he took back the note and studied it again. "I've been trying to help that girl her entire life. Never once has she accepted it. There's irony in it, that this should be why she finally asks, don't you think?"

"From my reading of that note," said Cuthbert, "she is not asking for herself, but for him."

Edgard's smirk faded. He tucked the note away. "Be ready in one hour." And with that he turned and made for the door.

On his way out, his eye was caught by one of Cuthbert's many workbenches, upon which papers and other instruments of his trade were laid out. This one was an artificing table, cluttered with specialist tools, precious metals, gemstones, and other raw materials—the stuff of a jewelcrafter. Edgard stopped and picked up what appeared to be one of several examples of the finished product, a tiny emerald set within a gold enclosure. It was fine precision work, the intricately cut gem little more than the size of an apple seed. He held it up to the light, examining it closely and with interest. To the layman it might appear a mere ornament, but Cuthbert had told Edgard its true purpose, and it occurred to him that such a thing might be useful now. Indra was his daughter and he loved her, but he did not trust her entirely, and he suspected that she did not trust him at all.

He turned to Cuthbert, holding up the small jeweled object. "Does this actually work?" he asked.

"Oh, yes," said Cuthbert, always happy to talk about one of his projects. "My test results have been extremely encouraging. In fact, that one you're holding has been the most accurate so far."

Edgard nodded, considering for a moment, then pocketed the golden trinket before continuing on his way out.

"My lord." Cuthbert watched from behind his desk, a look of concern visible in the warm green light.

Edgard stopped at the door and looked back.

"You and I have differed on this in the past," said Cuthbert. "I concede that perhaps it was avoidable before. But no longer. You have to—"

Edgard silenced him with a raised palm and a look so stern that the shadow he cast on the wall seemed to grow larger around him. "We have had this conversation before, too many times. Do not bring up the subject again."

And then he was gone, the door swinging closed behind him. Cuthbert slumped back into his chair and twisted the knob on his desk lamp, bringing the unburning flame down to its lowest setting. At times like this, when he needed to think, darkness was better.

TWENTY-SIX

They had eaten together in silence, Wulfric somewhat hesitant, and Indra, for all her desire, knowing it was wiser not to press him to talk further. Though Venator did most of their hunting, she had done her share, and she had come to see Wulfric as much like the wild deer she had learned to stalk; they so easily took flight if you were careless and allowed them to sense that you were coming too close.

To Wulfric, unlike the deer, she meant no harm. And therein lay the irony: he *wanted* her to harm him, to kill him; it was her offer of help that disconcerted him so.

And she so wanted to help him. Never before in her life had she encountered such a pitiable soul, and in this day and age that was no meager claim. Yet for all her promises and protestations, she had no idea what she could actually do for him. For all she knew, he was right, and he was beyond any form of aid other than a merciful death. Though the church forbade it as a remedy for those blighted by maladies beyond the help of medicine, warriors grievously crippled or maimed beyond salvation in battle were routinely dispatched by their comrades to put an end to their suffering.

Whether Wulfric could be considered such a case, Indra did not know; all she knew was that his proposed solution revolted her. There had to be a better way. Wulfric was cursed by such magick as she had never seen, but she felt certain—or at least hoped so strongly that it felt to her like certainty—that someone within the Order would know how to help him. That was why she had sent Venator back to Canterbury. There was one man in particular she was pinning her hopes on, the cleverest man she knew, the man who had taught her everything she knew about magick. Surely Cuthbert would know what to do. Surely.

She looked up at the sky, where the sun rose toward its noonday zenith. She could not be sure when Venator might have reached Canterbury or how long the help she had requested might take to get here. All she could hope to do was stay close to Wulfric, to keep him from taking flight before they arrived. She was certain that she would lose him if she told him the truth. It had been hard enough keeping him here this morning as things were; if he knew others were coming, that would surely be the last she would see of him. No, it was better this way.

Still, the problem of her father remained. Though she had not specifically requested he come in person, she knew that he would. It would be a reunion difficult enough under the best of circumstances. But this . . . She had known the man her entire life, had believed she knew him well enough, but as she thought on it now she realized she could not predict how he would react to this unique conundrum.

She herself had started out on a quest to hunt and kill an abomination, yet the one she had found confounded all her expectations and caused her to see things differently. What would her father see? He was a man of war, set in his ways, who always returned from the Order's hunting expeditions with a look of satisfied glee—the look of a man who took pleasure in something that should be seen only as a grim but necessary duty. But then, hadn't she set out on her own quest relishing the prospect of killing such a beast? Her father had been assigned the task of killing abominations by royal command, while she had sought it out, had asked for it eagerly. More than that, she had demanded it, despite her father's repeated attempts to dissuade her, even forbid her. She had wanted so much to kill one; what made her any better than him?

That was different, she told herself. She had her reasons, the very best there were.

But the more she thought, the more she began to worry that she had made a mistake. Her father would come with a force of men, chosen from the best under his command. Veterans who would obey his orders—and his alone. Once they arrived, her ability to control the situation would depend solely on persuading her father to see things as she did, and she realized now that she had little faith in that endeavor. What had she done? In her haste to help this man, had she inadvertently condemned him?

She looked up at the sun again, wondering how much time she had before they would arrive. She needed to think. Stern and unyielding though her father was, she had proven a match for him before, or she would not be here. She might yet convince him to help this man—convince him that Wulfric was different from all the abominations her father had killed without a moment's thought—if she had the time and freedom to do so. If she could meet him and speak with him on terms that were favorable to her, that would prevent him from acting rashly, even if she failed to persuade him. But how? Her eyes drifted over to her twin swords, propped against the rock, their blades gleaming in the light of the sun. Perhaps—

"What exactly did you do to me?"

Wulfric's voice snapped Indra from her thoughts. She looked up to see him holding his arms out before him, examining them as though the sight of his own skin was strange to him. Something about that amused her.

"I unchained you and pulled you from the ashes while you still slept, washed you with water from the stream," she said. "Is that not—I mean to say, do you not normally . . ." She floundered, realizing suddenly how awkward it is to ask a man how often he bathes.

Wulfric seemed to understand her anyway. "At first, I washed off what I could each day. But I soon realized it was a waste of time. The ashes return each morning, cover me anew." He looked now at his hands, pink and clean as a newborn baby. "After a while I came to see it as just part of my skin. Part of me."

"Well, if I may," said Indra, "you are much improved this way. Before, you looked like some kind of ghost, all covered in gray. But I suspected there was a man underneath there somewhere. I'm glad to have been proven right."

And it was true; the difference was remarkable. The filth that had covered Wulfric from head to foot had aged him deceptively. Though something in those haunted eyes seemed to belong to a much older soul, it was clear that he could be little older than thirty. Aethelred had been dead fifteen years, so Wulfric must have been little more than a boy soldier when the mad archbishop's curse befell him. Just another tragic detail to add to an already sorry tale.

"Here," said Indra, "see for yourself." She took one of her swords from the rock it was propped against and offered it to Wulfric. He looked at it and blinked but made no move to take it. "I pride myself on keeping my blades polished bright as a mirror," she said, prompting Wulfric again to take it. "Go on, have a look."

Gingerly, Wulfric reached out and took the sword, then held it up, its blade gleaming in the sun. Indra watched him keenly as he regarded himself in the narrow sliver of steel, turning it this way and that so that he might see his whole face. She hoped for some sign of pleasant surprise, but all she saw was the disquieted look of a man who seemed not to recognize his own reflection. Or, perhaps, one who did but did not like what he saw. After a moment, his eyes grew distant and his hands limp, and he let the blade sag into the dirt.

Indra took the sword gently from him. "Now, if you would only do something about that rat's nest of a beard," she said, trying to lighten the mood and offering Wulfric a smile, but it did not prove contagious. He just gazed down at his hands with that far-away look, still ill at ease, still somehow strangely at odds with all of this. He glanced back at the tree where he had spent the night, the iron chain that had bitten into its trunk and shredded its bark now spooled loose around it. Indra could sense a question, but he seemed hesitant to ask it.

"You want to know what becomes of the beast?" she asked.

Wulfric looked back to her. "You saw it?"

Indra nodded. "As dawn broke, it began to howl in pain, and it grew weaker until finally it lost all strength and simply died. For a moment it was still, then its body glowed as though a fire were burning within it. And then it was ablaze, consumed by flames stranger than I have ever seen, until nothing was left of it but a great pile of smoldering ash. And at the center of it, you, sleeping like a newborn child. After the ashes cooled, I pulled you out of there and tried to wake you, but you were dead to the world. Since I could think of no other way to make myself useful, I thought I'd clean you up."

Silence. Wulfric looked down at his robe, his fingers playing along the tears that Indra had mended with needle and thread. Her stitching was good, stronger probably than that which held the rest of it together.

"Why did you do all this?" he asked her.

"I thought that perhaps someone who spends only part of his life as a human should look like one while he was." Her eyes widened. "That reminds me!" she said, jumping to her feet. "I have something for you."

Wulfric watched as Indra walked around to the side of the rock, then returned holding a pile of clothes—shirt, tunic, breeches—neatly folded, with a pair of boots on top. They looked old and worn, and there was a bloodstain on the shirt surrounding a slit made by a blade. That had also been neatly stitched.

"What is this?" asked Wulfric.

"I took them from one of the men we killed. One of mine as I recall. He seemed to have no further use for them. It's not much, but far better surely than that flea-bitten old cloak. The boots, I think, are nearly new. Why don't you try them on?" She made a move toward him, but Wulfric scrambled to his feet and recoiled as though her gift were toxic.

"What's wrong?" she said. "There's no guilt in it. The man who wore these was scum. I doubt he acquired them any differently."

"No," said Wulfric. "It is not that. You are too kind. Far too kind." He wheeled around and made his way across the clearing to the tree, where he unwound the chain from around its base and made fast work of hauling it up onto his body, crisscrossing it over his shoulders. Indra followed him, still holding the pile of clothes. "They only go to waste if you refuse them. At least—"

"No!" Wulfric barked at her, and she startled and stopped in her tracks. He seemed to regret it instantly and softened his tone. "No. If I wanted to look like a man, to live like a man, I would have done so already. But that is not what I am. It is not what I deserve to be."

Wulfric had almost finished taking up the chain. There was still a length of it to go, but already he was laden with a burden heavier than any man should be able to carry, or should ever have to. Try as she might, Indra could not understand this man. "Why do you punish yourself like this?" she asked him.

"It is God who punishes me," said Wulfric as he wrapped the last of the chain around him and tucked it between the rest to hold it fast. "It is not for me to question his judgment."

As Wulfric checked that the chain was secure, Indra took a moment to contemplate what he had said.

"I, too, am a Christian, so forgive me when I say this," she began. "But that is quite possibly the stupidest thing that I have ever heard."

Wulfric looked up at Indra in surprise. She glared back at him, her expression confirming that she had, indeed, said what he thought she had.

"Punishing you for what?" she said. "What sin could you have committed that could possibly warrant . . . *this*?"

"Perhaps you did not read the same book I did," said Wulfric. "In mine, God's capacity for wrath is infinite."

"So, too, is his forgiveness," said Indra, taking a tentative step closer. "In my experience, it is men who have too much of one and too little of the other. No one would doubt the misery of your curse, but why must you compound it like this? You refuse all help, reject all hope, and seem intent on living the most abject existence possible. If anyone is punishing you, look inward, not upward."

Wulfric glared at her silently, the links of the iron chain across his body clinking gently against one another as his chest rose and fell with each breath. Indra stiffened her muscles, girding herself against a possible attack. But Wulfric only reached down and picked up the padlock and key from the ground at his feet, fastening it to the chain. "I thank you for your help, truly. But no more is needed," he said in a calm, measured tone that suggested some effort was required to maintain it. "Nor is it welcome. Good day to you." He turned his back on her.

Indra took a hesitant step after him, then stopped. "Why must you go?" she called after him.

"Do not waste your time attempting to follow me," Wulfric said without looking back. "I have eluded trackers far better than you." Wulfric reached the edge of the clearing and stepped into the dense and tangled wood, the trees' branches closing behind him like a curtain as he moved deeper into the forest, and was gone.

Indra stood there for a moment, alone, paralyzed by indecision. She thought again of her concern for what her father might decide when he arrived with his men, and she considered letting Wulfric go. But if the Order did not find him here when they arrived, they would surely search for him. And now they knew what to look for. Who to look for. Wulfric's one advantage, his ability to hide in plain sight by day, had been undone by a few lines in a note that she had written. She was now responsible for his fate, and his best chance—his only chance—was with her, the one person who might sway her father not to hunt down the beast, but to help the man.

As hopes went, relying on her father to do the right thing was a thin one, but that was not all she had. She had her wits, and if her luck improved just a little, one other thing that could make all the difference. *Please let Cuthbert be with them. He will know what to do.*

She heard a familiar sound and looked up, shielding her eyes against the sun, to see Venator circling in the sky above. She smiled, the sight of him bringing fresh hope to the day. He would have word from Canterbury that would help her prepare for what was to come—and his return meant something more besides. She had no doubt that Wulfric was right, and that she would not be able to follow him if he did not want to be followed. But she had never heard of any man or beast capable of shaking off that hawk.

TWENTY-SEVEN

The afternoon had been long and tiring, and Indra was relieved when at last night began to draw in. Wulfric had proven true to his word; tracking him was all but impossible. He seemed to move far more nimbly than any man encumbered by such a heavy weight should, and along a route designed to make him difficult to pursue. He kept far from any beaten path, moving instead through only the most tangled and overgrown brushwood; thorns and other prickly things had been snagging on Indra's clothes and scratching at her skin all afternoon.

Had she been stalking him alone, she would have lost him hours ago, with no hope of finding him again, but fortunately she was not alone. Venator had caught sight of Wulfric without delay and, from his aerial vantage point, had had no difficulty following him. It was following Venator that proved so difficult; for every bramble or thicket above which the hawk glided effortlessly, Indra had to find her way over or around it. At one point Wulfric had crossed a shallow but wide river, which would have made him even more difficult to track had she not had Venator in the air. As it was, she still had to wade waist-deep through the frigid, fast-moving waters. An hour later, her saturated clothes only barely starting to dry in the sun, she was still chilled to the bone. And just how fast was this man moving that Venator had to maintain such a pace to keep him in sight? Several times the hawk had circled back to allow Indra to catch up, which was embarrassing, and she had to convince herself that her friend was not scowling at her reproachfully as he soared overhead.

As her exhaustion and frustration grew, Indra looked constantly toward the sun, tracking its progress across the sky. She knew that Wulfric had to stop sometime before it set, and with enough time to safely secure himself for the night. But it was not until the sun had sunk completely over the horizon that Venator landed on a treetop up ahead, indicating that Wulfric had finally come to a stop.

She sank down onto a fallen tree to rest and catch her breath, wondering how much ground they had covered. She guessed that it was no more than ten miles, but across terrain like this it felt more like fifty. Their course had not been a straight one, Venator banking left and right many times over the course of the day to follow Wulfric's own winding path, and Indra suspected they were not so far from the clearing from which they had set out that afternoon. That, at least, was good, as it meant that tonight's meeting place was not so far either.

Venator swooped down and settled on a branch nearby as Indra wiped the sweat from her brow. He, of course, appeared completely unflustered, not a feather out of place, and again Indra had to tell herself that he was not silently judging her. The hawk did not make a sound but moved keenly along the branch, nodding his head toward a dense wall of trees that the encroaching night had already begun to shroud in darkness. To Indra, his meaning was clear: Wulfric was close by, in that direction. She nodded in acknowledgment and, standing, gestured for the hawk to stay as she moved quietly toward the copse of trees he had indicated.

She crept low and slow between the trees, careful of every footfall, wondering if Wulfric might have set some trap with which to snare her—from what she knew of the man, it would not be surprising. But there were none, and she was able to close on the small glade where Wulfric had set himself up for the night without alerting him.

She caught sight of Wulfric beyond the trees directly in front of her and froze. Thirty yards away, but close enough that she could hear the soft jangling of his chain as he shed it from his body and began winding it around the trunk of a stout oak tree. Carefully, quietly, she hunkered down, and, from her hiding place, watched as Wulfric shrugged off his tattered cloak, tossed it aside, and sat naked at the base of the tree, pulling the chains over his head and around his chest. The same ritual Indra had witnessed the night before, only now she was doing so without his knowledge. Something about it felt wrong, as though she were intruding on the man's deepest, darkest secret, a moment of almost sacred privacy. She had to remind herself that everything she was doing was so that she could help him. *God, I hope so.*

The change came upon Wulfric less than a minute after he had secured the chain around him. As his body began to shudder and convulse, Indra turned away. She knew what happened next and had no desire to see it again. She headed back the way she came, more quickly this time. There was no need for stealth now. All she wanted now was to be away. Her heart was already beating faster, and when she heard the first howl of the beast echoing through the forest, she broke into a full sprint, bounding between the trees, running faster and faster, away from the nightmare unfolding behind her.

She was gasping for breath by the time she made her way back to Venator, who flew from his perch to her shoulder as she came to a halt. He sidled close to her face and nuzzled her, the touch of his silken feathers against her cheek helping to calm her. *Venator, ever my protector.* Over the sound of the wind she could still faintly hear the distant howling of the thing Wulfric had by now become, no less terrible for being so much farther away. She knew now that it was the same beast she had heard on the hillside several nights ago, the same dreadful wail. It had put a chill down her back then as it did now. She could not block it out; all she could do was distract herself by attending to what needed to be done.

She raised her forearm for Venator and he hopped onto it obediently. "Dinner," she said, and that was all the command the hawk needed. He took flight and within moments had disappeared into the night sky. Indra then drew both her swords and placed them on the ground before her, blades glimmering in the light of the rising moon. There was one more thing to do tonight before she could eat or rest. The thing she had been dreading ever since she sent her message to Canterbury, and could not put off any longer. It was time to go and meet her father.

Edgard had arrived at the old church a full hour before dusk. He and his men had ridden as hard as their horses were able, stopping for rest only once the entire journey, and so by day's end, man and horse alike had arrived at the meeting place tired and hungry, but ahead of time. Only then did he realize what a wasted effort it was; the time they had saved en route still had to be spent waiting for Indra to arrive, and as those dead hours passed, they only sharpened Edgard's sense of anticipation and, increasingly, impatience. What could be keeping her?

By now night had fallen and so she might arrive at any time, and every moment that passed dragged out interminably while his mind filled with worry. Was she all right? What if the beast had harmed her? What if she had changed her mind?

What if it was all some cruel trick, her childish idea of retribution for all the wrongs she imagined he had done her?

Was she capable of such a spiteful act, against her own father, the man who had raised her and cared for her and tried to keep her safe? He would not put it past her. For all that he had done for her, that girl had shown him nothing but ingratitude her entire life. He did not expect her, at so young an age, to understand the

hard choices he had been forced to make regarding her upbringing, but she could at least have tried to appreciate that he had
done the best he could under difficult circumstances—that every
decision he made had been in her best interests, for her own protection. Was that not what a father was supposed to do? Still, she
had resented him and rebelled against him at every opportunity.
Though he knew that was not uncommon with fathers and daughters, the anger Indra carried inside of her had made parenting her
an almost impossible task.

She had insisted, against his wishes, to be trained in combat,
almost from the day she was old enough to pick up a practice
sword. When he and others had tried to tell her that martial artistry was not an appropriate pursuit for a young lady, it had only
encouraged her more, as though she were determined to prove
otherwise. When he had refused to let her train with the initiates,
she had gone behind his back and saw to it herself, spying on and
following along with the daily sessions in the training yard from
the shadows, cajoling private lessons from the instructors whenever she could, and practicing. Always practicing. No punishment
or discouragement could deter her. He would take away her sword;
somewhere she would find another. He would confine her to her
room; she would find a way to sneak out. Eventually Edgard had
thrown up his hands and allowed her to train with the initiates, in
the hope that taking all rebelliousness out of the endeavor would
lead her to eventually lose interest. But she only became more
committed, and, over time, better and better.

By the time she was beating men five years her senior in the
sparring circle, it was clear that this was no idle hobby, nor could
her obvious talent be ignored, be she a girl or not. But when she
demanded to join the Order as an initiate herself, enough was
enough. He, of course, forbade it. The idea of a female initiate, much less a paladin, was as preposterous as it was unprece-
dented. But again, his refusal only fueled her determination. She
had become obsessed with the idea of slaying an abomination, as

though that would somehow make right what she saw as wrong with her life, and had given him an ultimatum: either she would do it as a fully trained, fully prepared member of the Order, or she would do it on her own, while vowing never to speak to him again. Either way, she would not be denied.

And so, against every parental urge, he had allowed her reckless quest, for fear of losing her entirely if he did otherwise. It was ten long months ago that he had watched her go, knowing that she might never return, but hoping that, if she should, her time away might have given her an opportunity to reflect, to come to appreciate all that he had tried to do for her.

He pulled himself from his reverie. His boots had scraped a shallow trench into the sodden earth where he had been pacing back and forth, back and forth. His men had made far better use of their time, setting up camp in the churchyard and making the other advance preparations he had ordered. Some of them were around the fire now, eating a hearty dinner. The smell of flame-cooked meat carried on the wind, and though Edgard's belly grumbled at the scent of it, he had no appetite. He was far too anxious—in part to see his daughter, to be sure, but also for what she had discovered.

An abomination like no other, a unique hybrid of man and beast. And a unique danger to him and Indra both. It was of vital importance that this be handled correctly. Which is why he had brought twenty of his best men. Indra might harbor some naive notion of saving this beast, whatever that meant, but he alone knew the threat it represented. And he alone knew how to deal with it.

Edgard looked up at the moon, wondering how long he had been waiting. Some of the men were already finished with dinner and had begun setting up tents in preparation for a night's stay. What could possibly be keeping her? He had chosen this place because it was the closest landmark to the area from which she had sent her message, so it should not take her so long to get here. *At nightfall*, he had said in the message he had sent back with Venator.

But then, since when had Indra followed any of his instructions to the letter, or at all? *Where the hell is she?*

"My lord."

One of his men, standing near the edge of the encampment, was looking into the nearby woods, his hand on the hilt of his sword. Edgard turned to see, just as a slight silhouette emerged from the darkness between the trees that formed the boundary to the churchyard. The figure stepped into the open to be caught by the moonlight. Indra. A great smile of relief widened across Edgard's face, and he moved across the open grass toward her, his pace quickening as he approached.

"My child," he said. "I cannot tell you how much it lifts my heart to see you." His arms came out, his first instinct to put them around her, but Indra stiffened and took a step backward, away from him.

Edgard's face fell as he halted; "Will you not embrace your own father?"

Her face said it all. Edgard's heart sank. He recognized that look. It was the one he had seen when she left him ten months ago, the same one she had turned toward him her entire life. She was as resistant toward him as she ever had been.

Perhaps she just needs time, he told himself. *I should not try to rush her.* He made no move closer, but tried to appear warm and hospitable. "You look well," he said, and indeed she did, far better than he expected. A few scrapes and bruises, but if anything it appeared that her Trial had strengthened her. There was steel in her eyes and in the way she carried herself, more than he remembered, and there had been plenty enough before. "How has your Trial treated you, these past ten months?"

"Well enough," she said. Her voice sounded different as well. More mature, more seasoned. Yes, the Trial had toughened her up all right. That could be a problem, though not an insurmountable one.

"Thank you for coming," she added.

Thank you? That may be a first. Edgard tried to remember a time before this one that Indra had expressed gratitude toward him in any form. But it told him something important. It told him that Indra needed him, and she knew it. She was willing to at least show him some respect, even if only to win his favor. *Not so much as to accept her own father's embrace, of course. That would be too much to ask.*

"How could I not come, for my only daughter?" he said with a warm smile, though the sentiment seemed only to make Indra cringe. It was still too much, too soon, he saw. How carefully must he tread for fear of offending this insolent child? Did she not realize how her own disrespectful behavior offended him?

"You will see that I am unarmed," she said, seemingly keen to get on with things. "I come here in good faith."

Edgard had not thought to notice it, but now he saw that the hilts of the two swords that would normally be visible over Indra's shoulders were not there. The fact that she thought this necessary concerned him.

"There was no need for that," he said, opening his hands in a conciliatory gesture. "You are not my enemy. And I hope you understand that I am not yours, either."

Indra nodded, though she seemed unconvinced. "Did you bring Cuthbert?"

Edgard sighed and motioned to one of the men behind him, who turned and ran back toward the encampment. Indra and Edgard regarded each other in silence, one reluctant to speak and the other unsure what to say. It came as a relief to both when Cuthbert finally appeared, gathering up his monastic robe at his feet to keep it from dragging through the mud as he trudged awkwardly toward them.

Indra brightened immediately at the sight of him, something Edgard did not fail to notice. As Cuthbert drew level with him, Edgard saw Indra smile at the scraggy priest in a way she never had toward him, her own father, and for a moment it made him hate them both.

"Cuthbert, it's good to see you," said Indra.

"My lady," replied Cuthbert with a bow.

Enough of this. "Well, here we all are. Where is it?"

Indra bristled. "I think you mean where is *he*?"

"Well, night has fallen," said Edgard with a thin smile. "If this man is as you described, I believe that, as of this moment, my wording is correct."

"He is close by," said Indra. "I couldn't convince him to stay with me, but I've been tracking him. He doesn't know."

"Did he try to harm you in any way?" Edgard asked.

"No. I don't believe he wants to harm anyone."

Edgard nodded, then motioned toward the woods from which Indra had come. "Well, then. We are ready. Lead the way." He made to step forward but Indra stayed him with an out-held palm.

"First, I will have your word," she said.

Edgard looked at her quizzically. "My word?"

"That you mean to help this man, not do him harm."

"Of course," said Edgard. "Was that not your request? Is that not why I have come? I will do all that I can for this unfortunate soul, if you will just bring me to him."

Edgard waited, but Indra did not move. She scrutinized his face as though trying to divine his true intent, then looked to the paladins of the Order assembled in the camp behind him. "If you came out here to help him," she said, "why bring a dozen armed men?"

"A precaution only," said Edgard in a reassuring tone. "We know nothing of this man other than the little that you wrote."

"I told you he means no harm. You don't trust me?"

"Of course I do. But you must trust me in return, or else what are we doing here?"

Indra appeared uncertain for a moment, then turned her attention to Cuthbert. "I know that you will tell me the truth," she said. "Can this man's curse be lifted?"

Edgard looked pointedly at the priest. Cuthbert looked away, then down at his feet, as he struggled with his conscience. Then, at last, his eyes returned to Indra's. "No," he said grimly. "But—" Edgard cut him off with a sharply raised hand.

Indra glared angrily at Edgard. "And of course you would have known that before you departed with a dozen men-at-arms at your back. I should have known better than to hope for the truth from you. You were feeding me lies when I was barely old enough to hear them."

"Enough!" Edgard barked at her, his patience at an end. "I am your father and you will obey me!"

Edgard's thundering voice rattled several of the armed men behind him, but Indra remained unmoved. "I believe I've made it clear, many times, how I feel about that," she said calmly.

Edgard took a step forward, scowling menacingly. "Very well. If you will not accept my authority as your father, you will accept it as your commanding officer. As lord marshal of the Order, I—"

"I won't allow you to harm this man," said Indra, still unbowed. "He is innocent and should not be punished for the actions of a beast beyond his control."

"I would not wish to punish a rabid dog for its actions either," said Edgard, "but still it must be put down." He put his hand to his forehead and looked to the sky, exasperated. "Why are we still talking about this as though it were a negotiation? You will take us to this man without further argument or obstruction. Now."

Indra heard a rustling behind her and looked around to see eight more of Edgard's men, swords drawn, emerging from the trees. They fanned out around her together with the dozen in front of her, circling her entirely. She looked back at Edgard as though part of her had expected this. "What was that you said about trust?"

Edgard shrugged. "As I said, useful only so long as it is mutual. If you will not trust me, then you force my hand. One way or another, you will lead us to this beast."

Indra looked at the faces of the men surrounding her. Hard and battle-scarred, every one. She recognized most of them. Some she had beaten and battered in the sparring circle, and she did not doubt that they would be only too happy to return the favor now, given the order. She looked back to Edgard. "You won't harm me. You know it won't work."

Edgard sighed; he had known the ploy was unlikely to succeed, but he still had cards left to play. "No. But I will have you tied and taken back to Canterbury while my men conduct a thorough search of this area. If this abomination of yours is not far from here, I doubt it will take them long to find it. Or you can take us to it and avoid a hunt that I am sure would go harder on the beast than on us. I leave the choice to you."

He hoped still to convince her, to do this without engendering still more resentment toward him. He stepped closer, close enough to reach out and touch her, but she retreated again.

"Indra, I only want what is best for you. Help us, and on our return to Canterbury you will be rewarded with full investiture into the Order. The youngest paladin there has ever been, and the first woman. Isn't that what you've always wanted?"

She looked at him with contempt and shook her head. "You don't understand at all, do you? You never will."

Edgard knew then that nothing he could say or do would overcome the disdain she still held for him. With a heavy sigh, he motioned to his men. She stood stock-still as they closed the circle around her, but when the nearest man reached for her arm, he stumbled, trying to grasp something that was not there. A moment later, a second man grabbed her with both arms from behind, only to fall forward, clean through the very spot where she stood. Edgard watched in astonishment as another man and another tried to take hold of her, their hands passing through the formless apparition.

Cuthbert was the first to comprehend what was happening, and he could not keep a smile from creeping across his lips. All he could do was turn his face away so that Edgard did not see it.

Edgard marched toward Indra and thrust out his hand. Like all the others, it passed cleanly through her body as though she were no more than a shadow. She met his gaze and gave him a crooked smile. "It would appear we trust each other equally," she said. And then she was gone, her ghost shimmering and fading into nothing before Edgard's eyes.

He stood there for a moment in bewilderment. Then he whirled and seized Cuthbert by the throat, the priest's legs pedaling backward frantically as Edgard marched him toward the nearest tree and pinned him against it, glaring in wild-eyed fury.

"You taught her magick?" he hissed, leaning in close, flecks of spit from between his gritted teeth landing on Cuthbert's face. "You taught her to *scry*?"

Cuthbert groped helplessly at the hand clamped around his neck. His face began to turn red, his mouth opening and closing like a fish flapping on a riverbank as he gasped for breath.

Edgard loosened his grip, just enough to allow Cuthbert to speak.

"She wanted to learn, and I could not dissuade her! My lord, you must understand, that girl can be most insistent when she is of a mind. She will not take no for an answer!"

Edgard released his grip and Cuthbert slipped to his knees against the tree, gulping in air.

"Truer words were never spoken," Edgard said as he looked toward the spot where Indra had disappeared. Then back to Cuthbert. "Idiot! What were you thinking, telling her the truth when she asked what could be done? Until then we had her! What other truths might you have told her had she asked, I wonder?"

Cuthbert looked up, pathetic, crumpled in the mud at the base of the tree, still trying to catch his breath. How the man had survived in this world so long on only his wits—ample though they were—was a mystery Edgard was sure he would never solve.

"None that are for me to tell her," the priest said in a hoarse voice.

Edgard took his meaning, and it was not appreciated. He drew back his hand to strike. Cuthbert flinched and threw up his arms, and that was enough for Edgard. He gave an amused smirk, then reached out and offered his hand. He still needed the priest, after all.

Gingerly, Cuthbert took Edgard's hand and was pulled to his feet. Edgard turned his attention back to the darkened woods surrounding them. "How far away might she be?" he asked.

"It depends on the level of her ability," said Cuthbert. "At best, she could be as far as five miles in any direction."

Edgard frowned. Under normal circumstances, finding her might be impossible. Fortunately, he knew Indra well enough to suspect some trickery on her part and had come well prepared. "It is a good thing for you," he said to Cuthbert as the priest brushed the mud from his robes, "that she is not the only one with magickal tricks up her sleeve."

TWENTY-EIGHT

Wulfric woke among the ashes, squinting against the warm rays of the rising sun. He groaned, his body ringing from head to toe with the aches and pains that had become as familiar a part of his waking as the morning light. He shook the smoldering gray dust from his hair, then swept his hand through the ash at his side until he found where he had left the key, which he used to release the padlock. The chain around him fell slack. He shrugged it loose and, standing, stepped free of it, the warm ash crunching beneath his feet.

Once again, he was coated in its gray residue, with no trace left of the human flesh beneath. In a way, he found it almost comforting. It had been strange to see himself as he had yesterday, as a man he once knew but barely remembered. His skin of ash was part of who he was now, and it felt wrong to have it cast off, though he did not blame the girl for doing it. Her intentions had been born out of kindness. He could not have expected her to understand.

What was it she had called him? A gray ghost? That was accurate enough a description, he supposed. The ghost of a man who once lived, long ago.

He found his cloak and threw it on, then began unwinding the chain from the tree. As usual, the bark was tattered and stripped bare where the beast had strained against it, trying to break free.

As usual, he would have to check every link in the chain to ensure that none had bent or weakened. If even one had—

"Wulfric."

She was standing on the other side of the tree.

Wulfric let out a groan of exasperation. Though he had known she would try to follow him, he had been certain that he had lost her yesterday; the path he had taken should have been enough to lose anyone. This girl seemed to have a way of confounding his estimation of her. And of not understanding the simple concept of *no*.

"Girl," he said wearily, "I will not tell you again—"

She moved toward him, and now Wulfric saw that there was something different in her demeanor. There was an urgency about her, bordering on fear, and she looked as though she had barely slept since last he saw her.

"Listen to me," she said. "We need to go, as far from here as we can, as quickly as we can. I will explain, but first we must get moving. Enough time has been lost already."

"We?" said Wulfric. "I thought I had made myself clear."

"You don't understand!" she said. "I have placed you in grave danger. We must go, now!"

Wulfric did not know quite what to make of this. So many times had he died and been reborn that he no longer thought of himself as capable of being in danger; he was more accustomed to thinking of those he might put in danger if he were careless.

"In danger how?" he asked.

"The Order is here. They're looking for you. Right now." He could see by the way she carried herself, shifting her weight fitfully from one foot to the other, that she was beside herself with worry.

"Wulfric, I'm sorry. My father is a powerful man; he commands the Order, and I thought I might persuade him to help you. I was wrong. He intends to hunt you down, and has brought the best of his men with him."

Wulfric took a moment to think on this. Then, calmly, he gathered his robe around himself and sat down, planting himself cross-legged at the base of the tree where he had slept.

"What are you doing?" said Indra. "This is not a joke! If they come here and find you they will kill you!"

"Good," said Wulfric. "Let them come."

Indra just gaped at him. "What?"

"If you will not grant my simple request, I am quite certain they will. Let them chain me up and kill the damned thing and me with it," he said, neatly arranging the folds of his tatty cloak across his knees. "I always avoided the Order, as I thought the beast unkillable and that any contact with them would only result in more needless slaughter. Now I have cause to believe otherwise."

Indra threw up her hands and shook her head at him. "You're impossible. I swear it, you're beyond help!"

"I have been trying to convince you of that for some time."

"What reason do you have to believe that killing the beast would even work, beyond a scar that passed from it to you?" said Indra. "What does that prove?"

"For me, it is proof enough," Wulfric said, still a calm sea against Indra's raging storm. "If you had lived my life these past fifteen years, you would take any sliver of hope that was offered, however thin it might be. God works in ways mysterious, but now I understand, and I thank him for sending you to me."

Indra blinked. "You think God sent me."

"I believe that you were his way of showing me that I have suffered enough for my sins. That it is time for my punishment to end."

Indra put her hands to her face and pulled on her skin, utterly exasperated. "You were cursed by the magick of an evil madman as you risked your own life trying to stop him, and you believe that this is all somehow a punishment from God."

"Yes," he said. "Punishment for a life spent killing, and for betraying my father and my mother."

She sank to one knee before him. She seemed calmer now, more levelheaded. "Wulfric. Explain this to me, so I can understand it, and I swear I will bother you no longer. I will leave you be, to whatever fate you believe you deserve. Just, please, help me understand."

Wulfric sighed. What difference did it make what he told the girl now? He would be dead soon enough, and perhaps if he satisfied her curiosity, she might actually stay true to her word and allow him to spend his final hours in some kind of peace.

"My father hoped that I would be a farmer, my mother, an artisan of some kind. Instead, I became a soldier and gave my life to war, where I discovered that I had a great talent for violence. Some thought it a gift. I did not. But I allowed it to flourish all the same. I nurtured and fed the killer in me with each life I took in battle, until it became all that I was.

"I tell you now what I believe. That this monster within me has always been there, from the day that I was born. It is within every man, and every man must conquer it, or else it conquers him. I lost that battle long before I ever met Aethelred. And so God used him to punish me by showing me what I had become. He sent him and his curse to draw the murderous thing inside of me outward, to give it form.

"But that was not the end of it. The curse, as I have come to realize, was only part punishment. It was also part test. God was offering me one final chance to redeem myself, to prove to him that I was not beyond salvation. When I returned home, and the beast was born for the first time, he challenged me to find it within myself to conquer it. I failed. It ran wild and slaughtered every man, woman, and child in my village, including my own beloved wife and newborn daughter. Both of them cut to pieces, butchered beyond recognition, because I had not the strength to stop it, even to protect those I loved most. The life that I had led so diminished the man, all that remained was the monster.

"This is why I know it is God who punishes me. Because only he could have conceived a justice so poetic."

Indra stared at Wulfric in a kind of stupefied shock. For a moment Wulfric felt guilty for burdening her with the full horror of his story, but then again, he had done all he could to keep it from her, until she insisted upon hearing it.

"Now, I hope that you will understand," he said. "And that you will keep your promise, and leave me to my end."

Indra did not respond, or even acknowledge that he had spoken. Still paralyzed, she had a distant look that suggested thoughts racing through her mind faster than she could marshal them. She leapt to her feet, paced up and down, more agitated now than she had seemed when she had first appeared to warn him.

She stopped, looked at him. "This was fifteen years ago. When the beast killed your wife and daughter, destroyed your village."

"Yes," said Wulfric.

Indra shook her head. "No, it's not possible," she said. "You are too young. You would have been little older than I am. Too young for a wife and child."

"I was born forty-four years ago," said Wulfric. "But since the time I was cursed, I have not aged a day. Part of my punishment, I suppose, that I should not find relief even in death by decrepitude."

Wulfric paused. "Child, what is wrong with you?" Indra's expression had become entirely ashen. Not for the first time, she looked at Wulfric as though he were a dead man risen from the grave.

"I was told that my parents were killed by an abomination," she said. "Along with their entire village. That is what I was raised to believe."

Wulfric was confused. "You said your father commanded—"

"He is my father in name only. He took me from my crib when he found my village in ruins. Fifteen years ago. He tried to raise me as his own, but I always suspected that something was amiss, and when at last I demanded to know the truth, he told me that my real father was a man named Wulfric, a peasant who had died with my mother in the massacre on my home. I thought little of it when you told me your name, as it is not so uncommon, but . . ."

Now Wulfric's heart was racing as well. Now he, like Indra, tried to make sense of the seemingly impossible.

His wife and daughter were both dead. He had seen it for himself. Cwen had been torn to pieces, of that there could be no doubt. And the infant? Though he had looked for only a moment, his memory of the horror he had seen in his daughter's crib was seared indelibly into his mind, as vivid today as fifteen years ago. Nothing but bloody, unrecognizable scraps of torn flesh and splintered bone. But whose?

Turning the image over and over in his mind, he realized now that, amidst such carnage, he could not be sure. He could not—

"No," he said, hitting upon a detail that undermined the possibility of it being true. "You are too old. You are eighteen, that is what you said. You said—"

"I lied so that you would not dismiss me," she admitted. "I will be sixteen in October."

October. The month his daughter had been born.

"Your mother, what was her name?" he asked Indra.

"Cwen," she answered, and Wulfric flushed from head to toe and felt his heart quicken. He opened his mouth to speak, but found that now he barely had the strength. His voice was little more than a whisper, but he was close enough for Indra to hear.

"My wife."

Venator flew into the grove and glided to a landing close to where they stood, carrying a fat white-bellied salmon in his beak, the spoils of his morning hunt. Neither Wulfric nor Indra noticed, for at that moment nothing in the world existed save the two of them.

Wulfric rose slowly to his feet. He looked at Indra, as she looked at him. Both afraid to move, or speak, for fear of shattering this moment. The truth seemed beyond doubt, and yet so fragile that the slightest thing might undo it. In the end, it was Wulfric who dared first, taking a tentative step toward Indra, his hand leaving his side as he began to reach for hers. Then she did the same, the distance closing between them—

"Hold!"

They froze, but a few feet from one another, as twenty men of the Order emerged from the woods on horseback, swords and bows drawn, surrounding the two of them. Then followed Edgard, his jaw set sternly, Cuthbert riding just behind him, head down and forlorn.

Though it had been fifteen years, Wulfric recognized his old friend and comrade immediately. Edgard's hair was thinning, and he had grown fatter, but he had that same unmistakably overbearing look about him. It was a look that he had worn far better as a younger man. Back then it had seemed a well-earned surplus of confidence. Now it looked more like arrogance.

Edgard appeared not to recognize Wulfric so readily; or rather, he seemed disconcerted by the sight of him, and he turned his attention quickly to Indra.

"I told you that you would lead us to this beast," he said with a self-satisfied smile. "One way or the other."

TWENTY-NINE

"Venator, to me."

The hawk seemed at first conflicted, then flew onto Edgard's arm as commanded. Edgard removed the leather glove from his right hand and, carefully, unfastened the copper message ring from around Venator's leg, opening it at its hinge and holding it so that Indra could see. On its inner surface a miniature fine-cut emerald had been embedded, so small and so carefully hidden that she had failed to notice it when Venator had returned from Canterbury.

"An enchanted gem," said Edgard with a pronounced air of satisfaction. "Just one of the minor miracles we have wrought from our study of Aethelred's works over the years. I don't pretend to understand how the magick works, but the emerald is traceable, by those with the expertise, across any distance to wherever in the world it might be. I had planned to use them to tag any abominations we might capture and bring to Canterbury for study, should they escape, but it seems they work just as well for finding errant children who betray their father's trust."

Wulfric glowered at Edgard. "This is the man who found you, who raised you as his own?" he asked Indra in a low, restrained voice.

Indra was astonished. "You *know* him?"

"He was once my friend."

Edgard pocketed the emerald, seeming disappointed that his ingenuity and cunning had not been better appreciated. He pulled his glove back on. "Separate them."

His men responded, dismounting to take Wulfric and Indra by the arms and pull them apart. Wulfric did not resist, but the first man who tried to lay a hand on Indra was greeted with an elbow to the face and crashed to the ground with a bloody mouth. She struck the second man in the shin with the sole of her boot, and he limped away, cursing. Then, as she reached for her swords, three men grabbed her all at once, pinning her arms behind her, and there was nothing more she could do. They dragged her away from Wulfric while she struggled and kicked uselessly.

"Gently, please," Edgard said to the men who held her. "Treacherous as she is, she is still my daughter."

Indra stopped struggling and focused on Edgard, the whole of her filled with a loathing that went down to the bone. "I am not your daughter!" she growled, then looked over to where Edgard's men were holding Wulfric. "I am *his*! And you always knew, didn't you? You knew when you found me that his body was not among the dead, that he was out there somewhere, alive. You lying pig!"

Edgard flinched, unable to hide how Indra's words stung him. Then he swung his leg lazily over his saddle and dismounted. Indra stiffened at his approach; it was difficult to tell if, were she not held firmly by three men, she would run away from him or right at him, swords drawn.

He stood before her, all trace of conceit gone. Now there was only sincerity. Or, to Indra's eyes, an effort to create the illusion of it.

"Indra, my child," he said. "You must understand that what I did, I did only to protect you. I hid the truth from you because I knew it could bring you nothing but grief. You deserved better than that. You deserved a real father, not this . . ." He glanced over at Wulfric, careful not to meet his eye. "This pitiful creature."

Indra's anger was not lessened; it burned brighter. "It wasn't your choice to make but mine, and you robbed me of it," she hissed between gritted teeth. "All my life I knew that something was out of place, but not what, or why. Because you were too spineless, too selfish, to tell me the truth."

The reddening of Edgard's face as his temper began to fray should have warned Indra to go no further, but her anger had taken hold and consequences were no longer a part of her thinking. She would have her say no matter what.

"I always imagined there might be some other lie beyond those you had admitted to. I never imagined anything so low as this," she said. "Do you know how, even as a young girl, I suspected that you were not my real father, no matter how much you would insist? It wasn't just the whisperings of your men behind my back. It was because I recognized you for what you were, in your bones, and I knew that I could never be the natural-born child of such a fucking coward."

The words hung in the air. Several of Edgard's men exchanged nervous looks. Edgard himself clenched his jaw, his own anger now welling up within him. The wound Indra had dealt him was grievous, and he knew only one way to respond. He drew back his hand to strike her—

"Edgard."

He froze. Wulfric stood several yards away, watching intently. "Lay one hand on that girl and I will show you how a father protects his daughter."

Edgard knew that look in Wulfric's eyes; it was no idle threat. Still, three men had him under close guard.

He slapped Indra hard across the face with the back of his hand, leaving a stinging welt on her cheek.

The three men guarding Wulfric had perhaps been lulled by his lack of resistance when they first took him, and by his disheveled appearance. Now he gave each of them cause to reconsider. Before Edgard's blow had even completed its arc, one man was on the ground clutching his throat, his windpipe crushed. The second and third went down in short order after that, one wailing as he collapsed to his knees at the sight of the splintered bone protruding from his right arm, the other splayed out, unconscious, blood streaming from his nose. Free, Wulfric bolted toward Edgard. He made it halfway before the first arrow struck him in the shoulder and was still running when the next three hit him in the chest and the right knee. Indra let out a scream as Wulfric stumbled and pitched forward, crashing face-first to the ground, his outstretched arm just inches from where Edgard stood.

Edgard's mounted archers nocked fresh arrows as he stepped forward cautiously and nudged Wulfric's body with his boot. It did not move.

"Bastard!" Indra spat, kicking at Edgard with both feet as his men struggled to restrain her. "You fucking bastard!"

Edgard ignored her, motioning to two more of his men. They lifted up Wulfric's corpse and hauled him away, his feet dragging along the ground. Indra watched, distraught, as they slung his body over the back of a horse.

"Calm yourself, girl," said Edgard. "You know as well as I do that he will not be dead for long." He turned away and walked back to his steed, planting his foot in the stirrup and hoisting himself into the saddle. "Move out!" he commanded as his men helped up their injured. "We make Canterbury before nightfall, or not at all."

Indra was marched to a horse, all fight gone out of her. When the men were mounted, and the Order rode back into the forest, Cuthbert was the last to go, his head hung low in shame.

— —•◦⊰⊙⊱◦•— —

They made even better time than on their outward journey, returning to Canterbury as the sun was just beginning to set. Edgard's men had been well briefed on Wulfric's condition and what would happen if night fell before they had him secured within their fortress. This time they did not stop to rest.

Wulfric's body was brought inside and taken to a dungeon that had been built as part of Edgard's military renovations. Down flights of stone steps and past girded doors and iron-barred gates, he was carried until he was brought inside a large straw-lined cell and dumped unceremoniously atop the oak table at its center, a table heavily bolstered with iron and bolted to the floor. The six men assigned to this task made hasty work of it; down here in the bowels of the old church, the only light came from the torches flickering on the walls; there were no windows to show how far the sun was from setting, and so no way of knowing how soon this dead man would become something far more dangerous.

They laid out Wulfric's body and wrapped it in chains that ran through iron rings around the table's edges. The moment the chains were secured, the men fled from the cell and back along the stone-walled corridor from which they had come. Most were already on the stairs leading back to the surface before the last of them scurried out of the cell and slammed the heavy iron gate behind him. Even among the deep shadows inside the cell, the man could have sworn he saw Wulfric's body move as he inserted the key with trembling hands and turned it in the lock. Then he, too, was gone, his ring of keys jangling as he pelted along the hallway and disappeared around the bend in the spiral stairs.

Some minutes later, Edgard appeared, carrying with him a straight-backed wooden chair. He placed the chair several feet short of the cell's iron gate and sat, peering into the gloom beyond the bars. In the dim glow of the torchlight he could see a dark shape, motionless and chained to the reinforced table, but little else.

He sat. And watched. And waited. After fifteen minutes had passed, he started to wonder if something was wrong, but just as he began to fidget, so, too, did Wulfric.

Edgard leaned forward in fascination; he had seen every form of abomination under the sun, had hunted and killed them all, but he had never seen anything like this. And as Wulfric's body began to jerk against the chains that held him to the table, began to split apart and spill out foul black blood that reeked of sulfur, it dawned on Edgard that he might be able to put this beast to far greater use than simply another trophy.

Cuthbert paced in his study, the light from his lamp turned low. The darkness was doing little to help him think this time. It was not that he lacked an idea; it was the matter of whether the plan would work and, more pertinently, whether he had the courage to carry it out, that he wrestled with.

He had never considered himself a brave man. Part of the reason he had entered the priesthood, in a time of seemingly unending war, had been to avoid conscription into some military profession for which he knew he had not the mettle. God had found a way to test that mettle anyway. His unique understanding of Aethelred's discoveries and his subsequent forced recruitment into the Order had subjected him to horrors far beyond anything he imagined conventional war could bring. His service had hardened him, to be sure, but still he knew that he had never fully stepped out of the shadow of the callow cleric he had been fifteen years before.

No greater proof of that existed than the fact that he had betrayed his friend. His years under Edgard's command at Canterbury had been mostly miserable. The knights he served with, all red meat and bravado, saw him as an odd little weakling to be hectored and ridiculed, and Edgard had done nothing to discourage it. Indra was the only one who had ever shown him any kindness or generosity. He had known her since she was a babe in arms, since the day Edgard had brought her back from Wulfric's devastated village, cradled in his arm. He had watched her grow and, in time, she had become his only friend.

It was no mystery to him where her skill with a sword, her upstanding character, her quick wits, and her thirst for knowledge came from—all traits so clearly inherited from her natural father, and, swordsmanship aside, so very unlike those of the man she had been raised by. Eventually, Indra's dogged persistence in pursuit of her own suspicions had wrought the truth from Edgard, but only part of it. The rest, the part that mattered most, had been kept a secret by Cuthbert and Edgard until today, and Cuthbert had never regretted that fact more. Now he had seen with his own eyes how much their years of separation had cost father and daughter both. He could have—should have—done so much more, so much longer ago. But at what cost to his own safety, his own life? *Once a coward, always a coward.*

There was a knock at his door. Cuthbert hoped it would not be Edgard; he had never wanted to see the man less than he did now. As the door swung open, Cuthbert turned up his lamp and saw, in the soft green light of the unburning flame, that it was Indra. He was at first relieved; then he wondered if he might wish to see her even less than Edgard. What was worse, fear or guilt? He managed a cautious smile as Indra let the door close behind her.

"I thought you were confined to your room," he said.

"That works as well today as it ever did," said Indra. Cuthbert found himself wondering what she had done to the poor bastard Edgard had assigned to stand guard outside her door.

"Well, as considerable as is my surprise to see you, my joy is far greater," he said, hoping for some indication that she felt the same. "Almost a year gone, with no word. I admit there were times when I feared the worst."

Indra looked at him impassively. If there was any indication of warm feeling toward him, it was lost in the shadows and gloom. "Did you think I wouldn't survive out there?" she asked, her tone giving his hopes equally little to cling to.

"At times," he admitted. "Then I remembered how good you were with those swords and that damned stick of yours and the feeling passed." He grinned sheepishly, hoping that his attempt at humor would cajole a favorable response from her. If not, at least he would know for sure where he stood. It was the uncertainty that was so agonizing.

Still nothing, not a flicker. Cuthbert began to feel queasy. "Indra, I—"

"Did you know?"

His shame was so great that he could no longer look her in the eye. He turned away, looked at the floor, at the leather-bound volumes on his shelves. Anywhere but at her. "Yes. I am the reason Edgard knew. When he first brought you here from your father's village, and could not account for his body among the others found there, I told him of my suspicion."

"What suspicion?" Indra stepped closer, into a brighter pool of light that only made it more difficult for Cuthbert to look at her. He made his way to his desk and began shuffling papers absentmindedly.

"Before Aethelred was killed, in the cathedral nave above us, he placed upon your father one final curse. The scar on his chest is the proof of it."

"So it was my father who killed Aethelred," he heard Indra say behind him. "Not Edgard, as he always claimed."

Cuthbert had not intended to reveal that; it had just slipped out in the telling. But he was glad of it. It was time for all the truths that had been rotting him away from the inside to come out, every one of them. He nodded.

"After he killed the archbishop, your father burned Aethelred's last writings, but I had already seen enough to further my study of his work and, in time, come to understand what it was that he had discovered: the means to create a new form of abomination, magick that could turn a man into a beast and back again, over and over, without end. When I learned what happened to your father's village, the day after he returned home, I knew what had become of him.

"I told Edgard what I had discovered; I begged him to take his men and search for Wulfric so that we might find some way to help him, but he would have none of it. He knew what I told him was true, but still he hid behind demands for proof, which he knew would be impossible to give. He was determined to raise you as his own, and so he abandoned Wulfric to the cursed life that he has lived.

"And he told me that if I should ever tell you any of this, he would see me tortured to death. So you see, it is my own coward-ice as much as Edgard's deceit that led you to believe your whole life that your true father was dead. God, it seems, found a way to correct my mistake. That makes me no less of a wretch for perpet-uating it all these years."

Finally he turned back to face her, surprised to see her stand-ing closer to him now. He trembled with guilt. "Indra . . . I can never apologize enough. I will understand if you can never forgive me for what I have done, but I hope that you will not hate me for it. In all the world you are my only friend, and that would be more than I could bear."

Silence so filled the room that all Cuthbert could hear was the sound of Indra's breathing. Then, at last, she reached out and took his hand in hers. As Cuthbert began to sob, she put her arms around him and held him close to her, as though she knew he might fall if she did not.

"I have few enough friends myself," she said as his body shook in her arms. "I don't discard them for telling me the truth, no mat-ter how overdue." She stepped back as Cuthbert steadied himself against his desk and wiped the sleeve of his robe across his eyes. "That doesn't mean, however, that you don't owe me a very, very large favor."

Cuthbert smiled, the relief still washing over him. "Anything," he said, his voice shaking.

"Before, in the churchyard, you said that the curse cannot be lifted. Are you absolutely sure?"

"Alas, yes," said Cuthbert. "I have spent fifteen years searching for a way, but the curse goes deep. The beast is in him down to the marrow, as much a part of him now as is his human half. If there is any way to exorcise it, it is beyond my ability."

Indra ran her hands through her hair, despondent. "You were my only hope," she said. "I was sure that you might know of some way . . ."

It tore at Cuthbert's soul to see her like this. *Enough is enough*, he thought. *Will you let fear rule you your whole life? So what if it doesn't work? You have to tell her. You have to try. You owe her that and more.*

"I know of no way to separate the man from the beast," he said. "But there is, perhaps, another way to save him. At least, in part."

Indra took Cuthbert by the arm, gripping him firmly.

"Tell me."

THIRTY

Wulfric was not accustomed to waking in darkness, or on his back, though little else was different. The aches, the grogginess, the raging thirst, and the smell of sulfur were all too familiar. The absence of bright sunlight was in some small way a mercy but no less confusing for it. He sat up with a pained groan and noticed that something else was strange: he was naked and coated in ashes, but there were none surrounding him.

As his hands groped in the gloom, he realized he was sitting on a wooden floor. Then he found the edges of it. Not a floor, but some kind of raised platform or table. He looked around blindly, trying to remember how he had come to be in this place, whatever this place was. His memory was a blur, a smear of half-formed images and sensations in nonsensical order. He remembered the pain of arrowheads piercing his flesh, a sudden flush of rage. A face, that he had come to know recently, and one that he had not seen in many years. The new face stilled, slowly becoming recognizable. A girl's face, young and beautiful, mouthing the same words again and again. Faraway and indistinct at first, her voice became clearer with each repetition.

. . . *a man named Wulfric my real father was a man named Wulfric my real father. . .*

The rest of it came back to him all at once and with such force that it made him giddy.

My daughter. My daughter is alive.

"Good morning."

He snapped his head around to see a dark figure silhouetted against the dim torchlight on the other side of a heavy, iron-barred gate. Wulfric could not see the man clearly, but he knew Edgard's voice. His every bone and muscle still protesting, he slowly made his way down off the table and planted his feet on the straw-lined floor. As he stood upright, Edgard took a step closer—though still beyond arm's reach of the bars—and now Wulfric saw his face.

"I saw no reason for you to be chained up like a beast during daylight, so I had my men release you and clear away the ashes after you returned to human form," said Edgard. "I must say, that was the most remarkable thing I have ever seen. After Cuthbert told me what you had become, I often wondered how the changing actually worked. But it is far more extraordinary than ever I imagined."

Wulfric's eyes had adjusted to the light, and he saw now that the oak table was charred black where he had slept on it, a ghostly imprint in the vague shape of a human seared into the wood. He slowly made his way toward the gate, feet shuffling in the straw, and saw Edgard retreat a step as he approached. Still dizzy, he reached out and gripped one of the thick iron bars to steady himself.

"Where is she?" His voice cracked, throat dry as a bone.

Edgard sighed. "Wulfric, you know that I have always been your friend. What I did for Indra, I did as much out of friendship to you as to protect her. You should be thankful that it was I who found her. Ask yourself, would you not have thought of me to raise her, if you and Cwen were to die? Who could have made a better godfather?"

"Alfred was to be her godfather," said Wulfric. It was true; that was the one thing Wulfric had planned to ask from his friend, the King, in return for all his years of bloody service. He had intended to ask Cwen for her blessing in it the day after he returned home. The day he had awoken to find her dead.

Edgard glanced away, disappointed. "Yes, well. Perhaps then it was fate that Alfred had his part to play. I returned to Winchester in your stead to inform him of Aethelred's death, and the King refused to hold any celebration in your absence. He dispatched me to your village to insist that you attend, and so it was that I discovered Indra, the sole survivor of the carnage you—*you!*—had wrought the night before, crying and covered in her own mother's blood. Had I not, who knows what manner of lowborn peasant might have found and raised her, if anyone at all. It is thanks to me that she survived and had a proper upbringing—not that she has ever shown me an ounce of appreciation for any of it.

"In truth, my friend, I did you a kindness in sparing you from raising her. The girl is willful and disobedient to the point of being impossible. No conception at all of what is to be expected of a daughter. Discipline? Ha! She spits on it!"

Wulfric remembered Edgard striking her across the face, and thought back to all the times he had seen his friend bully and browbeat the men in his charge during the wars.

"Did you beat her?"

Edgard raised his chin, sanctimonious. "You do not know her. I do. Her ingratitude would try the temper of any man. She was raised the daughter of a nobleman, in a house that would be the envy of kings. Her whole life she has wanted for nothing."

"Except her true father," said Wulfric. "You knew my fate. You could have searched for me, or told her the truth and freed her to do it. Yet you did nothing."

"You were damned. Beyond salvation," said Edgard, steadfast. "I did no wrong in this, Wulfric. Who was harmed? She was in want of a father, and you know that I had always wanted a child of my own."

"Then you should have *had* a child of your own!" Wulfric spat back. "Instead you forsook me so that you could steal mine." He seized the iron bars with both hands and shook them so hard they rattled. Edgard took another step back.

"You would have me condemn her to grow up with the knowledge that her father was accursed, a monster who killed her mother and was wandering the earth like a wraith, past all hope?" Edgard said, trying to remain resolute in the face of Wulfric's withering glare. "What would that have done to her?"

"That girl is stronger than you know," said Wulfric. "You should have trusted her with the truth. Instead, the wound you inflicted upon her with this lie has festered her entire life."

Edgard seemed less sure of himself now but determined to cling to his righteousness. He pointed accusingly at Wulfric. "You are wrong to hate me for this, old friend."

From behind the bars Wulfric shook his head. "You are not my friend. And I do not hate you. I pity you."

Edgard appeared surprised. "What?"

"I have seen up close my daughter's anger. It is a thing to be reckoned with. She has spent her life searching for the thing that created it. And now at last she has found it. Cursed though I am, I would sooner be in my position than yours."

Wulfric watched Edgard as those words sank in, saw the man's face turn sour. It took a moment for Edgard to regain his composure. "I came here to tell you that I bear you no ill will. You may think that God has cursed you with this affliction, but I believe that he still has a purpose for you. You founded this Order, and now, in its hour of greatest need, you may be the one to save it."

Wulfric just looked at him, not understanding.

"I have sent for an emissary of the King. He arrives before sundown. When my men come to secure you to the table, I advise you not to resist. I'm sure you would rather not have to die twice in two days." Edgard turned and marched away, toward the spiral steps at the end of the hallway.

"Edgard."

Edgard stopped, looked back. Wulfric glared at him from the shadows.

"You look old."

Suddenly self-conscious, Edgard brushed a strand of thinning hair away from his lined face. A small wound, but one that Wulfric knew would sting. *Still as vain as you were, only now with much less cause.*

Edgard looked back and forth between the stairs and the cell, as though trying to decide whether to let the slight pass. Then he marched back to the cell, stopping just out of Wulfric's reach. "You know, I never truly realized how close you and Alfred were," he said with a spiteful sneer. "Until I saw how devastated he was when I told him of your death. He never really recovered from it. The sickness came on shortly after that. I do believe that it was the beginning of the end of him. Such a shame."

He let that linger for a moment, then turned with a flourish of his cape and swept back down the hallway, dousing the torches on the wall as he went, until the dark had swallowed Wulfric whole.

Time has a way of bending and stretching strangely in total darkness, and Wulfric did not know how much had passed before the torch at the farthest end of the hallway was lit again, creating a tiny, flickering point of light. Then another, closer. Someone was moving along the corridor toward his cell, lighting the torches on the wall as they went.

Wulfric stood and made his way closer to the bars. It was not one figure approaching but two. At first he assumed it to be Edgard's men, as promised, but then he heard the two voices quietly bickering with one another as they went along. One voice he recognized immediately, the other was harder to place, but it was someway familiar to him, too.

The nearest torch was lit, and as the flames grew, casting a dim glow in front of the cell, Wulfric saw Indra and a slender man in a hooded robe, who fidgeted and wrung his hands nervously. But all Wulfric's attention was on his daughter. He pressed his body against the bars, reaching out for her. She took his hand and brought herself as close to him as the iron between them would allow.

Wulfric looked upon her, and even in the poor light it was obvious to him now. She had her mother's eyes. Her nose. Her smile. Her spirit. It was uncanny. How had he not seen it before? *Because who sees the impossible, even when it is standing right in front of them?*

"Father," she said, her eyes welling up.

"My girl." Wulfric gripped her hand tightly.

In the end it was the man in the hood who brought them back to the world. He issued a polite cough as he drew back his hood.

"Um, perhaps there will be more time for this later?"

"Of course," said Indra. "Father, this is—"

"Cuthbert," said Wulfric in wonderment. He recognized him instantly. He had always liked the man, strange as he was, and though he had all but forgotten him in the years since, the sight of the priest now overjoyed Wulfric for reasons he could not explain. Something about the man, even in all his timidity and awkwardness, brought great reassurance. Wulfric might even have said hope, but for the fact that he had long ago forgotten how to recognize it.

"My lord," said Cuthbert. "I believe there may be a way to help you."

Wulfric's expression turned grim. "Do not think of trying to help me escape. You will only endanger yourselves. I will not—"

"Just listen to him," said Indra. "We don't have much time."

"No, not escape. Not really my specialty," said Cuthbert with a nervous smile. "Magick, however . . ."

Wulfric saw the glimmer of intent in Cuthbert's eyes and shook his head. "There is no way to break this curse."

"That is true," said the priest. "But if I am right, there may be a way to bend it a little."

"You are not beyond salvation, whether you can see that for yourself or not," said Indra. "This I know for a fact. And I can prove it to you."

Wulfric was perplexed. "What do you mean?"

"You believe that the monster within you destroyed the man you once were. But I know better. Those years ago, when it first came, it spared me while all around me were killed. Then a few nights ago, when I fought with it in the clearing, it did so again."

"No," said Wulfric. "You said the beast ran off after you wounded it."

Indra glanced away for a moment, embarrassed. "It's possible I may have . . . embellished my account somewhat in the first telling. The truth is, the beast did not run. The wound I gave it only enraged it more. It had me on the ground, disarmed and helpless. It could have killed me easily. It *should* have killed me. But it didn't. It left me alive.

"Don't you see? It spared me not once but twice, because you would not allow it to harm me. Because even within the beast, some part of you down deep knew that I was your own flesh and blood. And some part of you, conscious or not, was strong enough to stop it." She squeezed his hand more tightly. "Father, the man you were was not destroyed. That man still lives. He has defeated the monster twice already, and he can do so again. If he has the will to fight it."

Wulfric's mind reeled. What he had just heard made a lie of everything that he had long believed about himself, and yet something about it rang true. *Perhaps only because I so want to believe it.* He looked to Cuthbert, lost. The priest nodded soberly to confirm what Indra had said.

"There is a way to help you, but it begins with you believing that you are worthy of it," Cuthbert said, "It begins with you seeking not God's forgiveness, but your own. The guilt you carry with you proves that you are a man of conscience, but it is time now to

put it away. For this to work, you will need faith in yourself, conviction, and strength. And perhaps some luck.

"Wulfric, you are the strongest man I have ever known. But
you have to want this. More than you have ever wanted anything.
Do you?"

He looked at the daughter he believed he had forever lost, into
her eyes, so much like her mother's. "Yes," he said, his voice barely
a whisper.

"Good," said Cuthbert, drawing back his sleeves. He cracked
his knuckles, clapped his hands, and rubbed them together vigor-
ously. "Now, let us begin."

"Wait," said Indra. "There is something I must ask. Something
I'd given up hope of knowing." She looked at him imploringly.
"What is my name? My real name. Please tell me you remember."

There was much that Wulfric had forgotten, eroded by the passage of years or cast away by choice. But not that. Though his old
life had been crushed into dust, that one memory had remained
forever intact, as clear and indestructible as a diamond. It came to
him instantly.

"Beatrice," he told her. "Your name is Beatrice."

And Beatrice wept.

THIRTY-ONE

The King's emissary made his way down the spiral steps, Edgard before him, leading the way with a torch. Under different circumstances, Edgard might have been apprehensive about this visit; with King Edward so consumed with preparations for war, requesting any of his attention, even via a proxy, carried considerable risk of being deemed a waste of his time. But Edgard was quite sure that once the emissary had seen what he would see this night, he would return with exactly the message that Edgard intended. That is, if he still had the stomach to ride the next day. The man looked to be relatively young and had probably never seen an abomination in the flesh, much less the kind that Edgard was about to present to him.

He had already forgotten the man's name—what did it matter?—but he was a person of import at court. Some distant cousin to the Queen. No surprise there; the man looked to Edgard like the kind of spineless toad who could not have risen to such a high station on his own merits. If this was the sort with whom the King kept counsel these days, Edgard had serious concerns about this impending war against the Norse. It was foolhardy enough in conception; would it be executed in similar fashion?

Nevertheless, it was a good sign that Edward had sent such a man, particularly when Edgard had worried that he might not send anyone at all. It was a sign that the Order still commanded at least some respect from the King. Though that respect was greatly diminished since King Alfred's day, it would not be for much longer.

They arrived at the bottom of the stairs and Edgard set his torch into a sconce on the wall. The hallway down here was already lit, though it grew darker as it went, and what lay at its far end was all in shadow. Edgard made a sweeping gesture with his hand for the emissary to accompany him, then started down the hall, the King's man grumbling as he walked alongside. He had seemed vexed to be here from the moment he had arrived, and now, down here in this dimly lit dungeon, his consternation had only grown more apparent.

"I am sure you realize that the King does not appreciate unwarranted distractions at such a critical time," said the emissary with a pronounced frown. By Edgard's estimation, this was the fifth time that the man had pointed this out since he had arrived at the gate.

"Of course," he replied. "I would not dream of asking for His Majesty's attention on anything less than a matter of the greatest urgency. I am sure, when you have seen what I have to show you, that you will agree."

They were halfway down the hallway now, and the emissary's pace was slowing as perhaps some trepidation set in. From here he could see a small group of armed men standing guard in front of a barred gate at the end of the hall. The torches lit the bars of the cell but did not penetrate beyond them; whatever was inside was cloaked in utter darkness.

Edgard noticed that the emissary had fallen a few steps behind him and turned to see that the man had, in fact, come to a complete halt, staring apprehensively at the cell. "What have you got in there?" he asked.

Edgard smiled. "I assure you, you're quite safe," he said.

Warily, the emissary followed Edgard to where the guards awaited. He peered into the cell and saw Wulfric, shackled once more to the oaken table. Seeing that he was securely bound, and some distance behind the bars, the emissary stepped forward for a closer look, observing Wulfric with grim fascination. His skin, filthy with gray ash, his matted hair and beard, the faraway look in his eyes.

"What is that?" the emissary asked in a lowered voice. "Is that a Norseman?"

"No," replied Edgard. "Something far more dangerous."

The emissary could not look away. "He looks barely human."

"How funny you should say that," said Edgard knowingly. "He is only part human. The rest is abomination."

"Abomination?" The emissary appeared bemused. "But he is—"

"We believe that the blight Aethelred brought into this world years ago has somehow grown into a new, and far more dangerous, hybrid form: abominations that appear as men by day, and take on their true form only by night. Perhaps you have heard tales of such things."

The emissary looked more closely at Wulfric. Edgard's reading of him suggested that he was skeptical. Not for much longer.

"I have heard of them," said the emissary. "But the stuff of ghost stories, surely."

"I used to think the same. No longer. As we speak, this new menace spreads across the land like a plague. How far we cannot know, as this new threat is more difficult to detect than the abominations of old. We captured this one two days ago, but who knows how many more may be out there, hiding among us in plain sight?"

In spite of his doubts, the emissary, Edgard could see, was slowly being drawn in by the tale. The dread was creeping up on him as he kept his gaze fixed on Wulfric. "When night falls . . . he will change?"

Edgard nodded and tried not to smile. He had timed this well. It was only a few minutes until sunset, and then this little man would know what dread truly was.

"Have you eaten much today?"

The emissary appeared flummoxed by such an odd question. "What? No. Why?"

"Because what you are about to witness is best done on an empty stomach."

Edgard had set the stage well. Now all he had to do was wait. Once the emissary had seen the monstrosity Wulfric was about to become, he would return to Winchester, to the King, with word of this new and dire threat to the kingdom. He would convince the King of it, or at least convince him to come here and see Wulfric for himself, and that would surely be enough. Enough for the crown to once again lavish gold upon the Order so that Edgard could rebuild it to its former glory and strength—strength enough to combat this new menace.

What did it matter if the threat was imagined? During the darkest days of the scourge, the Order had been a symbol of hope for a populace living in fear. The scourge might be gone, but the need for symbols remained. People still needed something to fear, for that kept them loyal and dutiful. They still needed hope, for that kept them productive. They still needed someone better than themselves to look up to and respect. And young men still needed a place to come and be trained to fight in service of a higher cause.

Towns and villages all across the land still needed men like those of the Order to welcome as heroes so that they might be touched by reflected glory. It made common folk feel good to lavish Edgard and his brave paladins with gifts of tribute, and free ale, and to introduce their daughters to men as noble and valiant as he. Yes, England still needed the Order. It still needed him.

"My lord."

Edgard was snapped from his thoughts. One of his guards motioned toward the cell, and Edgard stepped forward to see that Wulfric's head had lolled to the side, his body slack. It was time. He placed his hand on the shoulder of the emissary, who was rooted to the spot, eyes wide with morbid anticipation. "It will be soon now," he said. "When it begins, do not run. The beast cannot escape the chains, and as the King's eyes, it is important that you see everything."

Edgard could sense the man's fear. He was trembling, and though the stone walls of the dungeon made it a cool place, his face was beaded with sweat. And nothing had even happened yet. Yes, this man was going to deliver His Majesty a very good report. Any moment now . . .

Minutes passed. A few of Edgard's men began to fidget, and the emissary's agitation was slowly starting to resemble impatience.

"When, exactly . . . ?"

"Any moment," said Edgard, his own consternation growing. It should not take this long. He was close to worrying that something was wrong when he saw Wulfric begin to quiver and twitch beneath the chains that bound him to the table. He gripped the emissary's arm firmly. "Now," he said. "Watch this."

A final moment passed. And then Wulfric's jaw fell slack and he began to snore. It was a great, thunderous, rasping sound, not unlike the sound of a blunted saw cutting through a tree, and the stone walls of the cell only amplified it, sending it echoing along the hall.

The emissary shot a look at Edgard. "What is this?"

Edgard scrambled for an answer. "Sometimes the transformation takes longer than . . . if you will only indulge me for a few moments longer . . ."

And so the emissary waited for three more minutes, during which time the cacophony of Wulfric's snorting and grunting as he slept grew louder and louder. Eventually the emissary turned on his heels and marched back toward the spiral steps. Edgard rushed after him.

"Please, if you will—"

"No, no!" said the emissary with mock seriousness. "I have seen quite enough! I will be sure to inform His Majesty of the great peril that England faces from noisy sleepers! I am certain that when I return and tell him what I have seen here, the King will waste no time in adjusting the Order's funding to an amount sufficient to combat this new threat."

The emissary began making his way up the stairs, and Edgard could see that he had lost the man. He gave up and stormed back down the hall toward the cell in red-faced fury. "Open that gate!"

One of the guards rushed to find the key and unlock the gate before Edgard arrived. As the key turned in the lock, Edgard shoved the man aside and barged into the cell where Wulfric was bound, and still waking the dead with his snoring. Edgard struck him hard across the face, bringing him fast awake.

Wulfric blinked as his eyes focused and found Edgard standing over him.

"Why have you not turned?"

Wulfric said nothing, but looked past Edgard as though he were not there. Edgard clamped his hand around Wulfric's cheeks and forced him to meet his eyes. "Look at me, and answer!" he bellowed, apoplectic. "Why have you not turned? What about this night is different?"

Nothing. Edgard released his hand and stepped back. He took a breath, controlled. "You will not make a mockery of me before the crown a second time. Tomorrow morning we depart for Winchester. I will take you to the King himself. If you must languish in his dungeon for a month, sooner or later he will see what you truly are. And if he does not, if you are of no use to me, I will bring you back here and bury you in chains beneath twenty feet of stone and you can suffer in darkness long after Indra and I are dust."

Still quivering with anger, he turned to his senior officer, a stocky, bull-necked man who trained initiates in unarmed combat and was known for going especially hard on them. "Unchain him and see that he remembers what I have said. Make sure he remembers it well."

The bull-necked man nodded and cocked his head toward the cell, gesturing for his men to follow him. Edgard watched as they unchained Wulfric from the table and lifted him from it. When the first punches began to land, Edgard turned and made for the stairs. He had no desire to watch. *This is a necessary evil,* he told himself as he walked away, *but I am not an evil man.*

THIRTY-TWO

Dawn came. The King's emissary had departed for Winchester, and Edgard's men were working in the stables, readying horses for the same journey. A wagon that held an iron cage was hitched to a pole that would allow two strong horses to draw it between them. The cage had been built to house abominations captured in the field to be returned to Canterbury for study, but had been used rarely as capturing a live specimen had proven all but impossible. They usually died fighting. Well, Edgard had found a purpose for it now. As the sun rose over Canterbury, a stableman moved around inside the cage, spilling straw from a sack onto the floor and spreading it about with his feet. He spread more than he would have for an animal; he knew that the cage's occupant would be human, for at least some of the time.

Meanwhile, four men moved down the spiral steps and into the gloom of the cathedral's dungeon, torches lighting their way along the corridor. Two of them carried a length of heavy chain. The foremost guard, a ring of keys jangling in his fist, barked at Wulfric to wake up and get on his feet; two of the others had been present for the previous night's beating and knew it would take more than that. They would probably have to carry him out, still unconscious.

The light from their torches did not extend far beyond the iron gate. They could see the bolted oak table and spots of dried blood on the flagstones around it, but the far recesses of the cell were cloaked in darkness. There was no sign of the prisoner, who was no doubt curled up in one of those dark corners.

The guard with the keys rapped the heavy iron ring against the bars noisily. "I said wake up! On your feet!"

There was a low grunt from the far corner of the cell and they saw something in the darkness as the prisoner began to move. Though no more than an indistinct shape amidst the gloom, he seemed only to be shifting his weight, a man turning restlessly in his sleep rather than one attempting to rise from it.

"Up and off your arse, now!" barked the key guard, losing patience.

It was the man standing beside him who first noticed that something was wrong. He had seen Wulfric before and knew that he was not a small man, but the shape in the darkness was too big. Far too big. It shifted again, still low to the ground, and made another guttural sound. And though it always smelled rank down here, it had never been this bad. Never like—

"Right, that's it." The lead guard jammed the key in the lock and was about to turn it when the man beside him grabbed his hand. "Wait! Something's—"

The tongue shot out from the darkened corner of the cell and between the bars of the gate, coiling itself around the throat of the man with the keys like a noose and constricting. Its coating of corrosive saliva boiled through the man's neck so swiftly he had no chance to scream. He let out a strained, breathless gurgle as his head came away from his body and fell at his own feet, a red geyser pumping from his neck.

The two guards behind him cried out and drew back in terror as the tongue recoiled into the darkness, but the one standing beside him was too paralyzed by shock to move away. He startled only when the thing that hid in the darkness leapt forward and into the light, and by then it was too late. The beast flung its great black body against the bars with such force that they bent outward, knocking the man on the other side clean off his feet and sending him crashing to the floor several feet away, unconscious.

The two remaining men retreated another step but did not flee. The bars of the cell had bent but held; the beast was still contained behind them, prowling in the darkness. They watched as its clawed limbs probed methodically at the bars, reaching around and through them as though looking for some weakness. The sight of this unsettled them greatly. This was not the behavior of the mindless abominations to which they were accustomed. Those were naught but animals, driven only by savage ferocity. There was deliberation in the way this one moved. Purpose. Intelligence. It was almost human.

Each man felt his stomach drop as the beast's groping claw found the key, still in the gate's lock, and turned it. The mechanism clicked, and the gate swung slowly open, the beast's low growl echoing along the walls. Whether real or just a trick of the shadows, the beast appeared to grow larger as it stepped out from inside the cell, its monstrous size taking up all of the narrow hallway. It lumbered toward them, carapace scraping against the low stone ceiling, its mouth yawning open and drooling saliva that landed in hissing droplets on the floor.

One of the two men had the presence of mind to draw his sword.

The beast stopped.

Its great black cluster of eyes blinked as it cocked its head, regarding the blade with apparent curiosity. And then it spat out a great gob of venom that struck the blade with force enough to knock it from the soldier's hand. Before it even clattered to the floor, half of its steel had been dissolved. As the acid ate away at what remained, down to the hilt, the two men turned and ran. The beast made no attempt to pursue, just watched as they fought each other to be the first up the stairs.

There was a dazed groan and the beast looked to the ground. The guard who had been thrown clear of the bars was lying at its

feet, slowly coming around. As the man's eyes fluttered open, he
saw the monster standing over him. Panic took him and he tried
to scramble away, then he cried out at the sharp pain lancing along
his leg. Broken. He could not move, or do anything but gaze up in
terror at the hideous thing that was looking down on him as a cat
might a wounded and cornered rat.

The monster considered the injured guard a moment longer,
then stepped over him and left him behind as it made its way down
the hall. The downed man watched, amazed to still be alive, as the
great thing squeezed its body into the spiral staircase and lurched
its way upward.

She paced back and forth in her room. Would the magick work?
How much longer would she have to wait to know? She so desperately wanted to go and find answers, but Edgard had placed
a second guard outside her room last night after learning of her
brief escape earlier that day—though thankfully not the purpose
of it—and now she couldn't get out without causing a commotion
that might upset everything.

Be patient. Stick to the plan. But what if the plan hadn't worked?
What then? Her father would be doomed, and all because she herself had delivered him into Edgard's hands. *Because you didn't
think. Stupid girl. Stupid, stupid—*

She heard the peal of bells outside. An alarm. As she ran to
the door, she heard more bells being rung, all over the cathedral. It
could only mean one thing.

Now.

She hammered on the door. "What's going on out there?"

A gruff voice from outside: "Nothing. Be quiet!" The man
sounded nervous. She kept on hammering, harder than before.

"I want to know what's happening! Open this door!"

She heard the turning of a key in the lock and gently took the door by the handle. It opened just enough for her guard to push his head inside, but she could see armed men rushing past him along the hallway.

"I won't tell you again, shut up and stay—"

She yanked on the door as hard as she could, dragging it open wide and pulling the guard, still gripping the handle, inside with it. As he stumbled toward her she thrust her knee up and caught him where it mattered most. He released a soundless breath as he collapsed to the floor.

The second guard rushed into the room and went for his sword. To his credit, his hand had almost made it to the hilt when her fist landed in his gut. He bent forward with a gasp. He was still fumbling for his sword though, still a threat, so she grabbed him by the collar and yanked his nose down to meet her forehead hard. He flew backward and landed on the stone floor of the hallway outside, limbs splayed. She stepped across the threshold, drew the sword from his belt—then stopped and turned back to her room. The man curled up on the ground there was conscious but could do nothing with his hands but cup them between his legs as he groaned quietly. He offered no resistance as she disarmed him, and she strode back out into the hallway with a sword in each hand. One was good, but two was better.

Edgard bellowed orders as his men flowed into the armory to equip themselves with every heavy weapon they could carry. Pikes, axes, swords, crossbows. They strapped armor plate onto their bodies, pieces that had been specially forged and treated to resist the corrosive spittle that many abominations were known to possess. Though Edgard knew the armor had been proven to have little effect, many of the men did not, and if it emboldened them in battle, then that was enough.

"I want it taken alive!" he barked as men fumbled nervously to buckle leather straps and fasten scabbards. "Any man who kills it will answer to me. We corral it back underground and seal it there."

The clamor of bells was near deafening, but above them all, Edgard could hear men shouting and screaming somewhere not far from here. The sounds of fear and panic—from hardened soldiers, trained to deal with just such a threat as this. It did not bode well. He looked at the faces of his men as they armed themselves, and wondered if they would be enough. Then he looked around for some sign of Cuthbert, who was nowhere to be found.

Thinking on it now, Edgard realized that he had not seen the man since late yesterday.

"Somebody find me the priest! Now!"

The beast made its way along the broad central aisle of the nave. Armed men rushed to meet it, and were flung left and right by sweeping blows from its great clawed limbs, their bodies thrown against the walls. When there were too many to cast aside one at a time, the beast lowered its head and went at them headlong like a bull. Those that did not scatter were knocked to the ground and sent crashing into pews. The beast was almost to the open doorway to the outer courtyard when still more men flooded inside and closed the heavy doors, barring them and forming a defensive screen, pikes and swords held outward.

The beast paused and let out a hot snort of breath. Each man bravely held his ground, knowing full well that the abomination would charge in a senseless frenzy—for that was all abominations knew—and that some of them would die.

But it did not charge. Instead it turned and moved away from them, smashing pews and supply crates into matchwood as it cleared a path toward an archway that led to a side passage. As it disappeared through the arch, the men at the door first slackened their posture in a mixture of relief and confusion, then ran in pursuit.

The beast lumbered along the stone-walled passage until it found its way into a small rotunda where several similar hallways met. Each looked much the same. The beast stood at the center of the room and circled slowly in place, turning its head this way and that. Lost. When it heard sounds behind it, it turned back, too slow. Six men appeared in the archway there, grouped in a tight phalanx, shields locked together before them, and charged.

They crashed into the beast as a single wall of steel, their combined weight knocking it off its feet and into the wall on the far side. It now rested sidelong against the wall, its soft, beating underbelly exposed as it struggled desperately to right itself.

The phalanx broke apart and the six men spread out around the beast, swords and pikes held ready. One of the men, zealous, lunged forward and drove the point of his pike into the beast's belly. It gave a hideous shriek. Black blood seeped from the wound and trickled onto the floor.

"Edgard wants it alive!" said one of the other pikemen.

"Bollocks to him," said the one who had stuck the beast. He stepped back and watched its blood run down his pike. "There's only a few of them left, and this one's mine." He drew back his arm, as if to hurl the pike like a javelin—then sank to his knees and toppled forward, the pike slipping from his hand and skittering away as he hit the tiled floor facedown, a sword buried deep in his back.

His comrades looked through the archway behind the fallen man and saw the girl barreling toward them, her other sword in both hands. As they came into contact, her blade flashed, opening the throat of one man from ear to ear and taking the arm of another at the elbow. Two bodies fell aside, and the others quickly withdrew into the rotunda, fanning out into a better defensive position.

She saw the beast against the wall behind them, whimpering as its blood pooled on the floor, and she flushed red. She reached down and pulled the sword from the first man she had killed, then looked at the three men standing before her.

"You all know me. Any of you who doubt that I can and will kill every one of you here and now, remain where you are. All others, go."

The men hesitated, exchanging uncertain glances. Then they scattered, each of them down a different hallway.

She rushed to the beast's side. "Can you move?"

The beast made a sound, but what it meant, or if there was meaning behind it at all, she could not know.

"Hold on." She put down her swords and pressed herself between the beast and the wall it leaned against. Putting her back against the beast's and her boot to the wall, she strained with all her might to get it back onto its feet. It was like trying to right an overturned wagon. At first it seemed hopeless; the thing was simply too heavy. But she would not quit, and as she continued to push, she at last felt the beast begin to move. With one final effort she heaved, and then the beast's own weight did the rest and it keeled over onto its belly. It tried to regain its footing there, but the wound had weakened it and there was little purchase to be found on the floor, slick with the beast's own blood.

"Come on," she said, hearing the echoes of footsteps fast approaching, though from which direction she could not tell. "We have to go, now!" She looked around. Any one of the archways could lead to freedom, or to their capture. What were they to—

"Is this your father or your pet? It must be very confusing."

Her heart sank even as she turned to see Edgard, a dozen knights behind him. Then each of the other exits was depositing more men into the rotunda, and she realized that the reason the footsteps had sounded like they could be coming from anywhere was because they had been coming from everywhere.

Thirty, thirty-five men, by her rough count. So many that some of them were backed up in the hallways leading into the rotunda. On instinct she picked up her swords, though she knew that against these odds they were useless.

Edgard shook his head. "Indra, please. Enough blood has been spilled already today, and it's still morning. Step away from that thing and come to me. I promise, you will be in no trouble if you end this foolishness now."

She weighed the swords in her hands, gauging the distance, wondering if she could get a blade to his throat before his men stopped her. She doubted it, but thought it worth a try nonetheless. She had surprise on her side, after all. Edgard would not expect it, because even after all these years, he had never truly understood just how much she had come to hate him.

In a few seconds he would know, and it would be the last thing that he would ever know.

She coiled her muscles, preparing to throw herself at him. Then she sensed movement behind her and saw Edgard's men edge backward, tense. She glanced over her shoulder to see the beast rising slowly to its feet. It could move, but even at its best it had little chance against this many armed men. What could it hope to do?

It nudged her, and looked to the one exit from the rotunda that was not blocked by Edgard's men. A stairwell leading upward.

She knew where it went: all the way to the high ramparts that surrounded the cathedral. There was as little chance of escape up there as where they stood. But the beast shuffled toward the stairs, and as a group of Edgard's men moved to block its path, she quickly cut them off, positioning herself between them and the stairway. "No farther," she warned, holding them at bay with the point of a sword, her other held ready to strike.

Edgard marched forward, what remained of his patience coming apart. "Indra! Enough! What do you hope to accomplish here?

One more step and I swear I will make you regret it. Indra, listen to me!"

But she did not listen, or look at him, or even acknowledge that he was there. She kept her eyes fixed on the men closest to her, those who posed the most imminent threat to the beast as it started its slow climb. Then she backed onto the steps behind it and followed, never once lowering her swords.

She broke open the locked door with her shoulder and emerged onto the rampart's walkway. The sun was now fully up in a cloudless sky and she shielded her eyes as she stepped outside. The beast was behind her, lurking in the darkness at the top of the stairs, as though afraid to come out into the light.

"It's all right," she said, beckoning it to follow. Hearing footsteps on the stairs below, she gestured more urgently. "Come on."

Slowly, warily, it stepped out into daylight. Immediately it shrank from it, rolling its head and trying to cover its lidless eyes. Knowing that Edgard's men were not far behind, she took it by one of its claws and led it out onto the walkway. And she saw it clearly for the first time in the light of the sun. Separated from its hateful, violent nature, the creature itself was beautiful, in its own strange and terrible way. Perhaps not something God would create, but a thing of beauty nonetheless.

Edgard and his men spilled out onto the walkway and closed in. She looked around; there really was nowhere to run up here. This outer wall ran in a closed loop around the entire cathedral and was nearly a hundred feet high. If there had been a moat below, perhaps they could have jumped, but as things stood, the only way off this wall was a sheer drop to certain death.

The beast seemed slowly to be adjusting to the light. It looked up at the blue sky above, breathed in the warm, clear air. It turned to take in the beautiful rolling hills and plains of Canterbury that spread out in every direction beyond the wall. And looked at her, the girl who had risked her own life to try and save it. To try and save *him*.

Tears welled in her eyes. Edgard was just a few yards away, and behind him a small army that crowded the walkway eight men deep.

"I'm sorry," she said, all that she could find in herself to say.

The beast let out a roar and swept her up in one of its clawed limbs, pressing her tight against its body. Edgard and his men surged forward, but the beast was moving fast now, scuttling backward toward one of the towers that ran along the ramparts and scaling it, quickly climbing beyond the reach of any sword or pike. An archer nocked an arrow and made to aim but Edgard pushed his bow aside. "Idiot! You could hit her. No arrows!"

The beast climbed to the top of the tower and perched there, twenty feet above the ramparts. It looked at the dozens of armed men crowded and waiting below, and clutched the girl more tightly. She felt its strong, muscular limb squeeze around her waist, but did not struggle or resist. Impossible though it seemed, she had never in her life felt safer.

And then the beast flung itself, and her, from the tower and over the wall.

Edgard ran to the parapet and watched as they fell away from him, down through the air, tumbling as they went but never separating, falling together as one.

She saw the world whirling around her as they plummeted. She thought to close her eyes but did not. She thought that she might panic but did not. In her final moments, she knew that she was at least to die as she had always hoped to live: without fear, without surrender, and with her true family. And so she watched, unafraid, as the ground came rushing up to meet her, closer and closer—and suddenly away from her again. Now she was swooping upward, the ground receding beneath her, the horizon falling lower and lower as she rose higher and higher into the air.

It was difficult to look up, with the beast holding her so tightly, but she craned her neck enough to see the outer span of two great wings sprouting from its back, beating as rapidly as a hummingbird's, so fast they were a blur. As she marveled at the wind rushing past her face, at the sight of their shadow passing over the tiny villages and farms far below, at the horizon, farther away than she had ever seen it, she could think only a single thought: *What a thing it is to fly.*

She was still gazing in wonder at that distant horizon when she began to realize that something was wrong. The beast's flight was becoming unstable, the beating of its great wings erratic, and those little fields and farms below were fast becoming larger, closer. Then the beast dipped forward and dove toward the ground, barely clearing the roof of a dilapidated barn, and, with just a few feet of altitude left, released her to fall safely into a patch of earth before it finally crashed to the ground, plowing a deep furrow as it pitched end over end, battered and broken, and came to a stop.

She hauled herself up, winced as she realized her right ankle was badly hurt, and hopped lamely across the field to where the beast was slumped, unmoving. She shook it, trying to rouse it back to consciousness, but it would not stir. Then, as she tried once more, she felt the hard shell that encased its body grow warm, then hot, beneath her hands. She backed away, and the beast began to glow, then ignite, flames of ethereal blue fast consuming its entire body and burning it to cinders.

It took only moments, and when the flames died, all that remained was a smoldering pile of embers with Wulfric's naked body at its center, curled into a fetal ball and covered in a coat of gray ash. She went to touch him, but the ashes on and around him still burned hot, and she drew her hand away, cursing. She knew that it would be a while longer before she could pull him free and even longer before he woke.

She heard the distant thundering of hooves and looked back toward the cathedral, now just a miniature on the horizon, to see a lone figure riding toward them. The man was too far away to recognize, but there was no mistaking the horse he rode on. The brilliant white steed was the only one of its kind at Canterbury, and it belonged to Edgard.

No, no, no . . .

She had no sword, no weapon of any kind, no horse on which to make an escape, nor even two good legs with which to run. And there was her father, unconscious and helpless. Even if she could get away, she would not leave him. She stood in front of Wulfric as Edgard drew closer, until the approach of his horse shook the ground beneath her feet.

At several yards' distance, Edgard reined in his horse. He dismounted before it even came to a halt, and marched toward her with sword drawn.

"Stand aside, child. I am in no mood."

She stood firm. "You will not touch him."

He paused for a long drawn-out breath. She recognized the calm before the storm, the look that would come over him before the thrashings he had dealt out when she was younger, before she taught herself how to fight back. "My patience with you is at an end," he said, flat and expressionless. "You are coming back with me, you and him both. Or do you intend to fight me, injured and unarmed?"

"I intend to fight you," she said. "Injured and unarmed. Let's see which one of us kills the other. But I will not go back with you, now or ever."

Edgard just shook his head sadly as he started toward her. "What a pity."

She had learned to fight with fluidity and grace, but she had neither the ability nor the inclination for that now. Her ankle would not allow her to move nearly as well as she would need to if it came to trading blows; her only chance was to surprise him and take him down quickly. She waited, and when he came close enough, she launched herself at him headfirst, barreling her shoulder into his chest and sending them both down into the dirt.

Before Edgard could recover, she was on top of him, fists raining down, breaking his nose and bloodying his lip. She was furious, and relentless, yet Edgard was able to break the attack, grabbing her wrist with one hand and striking out with the other. He hit her hard across the jaw and knocked her off him.

As she floundered groggily on the ground, Edgard staggered to his feet and recovered his fallen sword. Then he made his way to where she was still struggling to get up and drew back his sword to strike. He was about to swing when something swooped out of the sun and hit his face, scratching and tearing and sending him scrambling backward in a sudden, desperate panic. From down on the ground, she saw Edgard batter at the bird with his free hand, then drop his sword to fight it off with both. She clambered to her feet and hobbled over to pick up the sword.

"Venator, to me."

Only then did the hawk break off his attack and fly to her shoulder.

Edgard was still holding his hands to his face, but she saw that his right eye had been put out, leaving just a bloody socket. He slumped to his knees and saw her standing over him, holding his sword in her hand. He spat out a bloody tooth and glared at her with loathing. "All I ever wanted was to be a father to you, Indra," he said feebly, his lip cut and swollen. "And this is how I am repaid. With a disrespectful, disobedient, hateful little bitch for a daughter. I rue the day I ever found you."

She thought about what he had said. Thought about how easy it would be to take his head from his shoulders right now. One clean swing and it would be done. She brought back the blade, and, as her shoulders turned, caught sight of Wulfric, lying in the ashes behind her.

"You are right," she said to Edgard, as she rotated the sword in her grip a quarter turn, "in every thing but one."

She swung the sword. The flat of the blade caught Edgard hard across the face, knocking him cold. She watched as he slumped sideways and fell to the ground, then tossed his sword down next to him.

"My name is Beatrice."

There were more horses coming now, more men. Not yet within sight, but she could see the cloud of dust on the horizon. She limped to Wulfric, and though the ashes around him had only partially cooled, she reached in and pulled him from them anyway, ignoring the pain as the embers burned her hands. Once he was free, she hauled him up onto her shoulder and did her best to carry him to Edgard's horse.

He was far less heavy than the beast but still more than she could carry easily on two strong legs, much less one. Twice she stumbled and fell; twice she got back up and lifted him again. Finally she was able to sling his body over the horse. She glanced toward Canterbury to see the riders approaching. Less than a minute out now.

She climbed into the saddle and set the horse running. It was renowned as the fastest at Canterbury; those pursuing would have little chance of keeping up, even with it carrying both of them. *Finally, an advantage.* She put her heels into its sides and the cathedral receded into the mist behind her until it was no more.

Miles and hours later, they sat together by a babbling stream, Wulfric wincing as Beatrice gently eased his arm into a sling she had fashioned from part of her shirt. It was broken, but not so badly that it would not mend. He bore a fresh scar also, just to the right of the beetle-shaped brand on his chest—the remnant of the pike wound the beast had sustained that morning. But like the older one, lower on his belly, it had been well on its way to healed before Wulfric woke. He shivered, naked save for the horse blanket he wore around him. The horse it had come from, Edgard's own white stallion, idled nearby, drinking from the stream as Venator sat watchfully on a branch overhead.

"We'll have to find you some clothes," said Beatrice as she adjusted the sling. Wulfric nodded, but something else was preoccupying him.

"Why did you not kill him?"

Beatrice looked into the woods as she sought her answer.

"I thought about it. I wanted to. But I thought also about what you said, about the guilt you carried all those years for the men you killed. I didn't want his death on my conscience."

She did not recognize the way that he was looking at her now. "Did I do wrong?"

"No," said Wulfric with pride. "You did right."

She was still conflicted. "Perhaps it would have been easier on us if I had killed him. He will come after us now."

Wulfric stood, wrapping the blanket around him. "All the more reason for us to get as far from him as possible."

"Where will we go?"

He thought, but had no answer. He had spent so many years in transience, with no destination in mind, living without purpose from day to day, moving from place to place, never a thought for tomorrow. Now . . . now he had a purpose, a tomorrow.

"What do you think?" he asked her.

She looked around, considering. "I've heard that the highlands to the far north are quite beautiful."

Wulfric smiled. "So have I."

She went to the stream to take the horse by its reins, careful how she moved over the uneven terrain with her ankle still troubling her. Her hands were wrapped in linen, also torn from her shirt, to cover the burns she had sustained pulling Wulfric from his nest of ashes.

"Thank you," he said. "For saving me back there."

She looked at him warmly. "On that score, I believe we're even."

She checked the horse's saddle, looked up at the sky. "It will be dark soon. Will you . . . I mean, can you—"

"We shall have to see," said Wulfric. "Cuthbert showed me how to contain the beast, and it seems to have worked well enough so far, but I am still learning. Each night will be a new test. Of one thing I can be sure: if it should come, it will not harm you."

Venator took to the air as Wulfric pulled himself into the saddle and reached down to help Beatrice up behind him.

One question still puzzled her. "How did you know that it could fly?"

"I didn't," he said. "God works in ways mysterious."

And on they rode.

EPILOGUE

Wulfric was almost finished with the note. He had taken his time over it, since it was the only one he ever intended to send, and he wanted to make sure that all that needed to be said was said. He rubbed his chin as he looked it over once more. His face felt strange since he had shaved off the beard, though Beatrice kept assuring him that he was far better for it.

He told himself that he was satisfied enough with the note, then put his initial to it. He was no author, but he believed his point was made.

Edgard,

I know that you care for Beatrice, in your way, so know that she is safe and well with me. She is in no danger from the beast. In these past months, I have learned to contain it, to allow it forth only when I bid it, and to control it when I do. Rest assured, it will never harm her— only those who would try to.

I hear word that the Order is to be disbanded by royal decree, and that your remaining time at Canterbury before it is given back to the church is short. I wish you peace on whatever road you next choose to follow, but tell you this: you would be unwise to think of seeking us out. Beatrice has no wish to see you. For that reason, we have been careful to ensure that you will never find us, and for that reason, too, I am quite certain that you would regret it if you ever should. Truth be told, you have far more to fear from her than you do from me, or the beast.

I know also that Cuthbert has left your service and makes now a new life for himself. He sends us word from time to time that he is well. Should he ever fail to do so, know that you will not need to try to find us. We will find you.

My daughter and I are happy, both of us for the first time in many years. Leave us be. And all will be well.

W.

"Venator, to me."

The hawk flew to him from his perch outside the humble farmhouse. Wulfric folded the parchment and tucked it into the copper ring around the bird's ankle, then let him fly. From the rock where he had been sitting, he watched as Venator soared away across the loch toward the highlands beyond until he was gone, swallowed up by the mist.

Wulfric turned back to the farmhouse. It was not much, but then, what more had he ever needed? *What more than her*, he thought, as he looked across the field at his daughter, tilling the soil in preparation for the sowing of a new crop. Just as he had taught her.

She had been a fast learner, already as good a steward of the land as his father had taught him to be. He saw her smile at him as he approached. *So much like her mother.* She planted her spade in the earth so that it stood freely and wiped her brow, happy for a moment's rest.

"I saw Venator leave," she said. "It's done?"

He nodded, surveying the freshly tilled earth. "You have quite the makings of a farmer. As good with that shovel as you ever were with a sword."

She pulled it from the earth, hefted it. "Not quite as useful in a battle," she said playfully.

"No," said Wulfric. "But then a sword never fed anyone."

She stuck the shovel back into the ground. "What are we planting?"

"Carrots. By autumn, this will all be carrots. Wait and see." He reached into the pocket of his coat. "Here, I have something for you." He produced a looped leather cord around which hung a simple pewter pendant set with a bright red gemstone. "I saw this at the market when I went to buy the parchment," he said, holding it out to her. After a moment's hesitation, she reached out and took it, turning it over in her hand, watching as the gem caught the sunlight.

"What is this stone?" she asked.

"A red garnet," said Wulfric. "The merchant said it is also called a carbuncle. I remember once I called you that. At the time, I did not know what a beautiful thing it was."

She blinked back a tear. "I'm sorry. I don't know what to say. Never in my life have I been given anything like this."

"Never in my life was I given anything like you," said Wulfric with a smile. "So on that score, I believe we're even."

A beetle crept its way up from the plowed earth and along the handle of the spade. Beatrice saw it, allowed it to crawl onto her hand for both of them to see. "What is this one?" She had been trying to stump Wulfric on his knowledge of bugs and beetles since he told her how he had learned them from his father, but she had not managed it yet.

"Common dung beetle," said Wulfric. "Also known as a scarab beetle."

He saw her face light up with the simple delight that she took in newfound knowledge, and it brought him a sense of joy that he had not known since he first held her as a baby. He had no idea how to be a father to a daughter. But he would learn. For now, just to be here with her was enough.

I am a father. I have a daughter.

Yes, it was more than enough.

HONORARY MEMBERS OF THE ORDER

Abomination was in large part made possible by the individuals named below, who lent critical early support and patronage via Inkshares. They are hereby inducted as Honorary Members of The Order. *Contra Omnia Monstra!*

Adam Gomolin

Alan Hinchcliffe

Austin Wintory

Brian Kirchhoff

Danny Hertz

Emma Mann-Meginniss

Genevieve Waldman

Geoffrey Bernstein

Howard Sanders

Jay Wilbur

Jeff Harjo

Ken Fabrizio

Kevin Becker

Kiki Wolfkill

Laurie Johnson

Linda Wells

Logan Decker

Mace Mamlok

Meggan Scavio

Mekka Okereke

Michael Pachter

Michael Sawyer

Michael Seils

Patrik Stedt

Peter "KmanSweden" Koskimäki

Piotr Jegier

Ray L. Cox

Robbie D. Meadows

Ronald Tang

Samuel Parrott

Simon Kirrane

Steve Lin

Thomas Grinnell

Timothy E. Thomas

Tony Dillon

Tricia Gray

ABOUT THE AUTHOR

Gary Whitta is an award-winning screenwriter best known for the postapocalyptic thriller *The Book of Eli*. He was also a writer and story consultant on Telltale Games' interactive adaptation of *The Walking Dead*, for which he was the co-recipient of a BAFTA award. Most recently he served as a writer on Lucasfilm's new generation of *Star Wars* projects for film and television. *Abomination* is his first novel.

Please visit and share the link below. You can learn more about the story behind the story, sign up to receive updates, and order copies of the book. Reviews are ardently invited and may be submitted to editor@inkshares.com.

—Inkshares

http://inkshares.com/projects/abomination